Praise for *Tyler*:

"Steamy… The passion is electrifying."
—*RT Book Reviews*

"Fantastic… multifaceted and interesting."
—*Night Owl Romance* Reviewer Top Pick

"An interesting, potent, provocative love story. Perfect for those who love cowboys and strong men."
—*Love Romance Passion*

"Sexy, sizzling hot… The characters are vibrant and the pages race by."
—*Minding Spot*

"Admirand has penned an entertaining, enchanting story that is sure to have readers hanging on to every word."
—*Fallen Angel Reviews*

"Tyler is one hundred percent genuine cowboy and all man… I cannot wait to rope myself up the next book, *Dylan*."
—*Cheryl's Book Nook*

"C.H. Admirand keeps things fresh… a book that's guaranteed to sizzle in your hands."
—*Long and Short Reviews*

THE SECRET LIFE OF
·COWBOYS·

Dylan

C.H. ADMIRAND

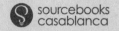

sourcebooks
casablanca

Published by Sourcebooks Casablanca, an imprint of Sourcebooks, Inc.
P.O. Box 4410, Naperville, Illinois 60567-4410
(630) 961-3900
FAX: (630) 961-2168
www.sourcebooks.com

Printed and bound in Canada
WC 10 9 8 7 6 5 4 3 2 1

Chapter 1

Dᴙʟᴀɴ Gᴀʀᴀʜᴀɴ ɴᴀʀʀᴏᴡᴇᴅ ʜɪs ɢᴀᴢᴇ, ᴛʀʏɪɴɢ ᴛᴏ focus in the glare of the spotlight, searching the crowd for her face. It was time for the big move in his act—the showstopper.

Where was she?

Jolene would kill him if he messed this up, but he'd made it through the last two nights and would make it through tonight. The redheaded owner of the club should have no complaints about the middle Garahan brother not keeping his word or holding up his end of the bargain. Damn the woman and her tests!

Controlling the urge to turn on his heel and walk off the stage, he dug deep and found the grit to stick it out. *Hell, if Tyler could handle this job, so could he. Garahans went down fighting!*

Oblivious to the adoring gazes of the women around him, he moved toward center stage, bent, and picked up the coiled rope. He looked up as a blonde, a brunette, and a redhead walked into the bar… right on schedule… but there was something different about the brunette. Maybe it was the blindfold. He struggled not to laugh, but he couldn't keep from smiling, wondering why the cloak-and-dagger bit.

Looping the lasso in his hands, he started the slow circular motion. Getting the rhythm going until it was smooth and sweet, he raised it above his head and locked gazes with the blonde. When she nodded, he let the lasso fly, as the blonde whipped the blindfold off the brunette.

The woman's stunned expression as the rope slipped around her upper body didn't stop him from tugging on the rope and reeling her in. The patrons of the Lucky Star hooted and hollered, encouraging him to pull faster, but he didn't want the little lady to trip and fall on her pretty face.

Glad that the focus of the crowd wasn't totally on him, he gently pulled her toward him. The brunette's gypsy-dark skin, full red lips, and almond-shaped eyes captivated him. The promise of pain-filled death in her dark green eyes, as she struggled against the bonds that held her, had his lips twitching, fighting not to smile.

She dug in her heels, but he used his strength to subdue her. Undeterred, he yanked on the rope. When her eyes widened in shock, he used her surprise to his advantage and reeled her in the last few feet. When they were a few inches apart, he tipped his hat, smiled, and rumbled, "Happy birthday, darlin'."

Her eyes narrowed, and her nostrils flared; Dylan recognized the signs of a fractious filly about to raise a ruckus. Not a problem, he was ready. Wrapping his free hand around her, he hauled her in close, pinning her to him before she could let loose and kick him.

The crowd roared its approval.

"Let me go," she demanded, her sweet breath tickling the hollow of his throat.

Enjoying himself for the first time since he'd hit the stage, he chuckled and bent his head closer to her full red lips. "Why?" His gaze locked with hers. "So you can have more room to do more damage?"

"I don't like being manhandled."

Her vehement protest didn't deter him; he had a job to do and an act to finish. "Well now, darlin'," he drawled, "that's not what your friends said."

Her eyes sparkled with temper, and her willowy body trembled with anger. Dylan's body stood up and said *hell yeah*! It'd been a long time since he'd had a woman tempt him. The sultry brunette in his arms looked like she wanted to tear a few strips off of his hide... right before she killed him.

Damn, but that turned him on.

Perverse. That's what his grandpa would say. He grinned and would swear he heard her grinding her teeth in frustration.

"Let me go." She struggled against him, but he'd trapped her slender curves against him so not a breath of air was between them. "I'm not one of those desperately lonely women, or buckle bunnies coming in here look-ing for some eye candy."

Lord, he really loved the husky sound of her voice. Even angry, it sounded sexy. He fought against the in-stant attraction he'd felt and shrugged. "I'm not the one whose friends blindfolded me."

She closed her eyes and stopped struggling. Dylan could feel the anger leaving her by degrees.

"They're just trying to help."

"With a face like an angel and a body made for lovin', why would you need any?"

Tears gathered in her eyes. "None of your business."

Well, hell. His one weakness cut him off at the knees. *A woman's tears.* "I'm about to make it my business."

The music ended and house lights went on, his cue to

release his captive and take a bow. Cursing his job and his redheaded boss, he brushed her tears away. Moved by the split second of vulnerability, before she covered it with the toss of her long, dark, wavy mane, he hungered for a long, slow tasting kiss.

He wasn't sure if he wanted to reassure her that whoever had put the sadness in her eyes wasn't worth her time, and that he would be, or if he had been too long without a woman and was letting certain parts of his anatomy take his mind hostage.

Dylan slid his hands around to the small of her back and watched her eyes turn an even deeper green, the color of the tumbled sea glass he'd found as a kid, on a beach down on the Gulf Coast. When the go-to-hell expression on her face morphed into shocked surprise, he dipped his head low so their mouths were lined up.

He could feel her heart begin to pound, but from the dazed expression in her eyes it wasn't from fear; it was something darker and a hell of a lot more fun. He brushed his lips across hers and felt the bottom drop out of his stomach. She tasted like sin, and he was ready to burn.

Need tied his guts into knots, but he'd be damned if he'd be letting go of this little filly before he'd taken his fill. He gentled her with soft, tentative kisses until she relaxed in his arms. When she moaned low in her throat, the knots inside him pulled tighter a heartbeat before she melted in his arms.

"Darlin', you're killing me."

Her eyes met his, and he knew she was going to kiss him back. He didn't ask; he simply plundered. Surrounded by the dark, sensuous taste of her, he couldn't get enough. Splaying his hands to the small of her back, he molded her to him, drinking from her lips like a dying man, three days without water.

Hungry for more, he slid the tip of his tongue along the seam of her lips, coaxing her to let him fully taste her dark, sweet flavor. When she parted her lips, he devoured her. Two years of frustrated need, anger, and desire swirled inside of him and struggled to let loose.

"Happy birthday, Ronnie!"

He snapped to attention and loosened his hold, though it nearly tore him apart. He was not done. He wanted more, ached for more, needed more from this woman.

"Will you wait for me?"

"Break it up, cowboy." Jolene Langley brushed against him so that he had no choice but to step back or get stepped on.

So the sweet thing with the dark hair and kissable lips was one of Emily's new friends, and just his good fortune she was the first carpentry job Tyler's fiancée had lined up for him. Life couldn't get any better. The woman was gorgeous and kissed like an angel. He wondered if she knew that he'd be calling on her tomorrow night. That thought distracted him for a moment, but a more pressing matter was at hand; she still hadn't answered his question. "Sorry, boss." He removed his hat and raked his hand through his hair. "Ronnie, darlin'," he rumbled. "Will you?"

She narrowed her gaze at him. "Will I what?"

Hmmm… the woman got her grit back along with her voice. For too long he'd been hung up on the fact that the woman he'd thought to marry hadn't wanted to stay in Pleasure and he hadn't been interested in any woman in particular since.

But this little brunette intrigued him on a level that his former girlfriend hadn't. His libido stood up and saluted him... he was ready, willing, and able to get back on that particular horse and ride it all night long. Ronnie might not be Ms. Right, but she sure looked to him like Ms. Right Now. No time like the present to find out. "Will you be here when I get back? It'll take me a couple of minutes to change."

If possible her eyes darkened to a dangerous shade of green—the color the sky turned before a tornado touched down and all hell broke loose—that had him wondering if he'd read her wrong. He licked his lips and could still taste her. No, he reasoned, she'd kissed him back and gave every indication that she was just as interested in him, and he was holding on to that truth with both hands. Hell, if he had to, he'd hit his little brother up for pointers on being charming. Normally he didn't care, but right now...

"I don't think so, cowboy."

His gut burned with the icy chill of her rejection. He didn't mind when Jolene called him cowboy, but for some reason when this woman said it, it bothered him. The toss of her wavy dark hair and the sneer of her succulent lips had the knots in his stomach freezing.

Ignoring the cold lump of need, he put his Stetson back on his head and nodded. He would let her think she was getting her way for now. Dylan could be a patient man and bide his time. His gut told him she'd be worth the wait. Besides, he'd be seeing her for the next little while until he'd finished the job, and from what Emily had told him, the damage to Ronnie's shop had been substantial.

"Ladies."

At least that mind-boggling kiss had done one thing for him: it had shaken him up and had him realizing that he'd gone too long without a woman and it was past time to remedy that particular situation. Once he made up his mind, he'd stick… and his mind was set on having Ronnie. He'd give her all the time she needed to decide whether or not she wanted to get to know him better on a personal level—the first order of business on his agenda was to see if he could tempt her to get to know him on a physical level.

"Did you know about this, Jolene?" Ronnie demanded.

She didn't seem happy with her present. Hell, most of the other women he'd had to lasso or haul up into his arms while on stage usually grabbed at him, held on for dear life, and were ecstatic with their birthday gift courtesy of the Lucky Star. Extracting himself from their grasping fingers usually left a mark. He'd be carrying the few he had already earned working there for a couple more days.

The owner of the club smiled. "Of course, how else do you think my latest headliner would know to pick you out of the crowd?"

Dylan clamped his jaw shut. His boss surely knew how to make a man feel like a hunk of meat on display. He knew it wasn't personal, but he was beyond tired and had had enough of this place. Planting the heel of his boot to the floor, he spun around, intending to walk away.

"Could have been the blindfold," Ronnie rasped, wrapping her arms around her slender waist. "Jolene, you know I hate surprises."

The brunette's distress had him pausing. He watched

his boss smile and link her arm through Ronnie's. "Honey, I couldn't say no to your friends; they wanted your twenty-fifth to be a birthday to remember."

Ronnie's gaze shifted to meet his. "I'll never forget it."

And just what did that mean? His pride still stung from the direct hit he suffered when she'd turned him down. Was she one of those women who said no but meant yes? Hell, if only he had the energy to stick around to find out. It was time to get out of Dodge, head back to the ranch, and regroup. Women were trouble with a capital *T* and only wanted one thing from him anyway, and it sure as hell wasn't his heart. Normally being wanted because of work-hardened muscles and the way he dressed didn't bother him, but not being wanted by the sultry brunette because of the way he dressed—or was it the way he undressed—got to him. Maybe it was because he was desperate to get back to the ranch and get some sleep. Shaking off the odd feeling, he tipped his hat to the women, coiled the rope, and headed for the door by the side of the stage.

The Circle G was waiting… for how much longer, well now that would be up to him and how long he could put up with raucous women hootin' and hollerin' while they tried to stuff money in his black spandex briefs, but if the replacement dancer Jolene had found worked out, then he'd be able to move on to the handful of carpentry jobs he'd lined up with Emily's help. Truth be told, he'd do just about any type of manual labor, as long as it wasn't plumbing—he couldn't wait to get started on the repairs to Ronnie's shop. He was that partial to carpentry.

Shaking his head, he dodged the women waiting by the stage door and slipped through into the back room.

Changing his clothes, he couldn't get the birthday girl, or the memory of her tears, out of his exhausted brain. *Maybe I should forget about her. Besides, she's just a temptation*, he reminded himself. *She's not interested in me.*

Liar. He ignored the voice in his head.

"I don't have time for women."

Make the time.

Hell, now he was imagining he was hearing his grandpa's voice in his head. "Definitely time to hit the hay," he grumbled. "I'm hearing things."

Listen up, Son.

Aw, hell, maybe he was going crazy after all.

Dylan looked both ways to make sure the coast was clear and that no one was waiting by the stage door to ambush him. Hell, three nights of working the same job as Tyler, and he'd had enough! The redhead from the night before had been convinced Dylan couldn't resist her. She and a handful of others who'd tried to get his attention had been wrong. If and when he wanted a woman, he would be calling the shots, not an out-of-control, tipsy succubus with time on her hands and spurring him on her mind. His mind drifted back to the woman he lassoed; he might make the time for an emerald-eyed woman with attitude to spare who sounded like she'd just stepped off the bus from the East Coast. Time would tell.

No one was there. *Good.* He hightailed it out the door and down the hallway; he was done. He needed to go home.

Home… the Circle G. Too bad his mom and grand-father wouldn't be there. Days like today, when he'd run dry, he could have used a hug from his mom, or one of his grandfather's affectionate cuffs on the back of the head.

We're here, Son. His grandfather's voice echoed in his head. *Don't doubt it for a moment.* He'd heard the words so many times growing up, when he was tired, he could call up any one of a hundred times his grandfather had spoken them.

Oddly relieved, he reached for the front door.

"Going somewhere, cowboy?"

His sigh was loud and long as he turned around to face his boss. "Jolene, I'm dead on my feet and know I've done everything you've asked for the last three nights." He waited for one of her long-winded speeches about how important the dancers were to the lonely women who came to her place to dream about what kind of man they really wanted in their lives. Go figure, every last one of them wanted a cowboy.

But instead, she surprised him and agreed. "Yes. You've more than held up your end of the bargain. I'm impressed by how hard the Garahan brothers work."

"You still need me tomorrow night?" He actually held his breath, hoping she'd say no.

Jolene shook her head. "We hired a dancer today, he starts tomorrow night."

He breathed a sigh of relief.

"I'm sure you're heartbroken."

"Well," he said slowly, "if it doesn't work out…" He let his words drift off; he didn't want to commit to working any more nights at the Lucky Star. Three had been more than enough for him, but now that meant that he'd have a chance to get started on the first carpentry job on his list and see if he could get to know Ronnie while setting her store to rights. It wasn't a large job, but at least for the time being, he'd be able to bring in the extra money they needed until the ranch was out of the red. He hoped he'd be a lot closer to sweet-talking Ronnie into bed before the job was over. He had a gut-deep feeling she'd be one hellacious ride.

"I'll keep you and your brother Jesse in mind in case this latest dancer doesn't work out. Would you mind if I asked you to be on standby for the next few nights?"

He tipped his hat. "My pleasure, ma'am."

Dylan turned to go, but Jolene held out a hand to stop him. "I know how hard it was for you to get up there on stage, Dylan."

He shrugged.

"You and Tyler have been fabulous for business, and your work ethic can't be beat. I have a feeling Jesse would work just as hard."

Knowing she had something on her mind, he waited until she finally got to the point. "Would you and your brothers be interested in being part of an all-male revue?"

His stomach knotted. "Does that mean what I think it does?"

She tilted her chin up and frowned at him. "I have no idea what you think, but before you go jumping to any conclusions, I'll tell you. Emily and I have been talking it over with Gwen, Natalie, and Jennifer, and we've decided to add to the entertainment part of Take Pride in Pleasure Day by having the Lucky Star represented with a lineup of dancers."

He felt the blood rush from his head to his toes and dug deep for the strength to keep standing. It was hard to speak with his jaw clenched, but he managed to grind out, "Are you nuts? There's no way my brothers or I would strip in public."

When Jolene's eyes twinkled and she started to laugh, he was transported back in time to the first day of sixth grade, when he'd felt like he'd landed in an alternate universe and everyone but him spoke a foreign language.

He shook his head to clear out the unwanted memory. When she realized he wasn't laughing with her, she closed her mouth and swallowed gamely. "I'm not laughing at you."

"Yeah," he said. "You are."

"Well, maybe just a little," she said laying a hand on his arm. "The revue will have a lineup of four or six dancers dressed up as cowboys: jeans, boots, hats, and vests—no shirts."

He snorted. "Who're you gonna find to dress up?"

"I thought I'd ask a couple of real cowboys to round out the lineup. How about it, Dylan? Would you ask your brothers and let me know? It'd be a big favor if all y'all agreed."

He felt as if he'd been lassoed around the chest, and Jolene was pulling the rope tighter. The expectant look on her face was hard to say no to. *Damn.* "Do I have to answer you right now?"

"You can let me know in the next couple of days."

He nodded and turned to go, and damned if she didn't call out to him again. "Jolene, not that I don't want to stay and chat, but hell, what part of 'I'm done' didn't you get?"

"Relax, cowboy. I just wanted to tell you that you made Ronnie's birthday."

He narrowed his gaze at her and waited for the rest. With women, there was always more than a simple statement.

Like before, Jolene didn't disappoint him.

"She still looks dazed from that kiss you stole."

He tipped his hat to the back of his head. "That a fact?"

His boss smiled at him, and he actually smiled back. "Why don't you ask her yourself?"

Dylan's gut twisted remembering the chill of her rejection. "Maybe later. See you, Jolene." When he'd stepped through the door, he paused and called out, "Hey boss?"

She turned to look over her shoulder. "Yeah?"

"Thanks."

Jolene shook her head. "My pleasure, cowboy. Now get on home."

He may have hated stripping, but he didn't mind working for Jolene. "You're not as tough as you let on, Ms. Langley."

Her laughter followed him out into the night.

———— ∿ ————

Ronnie DelVecchio's pulse still pounded wildly in time with her heart. *Forget him, forget that kiss!* she told herself. He's just another guy pretending to be someone he's not, dressing up like a cowboy, but paid to strip… and paid to make her feel special. But the calluses on his hands felt real, and his muscles felt like he used them for more than just show. *When will I learn?* Just because he'd mesmerized her with the dark and dangerous promise deep in his molten chocolate eyes was no reason to do something so stupid as to let him kiss her brainless and fall all over him. He was just a man... period. *A cowboy wannabe*.

Now that he'd gone, the sizzling kiss they'd shared kept replaying over and over in her mind along with the feeling that she'd met him before. Damn, she'd always loved watching those old TV Westerns with her grandmother, and the man who'd lassoed her looked like a combination of John Wayne, Gary Cooper, and Roy Rogers all rolled up into one dangerously attractive man. Dark hair, dark eyes, gorgeous hunk of cowboy—he had to be one of Tyler Garahan's brothers. The handsome hunk now had a name, and Garahan men spelled trouble. She had a reason to steer clear of him.

Why am I talking to myself? I should be giving my friends hell for talking me into letting them blindfold me and setting me up to get lassoed and kissed by that hunkalicious cowboy. Her temper simmered, heating dangerously close to a boil. She would refuse to accept the blame for locking lips with the muscle-bound cowboy. *That way you can take your anger at yourself out on everybody else*.

Her grandmother said it often enough that her own conscience replayed the words at the most irritating moments. The last time she'd heard the words she'd been getting into her cousin's truck, preparing to leave her former life behind her to start a new one out West. Her grandmother hadn't wanted her to leave but had accepted Ronnie's decision to go as long as Ronnie promised to stay in touch, calling home often. Well, this was something she wouldn't be telling her grandmother about.

Besides, Ronnie was a grown woman and could

accept blame… or place the blame on whomever she wished. *As long as you're honest with yourself.* She looked over her shoulder and sighed. Having a conscience was a royal pain in the ass.

Draining the Mega-Margarita, wishing she'd declined and gone for her usual longneck bottle of beer, Ronnie set the glass on the tabletop. The memory of the cowboy's lips lightly pressed to hers, drawing her in, soothing her before he eased back and locked gazes with her, had her shivering. Remembering the way he'd waited for her to stop him—right before he rocked her world with that mind-blowing kiss. A kiss that sent sparks of desire screaming through her sensitized system like a shot of tequila. But she'd given up combining hard alcohol and men after her divorce; the two were not a good mix for her. Things always ended badly.

"Ready for another?"

Before she could answer, her friend Shannon signaled the bartender for another.

"I do not want another one of those." Ronnie moaned in a delayed reaction, as the frozen concoction hit her right between the eyes with a serious case of brain freeze. Just like when the dark-eyed cowboy paralyzed her with his intentions right before he laid his lethal lips on hers.

"I thought you wanted to try something wild and wonderful for your birthday."

Ronnie raised her head. "Would that be the blindfold or having the cowboy lasso me?"

Shannon snickered into her oversized drink. "Actually, your friend Mavis came up with the second idea. Jolene suggested the blindfold and we ran with it."

Taking a sip of her own drink, Shannon licked her lips and sighed. "José is definitely *my* friend."

Ronnie looked at her and tried not to sigh. Shannon McKenna was blonde and beautiful. Too bad she was so likeable, or else Ronnie could toss the drink she'd just been handed into her friend's face or dump it over her head. "You know I like beer. Tequila is not my friend. Besides, I wanted to go somewhere different for my birthday."

"You didn't say somewhere when you mentioned that little tidbit a few weeks ago," Shannon reminded her. "You said *something* different."

Ronnie shrugged. "Same thing."

"No, it's not," Shannon grumbled into her glass. "By the way, what did you think of Dylan the Delicious?"

Ronnie paused with the drink a fraction away from her lips and had to laugh. "He certainly was." Taking a healthy sip, she swallowed and licked her lips. "Which one of Tyler's brothers is he: the middle or the youngest?" One of them would be very important in her life, helping her rebuild Guilty Pleasures.

Totally clueless to Ronnie's inner turmoil, Shannon shrugged in answer, set her half-empty drink on the table, and leaned toward Ronnie. "I have to ask." She leaned closer. "What was it like when he tossed the lasso around you and reeled you in?"

Turmoil evaporated like morning dew under the heat of the morning sun. An involuntary shiver raced up Ronnie's spine as heat filled her cheeks.

Shannon's eyes widened. "Wow. That good?"

There was no use denying it. She sighed. "Yeah." The moment of impact, when their bodies collided and their hearts pounded in unison, would keep her up at night for days. Every hard muscled inch of him fitted against her, tempting her, but she wasn't interested in a one-night stand with a cowboy—was she?

Her friend nudged the silent member of their trio. "What did you think, Lenore?"

The redhead turned; she had a shell-shocked look on her face. "I can't say just yet, too much sensory overload." Their friend paused, letting her gaze drift up toward the stage.

Ronnie looked up to where another dancer stripped down to the tiniest pair of black spandex briefs and swiveled his hips in a really good imitation of Elvis. She shook her head; although her friends had misunderstood, they definitely went all out and did *something* different.

Gaze glued to the dancer, Lenore rasped, "I think I need another Mega-Margarita."

Ronnie exchanged a look with Shannon. Shannon's cousin had been in town for a week or so, but had apparently never been to a strip club or seen a half-naked cowboy up close before.

"Poor Lenore." Ronnie lifted her glass in salute to the next dancer up on the stage before turning to call out, "Hey, Gwen!" When the bartender looked their way, Ronnie wiggled her glass and held up three fingers. Gwen nodded. Part of being the birthday girl meant the perk of having her glass refilled all night long. She hadn't thought to celebrate her twenty-fifth birthday at the Lucky Star, but now that she was here, she relaxed.

"Where did you say Mavis was?" Ronnie had spent enough nights here listening to Mavis Beeton expounding on the fact that if more of the uptight residents of Pleasure quit worrying about what everyone in town was doing behind closed doors and adopted her philosophy—live and let live—there wouldn't be so many pinch-faced busybodies poking their noses in where they didn't belong.

Staring up at the stage, Ronnie recalled one of the conversations she and Mavis had had recently, when Mavis had surprised her by saying that sex was just part of life; everyone needs it now and again. Ronnie remembered that when she agreed, her friend had added that those that engaged in a healthy physical relationship on a regular basis sure were a lot easier to get along with than those who'd given it up for a more cerebral pastime... like collecting thimbles. Ronnie smiled to herself; she wanted to be like Mavis when she grew up.

Too bad she had no idea how much longer it would take until she found the right man and settled down for the long haul—for however long that might be. Her first choice had been a dismal one with disastrous results, but she'd accepted that she was partially to blame.

The Lord and fate had a lot to do with a person's happiness. Nonni DelVecchio had told her that just this past Sunday during their weekly late night chat, and even though she might not like what her grandmother said, she believed everything Nonni told her. Well, except for the family curse. Every other generation, one of the DelVecchio women met an Irishman and fell head over heels in love and had twins, and not necessarily after they were legally married. But she couldn't ever remember seeing it happen to anyone in their family and figured Nonni was given to exaggeration. Just to be on the safe side, Ronnie had gone to great lengths to avoid the dreaded curse by marrying a nice Italian boy from her hometown. Too bad he'd lived up to the rumors about him.

"Enjoy your drinks, ladies."

Ronnie smiled. "Thanks."

Three sips later, she couldn't feel the end of her nose, but she was feeling really, really loose. "Mmmm. Why do I always drink beer, when José is so delicious?"

Shannon and Lenore raised their glasses and started singing "Happy Birthday."

"No, stop!" Ronnie moaned. "Sing something else— anything else."

"But it's your birthday," Lenore said, as Shannon started to sing the Beatles version of "Birthday."

"Come on, Ron," Shannon urged, "get up and dance."

Just tipsy enough to oblige them, Ronnie stood up, glass in hand, and started dancing around their table. Her drink sloshed over the rim, and she stopped to lick every last drop off the back of her hand. Singing along, stopping only to cool her throat with the smooth, icy goodness of her new favorite drink, she wondered why she let that handsome hunk of cowboy kiss her, draining every thought from her head before letting him walk away. *Was she crazy?*

A few more sips, and she wondered why she hadn't told him she'd wait. Her heart knew why: he was gorgeous and so tempting, and she'd been afraid to take him up on his offer, knowing he'd expect her to do a little mattress dancing with him after the way she'd spontaneously combusted when he'd hauled her in and kissed her. In his defense, she had totally given him that impression, but if she ever saw him again, and he asked, she'd plead the fifth.

Once burned, she thought. Well, she was nobody's fool, and she wasn't going to let a dark-eyed cowboy talk her into bed unless she was sober—no matter how amazing his kisses were or how hard his body was. Besides, from now on she was going to be the one who'd initiate any invitations that would end between the sheets.

Damn, she thought, staring in the direction he'd walked down the long mirror-lined hallway. He'd ignited a spark inside of her that flared into a slow-burning fire. Too bad she had a feeling that Dylan Garahan was the only one who could put it out. She'd be doing a lot of yoga to get that man out of her system.

"So what else do you want to do for your birthday?" Shannon asked after Ronnie sat down.

"Find that dark-haired cowboy and lick every inch of his hard body."

"Sounds good to me," her friends answered as one.

"Oh, crap," Ronnie said sinking onto her chair. "Did I just say that out loud?"

Shannon and Lenore grinned at one another and then her. "Yep."

Ronnie put her head in her hands and noticed the room tilted just a bit off to the left. She closed one eye to see if her perspective changed. It did; now the room tilted to the right.

"Hey, are you OK?" Lenore asked.

Ronnie shook her head the room started to spin. "I was wrong. José is *not* my friend."

Shannon and Lenore got on either side of their friend

and eased her to her feet. "Come on, Ron," Shannon soothed. "We'll take you home so you can sleep it off."

As they walked toward the entrance, Lenore added, "You'll feel better in the morning."

"Are all y'all leaving so soon?" Jolene called out from the side of the stage.

Ronnie started to shake her head, but her stomach flipped and she froze.

Taking pity on her, Shannon patted Ronnie's shoulder and said, "I think the birthday girl has had one too many Mega-Margaritas."

Jolene nodded in sympathy. "Do you need help getting her home?"

"No thanks. We'll make sure she gets there in one piece so she can sleep it off."

"I don't want to go home," Ronnie protested, although her friends didn't seem to be listening. "I want to go find Dylan the Delicious."

"Y'all come back tomorrow," Jolene said. "I'll tell you where to find him."

"Ish that a promise?" Ronnie slurred.

"Absolutely. See you tomorrow," Jolene called out as they made their way down the hall.

"When I find 'em, I'm gonna shtart with the hollow of hish throat," Ronnie said, stumbling on wobbly legs, wondering why she couldn't make her tongue work. The words sounded funny.

"That's José talking," Lenore said, helping her cousin pour Ronnie into their car. "Don't worry, you'll feel better tomorrow."

It was only a couple of blocks from the Lucky Star to Ronnie's apartment over her store, but she'd never have been able to walk that far without tripping and falling on her face.

"You'd better be careful what you wish for," Shannon warned, as they helped her inside and up the stairs. "Birthday wishes sometimes come true."

Two hours later Ronnie was still praying to the porcelain god. Exhausted and shaky, and halfway sober, she leaned her arm on the toilet seat and rested her head against it. Purging her system of the tequila hadn't been easy, but it would sure as hell be easier than forgetting the dark-eyed cowboy… that would be impossible.

"His lips were lethal," she moaned. Her stomach felt raw and her head ached, and all she could think about was being lifted into a strong pair of arms and held against a wonderfully warm, muscled chest—Dylan's.

She couldn't stop thinking about him and was already making plans to ask Jolene where he lived so she could just happen to run into him again.

Beware of the curse! her grandmother's voice echoed in her head.

She'd been raised to fear the DelVecchio Curse. Generations of DelVecchio women had been warned not to taint their pure Italian blood, but in the end fate always had her way.

Her tired brain tried to sort out everything that had happened tonight. Maybe Dylan was only part Irish, so she might be safe in that regard. She couldn't remember the last time someone in her family had married an Irishman, but she ran through the names of all of her female cousins and then started on her aunts, just to be sure.

Too tired to think straight, she gave up before she

could go through all of her aunts' married names. She couldn't think of one instance that would give credence to her grandmother's warning.

"Besides," she murmured, as her eyes drifted closed, "fate doesn't always win."

Poor bambina, she could almost hear her grandmother's voice crooning in her aching head. How many times had Nonni warned her not to try to drown her sorrows in alcohol?

Her stomach finally settled down. As her body gave in to exhaustion, she drifted off to sleep on the tile floor.

Chapter 2

DYLAN SMELLED COFFEE. HE ROLLED OVER, LIFTED HIS head, and sniffed the air. He wasn't dreaming; the scent of fresh brewed coffee was so close he could taste it.

"'Bout time you got up."

He ignored the grumpy voice and shifted so he was sitting up, leaning against the headboard. Without opening his eyes, he reached out his hand.

"We Garahans are so alike sometimes, it's scary."

His little brother was still grumbling at him, but his brain couldn't quite wrap around what Jesse was saying. If Dylan wanted that mug of hot coffee, he was going to have to open his eyes and find out what was going on. Not that he expected Jesse to be in a good mood every morning. Hell, Dylan spent half of the weekdays waking up in a bad mood himself.

That's because you're jealous of your older brother and what he's found with Emily—that and you're missing something sweet in your life.

It was an effort, but he ignored the voice and opened one eye and saw Jesse leaning against the doorjamb, looking like he'd been in a wreck out on I-635. "What the hell happened to you?"

Jesse shoved one of the mugs at him but didn't say anything. Something was definitely wrong with his brother. The youngest of the three brothers talked like he'd been vaccinated with a phonograph needle at birth, or at least that's what their grandfather always used to say. They'd always gotten a kick out of listening to old records on his grandfather's record player, and heck, Jesse talked nonstop, just like those records played— nonstop until the record was over.

Dylan swallowed a mouthful of hot coffee and grimaced. "Damn, did Tyler make the coffee this morning?" When Jesse didn't answer right away, he added, "You couldn't have made it. I'd be able to drink it if you had."

That got the reaction out of his brother that he was hoping for. Jesse snickered and bit out, "Some habits die hard, Bro. If Tyler's up first, he makes the first pot."

"But the first pot must be gone by now. Is something wrong with Lori?"

At the mention of their cook and childhood friend's name, Jesse stiffened up and turned to leave. "Hey wait up, Jess." Dylan set his mug down so he wouldn't spill it and got out of bed. A quick glance down reminded him of their grandfather's rule about women and breakfast. "Is Lori in the kitchen?"

Jesse shook his head and kept walking. Something wasn't right. "Is Emily still here, or did she leave for work?"

"She left fifteen minutes ago."

Good, he could ignore his grandfather's rule about putting on his damned pants for breakfast, since there weren't any females in the house. Grabbing his mug, he followed after his brother. "Hey, Jess," he hollered. "Wait up!"

His brother had other ideas. Dylan heard the back door slam as he walked into the kitchen. "Perfect."

Since Lori had been back at the ranch, she'd twisted the youngest Garahan brother into knots again... just like she had a few years back, before she'd run off with that shit-for-brains excuse for a man she'd married.

She wouldn't have run off with the same man again and left Jesse twisting in the wind, would she? Dylan started to think about it, but knew it was useless; women operated on their own plane of existence sometimes, leaving men without a clue as to their thoughts.

"Not my worry, not my problem." That was Dylan's motto since his girlfriend had left him to make her mark on the archaeological community.

He poured water and measured scoops of coffee into the drip pot. Banging open cabinet doors, prowling over to the refrigerator, he opened up the meat drawer and found a ham steak, snagged three eggs and the margarine, and finally had everything he needed to fix his breakfast except bread.

"Maybe I could ask Emily if she knows how to make Irish soda bread," he mused, hunting up and finding two clean frying pans. "There's just something about it toasted, slathered with sweet cream butter."

While the meat was heating in one frying pan, he cracked the eggs against the side of another one-handed. He'd inherited his big hands from his grandfather; all three brothers had. Good thing. They needed them to work the ranch and keep the place from falling down around their ears.

With his hands busy, his mind wandered, replaying events from the night before with a twist. The image of the blindfolded brunette got stuck in it. As he lassoed and reeled her in, the desire in her eyes beckoned to him.

He knew without asking that she'd wait for him, ready to run her hands up and over his shoulders, sliding them down to grab him by his ass—

Grease from the pan spattered the bare skin below his navel. "Shit!" Grabbing the dishcloth, he ran it under cold water and tried to cool the heat of the burn. "Damn, it's a good thing I'm not as tall as Jesse, or that'd have burned something important." Still grumbling he added, "That woman's trouble and she's not even here!"

You should have put your pants on. You're burning daylight, Son.

"Gee, thanks for the advice, but you always said we only had to dress if a woman was in the house."

His grandfather had always reminded them that dungarees were made of tough material that would save their legs riding the range—and would have saved his skin from grease burns. They were always trying to beat the clock, getting their chores done before they ran out of daylight. The old man had taught them that putting their pants on before breakfast would save time if they didn't have to go back upstairs to get dressed before going outside.

Irritated that he was seeing visions of the beauty from last night who'd turned him down and imagining that he was hearing voices in his head, he bit out, "Maybe I should saddle up wearing my damned boxers, like that time I was eight years old and hell-bent on riding out in my underwear."

He shook his head, remembering the beating his legs had taken after riding a few short miles before he turned back to doctor the scratches on his legs and put on his jeans. His mind wandered back to last night and the dark-haired woman who'd captured his eye and then stomped on his heart when she refused to wait for him, ignoring the sensual pull they both felt when their lips met. Sizzling and the scent of meat about to burn brought him back to the present. "Damn. I'm gonna have to work hard to keep my mind focused today until I can get my hands on that female." He grinned. "Just because she turned me down is no reason to back off."

By the time he'd fried the ham and eggs and ate them, he'd used up half an hour's time. "At this rate, I'll never get to the repairs on the barn roof, which I can't start until after I help round up those strays." His never-ending list of chores dwindled by the end of each day, but seemed to grow by leaps and bounds overnight. Tyler was handy with plumbing, but Dylan's expertise was carpentry.

He'd learned his skills the hard way, in exchange for staying out of jail when he was twelve. A chuckle escaped, surprising him. He hadn't thought about that time in his life for a long while. His grandfather had stepped up to the plate and had gone to bat for him, going head-to-head with Sheriff Wallace. Dylan had been scared spitless by the mountain of a lawman, but his grandfather had just smiled and turned his Irish charm up to brilliant.

Pouring his second cup of coffee, which was a whole lot closer to the real thing than Tyler's sludge, Dylan noticed something sticking out from behind the coffee-maker. Reaching in, he pulled out a tightly wrapped heel of soda bread someone—probably his pain-in-the-ass younger brother—had tucked behind the coffeemaker to hide it and save it for later.

"It'd serve him right if I ate the whole thing." And he would have too, if he didn't have to get dressed and head on out to the western border of their land to meet his brothers. Tyler'd end up hurting himself if Dylan wasn't there to keep their older brother from ripping out his stitches or breaking a few more ribs.

Slathering butter on a slice of soda bread warm from the toaster, he bit into it and sighed. He should have asked Lori to marry him. Man that woman could cook. Polishing off the second piece, he knew he'd have to get in line or fight Jesse to marry Lori. Jesse'd been stuck on Lori a few years back, and from what Dylan had noticed recently, still was.

"Women," he grumbled, as the image of the black-haired, green-eyed female filled his head again. Luscious lips curved up in a smile, had his heart pounding and his libido standing at full attention.

He'd have to ask Tyler what happened with Lori; odds were that if he asked Jesse, he'd get sucker punched. Their little brother had a mean streak a mile wide. Dylan grinned; he really admired that trait. Now that he thought about it, Jesse was definitely the one who'd hid the soda bread. Mean and greedy.

Piling his dirty dishes in the sink, he didn't even think about washing them. He was already behind schedule and would have to ride hard to catch up to his brothers. They'd be chasing down a couple of strays who had wandered through a break in the fence. He couldn't keep his older brother from riding out; broken ribs and stitches hadn't kept Tyler down for long. Dylan and Jesse had thought about tying their brother to a chair, but figured Emily'd just untie him. She was partial to their brother.

And now he'd have to deal with one brother in a good mood—because Tyler got to sleep beside the curvaceous redhead who had stolen his heart—and the other brother in a foul mood—because for some reason Lori had left.

Thinking of Tyler's injury had him flinching. All that blood… He should have shot first—right between that damned bull Widowmaker's eyes—and asked questions second. He owed that bull for head-butting Tyler into a barbed wire fence, slicing him up, and breaking a couple of Tyler's ribs.

He walked to the stairs, then took them two at a time, hoping to cut down on the time he'd already spent making his own damned breakfast. "Lori better not have cut out on Jesse again," he grumbled, grabbing the pair of jeans off the floor where he'd shucked them the night before. Pulling on clean socks and his boots, he nabbed a shirt from the pile of clean clothes he'd left on the top of his dresser. Why bother to put them away, when he'd only have to dig them back out to wear them? Besides he had a system: clean clothes on top of the dresser and dirty ones in the corner on the floor.

Dylan caught up to his brothers a little while later. The heat from the sun soaked in through his tired, over-worked muscles all the way to the bone, warming him. His horse responded when Dylan tightened his quads and leaned to the right. "Atta boy," he murmured, when the horse started after one of the stray steer, "let's go get that ornery little sonofabitch."

With his help, the three of them were able to round up all of the strays and coax them back in through the break in the fence. "Hell, we spend as much time mending fences and chasing down strays as we do tending stock."

"Easier now than when they didn't have as much of the land fenced in," Jesse grumbled. "It was tough when the open range started to close down all those years ago."

Tyler groaned then shifted his horse so he wasn't twisted in the saddle. "It must have been hard to change their way of doing things. Hell, letting the cattle graze wherever they wanted and rounding them up when it was time to drive them to market must have been one amazing trip."

"Not if Grandpa's stories are to be believed," Jesse said. "The trail was hard on the men and the cattle. Throw in the weather, acting like a pissed off female—all teeth and nails—and you've got yourself one bitch of a cattle drive."

Dylan listened to his brothers rambling and wondered what it would have been like. He wouldn't mind working harder than he did now, as long as he had a certain raven-haired beauty waiting on him when he dragged his sorry ass back to the ranch house at the end of the day.

He smiled imagining her waiting for him. He'd be heading in from the barn, using his Stetson to brush the dust of his day off of his jeans. He'd look up and their gazes would meet. She was such a welcome sight to a man who'd worked until his legs ached, his back screamed, and his hands were stiff from holding on to the reins.

He grinned and she leaped off the back porch and ran to his arms, not caring that he'd sweat through his shirt and smelled like the steer he'd been wrangling. Her lips were warm and welcoming as they molded to his. Diving in, he let his tongue tangle with hers as he slid his hand down to the sweet curve of her ass and...

"What the hell's wrong with you?" Jesse demanded punching Dylan in the shoulder.

"Hey, what? Ow!" Dylan rubbed the abused joint and mumbled to himself.

"Something on your mind, Bro?"

Dylan looked over at Tyler and noticed that his brother looked really tired, but knew neither he nor Jesse would be able to get their brother to stay behind unless they hog-tied him and left him there. Not that they hadn't tried a time or two when they were teenagers.

"Work," he finally answered.

"My ass," Jesse added.

"What the hell is your problem anyway?" Dylan demanded, glaring at Jesse. "You lit out of the house without telling me what happened to Lori."

Jesse's jaw clenched and his eyes narrowed, but he didn't say anything. He turned his horse and headed north to where the worst of the break was.

Tyler nudged his horse to follow. "I'll tell you later, Dylan. We'd better catch up and mend this section of fence. I've got other chores to see to."

Dylan snorted. "You've got a date with a bottle of aspirin, big Bro."

Tyler shook his head. "Already took it. Should hold me for another hour or so."

Working together, the Garahan brothers repaired the fence without speaking—just the way Dylan preferred to work, quietly, so he could focus on the job and get it done. But today, a certain female had worked her way under his skin and messed with his mind more than once, and he didn't like it.

"Damn," he ground out.

"Something on your mind?" Tyler urged.

Dylan shook his head. "Nothing worth mentioning."

His brother nodded and Jesse hollered, "I'm heading back to wait for the hay delivery."

They nodded and waited until he rode out of sight. "OK," Dylan said. "Tell me what happened. Where is she?"

"Gone," Tyler answered him, knowing without asking that Dylan had meant Lori. His brother sighed. "I guess you were too busy working over at the Lucky Star to notice she hasn't been around for a couple of days and before you ask, she'll be back."

Relief flowed through Dylan. "Well, that's all right then."

"After the wedding…"

Dylan's gut clenched as dread swamped the relief. "Hers?"

Tyler nodded.

"Shit."

"Yeah, so ease up on our little brother."

"Just one more question," Dylan said. "Did she go chasing after that shit-for-brains—"

Tyler cut him off, answering, "Yep. Emily's worked hard to find someone to pick up the slack now that Lori's gone."

"Yeah, you told me."

"You OK with bartering your carpentry skills?" Tyler began only to be interrupted by Dylan.

"Don't care, as long as we can eat."

Tyler looked as if he wanted to say more, but Dylan was done jawing and shook his head at his brother. Tyler shrugged and turned his horse toward home.

Riding back to the ranch house, Dylan wondered what would make a man like Jesse pine for a woman who didn't want him. The truth hit him right between the eyes: sometimes it was simply something about the woman that made a man want to sit up and beg, no matter how many times the woman had turned him down. Luscious red lips that begged to be kissed and siren-green eyes that lulled a man into thinking he was something special right before he crashed against the rocks.

———~~~———

Ronnie opened one eye and sighed. The room was no longer spinning, a sure sign that the worst was over. Sitting up, she brushed the hair out of her eyes and groaned. Her stomach felt like she'd ingested broken glass. Rubbing it, she knew she'd have to get going. Emily had promised that one of the Garahan brothers would be stopping by later today to help with the repairs to her shop downstairs. If she planned to be coherent by then, she'd better get started. Too bad she didn't remember which one of the Garahan brothers was the carpenter. Would it be the one from last night?

She shivered, stiff and chilly from spending the night on the bathroom floor. "Tea and toasted Italian bread, plain… no butter." Her grandmother's patented cure-all for an upset stomach.

With that in mind, she stumbled to the kitchen. "Why didn't I stick with my usual, a nice cold longneck bottle of beer?" Since coming out to Texas, she'd discovered one of its treasures: Shiner beer. Her favorite hangout, the Lucky Star, had three kinds of Shiner on tap: Bock, a rich dark beer; Blonde, a golden lager; and Light, a tasty light beer. She'd tried them all but still preferred hers in a bottle. She'd had a bad experience at a bar back in Jersey that hadn't cleaned out their taps properly, and she had been sick as a dog and emptied her stomach that time too. Too bad she hadn't remembered that last night. She reached for the teapot.

Ah well, she was twenty-five now, and she knew better. Last night was an aberration; she wouldn't make the same mistake again. She was older and therefore wiser. Turning the spigot on, she filled the glass teapot with water and carried it over to the stove. Her head felt just a bit too light. "Probably dehydrated myself." Disgusted with her total lack of brains last night, she berated herself, mumbling, "Idiot, moron, stupid... *stunad!*"

"No, Bambina... sei giovane." Her grandmother always told Ronnie that it was because she was young and not stupid, until the day she'd told Nonni that she planned to marry a nice Italian boy. Nonni had been in favor of Ronnie marrying one of the Murphy brothers. Even though she would have been in danger of fulfilling the DelVecchio Curse. Ronnie fought against it for all of the same reasons. Nonni wanted those grandbabies badly—just as badly as Ronnie wanted to prove that she was immune and not like the other DelVecchio women in her family rumored to have fallen like angels who'd just lost their wings.

Ronnie hadn't listened to her heart or her grandmother. She did everything she could to avoid the Murphy brothers after the oldest had told her best friend that he wanted to go out with Ronnie. But that had been high school and a long time ago. Ronnie was a firm believer that fate and destiny needed a push to make happen what *you* wanted to happen. You had total control, and she'd taken care of the curse when she'd married Anthony Faustino.

Too bad he'd lived up to the rumors she'd decided she could live with and *had* lived with—right up to and after their wedding day. She'd thought she could change the young Italian stallion that she'd married and could convince him to change his wandering ways. Nonni had been right about that too. The only person you have the power to change is yourself. Popping two slices of Italian bread in the toaster, she sat and waited for it to cook. Taking a tentative bite, she chewed slowly, not wanting to rush things and end up with a repeat of last night. By the time the first slice was gone, the tea water was ready.

"I hate tea." But she knew coffee wouldn't settle her stomach the same way tea always did. Grumbling, she scooped up a spoonful, blew across it, and sipped. "Yuck."

By the time she'd eaten the second slice of bread, half of the tea was gone and her stomach and head felt as if they were in sync. "Better," she sighed. "I'll live."

Her cell phone rang and she automatically reached for her purse, but it wasn't inside. She got up and followed the sound to the bathroom and the haphazard pile of clothes under the sink. The memory of stripping out of her jeans led to another: being lassoed and reeled in by a gorgeous hunk of cowboy.

Dylan the Delicious had lips that should be licensed as lethal weapons. Ronnie shivered remembering the way he'd coaxed a response from her. *Damn*. She had to get her mind on the major task at hand; the carpenter was coming in a couple of hours and there was more cleaning up to do before the man would be able to find the wood he'd be repairing. By the time she uncovered her phone, she'd missed the call. "Great," she mumbled. "Do not think about Dylan," she warned herself, pocketing her phone.

Too late.

The man filled her thoughts and messed with her mind. Unable to concentrate, only able to think about one thing: broad shoulders and a thickly muscled chest that were part and parcel of one towering example of pure unadulterated Texas cowboy. She'd always been a sucker for a man with broad shoulders. Ronnie wished he were here. She'd take back her last words to him and beg him to come home with her. If she had, she wouldn't have kept drinking and wouldn't have been in such sad shape this morning.

"Yeah, I know, wishing doesn't make it happen." Her head began to throb. "Time for aspirin."

A half hour later, her headache was under control and she'd donned a pair of yoga pants and her favorite T-shirt, one she'd stolen from her cousin Vito. It always shifted to one side and slid off her shoulder, but it was soft, roomy, and reminded her of home. Placing her phone on the bottom step so she wouldn't miss any other calls, she surveyed the situation.

"Why did I move to Texas anyway?" she grumbled, tucking her hair behind her ear as she bent over to reach for yet another ruined bit of satin and lace. What was left of the teddy was soft and supple, guaranteed to catch a man's eye and raise his blood pressure. The sudden thought that she'd like to raise Dylan's blood pressure irritated her. "He's not even here and the man's messing with my mind."

Focusing on cleaning, rather than what the mess used to be, was easier to deal with than the heartache of looking at the tattered remains of her fledgling business amidst chunks of wood, drywall, and glass—the result of what happens when some trigger-happy teenager with too much time on his hands goes on a rampage. Why else would someone she didn't know just break in and destroy the contents of her store?

The devastation had been complete—her collection of heirloom fragrances and reproduction perfume bottles, her selection of design-your-own-fragrance massage oil—all of it had been crushed, mangled, or poured out onto the hardwood floor. If that hadn't been enough, someone had broken in a second time and used a knife on her lingerie and a baseball bat on her walls, windows, and shelves.

Although she agreed with her friends and fellow female business owners that it was an act of boredom, she wondered about her collection of massage oils. A lot of towns didn't want anything X-rated within their borders, not that massage oil could be considered X-rated—well at least it hadn't been back home in New Jersey. But things were very different out here in Texas and she'd come up against a couple of narrow-minded individuals who'd rather strike the first verbal blow before even knowing what the facts were. Some towns wouldn't think twice before denying an application for a business permit. The town of Pleasure hadn't given her a hard time; the town clerk had written up the permit, stamped it, and handed it over with a smile, so she wondered if maybe one of those self-appointed do-gooders downtown had decided that her stock wasn't fit to sell in their town. Just because some of the lingerie was a bit on the risqué side didn't mean it had to be wrapped up in brown paper so no one would be offended by the see-through lace panels and teeny tiny thongs that were some of her best-selling items.

The break-ins and destruction of Guilty Pleasures had been a total shock and had ripped Ronnie's world apart. Tears filled her eyes, but she didn't want to give in to them. DelVecchio women weren't weak. She'd been accused of being stubborn, hardheaded, and loyal to the bone—but never weak. Too bad she hadn't found a man who appreciated her best qualities… yet. But that didn't mean that there wasn't a man out there worth cultivating and convincing that she would be worth getting to know. She wasn't a native of Texas, but she'd met quite a few of the local women and didn't think she was that different from them.

Her cell phone buzzed across the bottom step, the only surface left intact… the staircase to her apartment… reminding her of the fact that not everyone she'd met since she came out to Pleasure had been honest with her. Someone out there resented the hell out of her. Finding out why would be the next step—right after she figured out who did the damage to her store. Ready for a break, she tossed the bits of satin and lace on top of the pile she'd begun and lunged for her phone.

"Hey, Ronnie. How's the head?"

She grimaced. "How do you think?"

Her friend Shannon chuckled. "Maybe you should have stuck with your usual. José isn't always friendly. He has he moments when he's everybody's friend, and then before you know it—"

"You wake up lying on the tile floor of your bathroom

and can't remember how you got there," Ronnie finished for her.

"Oh hey, Ron," Shannon said. "I didn't know you would get sick. I thought you were just buzzed."

Ronnie shrugged and tried to make light of one of the worst cases of overindulging that she'd ever had. "Not your fault. I didn't have to keep drinking."

"So what are you doing now that you've joined the quarter-century club?"

She snickered. "Sorting through what's left of my shop."

"Did Emily's carpenter friend show up yet?"

Ronnie walked over to the front window and looked out from between the boards that she'd painstakingly nailed across the opening wondering which brother it would be. "He's supposed to be here in an hour or so. I guess his day-job boss isn't flexible, so he can't get here until around seven o'clock."

It was Shannon's turn to snicker. "I hope it's the middle brother. You deserve something good happening today. Need any help sorting?" her friend asked.

Ronnie looked around her and wanted to cry. "Nope. I'm good."

"Call me later. I want to hear all about him."

"You just want me to fill in the details, like how well his stellar butt muscles fill out his battered jeans."

"That would definitely do for starters," Shannon agreed. "Besides, I know you're a sucker for a man wearing a tool belt."

"If he can fix what's left of my shop, I'll be forever grateful."

"So you really accepted their deal to cook for them in exchange for the labor to do the repairs to your shop?"

Ronnie walked back over and sat down on the bottom step. "I'll buy the materials and they supply the food. All I had to do was send over a fresh-baked pie and they'd agreed." She paused and shook her head. "I just wish I could remember which brother is coming." Tapping her finger to her bottom lip, she mused, "Now that I think of it, I don't remember Emily mentioning his name."

"Are you going to cook your awesome homemade lasagna crepes?"

"Absolutely."

"With your Nonni's red sauce?"

"That's the plan, but do you think a bunch of boys from Texas will appreciate Italian food?" Ronnie wasn't sure about that; most of the people she'd met seemed to eat barbecue beef, steak, and hamburgers.

"They'll be convinced once they've tasted ambrosia."

Ronnie laughed. "Nonni would love to hear her simple sauce referred to that way. I'll have to tell her when I talk to her on Sunday."

"There's nothing simple about her pasta sauce."

"I'll let you know how it goes, Shannon," Ronnie promised, remembering she didn't have all of the in-gredients she needed for the sauce. "I've got to pick up a few things before my cowboy carpenter gets here." A shiver of anticipation shot through her. Rubbing her palms together, she realized she was about to drool. Time to get ahold of herself; she didn't want to get all worked up if her carpenter was the wrong brother.

She ran upstairs and changed the yoga pants for a pair of worn-at-the-knees blue jeans she'd had for longer than she could remember. Mindful of the weather and wildlife she wasn't yet used to, she pulled on socks and reached for a pair of work boots. Turning them upside down to check for critters first, she put them on. Two minutes later, she was upside down on the driver's side of her cousin's ancient blue Ford pickup, using the exposed ignition wires to start it. Vito's generous offer to take his truck didn't include the keys because he'd lost them a few years back and never replaced them… with his larcenous talents, he didn't need keys.

"Come on," she begged the truck. "I'm running on borrowed time and I need to get fresh garlic and onion for Nonni's red sauce."

The engine caught and roared to life. Shifting so she could wiggle out from under the steering column, Ronnie brushed her hair out of her eyes, grabbed ahold of the wheel, and put it in drive.

The good thing about living in a small town was that you didn't have to drive too far to get whatever you needed. Dawson's didn't carry everything that she needed, but she'd been warned about the differences between East Coast living and the wide-open spaces out in Texas and had brought a bunch of her favorite spices with her. Even better, Nonni said she'd mailed a care package that should arrive any day. She couldn't wait to see what her grandmother had sent.

"Hey there, Ronnie."

"Mavis!" Ronnie turned to greet her friend. "Where were you last night?"

Mavis smiled. "I had things to do. I'm sure you had fun even though I wasn't there, didn't you?"

She wondered if she'd have ended up on her bathroom floor sick as a dog if Mavis had been with her. "Oh yeah, I had tons of fun."

"You don't sound like you mean that." The older woman frowned.

"Let's just say I didn't use my head and got distracted by a hunk of cowboy the likes of which I'd never seen or knew existed."

"And?" her friend prompted.

"He... um, asked me to..." Embarrassed, she couldn't finish.

Mavis linked arms with Ronnie and started walking. "Sounds like you need someone to talk to." She soothed, "Tell Auntie Mavis. I'm all ears."

Ronnie sighed, knowing she'd feel better once she'd told Mavis. She trusted the older woman and usually heeded her advice. "Did you know Shannon and Lenore were going to have me blindfolded and lassoed?"

Her friend's hoot of laughter wasn't exactly the reaction she expected. When Mavis came up for air, Ronnie grumbled, "Then you weren't in on it?"

"Only the lasso part. Damn. I wish I'd have thought of the blindfold. It must have done something to that poor boy, seeing you all helpless." When Ronnie stopped in her tracks, Mavis tugged and got her walking and talking. "So was it Dylan?"

"How'd you know?"

"I have my sources." Mavis preened. "Besides, I happen to know he and his brother—"

"Which brother is he?"

"Dylan's the middle brother."

Ronnie needed to know which one was the carpenter. "Then he's the one who's going to rebuild my shop?"

Mavis agreed and added, "They all have the Garahan dark good looks, but Tyler's leaner than Dylan and they're both shorter than Jesse. All of those boys have hidden talents and are good with their hands—as ranchers, they have to be."

"All I know from last night is that they called him Dylan the Delicious."

The soft smile had her suspecting that Mavis had known him for a long time. It was a look she'd seen more than once on Nonni's face when talking about one of the neighborhood boys. Ronnie asked, "What do you know about him?"

"He's honest and hardworking as the day is long. All of those boys are." Mavis shook her head. "There was a time when we'd thought they'd spend their formative years doing hard time for Sheriff Wallace, but old Hank, their grandfather, had a way with words and the sheriff relented and let Hank set those boys on the right path."

Ronnie wondered what had happened that the brothers had been headed toward the wrong side of the law, but wasn't comfortable asking—just yet. When Mavis's smile turned wistful, she knew there was a lot more to the story. Time would tell whether or not she'd be interested enough in Dylan to find out more.

To distract Mavis from her sad thoughts, Ronnie blurted out, "He kissed me."

Mavis's smile broadened and a spark of pure pleasure lit her eyes. "Did he? Tell me more."

While she selected the fresh garlic and onions for her sauce, she filled Mavis in on the details of last night's celebration. As she walked toward the checkout, Mavis asked, "And what did you do when he asked you to wait for him?"

"I told him no."

Mavis patted the back of Ronnie's hand. "Any reason, other than the obvious one, that he scared you?"

"I didn't say he scared me."

"Didn't you?" Mavis asked. "Sometimes when love hits us between the eyes, we put up all of our defenses at once in order to protect our hearts."

It was Ronnie's turn to laugh. "I just met him last night. How could I love him?"

"Oh, honey," Mavis said, hugging Ronnie. "You don't always recognize the love bug when it bites you."

"Well, I might have been interested, but—" She didn't have to finish what she was thinking. One look at Mavis's knowing smile told her the woman had already made up her mind about last night and the woman hadn't even been there.

"How did it feel when he reeled you in and locked lips with you?"

"You weren't there, how did you know?"

Mavis smiled and ignored her question. "So how was it? I've heard rumors that those boys are as wild as the wind, just like their daddy, God rest his soul."

Ronnie's heart did a little jig in her breast. Yet one more thing that she definitely would want to find out—if she decided she was interested in getting to know the man better. What happened to his father? The little sigh that escaped had Mavis tilting her head to one side. Ronnie admitted, "If I hadn't had too much to drink, I may have taken him up on his offer. The man's lips should be licensed as weapons of mass destruction."

Her friend nodded. "Wiser to wait until your head was clear. It's always a mistake to mix alcohol with sex."

Ronnie let out a snort of laughter. "Now you sound like my grandmother. Don't hold back how you feel, Mavis."

The older woman nodded. "Like I always say, there's lovin' and there's lust. Not that there's anything wrong with having a little bit of one or the other, but it's best to have a clear head so you can tell them apart, so you don't do anything you'd regret later."

Ronnie looked up in time to see the wide-eyed look on the cashier's face. She didn't recognize the girl, but smiled. The poor thing was too embarrassed to return the greeting. Paying the cashier, Ronnie reached for her bag. "I'm afraid I'll make another mistake like I did with my ex. I thought I knew what I was doing."

"Dylan isn't Anthony."

"I didn't say he was, but—"

"Sometimes you have to grab hold of life with both hands and enjoy the ride."

Ronnie snorted. "I'm a former barrel rider—not a bronc rider. Did you know that there's a famous rodeo in New Jersey? It's a place called Cowtown in South Jersey. I've competed there."

"Who'd have thought it?" Mavis said, walking with Ronnie out into the parking lot. "Now, dear, remember when the love bug bites—"

"It's not love, damn it."

"So you say," Mavis said cheerily, waving as she got into her car.

"Sometimes she makes me crazy," Ronnie grumbled getting into her truck. She hesitated and checked the parking lot to see if anyone was watching her. She used to worry that people would think she was stealing the truck when she started it from beneath the dashboard, but for some reason out here in Pleasure, people didn't seem to think it was unusual.

A glance at her watch had her relaxing; she still had time for a ride to settle her nerves. She headed out of town and felt the tension leaving her by degrees as she left the town limits behind her. Five miles out of town her truck coughed and died.

"Damn, I should have checked those plugs when I changed the oil." She got out and slammed the driver's side door. She didn't have time for this; she had to get back or she'd be late when Tyler's brother showed up. She looked under the hood and sighed. She didn't really know what everything was called but knew, with Vito's truck, she could wiggle a couple of things and if that didn't work, she could pull out the hammer... if worse came to worst.

She tightened a few things and crossed her fingers.

Hot, tired, and annoyed, she wiggled and shifted until she was upside down beneath the steering wheel again.

"Need any help?"

The deep voice had her jolting. The smooth baritone did things to her insides that should be illegal. Digging deep, she ignored the feeling and the offer of help.

"Hey, are you all right?"

The firm grip on her knee had her smacking her head on the base of the steering column.

"Ow! What is your problem, buddy?"

"Name's not buddy, ma'am," the deep voice answered. "You didn't answer my question so I figured you were hurt and needed help."

"I didn't answer your question because I didn't feel like it," Ronnie said in her defense.

She touched the wires together and the ignition turned over purring like a top.

——⁓——

Dylan's heart flipped in his chest and started beating double time. Holy shit! The little lady stuck upside down in the cab of her truck had just hot-wired it!

"How did you learn to do that?" he asked, amazed that anyone aside from himself had that particular skill.

"My cousin taught me," she said maneuvering so she could get out from beneath the wheel. Placing a knee on the slide-over-here-honey seat, she scooted backward until she was out of the cab. She turned around and Dylan watched as shock registered first, recognition second.

"Well, now, isn't this a surprise?" He couldn't have planned it better himself if he'd tried.

He'd tossed and turned all night, and the woman standing in front of him looking up at him had been responsible for that and for keeping him tied up in knots for most of the day. And damned if she wasn't frowning up at him. Perverse of him though it might be, it really turned him on.

Glaring at him, she didn't answer. When the engine coughed and died again, she turned her back on him and reached beneath the seat and found what she was looking for. The claw hammer was worn and dirty—looked like it had been well used over the years. Grabbing the wooden handle, she hefted the hammer and got back out of the cab.

"What are you going to do with that?"

She ignored his question a second time, getting under

his skin like a burr under his horse's saddle. Taking a
step back, he leaned against his truck's fender to watch
the show. When the sweet little thing whacked the side
of the starter with the hammer, his jaw dropped. When
the damned thing started, he laughed.

"Who'd have thought—"

"Are you still here?"

To say the woman was pissed would be an under-
statement. When she turned her lethal green gaze on
him, his libido shot straight to boil. He had to get his
hands on her again. He pushed away from the fender
and stalked toward her. She was bent over the fender,
fiddling with something under the hood. Her curvy
backside was cupped lovingly by the worn denim, making his mouth water.

Just one taste. Hands clenched at his sides, he tried
to hold back, but when she wiggled to get closer to the
engine, his heart stopped beating. Light-headed, he
smacked his palm against his chest and finally felt the
organ kick into overdrive.

"Who'd have thought that a pretty little filly from
back East would know how to fix a starter and hot-wire
a truck?" Admiration got all mixed up with his roaring
libido, and something more, nearly indefinable—the
feeling that this woman was going to matter.

"That and a couple of bucks would get you a cappuc-
cino with the works back home," she mumbled, finally
straightening up and turning to face him.

Their eyes met and the anger in her gaze flared into
something hot and wicked. *Hot damn and hallelujah…
she wants me!*

She shook her head as if to clear it and held out a

hand to keep him from reaching for her. "Stop right there, buddy."

"Name's Dylan, ma'am." He grabbed ahold of her hand and reeled her in until she bumped up against his chest and their jean-clad legs were plastered against one another. Her heat scorched him, and Lord, every cell in his body stood at attention.

"You were on my mind all day," he rasped into her hair as he leaned down and pressed his lips to the top of her head. He breathed in and was surrounded by her scent, a combination of sun-warmed woman working up a sweat and—he buried his nose again—some kind of berry.

"And smell good enough to eat, but damned if I can decide if you'll taste like strawberries or raspberries."

"You are not going to kiss me again."

He grinned. "Well now, darlin', I'm not much of a betting man, but I'll take that one." He swooped down and captured her lips with a kiss that had all of his cylinders firing. His engine was running smooth and hot. Sliding a hand down to her waist, he angled his head for a deeper taste.

Shock waves rolled up and over him as his lips devoured the berry-tart confection melting into his arms. He was breathing hard when he came up for air. "I've got to have more."

He was watching closely for her to say yes and follow him into the madness, but something in her eyes changed. She pushed out of his arms, and he let her go. "You gonna walk away from me a second time, when you know we'd burn each other up in bed?"

Her eyes were emerald bright with desire, and still

the little filly sneered up at him and said, "Watch me, cupcake." She turned and stalked to her truck, got in, slammed the door, and gunned the engine. Dirt and gravel ground beneath her tires and shot out as she tore off down the road toward town.

Wiping the grit from his chin, he shook his head. It was going to be a long and bloody battle, but he'd win and she'd thank him for it.

Chapter 3

DYLAN'S HAND GRIPPED THE STEERING WHEEL AS HE drove into town. He wanted to gas it and catch up to Ronnie, but changed his mind. Why be predictable? The enemy would never suspect that he was going to lie in wait for her, until the time was right, and then he would take no prisoners and offer no quarter.

He was grinning as he pulled up in front of the address Emily had given him: Ronnie's store. He had a feeling the woman hadn't put two and two together and figured out he was her new carpenter. He couldn't wait to see her reaction. Although he'd come a different way, it was just around the corner from the Lucky Star. Putting his truck in park, he got a good look at why Emily said the woman needed him. The place was a wreck. What was left of the front window had been boarded up with plywood... interior plywood.

"Waste of good lumber, won't stand up to the elements." When he got closer, he noticed the heads of the nails. "Hell, whoever nailed this up had no idea what they were doing." He shook his head at the choice of the roofing nails used to nail the veneer plywood over the window opening. "No wonder Emily said her friend needed my help."

Still smarting from his run-in with the hardheaded woman from back East, Dylan had to dig deep to lose the irritation. He'd never be charming like his younger brother Jesse, but at least he could find some patience for the owner of the ruined store before he went in and bit Ronnie's head off.

He knocked, but no one answered. "Figures." He tried the door and found it unlocked, so he went inside. "Anybody home?"

No answer.

"Great," he grumbled, "my luck someone'll call the local law and have me arrested for breaking and entering."

Looking around at the inside of the store, he whistled. "Somebody must have had it in for the shop owner." He could see where the display racks and shelves had been and the piles where someone had been painstakingly sorting through the wreckage. The froth of fractured lace caught his eye; he bent to pick it up. The silky material attached to the lace was in shreds. "Who'd the owner piss off enough to have them shoot up the store?"

"Damned if I know, cupcake."

His entire body went on red alert. Dylan clenched his jaw and dug bone deep to keep from grabbing the woman paused halfway down the stairs glaring daggers at him. He was torn between the need to take her by the shoulders and shake her until she stopped trying to irritate the crap out of him and hauling her close and kissing her until she shut that smart mouth of hers.

His sigh was long and low. It wasn't his normal MO to want to get his hands on a woman—with the intention of teaching her a lesson and not just for a little mattress dancing. One look at her angry expression and he realized it wouldn't do any good to remind her that his name was Dylan—and not buddy or cupcake. She was obviously set on digging her spurs into him to get his attention. It was working. He'd give her that much.

The dark-haired temptress who had haunted his dreams and distracted him while he was working alongside his brothers sauntered down the steps and walked over to stand toe to toe with him. "Why you? Why couldn't it have been Tyler's other brother?"

"Out here, people are usually bit more sociable, ma'am." Dylan refused to let her get any further under his skin. "We usually start off a conversation with 'how're you doing' or 'what's the good word today.' Besides," he said crossing his arms and staring down at her, "my brother Jesse's talents don't extend to a hammer and nail."

Her mouth opened and then closed. The light laughter surprised the both of them. He hadn't thought the sound of a woman laughing could be so sexy. He'd been wrong. The silky sound of her laughter sent a set of chills chasing up his spine. Dylan fought the need to shiver.

"We do back home too—well not quite the same expressions you used, but the meaning's the same."

Dylan swallowed a snort of laughter and noticed her eyes twinkled. She urged, "Admit it, DD."

"DD? What kind of insult does that stand for?" He almost didn't ask for fear that it would have to do with his manly pride, and the little woman had flung enough insults at him already.

Slashes of deep rose accentuated the luscious olive-toned skin that begged to be caressed. He noticed textures and colors, wanting to delve deep for another taste of her. His fingertips itched to trace the curve of her jaw and test the plumpness of her bottom lip. She dropped her hand and shifted from one foot to the other. Was he making her nervous? DD must be an East Coast insult.

"Come on," he urged, "tell me."

She shook her head.

"Lord, woman," he ground out. "You'd drive a saint crazy."

She narrowed her gaze and stared at him. "I don't think you'd qualify as one."

This time, he couldn't contain the rumble of laughter bubbling up from inside of him. "Probably not."

She crossed her arms beneath her breasts. Did she do that to distract him or to just plain torture him? His palms started to sweat. He brushed them against his thighs.

He noticed Ronnie was skittish and kept looking over her shoulder behind her. A thought shot through him. "Are you expecting someone to come back and finish the job?"

The split second of fear in her eyes had his need to protect her screaming to the surface. She shook her head and a second emotion, so close to the one he'd been living with lately, flashed in her gaze before it was gone. "I just need some time alone."

He'd bet his last dollar that something—make that someone—had hurt this little lady enough to scar her. Dylan didn't want to get involved, swore he wouldn't let his heart lead him down the primrose path again, but damned if he didn't reach out and brush the tears gathering at the corner of her eyes, determined to fix whatever or whoever had hurt her.

"Emily said you needed more than my carpentry skills. I'm wondering if she meant my services as a bodyguard."

Ronnie's face flushed and he wondered if she were thinking what he'd been thinking—he'd really love to get close enough to do more than guard her body. To diffuse some of the tension in the air, he looked around the downstairs store and pushed the brim of his Stetson back. "Emily's a sweet thing and the light of my brother's life." He let his gaze slide back to meet hers. "But now that she and Tyler have decided to pair up and get married, she's wanting to find women for Jesse and me." He paused and looked down at her. "Why do you females do that? We can find our own women."

Ronnie rubbed at her temples as if her head ached. "I'm just feeling a little out of place out here," she said looking around at the piles of organized destruction. "Believe me, Dylan, I only want to fix my store and reopen before I go bankrupt."

Her words were so close to what he and his brothers were feeling about their ranch that he blinked and nearly asked her to repeat what she just said. Dylan fought the urge to reach out and massage the tender skin at the edge of her cheekbones. The woman had distracted him from the start; now that she'd reawakened feelings he'd thought buried too deeply to resurface, Dylan figured he'd be a walking, talking lunatic before he could convince the little lady that he was interested in more than just a one-night stand. "Hell or high water," he mumbled.

"Is that another of your down-home Texas sayings?"

He didn't know what to say that wouldn't have her snapping off a sharp comeback. Females could be a real pain in the ass—or in other body parts left alone and aching for too long.

—◦◦◦—

Ronnie couldn't believe her luck. Why couldn't it have been the youngest Garahan brother that was the out-of-work carpenter Emily had been talking about? She'd be able to focus on what needed to be done instead of replaying that scorching kiss they'd shared. Emily knew that Ronnie had been attracted to and distracted by the brother who'd been headlining at the Lucky Star the other night. Couldn't her friend have warned her so she'd be prepared to handle the six-foot-plus, dark-haired, dark-eyed man currently starring in her dreams? "I'll kill her later."

"Who?"

"Nobody," she lied, as she gathered her courage, braced herself, and looked into soulful brown eyes reminding her of warm, gooey chocolate, melted and swirled into her favorite raspberry fudge. She licked her lips wondering if he'd taste just as delectable. Could she give in to the need overwhelming her, beckoning her to follow down the wrong road for the second time in her life? No! She would not give in to the need to touch, no matter how beautifully sculpted his lips were and how badly she wanted to test their firmness with her own. *Ignore the breadth of his shoulders and the strength in his hands... history will not repeat itself.*

Before she could think what to say that wouldn't make her come across as a candidate for the psych ward, he said, "Look, if you've changed your mind and you're not looking for help—"

"I didn't say that," she interrupted, "it's just that so much has happened in the last few days, and I'm having trouble getting my bearings."

His gaze met hers and he nodded. "I can appreciate that." His dark eyes dropped to her hands and she felt the flush creep up her neck into her cheeks. "So what are you fixin' for dinner tonight?"

She had trouble switching gears and pulling her thoughts up out of the gutter, imagining what he'd been thinking staring at her hands. *Cooking!* Go figure, she'd been working up a really interesting scenario where he was putty in her hands as she started stroking his amazing pecs before working down to his abs and then—

"Ronnie, darlin'?"

She jumped. Damn! He'd done it again—distracting her when she should be paying attention. "What?"

He rubbed his chin and looked like he was fighting not to smile. Had he guessed the direction of her thoughts? "I've worked up a hunger working today and I know my brothers will be starving, so if you wouldn't mind telling me, I can give them a call and let them know what you'll be cooking for dinner tomorrow."

Ronnie couldn't help it; she laughed again. She hadn't in a long time, but somehow this cowboy had drawn it out of her. "I promise you'll like it. Why don't we keep it a surprise until we get to your house?"

"Ranch."

"OK, until we get to your ranch house."

He shook his head. "Out here, we call it the ranch—or the Circle G."

"Why?"

He looked down at her and she shivered under the intensity of his gaze. Lord, she wanted the opportunity to get to know this man better. If they connected on a cerebral level like they obviously would on a physical level, she could be… in really big trouble. She took a mental step back and stared into his eyes, waiting for him to speak.

Nonni always said that you could tell if someone was lying, or what they were thinking, by looking into their eyes. *Eyes don't lie*. Dylan's were a warm, deep brown. He didn't look away or flinch under her scrutiny. She liked that about him; she'd have to tell Nonni about him soon.

Trusting in her grandmother's oft-quoted advice, she held out her hand and said, "How 'bout if we shake on it."

Dylan paused as if considering. "You're not gonna fix some kind of weird healthy food—the kind that doesn't include meat, are you?"

The pained look on his face had her chuckling. "Well, I don't think my Nonni's lasagna crepes are weird."

"What's a crepe?"

"In this case, a very thin pancake—"

Dylan crossed his arms and stared at her as if he couldn't decide if she was joking with him or not. "Heck out here we put syrup on our flapjacks."

She shook her head at him. "Crepes are French, and very thin and light, and when you stuff them with cheese and sweet sausage, roll them up and pour my Nonni's red sauce on top, you'll think you died and went to heaven."

He was looking at her as if her elevator didn't go to the top floor. Wouldn't be the first time someone who didn't appreciate good cooking or understand her love for food thought she was nuts.

"Trust me."

He nodded and stuck out his hand. "All right, darlin'. Let's shake on it."

She took his hand and felt the jolt all the way to her shoulder. Trying to ignore the pinpricks of awareness sparking in places that hadn't been interested in a long, long time, she smiled up at him.

He frowned, and added, "I don't eat any of that tofu crap."

"Bean curd is good for you."

"Hell, I'll eat baked beans or green beans, just don't grind 'em up and make 'em into that white pasty stuff."

She struggled not to laugh, sensing that he was dead serious. "Deal."

His frown eased and his eyes twinkled. "Now, darlin', about that lacy stuff... just what did you sell in here?"

"Lingerie. Something for all tastes." She looked over her shoulder and sighed. "I had a collection of heirloom fragrances and reproduction perfume bottles and a display of essential oils so customers could design their own fragrance massage oil."

He swallowed and his Adam's apple bobbed up and down. "You don't say."

Longing sprinted through her and settled low in her belly. She wanted him to let loose and go with the emotions she saw swirling in the depths of his velvet dark eyes. "Back home, the massage oil was a close second in sales to the lingerie."

The man opened his mouth to speak, but no words came out. He flushed an adorable shade of pink, right before he tucked his hands in his back pockets and rocked on his boot heels. Pushing his Stetson to the back of his head, he scratched his forehead and settled his hat back in place. "I thought you sold underwear."

"I do, but I sell the other items too." She paused and said, "And it's not just underwear, I sell chemises, garter belts, peignoir sets—"

"Look, Ronnie. I'll be honest. I don't need this job bad enough to put up with you calling me names and then just plain laughing at me. I know a couple of guys who are looking for work and can give you a list of names and numbers."

There was more here than she could put her finger on. Just what that was she didn't know, but she needed to fix this so he didn't leave when all of her emotions were tumbling in a mass of confusion like this. She sensed they had a future that needed to be explored— thoroughly. A flicker of warning about the DelVecchio Curse tried to make itself known, but she tamped it down and rasped, "I'm sorry, Dylan."

His eyebrows shot up, and then he frowned.

"I promise I wasn't laughing at you."

"I've got two brothers who've been taking care of that particular job for years. Family's allowed to; strangers aren't."

She sensed there was something else that went much deeper, but knew enough not to ask right now. She needed Dylan Garahan's help and would use whatever she had in her arsenal to ensure she got that help. "Emily said that once a Garahan gave his word, he kept it." He toed the pile of wood with the tip of his boot and brushed his hands on his thighs. A master of distracting her grandmother, Ronnie knew she'd scored a direct hit to his conscience.

He sighed. "If this is gonna work, no name calling and no making fun just because I ain't never been in a fancy underwear store before."

"Dylan." She reached for his arm and squeezed it quickly before letting go. "I really am sorry." She wished she could make him believe it. "So then Emily was right about you keeping your word?"

He stopped in his tracks and turned to face her; letting his eyes met hers, he cleared his throat. "I give you my word."

"You'll stick until my shop's been put back together?"

He removed the hat from his head and raked his hand through his hair before answering. "Yes, ma'am."

"And I promise that I'll cook dinner for you and your brothers out at the Circle G and pay you for the materials to complete the job." Pausing, she rubbed at the ache that moved down to the base of her neck. "I just hope the insurance check will cover the damage and help replace what I lost, especially the massage oil. It's a specific grade that I buy that mixes well with my signature fragrances, so the scent isn't overpowering."

He stared at her long and hard. "You're not kidding?"

"About what: the insurance check covering the damage or the massage oil?"

He shut his eyes and groaned. "Darlin', my mind's working overtime wondering who'd have the time or energy to use that oil. Besides, why would someone with an angel's face need anything like that?"

"Because there are plenty of women out there who don't have a man in their life, or the time or energy to go out and find one, and the fragrant oil is simply for their pleasure."

"Are you talking about Texas women or women from back East?"

"Women are the same everywhere."

His laugh was bold and booming. "Oh, darlin', you haven't been in Texas long enough if you believe that." He stared down at her finally asking, "So what… uh… do you use the oil for?"

She smiled but didn't turn around. "It feels wonderful when you stroke it from your shoulders to your fingertips for starters." Ronnie thought she heard a groan coming from the big man following behind her, and no matter how badly she wanted to tease him, she remembered their agreement. "After a long day on your feet, nothing feels better than a long hot soak in the tub with a splash of my signature lavender and lemon balm massage oil mixed in."

Poor man sounded like he was choking. "Are you all right, Dylan?"

"Yes, ma'am."

"Are you still mad?"

He shook his head. "No. Why don't you tell me how the inside of your shop used to look. Then you can tell me about the sweet stuff you're gonna be baking for me and my brothers."

Relief filled her. Ronnie blinked back tears of gratitude at being given this chance to rebuild. She grinned up at him. Aside from the bone-deep integrity, the man standing beside her was as volatile as dynamite. She knew in that moment looking up at him that she'd definitely be sticking around long enough to see if that powder keg building inside of him would be safe enough to set a match to. She had a feeling they'd either both

spontaneously combust and burn each other alive with
passion or kill each other.

Knowing the way to a hungry man's heart, she smiled
and told him, "I've got this butter cake recipe that will
just melt in your mouth."

"Do tell, darlin'." Dylan grinned. "Do tell."

The memory of him tossing a rope around her and
slowly reeling her in while she remained helplessly
under his control chose that moment to pop into her
thoughts, distracting her. Sensing that it might be at the
root of her constant need to take verbal jabs at the man,
she realized she would have to be vigilant in order to
keep her promise to him too. But if she was truly honest
with herself, she'd have to admit it wasn't just the way
he'd lassoed her that had her entire body melting against
his when the hunkalicious cowboy's lips claimed pos-
session of her own. It was lust, pure and simple… wasn't
it? "I wish I could forget that."

"Forget what?"

Her head shot up, and her face burned with the heat
of her embarrassment. *Damn, she must have said that
out loud.* "Um, nothing. Why don't I just show you the
basic layout of the store."

Dylan stared down at her for the longest time, and
Ronnie had to keep her hands clenched at her sides, or
else she'd reach up and grab him by the collar and yank
him down until his lips were a breath away from hers.
Her body craved another taste, a long slow, deep tasting.

Would his lips be as lethal, or was it just a José-
induced memory from the night before? Afraid he could
read her mind, she buried the need deep, right alongside
the memory of her failed first marriage. She shuddered.

The two were on opposite ends of the spectrum as far as experiences go… maybe someday she'd find someone right in the middle who could balance out the scales. Someone quiet, calm, and boring as hell—but not Irish. She had no intention of fulfilling the curse, not matter how badly she wanted to spend time exploring the strength of the handsome cowboy's muscles, the breadth of his shoulders, or the taste of his lips.

Was she nuts? She'd never settle for boring again. Well, not as long as she could conjure up the delicious sensation of Dylan's firm, warm lips tentatively tasting her own. She shivered.

"You cold?"

The concern in his voice was genuine and went a long way toward easing the sharper edges of the unwanted memory of her first husband. They were both to blame. Her ex more than her, but he hadn't changed his colors; he'd been consistent—and unable to be faithful—she'd chosen to handle it until she began to suspect that he was having an affair with her best friend.

She sighed and shook her head and walked over toward the largest pile. "I wasn't sure what to do," she explained, "so I started putting pieces of wood together—sort of by size." Looking down, Ronnie wondered if she should have considered the thickness of the wood instead. "Maybe I made more work for you."

Dylan gaze met hers before sliding away to focus on the waist-high pile of wood. He shook his head. "Damn, but that's a waste. You ever figure out why your shop was the target?"

She shrugged. "Not really, just that it was one of three… all owned by women."

"Right," he mumbled. "I remember Mrs. Beeton explaining that a few days ago—the day Widowmaker tried to make sausage out of my brother's guts."

Ronnie watched as one emotion chased another across Dylan's handsome face. Anger, followed by pain, hot on the heels of resignation, until finally relief settled in and smoothed out the lines of frustration between his dark eyebrows. The man was a mystery she hadn't planned on wanting to solve. The last time she'd gotten in deep, she'd realized there wasn't anything beneath the surface calm of the man she'd married. He was all show on the surface, good-looking and smooth-talking, but she'd known him all her life and thought her ex was what she wanted. She'd been wrong.

He drew in a deep breath and slowly blew it out. She watched in helpless fascination as the fabric of his soft cotton shirt expanded, straining the seams to a fraction of an inch before they threatened to split wide open. *Darn*. The worn material must have been stitched with heavy-duty cotton threads; they held.

Get your mind on the job at hand, dear. "Yes, Nonni."

"Who's Nonni?"

"Hmmm?" She didn't want to answer the question and have to go into a long explanation as to why she heard her grandmother in her head and answered her out loud, when all she had to do was pick up the phone and call her. It was a comforting connection to home back East.

When she kept silent, Dylan didn't prod her to answer. She appreciated that fact. The longer she was in his company, the more things she found that appealed to her. Add them to the fact that he had a mouth that had

her thinking about sampling a deeper taste of him, and
she was in trouble with a capital *T*!

"Look, if you're all right down here…" She hesitated
and looked up at him for confirmation. When he nodded, she continued, "Then I've got some paperwork to
finish upstairs."

———∿∿———

Dylan watched her run off and wondered what had made
her so skittish. He hadn't done or said anything that he
knew of, but women were difficult to understand at the
best of times and impossible the rest of the time.

Shaking his head, he picked up the abbreviated length
of shelving and turned it on its edge to see if it was still
true. The wood still looked straight enough to reuse,
even though it was shorter than it had originally been.
He placed it on the floor, reached for the next piece, and
stifled a chuckle. A glance at the stairs reassured him
that she hadn't come back down. He didn't want her to
think he was laughing at her; he wasn't, it was the idea
that anyone would think to sort wood by length and not
type or thickness.

Getting to work, he soon had a couple of stacks
going, sorted to his satisfaction. What bothered him was
the biggest stack… it wasn't fit to use for anything but
a bonfire. At the current price per board foot, it would
be a damn costly fire. He wasn't sure if Ronnie had any
idea just how much material he'd need to reconstruct
her shop. He'd have to work hard to keep his price
within what he suspected was a very tight budget. But
he had connections in town and could probably work
something out to their mutual satisfaction, especially if

he could convince her to purchase used lumber. Done right, it would add to the appeal of her shop, giving it a vintage look that might complement her collection of bottles and such.

Going back out to his truck, he grabbed his tape measure, carpenter's pencil, and pad of paper from the front seat. His skin had finally stopped tingling once Ronnie had gone upstairs. Her lovely green eyes had begged him to follow, though he doubted she'd really wanted him to consciously… and it had taken all of his control not to. It was going to take some time to come to terms with the way she got to him, by turns good and bad.

He would have to deal with the bad as long as he could get to the good. He salivated imagining trailing his tongue from beneath her left ear to the hollow of her throat, where he'd stop to inhale the distracting scent that was pure woman—

Get your mind back on the job.

"Yeah, yeah," he grumbled. "I heard you, Grandpa. Geez, a man can't even pause to savor the thought of sampling a pretty woman." He slammed the door and walked back to the shop. Why he glanced up he couldn't exactly say, but the pretty face staring down at him had him wondering how long it would be before the woman put him out of his misery and let him taste the sweetness of her curves. He didn't want to rush her, but his newly awakened libido was like his horse Wildfire: champing at the bit, raring to go. He shook his head. He had more control than his horse—didn't he? Damn, but the woman messed with his mind.

Digging deep for control, he broke eye contact and reached for the door. He had a hell of a job ahead of him. It would take time, but he'd write up two estimates for her. One starting from scratch with new, scrapping what was left of her shop, and the other utilizing what could be salvaged and adding in used lumber when he could. It would take longer, but he had a feeling it was the option she'd want to go with. Not that it would help pay off the mortgage at the Circle G, but hell, they'd be guaranteed home-cooked meals. He savored the thought, grateful that the barter system was still alive and well in Pleasure, Texas.

Instead of the meals promised, Dylan envisioned another way the delectably disturbing brunette could pay him for the carpentry work. *Clothing optional…*

But reality and an empty belly had him getting back to work, and for the next hour, he measured and drew out plans to reconstruct. He raked a hand through his hair and straightened; he needed a break. The sound of footsteps had him looking up. The smile came easily. The woman was real easy on the eyes.

"Hungry?"

He swallowed the bark of laughter that threatened to escape. Lord above, did she have any idea how hungry he was for a taste of her? She stared down at him and all he could think was where he'd start sampling. The T-shirt she had on slid off her shoulder, leaving the gleaming skin exposed. The bare skin begged to be caressed. He walked toward her like a man in a trance, unable to look away, focusing on the beauty before him.

"I've got a loaf of bread, some pasta, and a pot of Nonni's red sauce simmering on the stove. I thought you'd like to take a break and have something to eat." She hesitated and not for the first time he wondered who'd hurt her and whether or not she'd be letting him get close enough to find out... close enough to convince her he'd be able to make her forget the jerk from her past.

Though he couldn't say for sure, he'd bet the way he answered her would either make or break their budding working relationship. He pushed all thoughts of tasting the woman aside and dug deep for the civility that he hadn't used in a while, hadn't needed to. Men only needed to appear civilized when women were around.

Men understood one another and didn't have to worry about what they said, how they dressed or acted. But when a woman was involved—he sighed deeply and looked down at his hands. "I need to wash up first."

"Bathroom's down the hall."

"I'll be right back." As soon as Dylan walked through the door, the subtle scent surrounded him. He drew in a deep breath and was assailed with the memory of sparks igniting in the air around them and the sweet, tart flavor he had come to crave.

Down, boy. He'd been invited to eat—food.

The upstairs apartment was small, so finding the kitchen was a no-brainer; he just followed his nose and the scent of simmering spaghetti sauce. "Smells good."

She looked over her shoulder at him and smiled. "That'd be a plus since you're going to be eating my cooking for the next month or so."

Dylan expected to be handed the serving spoon and told to fend for himself; he was surprised when she motioned for him to go sit down at the table by the picture window. Looking out, he noticed that the window was huge and it faced the parking lot, explaining why he could see so much of her. Gauging the height of the sun, he realized his brothers would be heading back to the ranch and having to eat whatever sandwich fixings were left in the fridge at home. He should probably be feeling sorry for them, if he didn't already know that the promise of an excellent meal was in the future for all of them, starting tomorrow.

She carried out a plate heaped with pasta and covered with sauce and a basket of sliced bread. "Please," she urged, "sit down."

He breathed in the mouth-watering scent before pulling out her chair and waiting while she placed the plates on the table. She shook her head at him and smiled. "I've got a few more things to bring in."

"Let me help."

She hesitated, then agreed. "Would you like wine with your pasta?" When he frowned, she offered, "I've got a couple of longnecks in the fridge."

He felt at ease for the first time since he walked through her door. "Beer'd be good, thanks."

She handed him two bottles of beer and nodded for him to precede her. Not wanting to make her feel ill at ease, he did as she asked. He set the beer down and took the plate from her hands, setting it down on the table. "You look a little pale. Do you feel all right?"

The pained expression on her face intrigued him, but he didn't know her well enough to push... yet.

"After you left, I had a run in with José last night."

"Ahhh." He helped her scoot closer to the table before he sat. "First meal today?"

She flushed, a hint of color tingeing the curve of her cheeks. Ronnie was a delight to observe. Maybe it wasn't just lust that had him by the throat. There was more here, and if he was patient, he just might discover the woman beneath the surface... the real Ronnie. Suddenly, he couldn't wait.

Digging in, he slipped the forkful of sauce-covered pasta into his mouth and groaned as his taste buds stood at full attention. Chewing, he savored the spices and full-bodied flavor. "If everything you cook tastes this good, I may not ever let you go, darlin'."

If he hadn't been looking at her, he would have missed the flash of fear. Every damned time she tried to hide what she was thinking or feeling, it made him want to stick around for the long haul. He hadn't felt this way since he and Sandy had been fourteen years old and pledged to spend the rest of their lives together. It was a distinctly uncomfortable feeling, but one he sus-. pected would accompany him each and every time he was within three feet of this East Coast woman.

When she still didn't speak, he sampled another forkful, chewed, and swallowed before asking, "Please pass the bread."

He deliberately brushed the tips of his fingers across her knuckles before grasping the basket of bread. Watching for a reaction, he was deeply satisfied when her eyes deepened to the emerald he remembered from the night before. She was interested right back. *Hot damn!* "Thanks."

They ate in silence. When his plate was empty, he remembered to use the napkin beside his plate and wiped his mouth. He could be polite if he had to.

"So, sweet thing," he drawled. "Are you dessert?"

Ronnie's mouth dropped open and then closed. Her

bright green gaze slashed across him, but he was ready and waiting for her reaction. "I already know how your smart mouth tastes, but I've got this hankerin' for a taste of your shoulder, your cheek, your—"

She got up so fast her chair banged against the windowsill. "Of all the—"

"Whoa there, filly," he soothed. "I forgot that hairtrigger of yours."

"What... I'm not... arrgggh..."

He took advantage of her sputtering and snagged her hand, pulling her close enough to plunder. He savored her flavor, enjoying the tartness mixing with the spices from the meal she'd cooked, slipping his tongue deep to sample the underlying sweetness. Lord, he'd die happy if her lips were the last thing on earth that he tasted.

Be careful what you wish for, Son.

Finally, her arms wrapped around him, and he broke the kiss, urging, "Kiss me back, Ronnie."

Her tongue tangled with his and he was lost.

Chapter 4

"No." Ronnie pushed out of Dylan's arms, shaking her head. "What am I doing?"

Dylan's eyes narrowed. "Smart woman like you ought to be able to figure it out."

"See what I mean?" Head swimming, heart pounding, she took another step back until she was no longer within the circle of his arms. Sweeping her hand toward the tiny table beneath the front window, she sighed. "We were eating. Two reasonable adults sharing a table and a meal."

His gaze snagged hers. "You kissed me."

She glared at him. "You started it!

Unbelievably, the man smiled at her.

"What is wrong with you? I fixed you dinner so you could sample my cooking." She folded her arms beneath her breasts. "Not the cook."

"Too late. My brothers and I demolished that pie and now that I've had a taste of you, I want more."

He grinned and she wanted to smack that look off his face. Her palms tingled and her fingertips flexed. It took every ounce of control that she had to keep from striking out at him. She hated to be laughed at almost as much as she hated to be misunderstood.

Once she had the urge to hit him under control, the overwhelming need to be in the man's arms had her breath catching and her heart beating double time. Her insides melted and damned if her traitorous body didn't weep with want in places better left unsaid.

His gaze snagged hers and his nostrils flared. He looked like a stallion who'd just scented a mare in heat.

Holy crap! It had been way too long since she'd let her body get her into trouble with the wrong man at the wrong time.

She hadn't tangled with any man since and had worn out two vibrators, lying to herself that it felt just as good. But vibrators can't snuggle and were a poor substitute when you had a smooth-talking, good-looking, towering example of pure unadulterated male standing three feet away, vibrating with need and the promise of heaven in his dark brown eyes.

Heat crept up her neck into her face. She smoothed her hands from the bridge of her nose along the line of her cheekbones; the heat singed her fingertips, but it wasn't embarrassment that sent a direct message to her center—it was lust. Plain and simple. But what did she know about the dark-eyed cowboy clenching his jaw, quivering with need, evidenced by the telltale bulge straining against his button-fly jeans? They'd only met the night before, and despite the fact that they'd spent the last few hours talking and then working in close proximity, they were still basically strangers.

Dylan ran his hands over his face and seemed to gather himself back under control. "Ronnie, I'm about to beg—I hate to beg."

Her inner muscles clenched and damned if her body didn't crank up the moisture to just shy of embarrassing. Trying to ignore her traitorous body, she drew in a breath and met his gaze. His eyes darkened and his breathing quickened. *Could he tell?* The need to cross her legs was almost impossible to resist.

"Dylan," she began, "I'm sorry if I gave you the wrong impression—"

He reached for her again but stopped when she held up her hand. He clenched his hands at his sides and she wondered how long she could keep this cowboy from tossing her over his shoulder and heading down the hall to her bedroom.

"I don't normally kiss a man I've never met before."

The look in his eyes chilled her. "We met last night, remember, darlin'?" He pantomimed circling a lasso with his hand, then letting it fly.

Fear and excitement had poured through her veins like molten rock last night, and only a large dash of common sense had kept her from agreeing to wait for him. "How could I forget?"

He stood at attention, his hands and his jaw clenching and unclenching as if to keep himself from grabbing her. The image of being hauled back into his arms flashed through her like lightning. Desire and lust combined into a ball of need so huge it threatened to close her throat. She swallowed against the lump. "You'd better go."

Something akin to pain flashed in his dark eyes, but it happened so fast she wasn't sure if she had imagined it or it had been real. Without another word, he turned on his heel and left.

A hollow, empty feeling filled the void his leaving had created. Ronnie wanted to rush after him, call him back, and apologize. "For what?"

Needing him?

Wanting him?

Lusting after him?

"All of the above."

Now that he'd gone, the sexual tension that had vibrated in the air around them dissipated, leaving her drained and wanting—wanting a man who could be all wrong for her. Besides, she didn't have the strength to go there again... did she?

Follow your heart, bambina. Maybe her grandmother wouldn't lecture Ronnie about sticking to her budget and not going over her minutes if she called her tonight and again on their usual day. With a heavy sigh, she cleared the table and straightened her tiny kitchen. It wasn't her dream kitchen... that would be the size of her entire apartment, with a fireplace that took up one whole wall. Just like the one she'd seen in a vintage Victorian magazine, one so large, you could roast a side of beef in it, complete with a double oven—so she could roast a turkey and bake pies—while the pasta and red sauce simmered on the stovetop.

Her eyes teared up at the thought of such culinary perfection, until she snapped out of it. "Hey, I'm not destitute. I have a damned stove to cook on and an oven to bake whatever I want in."

Yanking open the cabinet above the sink, she grabbed a container and carefully poured the leftover red sauce into it. Her Nonni called it gravy, but Ronnie's friends at school weren't Italian and thought she meant brown gravy whenever she called it that.

You come from solid peasant stock, Veronica, be proud of it and don't ever forget that.

She screwed on the lid and put the jar into the fridge, reminding herself to make that call as soon as she set the kitchen to rights. Once the dishes were washed and air drying in the dish drainer, she was ready to tackle the pots and pans.

Ronnie rubbed at her temples to soothe the growing ache. It didn't help. "At least I had my usual tonight." Rinsing out the empty beer bottles and placing them in the recycle canister next to her garbage, she smiled. Her grandmother would be pursing her lips right now; she never could understand how Ronnie could drink a beer and eat her grandmother's cooking. Nonni insisted on a robust red table wine. Ronnie could take it or leave it. Beer just tasted better to her. Must be something in her lineage somewhere that diluted her Italian heritage, rumors of *the curse* flitted through her beleaguered brain, but she ignored the thought and reached for the phone.

"Hi, Nonni, it's me."

"Veronica! Is everything all right? It's not Sunday."

The worry in her grandmother's voice soothed the rough edges that her night of overindulging had left behind. "Just missing you," Ronnie reassured her grandmother. Relieved, the dear woman launched into the latest news from back home. When she'd filled Ronnie in on who'd won at bingo, whose bridge partner had moved to Florida, and what new eligible man moved into their senior living complex, her grandmother asked, "So have you met any interesting men out in Texas?"

Ronnie's heart skipped a beat. "One or two." Wanting to give her grandmother something to think about until their next phone call, she added, "By the name of Garahan."

She could picture her grandmother's face smiling, which was as close as Ronnie could get to a hug right now. "Now don't go thinking it's anything serious, Nonni," she warned. "I… uh… met him last night when I was out with friends. He's going to be rebuilding my shop."

"*Bastardos!*" She agreed with her grandmother until Nonni started in on the curse. "You know Veronica, the Irish are just as hot-blooded as Italians."

Knowing there would be no stopping Nonni once she got going on her favorite subject, Ronnie pretended someone was at her door. "Hang on just a minute," she called out, "be right there." Waiting a moment, she said, "Nonni, I've got to go."

"Maybe it's that lovely Irishman from last night." Her grandmother sounded positively ecstatic about the idea. "You should save your pennies for our Sunday chats, dear."

"Yes, Nonni."

"I love you, *bambina*."

"I love you too, Nonni."

Half an hour later, she wandered back downstairs, amazed at how different it looked. Where there had been haphazard piles of lumber that she'd sorted were now neat piles of lumber that appeared to be all the same thickness and type.

"Must make sense to a carpenter." She smiled. Dylan was apparently a man of many talents; he could rope a woman, kiss her brainless, and sort wood. Time would tell if he was as good as Emily claimed he'd be repairing the front of her shop and rebuilding the shelves.

She turned and nearly swallowed her tongue; the pile of ruined lingerie had been painstakingly sorted by color, largest scraps on the bottom of each pile. The very thought of Dylan's hands touching the silky bits and pieces of what was left of the teddies and chemises she'd stocked and sold left her a bit breathless.

Remembering the callused hands that had gripped her upper arms and dragged her close, she closed her eyes, imagining what those hands would feel like caressing her shoulders, smoothing the hair off her neck, before pressing his lips where his hands had been.

"Arrgghh. Do. Not. Go. There!"

She spun on her heel and headed to the staircase, stomping her way up, feeling oddly better for taking some of her frustration out on the steps. When she reached the top she burst out laughing. If her grandmother was here, she'd be chastising Ronnie for *damning around*—that's what Nonni called it when Ronnie stomped out her anger as a child. And Nonni was rarely wrong. She had been mad and taking it out on an inanimate object: the poor stairs.

Alone, she was just a bit uneasy, wondering whether or not the teenagers who had trashed her store would be back. She didn't think they were that stupid, but she retraced her steps and locked the door at the top of the steps. The snick of the lock slipping into place reminded her that she called the shots; she was in charge and could lock up or not… it was her choice.

Desperately needing to have a choice was of the utmost importance to her. When she'd married, she thought it had been her choice, but looking back, she could see that it hadn't been. She'd been swept away by the idea of not fulfilling her grandmother's prophesies and the dreaded curse, choosing a boy she'd known all her life, one that she sensed wouldn't be all that concerned with fidelity, but would be able to provide for her. And wasn't that what she'd decided she wanted, rather than love: a big house, a fancy car, and designer clothes?

Her ex had said he loved her, but Ronnie had come to realize that what he had loved was his image of her. She'd never let him know the real her because she didn't love him enough to share her hopes and dreams with the man. He'd often told her he needed her, but she'd come to accept that what he needed was someone who would pick up after him and cook for him. She'd been content with their life until her best friend had started canceling dates to meet for coffee, shopping, and drinks. Her gut was never wrong—she'd wished it had been.

Now that the pain of their betrayal wasn't quite so sharp, she realized the only thing her ex really loved, wanted, or needed her for was her cooking. "Damn." Didn't that thought just turn her world upside down? Dylan needed her to cook for him too. Well, at least he'd been honest with her; Dylan had made no secret that he wanted a whole lot more from her.

"Double damn." Even knowing he only wanted her for her body didn't bother her as much as she'd thought it would because she'd been just as attracted to his amazing body from the get-go. Successful relationships had been built on initial physical attractions before—*just look at Nonni and Poppi*. Her grandparents had fallen in love at first sight—well, so maybe she and Dylan had fallen in lust at first sight. No biggie, there was time to sort things out while they spent time in one another's company at Guilty Pleasures.

Ronnie sighed as she flicked on the bathroom light. Her reflection smiled back at her as she admitted, "I really do want that man in my bed."

"No." Reaching for her cleanser, she opened the top and squeezed a dollop into the palm of her hand.

Smoothing it over her forehead and around the line of her cheekbones, she let her mind wander. Wasn't a surprise that it settled on the tall, dark, and handsome hunk of cowboy with the callused hands and kissable lips.

She studied her reflection. Her face had a rosy glow, but her eyes were troubled. "Stay away from that man's lips until you've built up an immunity to his charms." Her belly felt like it was filled with butterflies as she remembered the commanding way his mouth had claimed hers. Before those butterflies could travel south, she wondered if the curse would still be effective if he was only half Irish. She'd have to ask him.

The image of her grandmother laughing filled her. With shaky hands, she reached for her toothbrush and didn't look at the mirror again, even after she turned out the light.

———

Dylan drove up to the gate to the Circle G and put his truck in park. Sliding out, he unlatched and opened it without being conscious of doing so, his mind was stuck on the brunette with the slashing green eyes who'd both tempted and annoyed him to the bursting point.

"Hellfire." He didn't need a woman right now. Even if he did, he could go on over to Mesquite and find himself a willing woman any night of the week. He had a couple of times after Sandy had eviscerated him when she'd walked out the door for the last time. He scrubbed his hands over his face. He hadn't believed that she meant to make her life in the city, hadn't wanted to believe that she could make a life for herself where he wouldn't be a part of it. She'd gone to Southern Methodist University in Dallas to earn her degree in anthropology with a focus on archeology and had only come back for a couple of months—time that she'd spent living out at the Circle G—months that he'd spent trying to convince her that her place was here in Pleasure. With her degree still shiny and new beckoning her to travel where she'd always wanted to explore—the Pyramids of Giza and the ancient cities of the Middle East—his love and broken-down ranch hadn't been enough to hold her.

Sandy had warned him that she wanted more from life than the tiny town of Pleasure could give her. She wanted a career in archaeology, work that would take her to the other side of the world from him. When her parents relocated to the Southeast, he finally had to wake up and smell the coffee; she wasn't coming back to Texas… ever. Nearly two years later, he'd come to accept the fact that she'd been honest with him since the day she'd received the letter of acceptance to her dream college. He just hadn't believed that they didn't want the same things out of life and that she would eventually go.

He'd learned to listen the hard way; it was the mixed signals women often sent out that still confused the hell out of him. "Women need the words." He knew it now, learned it the hard way, watching his older brother Tyler and his girlfriend Emily as they struggled to make their relationship work. "Too bad I'm not much on talking."

Slamming the door, he got back into the truck, drove through the gate, got out, and repeated the process. Remembering the tender scene he'd walked in on between Tyler and Emily just that morning had been like taking a ball-peen hammer to his breastbone. He had frozen, unable to look away while Tyler slid his fingertips around the back of Emily's throat, brushing his thumbs along the line of her jaw. The beauty of Emily's surrender, as she leaned toward Tyler and lifted her lips, had had Dylan's heart pounding.

He'd been in a trance until Tyler slid the palm of his hand down the length of Emily's spine to cup her curvy backside.

Jealousy had hit him hard and deep, raking its claws along his nerve endings, breaking the spell. Without a sound, he backed up and walked out the front door rather than intrude on the lovers.

Raw and aching from the two-day hard-on Ronnie had caused, he slammed and damned his way into the house. Not caring if he woke anybody... not caring if they needed their sleep. What about him? He needed sleep, and damn it all, he needed someone to care about him too.

Jealous much? "Yeah. Damn woman's got me tangled up and tied in knots." *You just need to take a ride into Mesquite—relieve some of that tension so you can focus on your job at the ranch—and the one rebuilding Ronnie's store.*

He took off his Stetson and tossed it on the kitchen table, and the image of rose-dusted skin glistening in the moonlight sliced through him. The witchy woman with the raven hair lying on the rough wood farm table smugly smiled up at him, licked her lips, and opened her arms.

"Fuck me." Dylan scrubbed his hands over his face, afraid to look back at the table for fear that the glorious vision would either be gone or beckoning him to shuck his jeans and take what she offered.

"Coward." The table was empty but for the hat he'd tossed on it. "Crazy," he grumbled. "Plumb *loco*."

Shaking his head at his wild imagination, ignoring the bulge behind his button-fly jeans, he stalked through the kitchen, down the hall, and up the stairs, chastising himself the whole way for giving into his twisted need to watch his older brother and his girlfriend. Hell, he hadn't done that since Tyler was fourteen and Dylan thirteen—and horny as a three-peckered goat.

He paused reaching for the doorknob. *Now wasn't that an image, a goat with three—* "Jesus… I'm certifiable." Dylan opened the door and flicked on the light. It bathed his room in a soft glow for a moment before he heard an odd pop and the room went dark. "Figures." He didn't keep a stock of light bulbs in his bedroom and he sure as hell wasn't going back downstairs to rummage around in the kitchen drawers to find one.

He sat down on the edge of his bed, pulled off his boots and socks, and then stood to shuck off his jeans and strip off his shirt. He didn't need to worry about boxers; he'd forgotten to do the laundry, so he didn't have any clean pairs left.

He grinned as he hit the sack. *It sure as hell saved time getting dressed in the morning.*

Lying on his back, he stared up at the ceiling. Sleep eluded him, but the image of Ronnie tilting her head back and licking her lips haunted him.

"Damn… maybe she really is a witch."

Chapter 5

DYLAN WOKE WITH A START. WHATEVER OR WHOEVER had interrupted his sleep was going to die a slow and pain-filled death. He rolled over and groaned. "Jesse, what the hell is your problem?"

His brother shrugged. "I'm hungry. When are we gonna get some of that home-cooking Emily promised?"

Dylan's brain was still foggy from lack of sleep. "Emily's cooking for us?"

Jesse glared at his brother. "No, she promised that her friend would be cooking for us in exchange for you repairing her store, or did I dream all of that?"

The youngest Garahan looked like he'd been in a wreck out on I-635—again. Dylan rubbed his hands over his face, hoping it'd help clear his mind. It didn't, but a gallon of coffee might. "You want to talk about it?"

When his brother shrugged again, Dylan realized it would be a long time before Jesse would be able to get past the reality of Lori getting remarried to her loser ex-husband. With a heartfelt sigh, he admitted that women were more trouble than they were worth.

On the heels of that thought was an image of Ronnie... naked in the moonlight spread out like a feast on the farm table in their kitchen. Holy hell, he had it bad. Women—definitely trouble.

Jesse turned to walk away, but Dylan was already

out of bed following him. "Jess, you gotta get it out of
your system."

The pain in his younger brother's eyes cut him deep.
He knew exactly how Jesse felt. He'd been there until
Tyler had had a Garahan heart-to-heart with him—
which translated to fist-to-jaw, but it worked. After they
beat the tar out of each other, Dylan had started talking,
purging the hurt from his soul.

Knowing Jesse, he would keep it inside until they
were ready to kill him. Even though he liked beating on
his brothers, they'd never broken any serious bones—
just a nose or two… or three.

Jesse turned his back on Dylan and walked out the
door. Dylan tripped on his boots and slammed his shoulder into the doorjamb. "Damn it." His brother didn't turn
around, just kept walking. If Jesse made it outside, he'd
have to chase him down in order to beat on him. Dylan
was tired, grouchy, and needed a damn cup of coffee.

"Hey, wait up!"

His brother kept walking, never looking back. It
was like he was in a trance, following a voice only his
brother could hear, and it scared the crap out of Dylan.
"Jesse, don't make me chase after you."

"Got work to do."

"I thought you were hungry?"

"Changed my mind." From the way his brother
picked up the pace, he didn't want anybody stopping
him. Well, that was too damned bad. If Dylan had to
be brotherly and pick a fight with Jesse to get him to
talk, then that's what he'd have to do. "Damn," he said
staring at the coffeepot.

Watching out the window, he saw which direction

Jesse rode off in, filing it away for later. If he was going pick a fight with his brother, he needed to be awake enough to do it. Pouring a cup, he started thinking about why men were attracted to females who didn't want them back.

Perverse. "Yeah, Grandpa, I know." Reaching for the sugar, he bumped his cup, spilling hot coffee on his thigh. "Damn that's hot!" His leg was beet red and throbbing. "I know, I know," he said looking up at the ceiling. "I should have put my damned pants on."

Oddly, his grandfather's voice was silent. No sarcastic comments rang in his head. Just as well; he needed to focus on catching up to his brother, but if he didn't step it up, he'd be even further behind.

Dylan didn't start his morning without eating unless it was an emergency. Looking down at his leg, he figured he'd live. He should probably put cold water on it, but he kept remembering the pain in his brother's dark eyes. It was like looking in a mirror. Dylan remembered the pain, remembered the hurt.

He grabbed two apples from the bowl on the counter and a banana from the hanging basket by the window and set them on the table. Running for the stairs, he took them two at a time. He was dressed and back downstairs inside of six minutes. Grabbing the fruit, he shoved his Stetson on his head and shoved the back door open so hard it slammed twice before closing.

He inhaled the banana and was halfway through the apple when he got to the barn. A soft whicker let him know that his horse caught the scent of apple. He smiled. Wildfire was one of his favorite cutting horses, a sorrel American Quarter Horse. He snickered thinking about the cowboys that trained to ride in rodeos; they might think they knew what riding a good cutting horse was all about, but he rode one every day. He and Wildfire worked the ranch and cut steer out of the herd when they needed to, whether it was to vaccinate them, castrate them, or sort them getting ready to go to market.

Walking toward the stall where his horse waited, he grinned. "You think I'm gonna give you this other apple?" Smart horse that he was, Wildfire nudged Dylan's hand while he pulled out his pocketknife and cut it into quarters. The horse whickered again, impatiently waiting until Dylan offered him his treat.

Wildfire munched while Dylan got the tack he needed and then went through his normal routine, checking the animal's legs and hooves before tossing the saddle blanket on Wildfire's back and smoothing it out. When he was twelve, he hadn't been as careful and had ended up causing one of his grandfather's horses to have a raw spot where the blanket had been folded beneath the saddle. He'd actually felt the horse's pain when he saw the damage he'd caused. He never made that mistake again.

He led his horse out of the barn, put his foot in the stirrup, and settled into the saddle, the motion smooth and fluid, and second nature to him. He'd been riding since before he could walk. With the gentle pressure of his thighs, he guided his mount in the direction he'd seen Jesse ride.

Half an hour later, he caught up to his brother. Working silently, they got down to the business of checking the herd and making sure the water supply in the south pasture was available. When the herd was grazing on the east side of their ranch, they didn't have to worry about water; there was a river that ran through their land.

Garahans had fought and died over that water. But in the end, they'd kept their water rights, and no one had tried to wrest control of it from them again. He shook his head. *The things you remember when your body's beyond tired and your mind's working on autopilot.*

When Jesse pulled up alongside of him, Dylan let his gaze slide to the left. He didn't want his brother to think he was plotting on how best to knock him out of the saddle… his little brother had a hair-trigger temper and might just get the jump on him.

Riding along in silence, he figured they were far enough away not to spook any of the cattle and took his chance. "So, you ready?"

Interest lit the darkness in his brother's eyes a moment before Jesse launched himself out of the saddle and into his brother. They fell off their horses and hit the ground hard. Dylan's shoulder ached like a sonofabitch, but he ignored it, getting in a few well-placed punches to his brother's ribs.

"Shit, that hurt!"

"'Supposed to, you moron."

Jesse retaliated with an uppercut, snapping Dylan's head back. Now his jaw throbbed in time with his shoulder, but he didn't let that stop him from sucker-punching Jesse. Bending over his brother, he put his hands on his knees and grinned down at him. "You 'bout ready to talk?"

"Fuck yourself, Bro."

Dylan chuckled. "Can't. I'm not that flexible."

Jesse struggled not to smile. That just made Dylan more determined to get through his brother's thick skull. "Besides, I'm kind of partial to doing it with a partner... the feminine kind."

Instead of smiling, Jesse was now frowning. "They're nothing but trouble."

"Amen to that." Dylan offered his hand and helped his brother to his feet. "But sometimes it's worth it."

"I thought she was."

They saddled up and rode back to the barn. "You ever think you found the right woman?"

Dylan's gut clenched at the thought and wondered if Jesse had meant to stab him through the heart. One look at his younger brother, and he knew it had been unintentional. "Yeah, but I was wrong."

"I've been wrong twice now... with the same woman." Jesse sighed. "Now I sound like I'm whipped."

"Naw," Dylan said, rubbing his hand along his sore jaw. "Just mistaken. Women'll blind you with their soft, curvaceous forms and sweet-smelling hair."

Jesse stared at him and finally asked, "You been blinded lately, Bro?"

Dylan's first instinct was not to answer, but knowing how badly Jesse was hurting, he nodded. "I've been broadsided by the sweetest little filly with ruby-red lips and siren-green eyes."

Jesse slowly grinned at him. "That a fact?"

"Yep."

"Where'd you meet her?"

"My last night at the Lucky Star."

"Well, shit, Dylan. I told Jolene I wanted to work for her. Why hasn't she called me yet?"

"Because she just hired a new guy and she's busy teaching him the ropes."

Jesse's eyes gleamed. "That how you met your green-eyed filly?"

"You know it." Dylan remembered the shocked expression on Ronnie's face when he tossed the lasso and started to reel her in.

"She fight it?"

"Hell yeah, but in the end, she couldn't resist my charms."

"Right," Jesse grumbled, stretching his arm over his head and groaning. "You probably didn't give her a chance to say anything once you got your rope around her."

Dylan's smile started on the inside, warming him up. They'd beat on each other until they'd just started to feel the pain; it made everything tangled up inside of them hurt less. "How would you know?"

"Emily told me."

A couple hundred feet from the barn, Jesse finally opened up. "I was gonna marry her."

"I know."

"It hurts like hell." Jesse turned toward him and slid from the saddle. "When's it stop?"

Dylan shrugged. "If you keep busy enough, one day, you just forget."

Working silently, they cared for their horses. Saddles and tack stored, they rubbed down their mounts. The quiet eased the tension between the brothers. "Grandpa always said a body'd think straighter if his hands were busy."

Jesse nodded.

Dylan tried again, "Said it was better to get it out than holding it inside to fester."

Jesse laid his forehead against his horse's strong neck and hooked an arm around him. His brother's pain was alive and breathing... tangible. A stronger man would just walk away and let him sort it out, but Dylan had a soft spot for his brothers. They'd grown up leaning on one another. The death of their father hit them hard at a young age, then not even five years later, they'd lost their mother too. If not for their grandfather stepping in and riding herd on the wild-eyed preteens spoiling for a fight to happen, they'd all be in jail right now.

Well, at least Dylan would. Jesse lifted his head and continued to curry his horse, combing in long strong strokes that Dylan knew both man and horse needed. Turning back to Wildfire, he mirrored his brother's movements, letting his mind wander. Dylan'd been twelve years old and nursing a hurt so big, only tearing down a self-destructive path buried the pain.

He snuck onto neighboring ranches and hot-wired tractors, hiding them on the rancher's property, smiling innocently the next day when his grandfather shared the tale of yet another rancher's tractor being stolen.

Heck, he knew that wasn't the truth—he'd been the one doing the stealing... well, not stealing exactly... just moving the tractors from one side of the ranch to another spot, a spot guaranteed to take the rancher a day or so to find.

He grinned remembering how his grandfather had cuffed him on the back of the head and then dragged him down to have a chat with the sheriff. He'd been scared shitless and nearly passed out, but Garahans went down fighting. Prepared to do just that, he'd been surprised when his grandfather had turned up his charm and convinced the sheriff to let them visit each of the ranchers who'd had tractors stolen and offer Dylan's services, first in locating the missing tractors and then in doing any repairs on their ranches in exchange for not pressing charges against him.

It was tough at first, but by the time they'd visited all six ranches, he'd gotten better at apologizing without sneering. Might've been the headache he'd developed from being smacked repeatedly in the back of his head every time his lips started to curl up. He wasn't stupid, just stubborn… but not half as stubborn as old Patrick Henry Garahan, Hank to his close friends.

Six months later, Dylan had developed some serious carpentry skills that he'd learned to be thankful for and depend on over the years.

"…I said are you coming?"

Dylan blinked, looked down at his hands and then over his shoulder. "Yeah. Gimme a minute."

His brother grumbled but waited while Dylan put away his grooming tools, then fed and watered his horse. They were both moving slower than they would have if they hadn't indulged in beating on each other, but stiff ribs, aching jaw, and sore knuckles aside, they'd both purged some of the ache twisting them into knots.

Walking from the barn to the house, they stopped at the well pump and took turns sticking their heads beneath the cold, clear, life-giving water.

"Man, Dylan," Jesse said coming up for air, shaking his head like their old dog used to after swimming in the pond. "Remember when we were kids and Mom used to holler at us for wasting perfectly good drinking water on our hard heads?"

Dylan grinned as the memory of their mom standing on the back porch, hands on her hips, glaring at them filled him. "She sure did have a hair-trigger temper." He turned toward his younger brother and nodded. "A lot like yours."

Their gazes met and held. Dylan wished he could turn back time and be that little kid again. Life was simpler; times were easier. But, then, as his grandpa always told them, life wasn't for the weakhearted. "So, you ready to spill your guts yet?"

Jesse's eyes darkened with anger, but he finally drew in a deep breath and shook his head. "I'm not a wimp, Dylan."

"Is whoever said you were still standing?"

His brother snorted, trying not to laugh, but when their eyes met again, Jesse asked, "You think it's true?"

"Garahans are not wimps." Dylan paused. "We feel more deeply than most men—it's our Irish hearts."

When his brother looked out toward the clothesline, Dylan knew what he was thinking. "Some mornings, I wake up expecting to see Mom hanging out freshly washed sheets. Sometimes when I'm making up my bed with clean sheets, I hold 'em to my nose and breathe in—" Dylan paused and cleared his throat. "And I'd swear I hear her singing in my head."

"Lori was always singing, especially when she thought no one was around and listening."

Wanting his brother to open up and flush out the festering wound Lori's leaving had left behind, Dylan waited.

"She kind of looked like mom."

"A sweet faced, blonde-haired, blue-eyed lady," Dylan rasped. "Yeah. At first it used to throw me for a loop when I'd be reaching for that first cup of coffee, hearing the singing and seeing a slender bit of woman with blonde hair hanging up the clothes. I broke four mugs until Lori started leaving a cup on my dresser."

A glance at his brother had Dylan apologizing. "Hey, I didn't mean to make it worse—aw, hell."

Jesse scrubbed his hands over his face. "It took you eight months to come around the last time."

Dylan snorted. "That was a year ago, and up until the other night I swore off getting involved with women."

"Gimme seventh months and three and a half weeks, and I'll be ready to come around."

"No way, Bro, we can't afford to have you leave the living like I did." Wracking his brain to come up with a way to keep Jesse in the here and now, he finally hit on an idea. "So what time are Timmy and his buds coming over to work with Tyler?"

"'Round three o'clock, why?"

Dylan wrapped an arm around his brother's neck. "'Cause I'm about to fulfill one of your dearest wishes."

Jesse snickered. "Too late, she's already remarried by now."

Dylan smacked him in the back of the head. "Not that one. The one you've been pestering me and Tyler about since you were fifteen."

Jesse's eyes lit up like a kid spotting a pile of presents on Christmas Day. "Woo-hoo! Call Pete and tell him to break out his tattoo gun!"

Dylan watched his brother take off like a shot toward the house. "Hey, wait up."

"No way, we've got a lot to do before Timmy and company get here, and I'm still not sure what I want tattooed on me."

Hot on his brother's heels, Dylan opened the kitchen door, and said, "I think we should proclaim our heritage over our hearts."

Jesse looked over his shoulder and got a glazed look in his eyes. "Yeah... like a flag or something..." He turned back to rummage through the fridge.

Dylan grabbed two paper towels to use as plates, two glasses, and the bag of chips from the pantry. "Hey, is there any iced tea left?"

His brother grunted and set down the armload of sandwich makings before turning back to grab the pitcher. By the time Tyler limped into the house, they were plowing through their first set of sandwiches. Dylan shook his head at his older brother. "You're supposed to be taking it easy."

Tyler laughed. "Did that for the last couple of days, had to get back to it today."

Without asking, Jesse and Dylan slid one of their sandwiches in front of their brother and waited for him to sit down. "So, Ty," Dylan began, "Jess and me are goin' into town to Harrison's so we can save on the delivery fee."

"Wouldn't be a delivery fee if we weren't so far behind in paying Ms. Minnie."

"Yeah, well, we figured since Timmy's coming around three, you won't be out here busting your ass alone."

Tyler looked from one brother to the other and slowly grinned. "So what're you two really gonna do in town?"

"Shoot, Ty," Jesse grumbled, "what makes you think we're up to something?"

Tyler chuckled. "Hell, we're related."

Dylan reached for another glass, filled it with tea, and passed it to his older brother. "We're going to Pete's."

Taking a bite of his roast beef on rye, he chewed slowly then set his sandwich back down. "What kind of tattoos are you getting?"

"We're not sure, but something that'll proclaim our heritage."

Tyler nodded, tipping his head back to drain the rest of his tea. "How about a shamrock?"

"Yeah," Jesse agreed. "Right over our hearts, right, Dylan?"

Dylan groaned. "Sure, but we'd best be getting the rest of our chores done so we're ready to leave at three."

Jess took off like a shot, leaving the two older brothers alone. "He's hurting, Ty."

Tyler rolled his empty glass in his hands. "I know. It takes time before the healing'll start."

Dylan already knew that firsthand. "I'm hoping to jump start it. I don't think I could live with him if he acted like I did when—"

"Don't say her name," Tyler warned. "We agreed."

A lump of gratitude got stuck in his throat, but he swallowed past it and nodded. "I'd have been lost without you and Jess poking at me until I got it all out of my system."

Tyler's laugh was from the heart. "You mean until we got you so mad that you started swinging."

"Yeah," Dylan rumbled, "and when the fighting was over, we were all bruised and battered, but it didn't hurt so much inside."

Tyler agreed. "You don't think you can give Jesse the time to heal his heart?"

Dylan shook his head. "I heard that Lori and her man are moving back to Pleasure when I was over at the feed store the other day."

"Shit."

"He's bound to run into the two of them in town inside of two weeks, so we'd better get him to explode now where we can control it, instead of in town where people would probably call the sheriff instead of letting Jess beat the tar out of Lori's loser ex-husband."

Tyler's grim expression morphed into a grin. "Well, hell, I wouldn't mind if our little brother spent a couple of hours in the hoosegow."

Dylan smiled at his brother. "Yeah… maybe we should wait a couple of days."

—∿∿—

Ronnie couldn't get Dylan off of her mind. She'd already stretched and gone through her morning yoga routine. Normally, it helped balance her, so she was ready to face the day. But today, something was off—maybe it was her Chi—maybe she needed to round out her morning with a session of Tai Chi.

"Face it, you know what's wrong with you, and all of the exercise videos in the world won't cure what you need." She sighed and drew in a deep breath and started chuckling. "But maybe a little co-ed naked yoga might."

It was too soon; she wasn't ready for an intimate relationship with Dylan yet. Her insides clenched with need… *liar*… OK, well maybe her heart wasn't ready for it, but her body was.

"I'm going crazy," she grumbled. "That's the only explanation I can come up with. I can't think, I can't focus, and all I want is a long, tall, gorgeous hunk of cowboy. Guaranteed to feel like satin over steel…"

"Arrggh." She yanked on her hair and winced. "He's making me crazy."

Her cell phone started playing a song she remembered her grandmother singing to her when she was little: "Ronnie" by the Four Seasons. "Damn it, Shannon!" Her friend must have reprogrammed her ringtone when she'd laid her phone on the bar the other night. She picked up her phone and checked out the screen. It was a number she didn't recognize, but she answered it anyway.

"Wrong number." She disconnected and stalked toward the bathroom. "Figures." A hot shower should loosen out all of those kinks and wash away her stress. Besides, she had dessert to bake to bring along with the dinner she'd be bringing out to the Garahan brothers. She indulged in a head-to-toe scrubbing with her homemade sugar scrub. Today she decided to go with the vanilla, tomorrow, maybe she'd try the almond-scented scrub. "Mmmm." She just loved the way it left her skin so smooth. "Time to get down to the business of finding out a little bit more about Dylan."

A little while later, after hanging up with Emily, she sat down and stared at her phone and let go of the breath she'd held. "Well… I wanted to know."

Her lips tingled remembering the way he expertly drew a response from her. She hadn't wanted to be attracted to him. "Maybe I can pretend it never happened. Damn it! I should have figured he'd be one hundred percent Irish."

The family curse echoed in her head. Every other

generation a DelVecchio woman falls for an Irishman, there's usually an unmistakable sign, then she falls in love, marries him, and delivers their first set of twins.

"No. No. No. No, and most definitely no! There will be no falling for Dylan Garahan, no mystic sign, no *L* word, no marrying… again, and I'm not ready to have one baby, let alone two. I'll just avoid him."

She smacked the palm of her hand against her forehead. "*Stunad*." Stupid! "How can I avoid him when he's going to be here later today to pick up where he left off last night?"

Ronnie stared down at her phone. Mavis Beeton was on speed dial for emergencies. With the threat of the family curse looming, and the prospect of the handsome cowboy coming back tonight having her holding her breath, she hit the number.

"Mavis? I'm in trouble."

Chapter 6

"SO TELL ME AGAIN," MAVIS URGED, STEERING RONNIE toward her kitchen table. "Just what kind of a sign will it be?"

Ronnie slumped onto a chair and put her head in her hands. "That's just it. I don't know."

The older woman patted the back of Ronnie's hand and sat across from her. "Well now, I don't guess it would be someone who tossed a lasso around you."

Ronnie's head shot up. "No, I don't guess it would."

Mavis chuckled. "Don't get all sulky on me. You asked for my help, remember?"

Her head hit her hands again and Ronnie was tempted to pull her hair out—the frustration was killing her. She heard her friend get up from the table, and her manners returned. "I'm sorry, Mavis. I'm just so tied up about this."

Her friend's smile lit the room. "Interesting choice of words."

"I am so screwed."

"No, dear, I wouldn't say that, but you may be passing up the chance of a lifetime if you don't give in to the urge to get to know that young man better."

Ronnie's stomach knotted. "I'm tempted."

"Then what's the problem?"

"I can't take the chance."

"Then you're talking to the wrong person. I'm a firm believer in diving in headfirst."

Ronnie sighed. "I already did that once, and it didn't work out."

"I know things didn't work out with your first husband, but I don't know all of the details. Why don't you tell me what happened."

She didn't want to relive the agony, didn't want to dredge up the pain she'd finally learned to live with.

As if she could sense Ronnie's inner struggle, Mavis gently urged, "Sometimes love is meant to be for a brief time, just a couple of years. Or, for the lucky ones, a lifetime."

Their eyes met, and Ronnie remembered the story Mavis had shared a few weeks ago about how her rodeo-cowboy husband had been killed by a bull. "I'm sorry, Mavis. I shouldn't be complaining."

The older woman smiled at her. "I wouldn't trade one minute of the time I had to spend with my man. We fought hard and loved hard. Sometimes you need to grab the bull by the horns to shake things up in your life. Just because you've had one man in your life that wasn't the right one doesn't mean there isn't another one you should try on for size."

Ronnie felt her mouth drop open. "You don't really mean—"

Mavis grinned. "Honey, there's times in life when good old-fashioned plain-speaking is called for. Now is one of those times. You don't need anyone trying to pretty up words when your mind's already muddled and befuddled by that good-looking Garahan boy."

Ronnie cleared her throat. "Well, I—"

Mavis sat down across from Ronnie and interrupted. "Sex is necessary."

Ronnie didn't know what to say to that. "Well, I—"

Before she could speak, Mavis interrupted again. "And anyone who thinks they can substitute a battery-operated contraption for the real thing would be sadly mistaken."

Ronnie waited a beat, then agreed. "I can honestly say that while it does take the edge off, there's a lot to be said for a long night of lovin' and the cuddling that comes afterward."

"Amen!" Mavis said as she jumped up from the table. "I take it your first marriage didn't end well."

"It was a joint mistake."

Mavis crossed her arms beneath her breasts and frowned. "Did he cheat on you?"

Ronnie nodded. "But I knew he didn't have it in him to be faithful to one woman."

"He must have been something for you to marry him, knowing he had fidelity issues."

"Did you ever want something so badly that you'd be willing to do just about anything to get what you wanted?"

Mavis smiled. "I have."

"And afterward?"

Mavis shrugged. "Life happens, dear. We learn to roll with it and keep moving forward. By the way," her friend added, "if you ever need any help fixing a problem, I have a couple of friends from the circuit—"

"The what?"

"Rodeo circuit," Mavis explained. "They might be able to drop by and visit your ex when they're on the East Coast. It'd be a trek up from Tennessee, but they'd do it for me."

"I'll let you know."

"Well, all right then," her friend said. "Now, why don't you and I just ride on over to the Circle G and surprise those boys with whatever you've got prepared for them?"

"I haven't decided which dessert to bring yet, but I do have a pot filled with meatballs and my grandmother's special gravy."

"In my experience, men, especially Texans, love to eat meat. Meatballs and brown gravy does sound good."

Ronnie shook her head. "Sorry, I meant red sauce."

"Oh, why didn't you say so?"

"My grandmother always called it gravy... it's an Italian thing."

"Do yours have lots of garlic and spices?"

Ronnie nodded. "Dylan tried it last night and seemed to like it; do you think he'd mind eating the same thing two nights in a row?"

"Honey, as long as he doesn't have to cook it, I'm sure he'll be fine with it. Those boys work so hard during the day, they drag themselves back to the ranch house at night. Half the time, I don't think they even know what they eat, let alone remember that they did."

"Good to know they'll be easy to please."

"What did you bake?"

"Buttered pecan pie and pound cake."

"Maybe I'll just have to angle an invitation to dinner out at the Circle G tonight."

Ronnie smiled. "I could bake you a pie—"

"I haven't had pound cake in years," Mavis interrupted.

"Then I'll make one just for you. This one's a killer though; it has half a pound of sweet butter, half a pound of cream cheese, and six eggs!"

"My daddy would have loved that." Mavis smiled. "Melt in your mouth heart attack."

Ronnie laughed. "My mom got the recipe from a friend of hers. We adopted it and amped it up by adding cream cheese to it. The funny thing is when it's done baking, it weighs more than a pound!"

"That I'd have to see for myself."

Ronnie paused and confessed, "I've never been on a working ranch before, but I did spend a lot of time out at my friend's farm when I was learning to be a barrel rider."

Mavis smiled. "Isn't it interesting that you come from back East, but you love horses and learned to ride around barrels?"

"A lot of people back home raise horses."

Mavis shook her head. "Imagine that. People in New Jersey raising horses and riding them. There's an awful lot of people crammed into one tiny state. It's hard to imagine."

Ronnie had to agree. "But we still have a lot of open land where people keep horses."

"But not like the wide open spaces out here."

"No, but still…"

Mavis narrowed her eyes and glared at Ronnie. "You're stalling."

Ronnie's gut knotted. "Busted. I'm afraid."

"That's the first part of winning the battle."

"What battle?"

"The one to win your man."

"I'm not interested in winning any man." Ronnie's protest didn't seem to faze Mavis one bit. If anything, it had the woman grinning ear to ear.

"Texas men like a woman with a lot of fire in her."

"I give up."

"No, you won't," Mavis said. "You're going to keep moving forward with your life. A smart woman like you can maneuver around anything in her way."

"What if I'm not ready to take the chance that Dylan is the one who'll bring down my generation's curse?"

"Don't you want that big, strong, hunk of cowboy in your bed?"

The image brought everything Ronnie felt for Dylan back to life and stoked the flames burning inside of her. She licked her lips, surprised that her mouth had gone dry. "Must be the heat."

Mavis stared at her. "Well, at least you're admitting that the boy can surely start a wildfire and keep the flames burning hot."

Ronnie fanned her face and asked, "Can I have a glass of water?"

Mavis chuckled. Handing her a glass, she asked, "So are you ready to start living again?"

"Oh, hell," Ronnie grumbled. "We have to stop at my place and pick up the food!"

A short time later, the two were driving east, headed out of town. The gate with the letter *G* inside of a circle loomed ahead. "We're almost there," Mavis said as she put the car in park and opened her door.

"Wait," Ronnie said, putting her hand on the older woman's arm. "Let me." Ronnie got out and pushed the big gate open, waiting for Mavis to pull through to the other side before closing the gate and getting back in the car.

At the fork in the road, her friend turned right and

Ronnie saw the ranch house for the first time. It was white, two stories, with a huge wraparound porch.

"This house needs a woman's touch," Mavis said.

Ronnie agreed. "Well, maybe some more flowers. Is that a honeysuckle vine over there by the overgrown garden?"

Mavis nodded. "It used to be a sight when their mother was alive."

Despite not wanting to get involved, Ronnie found herself asking, "Has she been gone long?"

Her friend paused to think. "It's been so long, I'd have to stop and think about it. Tyler's thirty-two, and he was thirteen when she was in that awful wreck out on I-635. Those poor boys were so young to have to deal with such heartache."

No stranger to the emotion, she felt for the young boys the men had been. "Too young," she agreed. "So no one's taken care of the garden since then?"

Mavis smiled. "I didn't say that. Off and on over the years, one of them would have a spare moment and try to tame the garden out back. Times have been tough lately, so I guess no one's had the time." She turned and looked right at Ronnie. "Are you feeling the need to get your hands in Garahan dirt?"

"Just making a comment about the garden is all." She didn't want to admit that parts of Dylan's history had struck a chord deep inside of her, setting off warning bells in her brain to pay attention to this one.

Fate and destiny could be evil bitches. She'd already gone one round with them and lost. Was she up to another?

Mavis parked the car and got out. "Looks like

everyone's out riding the range or doing chores." Getting out, she walked around to the trunk. "I'll grab the baked goodies if you bring the pot of sauce and meatballs."

Ronnie got out and opened the door to the back seat, reached in, and grabbed the enameled stockpot. "Are we just going to go inside? No one seems to be here."

"Those Garahan boys'll be glad we did. Just smelling those meatballs driving all the way out here has made me hungry."

"If you think they won't mind…" Ronnie wasn't sure about walking into someone's house unannounced, but followed along behind, trying not to drag her feet. Her grandmother would not approve… well, unless you were family, then of course you should go right on in without knocking. Nonni was funny that way.

"Cool… they've got a swing." Ronnie sat down just to try it out, but almost upended the pot of meatballs. "I'll have to try it out later."

Mavis was just smiling at her, an odd light in her eyes. "What are you thinking, Mavis?"

Her friend smiled at her. "Hmmm? Oh, nothing in particular. I've always loved visiting out here. I miss my friend."

"You knew Mrs. Garahan?"

Her friend nodded. "I grew up in Pleasure and pretty much knew everyone. Small towns are special that way. We care about our own, and when one of the young people steps out of line, one of us older folks are around to help nudge them back onto the right path."

"Shouldn't that be their parents' job?"

Mavis's smile faded. "Only if their parents are still among the living."

Ronnie sensed there was more that her friend wanted to say, but she hesitated pushing Mavis. They set their burdens down in the middle of a huge farm table. "My grandmother had a huge table like this in her kitchen; my cousins and I used to play underneath it as kids." Ronnie smiled. "Scared her a couple of times, jumping out at her first thing in the morning on nights when we'd all sleep over."

"No doubt she loved every minute of it."

Ronnie's heart warmed as she savored the memory. "She's hoping for a couple of grandbabies who will do the same thing."

Mavis just smiled and changed the subject. "Well, if you don't want the boys to eat up both desserts, do you want to put one in the freezer?"

Ronnie laughed. "You don't think they'd polish off both desserts, do you? There are only three of them."

Mavis's eyes positively twinkled. "I've known those boys since they were in diapers. Given the chance, they'd eat sweets morning, noon, and night, so if you don't want them to polish off the cake and the pie…"

Her stomach fluttered. She was nervous and not sure if she should admit it. She'd never really cooked for anyone but family and friends. The Garahan brothers weren't quite friends yet, more like acquaintances, and Dylan… her body started to tingle from her head right down to her toes remembering the molten kisses they'd shared and the way he set her body on fire.

"Ronnie?"

The light touch on her arm jolted her out of her

lustful thoughts. Her cheeks were warm and she knew it wouldn't be a secret what she'd been thinking… or who she'd been thinking about.

"Mrs. Beeton," a deep voice called from behind them. "I thought that was your car."

"Tyler," the older woman replied. "You look so much better than the last time I saw you." She walked over to get a closer look. "I'd hug you, but I'm betting those ribs of yours are still a bit sore."

His grin was so like his brother's that it was all Ronnie could do to keep her traitorous body from calling attention to itself by moaning in pure pleasure. Damn, those Garahan brothers could make the angels weep they were so beautiful. Her tongue got tied up in a knot. Even carrying a layer of dust, the oldest Garahan was a guaranteed heartbreaker.

He turned and smiled at her. "How're you doin', Ronnie?"

She found her voice and answered, "OK. Mavis is right; you do look better. Have you been resting up?"

His laugh was deep and so like Dylan's her insides just melted. Good grief! She'd have to be on her guard whenever one of them was around.

"Restin' in the saddle every day."

Mavis shook her head. "Broken ribs don't mend if you're not resting. You don't want one of them to snap clean through and puncture a lung, do you?"

Tyler's face lost its healthy glow. "I, uh… no. I don't."

Satisfied she'd made her point, Mavis patted his cheek. "A man needs to be aware of the consequences of his actions."

Tyler rolled his eyes and looked over at Ronnie. She

grinned back at him. "I've only known Mavis a couple of months, and I can definitely tell you: don't mess with Mavis. She's never wrong."

Tyler laughed. "She's got you pegged, Mrs. Beeton."

"Ronnie brought meatballs and sauce for dinner—"

"Hot damn! We're gonna have real food for a change."

Intrigued at the thought, Ronnie asked, "How long have you gone without?"

"We've been scrounging for the last few days."

"I thought Lori had only been gone a day or so."

"Longer actually, and she wasn't thinking about stocking our freezer or fridge with food. She was thinking about that ex-loser she was hooking up with again."

"Don't hold back, Tyler." Ronnie laughed at the pained expression on his face. "Just tell us what you really think about Lori's situation."

Pain morphed into a dark and dangerous anger. "What she did to Jesse's criminal."

Ronnie looked over at Mavis to gauge her response. Her friend's mouth was clamped shut tight, so she decided not to add her two cents. A glance in Tyler's direction, and she knew she'd made the right choice. He was vibrating with anger, and she wasn't sure how to diffuse the situation. Finally, he seemed to get ahold of himself, drawing in a deep calming breath.

He pushed his Stetson to the back of his head, revealing a clean swatch of tanned skin that had been hidden beneath the hatband. "Sorry, ladies. He's pretty upset about her leaving and I—"

"We understand, Tyler," Mavis interrupted. "Best not to dwell on what can't be changed." She smiled up at him and swept her hand over to the farm table, drawing his attention away from his anger. "Look what Ronnie's baked for your dessert."

He swept his hat from head and held it in his hands. "Shoot, Ronnie," Tyler said, a hungry gleam in his eyes. "Can I taste test that pie?"

Her laughter bubbled up from inside and spread warmth through her, calming the nervous fluttering in her belly. "Are you willing to forfeit your dessert tonight to have a piece now?"

"No ma'am," he said eyeing the pie and cake beside it. "What kind of cake is that? It's not frosted."

She turned her attention to the man staring down at her baked goods, wondering if she should have baked a second pie. "It's pound cake; doesn't need frosting."

"Yeah?" Tyler looked from her back to the cake. "Maybe I should try a sliver of it to make sure you don't need to whip up a batch of frosting before I let you leave."

Mavis was laughing so hard, she had tears in her eyes. "Land sakes, Tyler Garahan, are you that hungry?"

He smiled sheepishly. "I didn't have much of a breakfast this morning—didn't have time."

Instantly concerned, Mavis patted his shoulder. "Now why don't you just wash up and Ronnie and I'll heat up those meatballs for you."

Before she could stop herself, Ronnie asked, "Where are your brothers?"

Tyler seemed distracted at the thought of satisfying his hunger. "In town… they had an errand to run."

Oddly disappointed, Ronnie sighed. "Oh. Well, I don't know if Emily mentioned it or not, but in exchange for your brother's carpentry skills, I'll be cooking for you."

He nodded. "She did, and that's why I feel it's my duty as the oldest Garahan brother to taste test your cooking—we know you're an awesome baker, but what about putting a meal together on the table?"

Tyler walked over to the sink and began to wash up.

Horrified at the idea of that kind of dirt near where she was going to prepare food, she said, "Um, Tyler."

He looked up at her. "Ma'am?"

"If I'm cooking in here, shouldn't you be washing up in the bathroom or something?"

He grinned at her. "No, ma'am."

Irritated, she bit back, "Why not?"

"Sink's too small."

Hands on her hips, she retorted, "Well, I don't like the idea of God knows what kind of dirt you've brought in the house with you ending up in the food I'm cooking for you."

Tyler smiled down at her while drying his hands. "That a fact?"

Was he laughing at her? "Do you think that's funny?"

If possible, his smile deepened, and she knew she'd be a goner if Dylan ever turned the full power of that Garahan charm on her.

"Mrs. Beeton, maybe you could explain things to our friend here from back East." With that he walked to the back door, leaned out, and yelled, "Hey, Timmy! Tell your friends to take a break. We've got company and they brought food."

"Now, Ronnie dear," Mavis said slowly, "don't mind Tyler and his high-handed ways. Not one of those Garahan men have been housebroken yet."

Tyler's sharp bark of laughter got under her skin,

annoying the crap out of her—not unlike his younger brother. She wondered if she could raid their medicine cabinet and find any laxative to add to his food. That'd teach him not to laugh at her.

"Not quite what I had in mind, Mrs. Beeton." He leaned against the doorjamb and crossed his arms in front of his chest, totally at ease, even with the tension in the room. "Since you're not from around here, you probably wouldn't understand, but out here we don't have time to worry about every speck of dirt that gets tracked into the house—"

"Newsflash, Tyler," she grumbled, "you've got a heck of a lot more than a speck of dirt on you."

His eyes were brimming with laughter and she softened a bit, remembering his brother's expressive dark eyes. Trouble—the Garahan brothers were chock-full of it.

"Yes, ma'am, my point exactly. We use the kitchen sink to wash up in and try not to track in too much of the pasture inside with us, but sometimes it happens. Time is short when there's work enough for ten men, and we're down to the three of us, plus my young friend Timmy and two of his hoodlum friends lending a hand."

"Well," she said slowly, "I guess it is your house."

"There you go," he said, obviously pleased that she understood.

"If you're going to be hanging around while we cook, you may as well make yourself useful." She nodded toward the table. "You can set the table."

"Yes, ma'am."

She was about to say more but was distracted by the

troop of boys coming in the back door. Ronnie started adding servings in her head, realizing that if these boys were as hungry as Tyler, there wouldn't be any leftovers. "Just how many boys do you have working for you?"

The tallest of the bunch answered, "Today, there's just three of us." He leaned closer to the pie and looked over at Tyler and grinned. "Some days four. Hey can I have some of that pie?"

Ronnie wanted to smack herself in the forehead for not baking that extra pie. "Why don't you boys wash up and Mrs. Beeton and I'll fix you a plate."

"You bring any biscuits to go with that?" Tyler wanted to know.

Her temper heated up another notch. "Did you set the table yet?" Tyler's crooked grin was starting to piss her off. "Are you laughing at me?"

Immediately contrite, he stopped laughing and answered, "No, ma'am. I know better than to do that. Besides, Emily'd kill me if I laughed at her when she was working up a good mad."

"Mavis, I could use a little help here."

Her friend was hustling the boys over to the sink where they were taking turns washing up when Timmy asked, "Hey, where're Dylan and Jesse at?"

"In town," Tyler answered, before adding, "they'll be back soon."

Those four little words set Ronnie's heart a pumping and her juices flowing, anticipating seeing the tall hunk of cowboy again. Lord, the things he had her dreaming about doing with him… to him… for him…

She must have been daydreaming, because when Mavis laid a hand on her arm, she jerked back to reality… that reality being four hungry men in her kitchen… well, the kitchen at the Circle G.

"Are you all right, dear?"

The concern in Mavis's voice brought her all the way back to earth. She lost enough sleep over that slow-walking, smooth-talking cowboy, which was her private fantasy—a tall, good-looking man wearing a cowboy hat, boots, and jeans, shirt optional, ready, willing, and able to take her on the ride of a lifetime.

"You're flushed, dear. Tyler," Mavis called out, "please get Ronnie a glass of cold water."

"Here, dear, sit down." By the time, she'd been pushed onto a chair and a glass shoved into her hand, she shook herself free of her favorite fantasy… it was harder now that the cowboy had a face and a name… Dylan.

"I'm sorry," she said. "I'm just tired. I didn't sleep much last night."

"Drink up, dear. Your color's coming back to normal, not quite so flushed."

Ronnie fought with her embarrassment and won, and felt the heat leaving her cheeks. She set the empty glass down and pushed to her feet. "I'm good," she said, looking at the concern-filled faces surrounding her. "Let's heat up those meatballs. It's my grandmother's special recipe."

Putting a hand to the side of the pot, she frowned. It had really cooled off on the ride over. "How much time do you have before you need to get back to your chores?"

Tyler looked at the bedraggled group of boys and over at the clock, "We could probably stretch it to forty-five minutes. How long will it take to heat up that pot?"

She sighed. "A lot longer than that if I don't want anything to stick to the bottom of the pot and burn."

"What about the microwave?" Mavis asked. "I'm not a fan of using it to cook in, but it's great for warming things up."

"In order to warm the meatballs all the way through, I'll have to cut them in half." She really hated to do that. It just wasn't the same, biting into a half a meatball.

"Sounds great!" Tyler's opinion was echoed by each of the boys.

"All right then, I'll need a couple of microwaveable plates."

Handing her what she needed, Tyler sniffed each and every plate he set down in front of the boys. Her opinion of him rose up a notch, because he set a plate in front of Mavis and offered her one before taking one himself.

She and Mavis shook their heads and Mavis said, "We'll eat later. Don't worry about us."

When Tyler had served everyone else, he finally took the steaming plate Ronnie handed him, breathed in deep, and sighed. "If this tastes even half as good as it smells, you're invited to come on out and live here with us... as long as you cook three squares a day for us."

"Who're you inviting to live with us, Ty?" a deep voice rumbled from behind her.

"You've already got a woman of your own," Dylan grumbled coming inside to stand beside Jesse. "I've got dibs on this one." He walked over to where she stood, eyes wide.

"Miss me, Ronnie?"

She licked her lips to keep from drooling. Oh man, did she, but she shrugged, playing it cool. "Maybe."

"Liar," he said, pulling her close and damned if each and every pore in her body didn't try to drink him in. Her body stood at attention as he started to slide his hand from her waist down to her—

"Watch your hands, buster," she bit out, grabbing ahold of his wandering hands and slipping out of his embrace. She looked over at the youngest of the brothers and sighed. He was bound to be as much trouble as his older brothers.

"Man, Dylan," Jesse said, walking over to the stack of plates. Grabbing one, he helped himself to a heaping serving and elbowed his way in between Timmy and the boy on his left. "Does this as taste as good as she smells?"

"Excuse me?" She couldn't believe what she'd just heard. "Did your brother just say—"

"Yeah," Dylan answered. "Ty?"

His brother looked up from his now empty plate. "Yeah?"

"Remind me to kill Jess later."

"Done." Tyler nodded at the youngest Garahan. "You should know better than to poach."

"Claiming dibs doesn't count when the woman hasn't acknowledged the claim."

"You're right," Tyler said slowly, eyeing his siblings.

But before he could start something that would end up involving fists, Mavis called their attention back to more important matters. "Who'd like pie and who wants cake?"

Dylan groaned out loud. "Man, is that pecan pie?" His gaze shifted from the pie to Ronnie. "Darlin', you free later?"

Suspicious, she asked, "Why?"

"We can find someone to marry us up, then you can bake your way to my heart."

Jesse snickered. "More like she should try to stroke your—"

"There's ladies present, Jess," Tyler warned.

The youngest Garahan tucked his head to his chest and mumbled, "Sorry... not used to it yet."

"Emily's been here for over a week."

"She don't count, Ty," Jesse said. "She's family."

Ronnie's heart melted at the thought of being a part of their family. Good thing, because it distracted her from thoughts of bashing Dylan over the head with the serving spoon in her hand, right before she laid a lip lock on him guaranteed to grab his attention. Talk about feeling conflicted!

"So how about it, Ronnie?" Dylan asked getting into her personal space again, setting every single cell in her body to vibrate and stoking the fire inside of her that only he could put out.

She was crazy. *He is so hot.* She was ten times a fool. *He is going to set my sheets on fire once I have him where I want him.*

No, no, and no! Step back from the hunkalicious cowboy with the darkly dangerous eyes and no one will get hurt.

He moved closer until not a breath was between them. His jean-clad legs were fused to hers, her breasts were squashed to his amazing pecs, driving her crazy—

"Shit that hurts!" He backed away from her as if he'd been burned.

"What happened, are you all right?" Concerned

because she couldn't remember if she'd set down the knife she was slicing bread with, she looked at her hands. They were empty.

Before she could blink, Dylan reached down, grabbed the hem of his T-shirt, and yanked it over his head in one smooth motion.

Her heart registered the shock of what he revealed before her head did; it skipped a beat, then two more before settling back into its normal rhythm. She sucked in a breath and stared; she couldn't help it.

The room started to spin as her vision grayed and her chest began to burn. Shock held her immobile while her brain frantically struggled to process what her heart had already accepted.

"The curse!" she rasped as everything went black.

Chapter 7

DYLAN SWEPT RONNIE INTO HIS ARMS BEFORE HER head hit the floor. "What the hell happened? What. The. Hell. Just. Happened?"

"Nice tattoo, Bro," Tyler drawled, ignoring the limp woman in his brother's arms. "Why did you back away from her like you'd been burned?"

"She leaned on my new damned tattoo."

Tyler and Jesse exchanged a look, while Dylan stared down into the angelic face of the woman who'd kept him twisted upside down and sideways all night.

"You need to lay her down." Mavis's words shot through him like a hot knife through butter.

But his brain wasn't working properly, hadn't been since he'd lassoed the woman two nights ago.

As if she could sense he wasn't capable of thought just now, Mavis placed her hand on his elbow and steered him toward the living room. Reluctantly, he set Ronnie down on the ancient overstuffed sofa. It had always looked so out of place out here at the ranch, but his mom had insisted if she was going to be working her butt off on the ranch during the day, she should at least have a comfy place to rest her weary bones at night.

Mavis had a washcloth in her hand, and she placed it gently on Ronnie's head.

Concern arrowed through him as she lay unmoving. "Is she sick?"

"I might ask the same of you, the way you were acting a few moments ago," Mavis said quietly, stroking the cool cloth over Ronnie's cheeks, forehead, and chin.

Dylan shook his head and looked down at her. The floor shifted beneath his feet and he knew in that moment that he'd never let Ronnie leave. Come hell or high water, this woman was not stepping one foot off of his ranch.

The elbow to his ribs had him spinning around.

"You keepin' her, Bro?" Jesse asked moving to stand on Dylan's right.

He looked from one brother to the other and nodded. "Yep."

"How are you gonna convince her to stay?" Tyler asked, coming to stand on his left.

"I won't need to convince her," Dylan boasted. "She'll stay."

Mavis shook her head, "Give the poor girl a moment to regain her composure, boys, before you start dictating where and what she'll be doing. Ronnie's an independent young woman and doesn't like to be told what to do."

Ronnie moaned softly as her eyelashes fluttered.

Dylan squatted down next to the sofa, to be there to reassure her when her eyes opened, but her first words were not quite the ones he'd hoped to hear.

"Frigging curse!"

"Nice mouth, DelVecchio." He waited a heartbeat then asked, "What curse?"

"It's more of a family legend."

"A legend that involves a curse?"

Her eyes narrowed as they focused on his face. "Yes."

He wanted to ask her more, but she was staring at his tattoo. Was she afraid of the sight of blood, or did it have more to do with the family curse? He grinned. The more he found out about Ronnie, the more he wanted to know.

———

"Could you please put a damned shirt on?" She shifted so she was leaning back against the arm of the sofa; if she sat up, she'd smack the reason she'd fainted with her face. She didn't need to be reminded to steer clear of this man. The evidence was proclaimed in kelly green in the form of a shamrock tattooed to his to-die-for left pec… right over his heart.

"Damned Irish pride," she mumbled.

"What's that?" Dylan leaned close enough to press his lips to hers, but she squirmed even farther into the cushion, moving her lips out of kissing range. She didn't trust the man as far as she could throw him. Looking at the breadth of his shoulders, the depth of his chest, and the size of his biceps, she figured she couldn't even budge him, let alone throw him.

Dylan Garahan was Grade A, prime Texas male. And wasn't it just her bad luck that he'd be sporting a sign even a dimwit should be able to notice. She wished Nonni was here so she could ask her more questions about the bane of the female DelVecchio's existence, a.k.a. the curse, instead of having to wait until she got back to her apartment to call her.

"Mrs. Beeton, I think Ronnie should stay here with us until she recovers."

Mavis coughed and Ronnie looked up at her for the first time since she'd come to. Was her friend trying to stifle a chuckle? What had she missed when she'd fainted?

"I'm fine," Ronnie protested. "Just let me up and I'll prove it."

His brothers backed up, but Dylan didn't. He put out a hand to stop her. "You blacked out in our kitchen and would have knocked yourself silly on the edge of the solid oak table if I hadn't kept you from falling."

"Oh really?" she sneered. "And how'd you do that?"

Dylan got into her personal space again, irritating her until she took a deep breath and his scent washed over her—clean and spicy, with a hint of what she could only describe as Texas air. Unless you'd been out to Texas you couldn't describe it, but it just didn't smell like back home. It was simply different... or maybe it was simply Dylan.

She shifted and eased back farther into the corner of the couch. "You going to answer me," she demanded, "or stare at me?"

"Darlin'," he drawled, "I could spend the rest of my life staring at you."

The breath she just drew in got caught in her lungs, black spots formed in front of her eyes, she swatted at them, but they got bigger as a funny buzzing filled her ears.

Mavis pushed Dylan out of the way and grabbed Ronnie's face in her hands. "Breathe, honey."

Ronnie obeyed, and to her relief, the buzzing dimmed and the spots disappeared. "Thanks, Mavis. I don't know what came over me."

Mavis leaned closer and smiled at her. "I think it's the *C* word."

Ronnie's stomach flipped over. *C for curse.* "I think you're right." Glancing first at Dylan, then his brothers, and finally the trio of boys standing silent in the doorway, she shook her head. "I need to get out of here."

Dylan slowly stood to his full height, and damned if it didn't impress the hell out of her. He was a man to be reckoned with—too bad she didn't have the time or the inclination.

You shouldn't lie to yourself, Veronica. Her grandmother's warning from her childhood would be apropos today.

"I think she should stay where someone can keep an eye on her. She's obviously got something wrong with her and needs someone to be with her in case she blacks out again."

Beneath the layer of frustration was concern. It was that emotion that had her looking to Mavis for advice. She didn't know what to do, but more, didn't trust herself to be alone with the man for five minutes afraid that she'd make the same mistake she had before and chose the wrong man for the wrong reasons. Only this time, she'd be choosing Dylan because of the feelings he stirred inside of her every time he looked at her—like a Texas wildfire, flaming hot and out of control.

He shifted his stance, muscles bunching and smoothing out again… make that three minutes.

Mavis nodded. "I think he's right, Ronnie. You shouldn't be alone right now, and I've got to go back into town. I have a meeting to go to."

Ronnie felt as if her one friend in the whole world was abandoning her to a pack of wild animals. A glance around the room and she felt as if she were the prey and the brothers were just waiting to pounce on her... make that one brother in particular: the one with the damned tattoo, the one who'd asked her to marry up with him.

"And who the heck asks someone to marry up with them two days after they meet? Is that another quaint Texas saying?"

Dylan's eyes narrowed, and she wondered if she pushed him just a little bit too far. It wasn't a good idea to prod the one with the black eyes and the really big muscles until he got mad.

The brothers looked at one another first and her second. "Our great-great-grandparents," Tyler answered.

"But that might have been an exception, due to the duress our great-great-grandfather was under at the time."

Ronnie didn't like the way they managed to join together as one against her, the outsider. When they simply waited, watching her, she finally asked. "OK, I'll bite, what duress?"

Dylan smiled, and her heart melted all over again. "He was in jail at the time."

"Come on, boys," Mavis said, corralling the young men and leading them back into the kitchen. "I'm sure Tyler has more chores for you boys and the day's not getting any younger."

Ronnie tried not to let her unease show. She wasn't quite as sure of herself as she let on, but the Garahans didn't know that, and if she were the woman she'd fought hard to become, they wouldn't figure it out anytime soon.

"What did your great-great-grandfather do to get arrested?"

The brothers looked at one another and then back at her. Tyler shrugged, Jesse shook his head, and Dylan answered, "Can't remember, but it must have been a trumped up charge."

She smiled. "Naturally, a Garahan couldn't be accused of committing a crime."

Dylan must not have appreciated her sarcasm. Not many people did until they got to know her better... but that was just it, he didn't know her better. Would he still want to?

To diffuse the anger she could see smoldering in his eyes, she asked, "So why did you jump back from me as if I'd sliced you with a switchblade?"

"Switchblade? Is that something that might have happened in a dark alleyway back East?"

She shrugged and didn't answer, instead prodding him, "Well?"

He leaned forward and damn if the man wasn't crowding her. She liked at least three feet or more between her and the person she was talking to... two feet if they were friends... make that a couple of inches if said friends had been drinking.

"You rubbed against my new tattoo and the skin's just a bit raw."

Her eyes shot to the bright green shamrock and she studied it closely. She could see a red outline around the leaf, and more red just beneath the color. "Why did they outline it in red?"

His mouth lifted on one side and his eyes twinkled. "Well now, that's not ink; that'd be blood... tattooing isn't for the faint of heart."

She felt the blood rush from her head to her toes and

for a moment, couldn't explain what was happening, other than she must have had an out of body experience. When her mind snapped back to the present, she was cradled in Dylan's arms once more.

The man was quick on his feet, she'd give him that much.

"And that just settled it; you're not going anywhere."

Wide awake now and in control of her body and her senses, Ronnie bristled at being told what to do. "I don't have to listen to you." She started squirming. "You can't keep me here."

She looked up at him, about to blast him until she saw the compassion-laced concern in his eyes, and came undone. Why that should appeal to her, deep inside, where she hadn't let anyone or any emotion touch her was a mystery to her. But right now, she needed to be strong, and remember not to let her misplaced feelings for the man confuse the issue.

At the moment the issue of the curse was paramount. She could not stay here… not if she wanted to have a say in her future. Did she really want to get involved with a man who probably spent most of his time working, and his spare time recovering from working? From all she'd heard since moving out to Texas, there were two types of people out here: those who owned and worked ranches and those who didn't. She rarely saw any ranchers in town, and from what Mavis had told her, probably wouldn't unless it was market day, usually the third or fourth Saturday of the month.

Shaking her head to break his hold over her, she was surprised when he didn't let go. Well, she wasn't really surprised; he'd proven to be hardheaded in his pursuit of her, maybe this was just another aspect of his not being able to accept the word no. "Did you have a hard time as a child?"

He blinked, then frowned. "With what?"

"Being told no."

Unbelievably, he tilted his head back and laughed, a deep, masculine sound that sent shivers up and down her spine. Afraid that the more she discovered about the man, the more she'd like, Ronnie knew she'd have to leave—now.

"Oh good," she murmured, "then if you'll just ease up on your grip, I'll be on my way."

"Darlin'," Dylan rumbled, the sound vibrating from deep inside his broad chest, "did you hit your head recently?"

She smacked him—just hauled off and smacked him with the flat of her hand on the back of his hard head and sweetly asked, "No, darlin', have you?"

The reaction she got was swift and unexpected. His mouth found hers and his talented lips shaped and molded hers as his kiss loosened the tension building inside of her. The tip of his tongue traced a lazy path around the rim of her mouth, filling her with pleasure, sharp and sweet.

Lord, the man could kiss.

Dylan changed the angle, slid his hand down the length of her spine, and cupped her backside, pulling her hard up against him, and all thought evaporated. It was hang on or fall off.

Need sprinted through her. She moaned, and his agile tongue took advantage and delved deep, teasing hers into response. His lips, mouth, and tongue were destroying her, but she met him taste for taste, stroke for stroke, and the wild, uninhibited side of her took over.

He might have a supremely talented mouth, but her hands were as quick as lightning as she moved them up his pecs, avoiding the tender area of his tattoo, over his shoulders, and around his back in a hypnotic motion until he moaned. Empowered by the sound, she took advantage of the moment and slid her hands down as far as she could reach, until finally, thank you Lord, she got ahold of his amazingly taut backside and grabbed on for dear life.

Holding him where she wanted him, her mouth went on a journey, licking and kissing a path along the line of his jaw to beneath his ear and along the tendon in his neck. He was breathing hard and fast by the time she'd latched on with her lips, adding suction. His grip changed from firm to punishing.

She reveled in his strength, not afraid of it or him. She wanted to make him forget about being careful with her, wanted to feel the power of him unleashed, raw and ready to mate. The man would be like a stallion, wild and free, taking what he could, when he could, and damn the consequences.

—∿∿—

Dylan felt the sharp, sweet sting of her love bite and felt the blood rush from his head to his boots and back up to flood the part of him that was proud to be a man. Ready, willing, and able to do his part, he moaned when his jeans constricted and cut into his erection.

The need to strip her bare and drive into her until they were both blind clawed at him. He slid his hands up from her backside to the hem of her T-shirt and grabbed ahold of it.

"Hey, Bro, you 'bout ready to—"

Dylan's heart slammed against his ribs, and his breath was roaring like a freight train. Looking down into Ronnie's slumberous green eyes, he knew one night with this woman would never be enough. The lacy, black bra peeking out from beneath the shirt he'd been about to tear off her had him groaning. The overwhelming need to kill the man interrupting him from taking what he wanted from the woman in his arms brought him up short.

"Whoa," Jesse said, holding up his hands and backing up. "I'll uh… just leave you two alone."

Dylan swore under his breath, leaned his forehead against Ronnie's, and let her shirt slide back down. "Darlin', it's getting too crowded here. How 'bout if I drive you out to your place where we can be alone?"

Before she could answer he heard Mrs. Beeton calling from the kitchen, "Ronnie, dear, if you're feeling better, you could come to my meeting with me and let Dylan get back to whatever he was doing before we interrupted. Besides," she said, coming to stand in the doorway, "the poor boy has to eat or he won't have any energy to finish up work here before he goes to your place."

And damned if that suggestion didn't stir his libido back to full boil. He let his gaze slide from Mrs. Beeton back to the woman in his arms and knew whatever madness had held them both by the throat had passed. The brazen look of desire had disappeared, and in its place was a wariness that he'd seen before.

Damn. He hoped he didn't have to start from scratch with her. She'd been just where he wanted her: hot, pliable, and his for the taking.

"Please," she rasped. "I… uh… have to go."

He wanted to keep her here and was about to ask, but the hint of desperation in her eyes stopped him cold. What had happened in her past that she couldn't trust herself to be alone with him and couldn't get away from him fast enough?

Need to be more than just the man who shared her bed until they burned each other out ripped through him, but deep down he was afraid he wouldn't get that chance. "Anything you want, darlin'." He eased his hold and slipped her out of his arms and onto the sofa. The emptiness had his gut churning, but he'd be damned if he'd let her know. They had a long way to go before they'd be sharing thoughts like that with one another. He hoped he could stand the wait.

"If you don't want to go with Mavis, I can leave now, get a few more shelves and walls put back together at your place and come back here to finish up."

The indecision in her eyes eased the riotous feeling in his stomach, soothing it. Her eyes told him all he needed to know. She wasn't sure what to do and sure as hell didn't want to leave. He fought the urge to smile. "Let me help you up." He held his hand out to her and waited.

She looked from his outstretched hand to his face and back again. Her hesitation started to work its way under his skin like a sliver of wood. He shrugged it off but couldn't keep from teasing, "I'm not the one who bites."

Her eyes changed in hue from soft spring green to emerald bright and from her expression, their color matched her mood. Getting a rise out of this woman was just one of the few pleasures he had in life. That is, until he talked her back into his arms and into bed, his or hers, didn't matter. Hell, they didn't even have to make love in a bed—table's fine.

"Are you coming, Ronnie?"

The woman he wanted, needed—oh hell, he may as well own up to it—craved. The woman he craved let her gaze slide from the top of his head all the way to his toes before she sighed and answered. "Wait up, Mavis."

Chapter 8

"RONNIE, ARE YOU SURE YOU DON'T WANT TO STAY here at the Circle G?"

Invisible hands squeezed her heart, the ache so real she rubbed a hand over it. "You know as well as I do that wouldn't be a good idea."

Mavis laughed as she put the car in reverse and turned around. "Oh, honey, if you don't think being alone with that gorgeous hunk of cowboy is a good idea, you should let me drive you on over to the health center to have your head examined."

On cue Ronnie's head started to ache with a flicker of pain behind her eyes. "You're supposed to be on my side."

Mavis pulled up in front of the gate and put it in park; before she got out, she reached over to pat Ronnie's hand where she rested it on the seat between them. "I am. But you're missing the point and the life lesson I learned some twenty years back."

Her friend slipped out of the car and opened the gate. Instead of offering to help, Ronnie sat there thinking over all that had happened since they'd driven out to the ranch. She needed to talk to someone, but was afraid Mavis would try to push her into Dylan's arms—not that she didn't want to be there, but she wasn't sure that would be wise with the DelVecchio Curse alive and well in Pleasure, Texas. The woman was just as bad as her grandmother!

Mavis got back into the car and drove through the opening, but before she could get back out, Ronnie pushed open the passenger door and did it for her. Drained of energy, it was heavier than she'd thought it'd be. A lot of things out in Texas weren't quite what she'd thought they'd be: her chance at a new life, leaving the old behind, opening her dream store.

"You're awfully quiet."

She sighed. "I have a lot on my mind."

Mavis didn't say anymore until they were a mile outside of town. "You know I'm not one to hold back."

Ronnie turned to look at her friend. "That's one of the things I admire most about you."

Mavis smiled but didn't take her eyes off the road. "Well, then listen up, because I'm about to give you some of my best advice."

Despite the urge not to, Ronnie did as she was told. "All right. I'm listening."

"If you let that man just walk away from you, I'm here to tell you, you'll regret it for the rest of your life. Men like Dylan Garahan are few and far between."

Playing devil's advocate, Ronnie said, "He's got a younger brother and I heard a rumor that he has four cousins in New York City and four more up in Colorado."

Mavis shook her head. "Why do you have to be so much like me?"

Ronnie laughed. "Maybe that's the connection I felt the first time I met you over at the Lucky Star."

Turning left onto North Main Street, Mavis drove past Guilty Pleasures and headed toward town hall, an old weathered building that housed the sheriff's office and jail, along with the rest of the local town offices.

"Who's your meeting with?" Ronnie asked.

"Sheriff McClure."

Worry filled her. "Are you in trouble, Mavis?"

Mavis shook her head, signaled, and parallel parked the car like a pro.

Impressed, Ronnie admitted, "It always takes at least two or three tries when I try to park on the street like this."

"I can help you practice if you need me to, dear."

"What I really need is some advice about the curse," Ronnie admitted.

"It should be a short meeting," Mavis said. "If you're up to it, would you go on over to Dawson's and tell Lettie that I'll be over to pick up the order I called in?"

Ronnie nodded. "I'm fine, no problem." She turned to go, then turned back and called out, "Mavis?"

Her friend paused with her hand on the door handle. "Yes?"

"I'm not trying to ignore your advice, it's just that…"

Mavis nodded. "I know, dear. I'll meet you over at Dawson's."

Tired and out of sorts, Ronnie walked across the street to one of the earliest establishments in the town of Pleasure: Dawson's General Store. The hardware side was doing a brisk business. Though new in town, she already knew quite a few of the local townspeople; it was only those who owned ranches on the outskirts that she wouldn't recognize by sight, but would by name. Well, except for those three dark-haired, dark-eyed Garahan brothers. The middle brother was hell on her heart. Add that to the worry over the family curse and she had her hands full.

"Hey, Ronnie."

She smiled at the young man bagging groceries on the food side of Dawson's. "Hey yourself, Shane. I missed you yesterday. How's business?"

He grinned and answered, "Busy for a Tuesday."

Leaving him to finish packing the order, she headed for the back of the store and the matchbox-sized office Lettie Dawson could be found in at this time of day. The door was open, so Ronnie knocked on the door frame. "Am I interrupting?"

Lettie's head shot up, and for a moment her eyes looked through Ronnie, but then they focused and the woman smiled at her. "Not a bit. How are you doing today? Is Dylan making any progress on your store?"

After the first few weeks living in Pleasure, Ronnie had stopped wondering how everybody kept so well-informed about her personal business and had learned to accept that it was just part of living in a small town. "He's sorted through the mess that I'd tried to organize and is getting ready to rebuild some shelves and walls where the baseball bat they must have bludgeoned it with tore it all apart."

Lettie stood up and pushed her chair under the battered oak desk that looked old enough to have been there since the store first opened its doors. "Well, that's a start, isn't it?"

Ronnie had to agree that it was.

"Well, then," Lettie smiled, "what can I do for you?"

"Mavis is over at the town hall—"

"Probably meeting with that handsome sheriff of ours."

Ronnie had to smile at the way Lettie's face lit up. "Yes, actually, she is."

"And you're here to pick up her order."

Ronnie narrowed her gaze at the older woman and asked, "Do you have spies all over town or just a network of informants?"

To her credit, Lettie didn't even miss a beat; she slipped her arm through Ronnie's and pulled her toward the front of the store. "I've got Mavis's order all packed and ready. Since you and she have become such good friends," Lettie said, "I expect a full report."

Confused, Ronnie asked, "On what?"

Lettie rolled her eyes at Ronnie. "Don't try to weasel out of telling me. I know she's cooking dinner for that heartbreaker, Zeke Eldridge."

"And you know that because?"

Lettie put her hands on her hips and frowned. "Zeke is partial to apple-stuffed pork chops, and Mavis bought a couple of pounds of pork chops, thick-sliced, and half a dozen apples. It doesn't take a rocket scientist to figure out what she's going to be cooking or for whom."

Sympathizing with the older woman, Ronnie asked, "Are you sweet on Zeke?"

"I'd have to be dumber than a stump to fall for that slow-walking, sweet-talking Texan, now wouldn't I?"

"How do you know that I'm not fond of pork chops and that Mavis is cooking for me?"

Lettie tilted her head back and laughed a joyful belly laugh. "Because you're spending your nights drooling over that handsome Garahan boy."

Ronnie bit her tongue to keep from lashing out at the woman. She was just a busybody—good-natured, like their mutual friend, Mavis, but a busybody just the same.

"Cat got your tongue?"

She shook her head and counted to ten before answering. "Dylan isn't spending the night at my place—"

"Well, he was seen arriving at your shop around seven p.m. and didn't leave until one o'clock in the morning."

Ronnie shook her head. "Your sources can't tell time. He only worked until midnight."

"And the job's not finished?"

"You're just fishing," Ronnie realized. "You didn't know for sure how long he was there, did you?"

The innocent look didn't fool Ronnie; she'd seen the same look on her grandmother's face hundreds of times over the years. The dear woman had been interfering in the lives of those she loved, hoping to give Cupid a little help, for as long as she could remember.

"That's neither here nor there," Lettie said with a frown. "What I need you to find out is whether or not Mavis'll be cooking for Zeke tonight."

How could she resist that sad look that had darkened Lettie's wide, blue eyes? She was a sucker for that look, having seen it so many mornings in her own mirror. "Before I make any promises, I need to know if Zeke made any to you."

Lettie turned at the jingling sound of the bells coming from the front of the store.

"Lettie?"

The woman sighed and looked back at her. "No. The scallywag didn't make any promises, he just…"

"Just?" Ronnie prompted, hoping the woman would confide in her. Her own experience with her best friend had broken her heart. While women who were friends could both be smitten with the same man, it was hell on a friendship when one friend started to suspect that the

other was avoiding her because she wasn't brave enough
to come clean about having an affair with your man.
Ronnie kept the lid on her emotions—anguish didn't
mix well with the anger she still felt. She really hoped
to prevent something similar from happening to these
two women. She'd come to know and really like both of
them since arriving in town.

"I guess he just lost interest."

"In a wonderful woman like you?" Ronnie found that
hard to believe. The first day she'd driven into Pleasure and
decided it was far enough from back East to start rebuilding
her life and dealing with the end of her marriage and the
betrayal of the two people closest to her, she'd ended up at
Dawson's and met Lettie and felt a close kinship.

"You've got a good heart, dear." Lettie frowned,
looking beyond Ronnie, and nodded. "Mavis."

Ronnie noticed the tension between the friends and
shook her head. Instead of the gossip fest that usually
started between the women, Mavis sniffed and tilted her
chin up, asking, "Is my order ready?"

"Hmmphf. When have I ever not had your darned
order ready, Mavis Beeton?"

The friends glared at one another, and Ronnie's heart
twisted. She knew what would come next: the friends
would start saying things guaranteed to slice at one another and leave wounds that would slowly bleed. She
didn't want that for these two women who'd befriended
her from the first. She had to do something.

"Would you two behave?"

Both women turned to glare at Ronnie. Good, she had
their attention. "And while you two are at it, how about
a little honesty? It goes a long way."

"What are you talking about?" Mavis demanded.

"Honesty? Hah!" Lettie grumbled.

"How long have you two been friends?"

They both crossed their arms and mumbled something she couldn't quite hear. Deciding to ignore the fact that neither one had answered her direct question, she dove in headfirst and said, "If this is about Zeke—"

"Are you cooking for that—" Lettie began.

While Mavis sputtered, "How could you believe that I'd—"

At that moment, Lettie's sister, Pam, walked over from the hardware side of their store. "Oh, would you two grow up," she said. "Zeke's sweet on Maryanne."

They both rounded on Pam. "Says who?"

"How do you know?" Ronnie asked.

Pam shook her head and nodded at the angry women. "I wonder if they'd spit and sputter if I tossed a bucket of cold water on them?"

Ronnie smiled but decided the best course of action would be to keep quiet.

Pam looked back at the pair and relented. "Because Sheriff McClure's new deputy was over here buying screening to repair his back door and mentioned that their dispatcher was always late coming back from her lunch break."

Both women had identical expressions on their faces. Ronnie felt their pain wash over her and wanted to take a piece out of Zeke's hide to even things. "It always starts out that way," she said. "First lunch, then they're lying to friends and family, breaking shopping dates, and standing you up instead of meeting you for coffee or drinks." She blinked the moisture from her eyes, not wanting to admit that it was tears filling them. "Then one day you come home and recognize the perfume lingering in your bedroom and know why your best friend couldn't meet you for drinks—she was too busy elsewhere."

The eerie silence that followed had Ronnie realizing that she'd said way more than she'd intended. "Perfect."

"Your best friend was having an affair with your husband?" Lettie asked, her voice pitched low, so they wouldn't be overheard.

Ronnie looked from Mavis, who nodded at her, to the Dawson sisters, and back. "My ex-best friend."

"Why couldn't she keep her lips to herself?" Lettie asked, glaring at Mavis.

"I thought I could change my ex-husband and that once he'd married me, he'd have no reason to stray. But I should have known better. The only person you have the power to change is yourself. Finding out that he'd been sneaking off to meet my best friend was the last straw and my wake-up call that it was time to start a new life over somewhere far away from where I grew up."

Pam's face fell. "Is he still alive?"

The snort of laughter surprised Ronnie more than the others. "Yeah, or I wouldn't be in Texas."

Lettie looked at her sister and then Ronnie. "Actually, a lot of people run to Texas to hide," she said. "It's a big state; a person could hide from the law for a long time."

Ronnie shook her head at them. "I was tempted to castrate him before I killed him, but decided he wasn't worth doing time for."

"So what did you do to him?"

Ronnie shrugged. "Actually, nothing. I figured if

they wanted to be together so badly, I'd let them. They deserve one another, and I figured I'd be vindicated when it was my best friend's turn to feel what I had felt when I learned there was another woman—because for a man like my ex, there will always be another woman." She paused then added, "I did tell my cousin, Vito, but made him promise not to do anything unless I ask him to."

"I think you should call your cousin," Mavis said, "and tell him you have a couple of friends out in Texas would want a piece of the action when he goes after your ex."

The three women nodded in unison. Lettie looked at Mavis, hesitated then asked, "Are you cooking dinner for Zeke tonight?"

Mavis's mouth opened, then closed, but no sound came out. "Now why on earth would you think that? Haven't we been friends forever?"

Lettie nodded. "But we both have a soft spot for that heartbreaker."

Mavis glared at Lettie and asked, "Would you have asked me if Ronnie hadn't spilled her guts just now?"

Lettie looked down at her feet, as if the toes of her boots were of particular interest.

"Oh hell, Sis," Pam grumbled. "You and Mavis have been friends for too long to let a man who's lower than a snake's belly come between you."

Mavis moved toward Lettie, When she was right in front of her friend, she held out her hand palm up and waited. Lettie smiled and did the same, and it was when Lettie turned her wrist to hold against Mavis's that Ronnie noticed they both had scars.

Pam leaned close and whispered, "It's an old Indian custom, to become blood brothers... well, in their case sisters."

Ronnie nodded. "I watched a lot of old TV Westerns with my grandmother as a kid. I was fascinated by the way they'd heat the knife, make a thin, shallow slice across their wrists, and place their wrists together, letting their blood mingle so they could become brothers... or sisters... of the heart."

Pam nodded at her. "It's important that they don't forget."

"So are you two good?" Ronnie asked.

They looked at one another and smiled. "Yes."

"So who are you cooking stuffed pork chops for?" Lettie asked.

"Rusty."

Lettie's eyes widened with shock. "LeDeux, the bull rider?"

Mavis smiled. "Retired bull rider."

"Are you up to handling another rodeo man in your life?"

Mavis drew in a breath, and Ronnie thought she'd have to blast the other woman, but in the end, Mavis answered her friend's question with a question. "Are you ready to give up on Zeke?"

Lettie's shoulders sagged. "Not that many interesting single men left in Pleasure that aren't already married."

Mavis smiled a secret smile and asked, "Are you two busy tonight?"

Ronnie wondered what her friend was up to.

"Rusty's in town with a couple of old friends of his from the circuit."

Interest flickered in the other women's eyes. "Anyone we know?"

Mavis laughed. "Tom Westin and J.T. Larame."

The names didn't mean anything to Ronnie, but from the awed expression on the sisters' faces, they did to the Dawsons. She asked, "Who are they?"

Mavis smiled. "Retired rodeo champs like their good friend Rusty."

"What are they doing in town, aside from visiting with you?" Ronnie wanted to know.

Her friend leaned in close so no one could overhear what she was about to say. "You remember when I asked if you wanted to give a demonstration of barrel racing in our Take Pride in Pleasure Day Celebration and Rodeo?"

"Yes. Why?"

"It's been a good fifteen years since these men have competed," she confided, "but each and every one of them has the rodeo in their blood. Garth Brooks wrote a song about it a lot of years ago. 'It's bulls and blood, it's dust and mud, it's the roar of a Sunday crowd.' And damned if each and every one of those rodeo cowboys didn't break nearly every bone in their bodies just like the song said, and they couldn't wait until they were almost healed so they could compete in the next go-round."

"It sounds like they're adrenaline junkies." Ronnie understood what that was like; her second cousin competed in drag racing down at Raceway Park back home.

The women agreed. "So, Mavis," Lettie said, her eyes light with excitement. "You think Rusty'll invite Tom and J.T. if I toss in a couple of fresh-baked pies?"

"Call him now," Ronnie suggested. "That way, you two can get back to what's important, saving a lifelong friendship."

"What about yours?" Pam asked.

"There's a lot I'd forgive," Ronnie said slowly. "Stupidity, an honest mistake, a faulty memory, but I cannot forgive infidelity, or lying to and cheating on your best friend."

"You've got the makings of a proper Texas woman, Ronnie," Mavis said with a smile.

"What do you say we buy a couple more chops and apples? Lettie, if you could make your grandma's buttermilk pie, maybe Pam could make her pecan pie."

Baking jobs assigned, everyone went their separate ways, lighter in spirit for having cleansed the wound that had been festering between two friends. Ronnie hoped that it would stay that way. She liked Mavis and both Dawson sisters and really hated the reminder of her own friend's betrayal. It still hurt to think about it, so she compartmentalized the hurt and shoved it down deep where it wouldn't work its way to the surface for a while.

Walking back to Mavis's parked car, Ronnie resolved to take charge of her life and not let a certain Irishman get under her skin and distract her from her goal. She had to rebuild what she'd recently lost. Her momentum had just started picking up. "Hey, Mavis?"

Her friend pointed her key fob toward the trunk and placed her bags inside. Ronnie unloaded the bags she carried and shut it. "What would you do if you were me?"

They got in the car and Mavis cranked it over. "Well,

dear, for one thing, I'd stop running away from what my heart wants."

Ronnie sighed, frustration simmering just below her surface calm. "How do I know it's my heart and not my coochie that's craving that wild-eyed handsome cowboy?"

Mavis flicked on her blinker and eased out of the parking space. "Sometimes you don't at first, but ask yourself this," she said, "what would my life be like without him in it?"

"Hell, I don't know. I've only just met the man."

Mavis rolled her eyes. "Good one, dear," she chuckled. "Try again."

Ronnie didn't want to think about how she'd feel, didn't want to have the worry of the curse hanging over her head. "Couldn't I just take my time to get to know him and not have to think about what it would be like without him?"

"Absolutely," Mavis said slowing down in front of Guilty Pleasures. "But think about this: the more time you invest getting to know Dylan, the more you'll want to know."

"That's crazy."

"Is it?"

"You know it is."

"How much time do you spend thinking about the man right now?"

Busted. "Too much."

"Then can you do any less than give the man a chance to get to know him?"

"He doesn't want to get to know the real me," Ronnie mumbled. "He just wants to slide into my bed and have his way with me."

Mavis smiled. "There is that, but think about it: what's not to like about a man who knows what he wants and isn't afraid to take it?"

"Couldn't he wait until I decide to give it to him?"

"Honey, a man like that isn't long on patience."

"Exactly. So, how do I know he'll be patient enough to find out all of the stuff I really don't want to tell him, but eventually will have to if he's in for the long haul?"

Mavis put the car in park and stared at her. "If that isn't the most convoluted thought I've ever heard. Call the man, let him know you're interested… invite him for dessert."

"He only likes me because I can cook."

"If I remember correctly," Mavis said, watching Ronnie open the door and get out, "it wasn't your cooking he tasted first."

Ronnie smacked herself in the forehead with the heel of her hand. "Anyone ever tell you that you're a pain in the backside, Mavis?"

She could hear her friend laughing as she drove off, leaving Ronnie standing on the sidewalk in front of her wreck of a store, wondering if she was crazy. Every fiber of her being stood at attention whenever Dylan Garahan was near. He was a distraction; by turns, he irritated her and intrigued her.

"That's still not reason enough to let him into my life," she grumbled, unlocking the door to her shop. She stopped and looked at the front of the store and shook her head. "Why lock the darn door, when all you have to do is remove a few boards and you'll be right inside?"

She paused on the threshold and looked around at the remnants of Ronnie DelVecchio's Life: Phase II.

Thanks to Dylan, it was more organized than her haphazard piles. The man was a miracle worker. She closed the door behind her, marveling that she could already see where he'd probably start working tonight—there was a section on either side of the front window that had been cleared of piles. Anger simmered the longer she stared at the debris and destruction. Needing to channel that anger, she breathed in, breathed out, and headed upstairs.

"Time for some yoga."

She tossed her keys on her bedside table and stripped out of her jeans and T-shirt. Ignoring the memory of Dylan's callused hands sliding the shirt up her belly, she pulled it over her head and unhooked her bra, tossing it on the bed. Donning her favorite pair of workout pants and sports bra, she walked to the living room. Her mat was stored beneath the sofa; she got down on her hands and knees, pulled it out, and laid it on the floor in front of her picture window.

Standing with her feet a hip's distance apart, she drew in a deep breath and brought her hands together. Two cleansing breaths later, she was ready to move from Mountain Pose to Downward Dog. She enjoyed the sensation of her muscles and mind working in tandem to strengthen and relax, rejuvenate, and renew. Her routine was her own; she preferred certain movements and poses to others, and knowing her body, she stuck with what worked for her.

Blocking out the world around her, she bent over into the Downward Dog Pose again.

—◁◁◁—

Dylan's tongue got stuck to the roof of his mouth. The woman he couldn't seem to get off of his mind, or coax into his bed, had the curviest ass he'd ever seen. *What the hell was she trying to do to him? Taunt him? Tease him? Kill him?*

Pick one. He sure as hell couldn't figure her out. "Nice ass, DelVecchio."

Her sharply indrawn breath told him she hadn't known he was standing there. *Maybe she wasn't trying to tease him.*

To give her credit she didn't stop; she moved smoothly from bent in half to flat on her belly. Parts of him that shouldn't be noticing how taut and toned said ass was noticed and sprang to life, alert and ready for action. He clenched his stomach muscles and rocked his hips forward, hoping to shift things around behind his zipper. He'd been hard since he stood at the top of her stairs, greeted by her sweet little backside. His johnson strained against denim, begging him to shuck his jeans and bury himself into the raven-haired witch who had him wrapped around her finger.

He scrubbed his hands over his face and cleared his throat. "Look, Ronnie," he bit out. "I need to get to work, but need you to take a look at where I'm starting. Can you please stop doing that?"

She was on all fours, curling her back up like a cat and then sticking her backside out as she arched up. His palms began to sweat. Need sliced through him, leaving him raw and wanting.

"DelVecchio, I swear—"

She slowly stood, drew in a deep breath, and looked at him. Funny thing was she didn't look so relaxed.

"Isn't yoga supposed to relax you?"

Emerald bright eyes glared at him. "Unless there's a distraction."

That thought appealed to him. He grinned. "You saying I'm distracting you, darlin'?"

She growled at him and he smiled. Lord, this woman suited him down to the ground. "Are you sure you don't want to take me up on my offer?"

She grabbed the T-shirt lying on the arm of the sofa and pulled it over her head, but she couldn't hide the fact that she was aroused. Her nipples saluted him. He wanted to yank her close and strip her bare. Inhaling, he caught the heady scent of her and had to control the urge to toss her over his shoulder and carry her off.

"Stop it."

He shook his head. "What?"

"Don't give me that innocent look," she ground out. "I'm warning you…"

Trying to be reasonable, he said, "If you don't tell me what I'm doing that's bothering you, I can't stop."

She closed her eyes and tilted her face toward the ceiling. Was she counting?

Finally, she lowered her head and crossed her arms beneath her breasts. "Stop looking at me like you'd like nothing better than to toss me on the floor and have your wicked way with me."

His gut clenched and his heart began to pound. If he got any harder, he could cut wood with his johnson—the hell with his power tools, he'd use the one God gave him.

"Darlin', give me a little credit."

She narrowed her gaze at him and put her hands on

her hips. "Do you mean to tell me you aren't thinking of ravaging me?"

He put his tongue in his cheek and rocked back on his heels. Shaking his head, he chuckled. "Well now, that thought has appeal, but I was hoping our first time might be in your bed... and not your floor, but I'm flexible." His gaze met hers. "Are you?"

She turned her back on him and bent over. If he didn't relieve the pressure soon, he'd embarrass himself and come in his jeans.

"Damn it, DelVecchio!"

Ronnie must have sensed his movement. She spun around to face him, her mat clutched across her chest like a shield. "Don't you have work to do?"

Reining in the need to take what she unknowingly offered cost him. But he'd be damned if he'd have her crying foul; he'd better get a grip and beat his libido senseless with mind-numbing work.

"A smart little filly wouldn't twitch her tail in front of a stallion."

"Is that a threat?"

"No," he bit out, "a warning."

"What are you talking about?"

"Don't bend over in front of me or else suffer the consequences."

"How the hell can I do yoga if I don't bend over?"

"Don't know," he growled, "don't care." Not breaking eye contact with her, he was satisfied that a hint of fear filled her siren-green eyes. *Good.* "Just see that you don't go flaunting what I want in front of my face."

"What you want? You make it sound as if I'm trying to get a rise out of you, forcing you to act like an animal when all I'm doing is trying to relieve some stress by working out."

"Darlin'," he purred, "I know a surefire way to relieve stress." He'd start with her legs, he thought, and work his way up to her amazing backside. "I'd be happy to stand in for your exercise mat. You can lie down on top of me and—"

"Shut up, Garahan." She stormed past him down the hall and slammed the bathroom door.

A few minutes later, he heard water running. The image of her standing beneath the steamy spray had the back of his neck knotting. Wiping his still-damp hands on his thighs, he rubbed his neck to loosen it. There was more than enough to keep him busy downstairs until he could ask her about the shelving for the far wall. It would have to wait; he had to do something with his hands before he imploded. Horny and hard as steel, he spun on his boot heel and stomped down the stairs.

An hour later, he'd replaced studs out both sides of the front door and was ready to close the space with the drywall. He ran a hand through his hair and wished he hadn't been so harsh with Ronnie earlier. He'd had a chance to settle down and cool off. That he wanted to make love with the green-eyed temptress was a given; that his body still ached with need was a little harder to handle. No stranger to lust, he figured a night or two might be enough to slake his need, but he wasn't sure about what to do with the other feelings sprinting inside of him.

After the way his body threatened to spontaneously combust, he wasn't so sure a night or two would be enough. *Maybe she's the one.*

"Hell," he muttered, "can't tell if I can't get her alone for more than five minutes."

Son, the state you're in, you wouldn't last five seconds.

"Gee thanks, Grandpa."

"Talking to yourself?"

He looked over his shoulder and damn if she didn't look good enough to eat. Her ruby-red lips would taste tart with a hint of honey-sweet if he slipped his tongue between her lips to tangle with hers.

The slim column of her throat beckoned to him, but would it taste of vanilla or almonds? He'd caught the scent of vanilla the first night he'd locked lips with her and almonds the next. A woman of moods… he could handle that.

He straightened to his full height and looked down at her. The wary expression added a hint of vulnerability that he hadn't noticed before. He'd seen a half a dozen moods reflected in the depths of those amazing eyes of hers: aroused, angry, irritated, intrigued, baffled, bewitched. Damn if each and every one wasn't a turn-on.

No surprise, he turned on like a light bulb, but he sure as hell didn't turn off like one; he smoldered like a pile of wet kindling.

She didn't back away from him this time; she stood her ground. He noted it and added it to the list of things he liked about her from the night he'd tossed his lasso around her and reeled her in.

"Are you thirsty or hungry?"

His gut clenched. "Thirsty for a sip from your lips and hungry for a taste of your lovin'."

Her eyes widened and her mouth opened, but no sound came out.

He reached over and touched the tip of his finger to her chin. She flushed a dusty rose but closed her mouth.

"Darlin', if you keep on reacting this way, I'm gonna have a hard time waiting for you to make up your mind."

"About what?"

"Come again?"

"Making up my mind about what?"

"About whether or not you're going let me park my boots under your bed for the next little while."

"Is that Texas slang for hooking up?"

She sure was a looker when she got all riled up. "Your fractiousness is a definite turn-on."

"What is it with you and your animal analogies?"

"I'm a rancher, darlin'. We're the salt of the earth."

"Wouldn't that be a farmer?"

He tilted his head back and laughed. "Yes, ma'am. If we get to town hall early enough, we can catch Judge Gambling on his way into the office and be married inside of twenty minutes."

Her eyes lost their glow, replaced with irritation... now what had he said that cause that to happen?

"You are clueless, just like the rest of the male population."

"Now don't go disparaging all of mankind just because you got your panties in a twist over something I said."

Irritation shot past angry and straight into mad as a hornet. The deep green beckoned to him, luring him into where he'd crash against the rocks. He'd pegged her as a siren the first time he laid eyes on her. He knew she'd either dig her nails into him until she was ready to set him free, or take bites out of him until she'd chewed him up and spit him back out.

Even knowing what she'd likely do to him, he was still ready and willing to let her. What kind of fool did that make him?

Don't know, how many kinds are there?

His grandmother always claimed his grandfather had a twisted sense of humor; sayings from his youth had him remembering why.

"Are you finished up for the night? It's late."

He reached into his pocket for his watch. He pushed in the button and the cover popped up. "It's only eleven fifteen."

"I'm tired, and I'm sure the neighbors would appreciate the quiet."

"Darlin', your neighbors are shop owners who all live on the other side of town, not upstairs like you do."

Her cheeks turned a delightful shade of dusty rose that he'd come to recognize as her body's reaction to his teasing when she didn't quite know what to say. Instead of the snappy comeback he expected, she turned around and walked upstairs.

"Well, hell." What female didn't have to have the last word?

The one you want.

Shaking his head, he watched her walk away, noticing the stiff set of her shoulders. There didn't seem to be anything that he said that didn't set her off. Maybe it was time to start gentling his little filly.

He collected his tools and stowed them in their proper place, that way he'd always have them. Looking around, he found the push broom he'd used the day before and swept up after himself. He carried his toolbox outside, set it in the truck bed, and on his way back inside, he heard the sweet sound of her voice calling his name. A slow burn ignited inside of him. He acknowledged the desire and dug deep to control the lust threatening to burn him alive.

"Are you coming?" she called from the open doorway.

He grinned. "Darlin', I'm just getting warmed up. I'm not even excited yet."

He'd used that line before but never meant it. With Veronica DelVecchio, everything was different.

Watch yourself, Son, there's quicksand ahead.

Chapter 9

SHE HAD TO TURN HER BACK ON HIM, OR ELSE HE'D see the desire sprinting through her system, setting off sparks of need so intense, she was sure it would light up the velvet dark sky. What was she going to do about Dylan?

He was a man with a capital *M*, wasn't afraid of hard work or getting his hands dirty. Her grandmother would have approved of him, as she never had Ronnie's first husband. Not that it mattered now.

"Wait up!"

She heard him bounding up the stairs behind her, but she didn't wait for him. She'd been working on an apology and it wouldn't be right if there wasn't the element of surprise. Setting out a plate with a slice of just-baked pecan pie and mug of coffee, she was ready when he walked through the door into her tiny kitchen.

He looked at her with a hunger so strong, it tugged at her core. Before she could open her mouth to speak, he seemed to draw within himself and take a step back. "Darlin', you must be a mind reader."

Unsure of whether he referred to the coffee or the pie, she waited.

"It was pure torture catching the smell of that pie baking as it wafted down the stairs and wondering if you'd offer me a bite." He paused and grinned. "Of pie."

They both laughed, and the tension in the room

eased. He'd put his Stetson on, but removed it when he walked into the kitchen. She reached a hand toward him, nodding to his hat. He hesitated before giving it to her. Placing it on the other side of the table, she didn't see him step toward her or pull out her chair until she backed up and bumped into it.

"Oops, sorry," he apologized. "I was just trying to be a gentleman."

It made her feel good inside that as tired as he was, he wanted to remember his manners for her. She felt special. "Thanks."

"My pleasure."

When he sat down, she passed him the sugar bowl. "I put two spoons in already, but wasn't sure just how sweet you liked it."

"How did you know I like it black with sugar?"

Her cheeks warmed, and she hated that she was blushing, but more than that, she was embarrassed that he'd know she'd asked how he liked his coffee. May as well fess up. "I… uh… I asked Mavis."

His dark eyes gleamed. She couldn't look away, caught in the crosshairs like a deer in the headlights. He didn't say anything, just shook his head and scooped up a forkful of pie.

Nerves dancing, she waited for his reaction. It was her friend's recipe—she'd never roasted her pecans before putting them in the pie before.

"Mmmm… Lord Almighty, this pie's sinful."

He took another bite and closed his eyes as he chewed and swallowed. He opened his eyes and his gaze met hers. "Ronnie darlin', you've got to move out to the Circle G so we don't have to wait for you to drive on out with meals. It worked for Lori… well, most of the time we thought it had, but her plans changed. There's a small room downstairs off the kitchen you could use if you want to."

"So, you just want me for my culinary abilities?" She couldn't believe she'd just said that… or felt disappointed that he might have changed his mind about wanting her. Teasing a man like Dylan, who had a dangerous edge to him, was like teasing a wild animal. You never knew when he'd turn and walk away or jump you. A shiver of anticipation raced up her spine.

He noticed. "Penny for your thoughts," he said, eating the last bite of his pie.

It was odd that he hadn't said anything about wanting her. Damn! Had he changed his mind? Was she too contradictory, sending him mixed messages? Mavis had warned her that men like Dylan Garahan didn't walk into your life more than once.

She'd missed her chance to test his strength against her own and run her hands all over his righteous muscles. She really wanted to taste the skin by his tattoo. *Would it be salty after spending the evening doing carpentry work downstairs?*

Her skin tingled thinking of the journey her tongue could take from the tattoo on his left pec over to his breastbone, tracing a path between his ribs, down the happy trail to heaven—

"Darlin', if you keep looking at me that way, we'll be burning up the sheets on your bed, and I don't think you're ready to trust me enough to get naked with me yet."

Her mouth dried up. He'd certainly put her fears to

rest. The man was still interested. She tried to clear her throat but couldn't; there wasn't an ounce of moisture left. He pushed her mug closer to her hand. She looked down and wondered if she would choke if she tried to sip it. Finally, she lifted it to her lips, sipped, and felt the moisture return to her mouth.

"You know it's gonna be good, but I won't push you. I can wait."

"Dylan, you don't know anything about me."

"You'd be wrong about that. You're not a quitter; you didn't turn tail and run when those teenagers busted up your shop and destroyed your stock."

She opened her mouth to speak, but he held up his hand, and she fell silent.

"You work hard; you're loyal to your friends. You cook like an angel, and Lord, I'm hoping you'll trust me soon, 'cause I just know you'll love me like the devil."

Shock waves rolled up from her feet and crashed over her head as his words hit her dead center, brushing against her frozen heart. She could feel the cold lump begin to thaw. Mavis was right about Dylan: there wasn't anyone else like him. She knew; she'd been looking for a long time.

He nodded to her, pushed back from the table, and grinned. "I'll just leave you with that thought. When you're ready to let me love you, darlin', you just give me a call. You know where to find me."

He grabbed his hat off the table and put it on his head, his movements smooth and sure. Just like the man. Nodding to her, he touched the brim of his hat and was gone.

What a study in contrasts he was: hard, yet not in

his heart where it counted; strong, but she sensed he wouldn't use it against someone weaker. Pure pleasure to look at, but if she told him that, he'd probably look at her like she was crazy. He wasn't arrogant about his looks, but he was sure of himself and what he could do with his two hands and the good sense God gave him.

"Oh crap!" She sank down on the chair as the realization washed over her. "I'm already in way over my head."

Nonni would tell her he's a nice young man and to give him a chance.

"I'm not ready to settle down, get married and have kids—let alone twins!"

Maybe she shouldn't tell Nonni too much about him. She'd probably urge Ronnie to open her heart and trust him.

"But, Nonni," she wailed. "Twins?"

One for each arm. Your heart's big enough... trust him. Damn it, her grandmother's words echoed through her heart. She really needed to talk to Nonni, despite the fact that her grandmother would likely urge her into Dylan's arms. Sunday was a couple of days away, and she'd already called her grandmother. "Time to stop worrying about it, and pick up the phone."

"Hello?"

"Nonni, it's me... I think I'm in big trouble."

———～～～———

Dylan's gut churned and his jeans were too tight; they cut into him when he slid onto the seat. He shifted until he could sit without causing any permanent damage.

"That woman's going to be the death of me." He shut

the door, put it in drive, and fought against the urge to spin his tires, peeling out of the parking space in front of her shop.

"When did I get so sucked in that I'd let a female tie me up in knots like this? She's not like—" He couldn't say his former girlfriend's name without seeing images of their years spent growing up together, as their relationship changed from friends to lovers. He'd survived that particular train wreck when he'd finally listened to what she was saying and realized she was leaving, but didn't think it was wise to revisit the scene of the accident.

"I should just turn this car back around and—" His hands tightened on the steering wheel. "No. I want her to open up and trust me, damn it!" The tension coiling inside of him eased, but his hand ached where he smashed it on the wheel. He'd learned that particular lesson the first time around: inanimate objects always win; too bad he couldn't think when he got riled.

You're stuck on her, Son.

Grandpa always liked to rub it in when he was in the right and Dylan or one of his brothers was in the wrong. *Fine time to remind me.* The knot of tension at the base of his skull started to throb. He rubbed at it, but he knew it wouldn't go away any time soon.

"She's got me hard all the time just thinking about her." He blew out a breath and let the drive back home distract him. Better off paying attention when he was driving—another lesson where the inanimate object won. "Women."

A little while later, he turned off the main road onto their land. Pushing the gate to the Circle G open, he got back into his truck. When he pulled through to the other side and got out to close the gate, he couldn't help but wonder if she was as frustrated as he was. Did women even get all hot and bothered just thinking about a man? Hell, he already knew that answer; he'd seen Ronnie's reaction to him a couple of times now. That first night he'd claimed her lips and she was his for the taking—too bad her conscience reined her in. She would have been explosive in bed.

Sitting in the cab of his truck, he looked into the rear-view mirror and an odd thought swirled around in his aching head. "Jesse and me should have gotten our brand tattooed right alongside of the shamrock." He shifted into drive and let that thought simmer while he drove up to the ranch house. His lights swept across the front porch and then moved on, illuminating the well pump and barn. He parked but didn't shut off the headlights.

He stared at the side of the barn and sighed. "Got a couple of boards that need nailing down, didn't get to it yet." Wildfire had gotten upset over something and kicked at the wall. "Probably that mare Tyler said O'Malley brought by a couple of days ago."

He shut off the engine and killed the lights. It was after midnight, but he wasn't tired and he was too wound up to sleep. Knowing his horse had heard the truck, he grabbed a handful of oats when he walked into the barn and past the other horses, promising to feed them in a few minutes. Wildfire came first with him. The horse always would; he'd saved Dylan's life zigging when Dylan wanted to zag. He'd have gotten trampled if he hadn't trusted his mount and given him his head. "Smart, aren't you, boy?"

Horse and man eyed one another over the top of the stall door. Finally, Wildfire tossed his head high and snorted. "You've always got an opinion, don't you?" The sorrel shook his head and nudged Dylan's elbow.

"Do you really care, or do you just want the oats?" He opened his hand and offered the treat to his horse, careful to keep his fingers out of the way; he'd been nipped before and it hurt like hell.

"She's killing me," he confessed, leaning his forehead against Wildfire's neck. As if sensing Dylan's mood, the horse blew out a breath. When Dylan didn't move, the horse tucked his head down, forcing Dylan to move or get caught in a headlock.

"Women are nothing but trouble." The answering whicker had him chuckling. He stroked the horse's forehead in long smooth motions down to his nose. Wildfire snuffled into the hand Dylan cupped beneath his muzzle. "Sorry, boy, that's all I have for tonight. Besides," he said giving him one last pat to his jaw, "your barn mates would be jealous and start kicking out their stalls if I don't deliver their promised treat."

Dylan always kept his promises. He passed out handfuls of oats to the rest of the horses, turned off the light, and was ready for bed; caring for the horses always soothed him. With no moon, the yard was dark, but the path from the barn to the house was well worn. Sometimes it soothed him when he thought of his mother and his grandfather walking the same cinder path from the barn to the house. There was another path that led out to the herb garden and a series of paths and old wagon roads that wound past the pond and headed in all directions to where they grazed their stock. The ranch house was at the center of it all—the heart of their land. The love for it kept the Garahan clan strong.

"Out pretty late aren't you, Bro?"

Dylan's heart jolted, not that he'd admit that to his little brother. "Up pretty late, aren't you, Jess?"

His brother's snort was as close to a chuckle as Jesse was liable to get these days. "Can't sleep."

Dylan walked up the steps and leaned against the porch railing opposite where his brother sat on the porch swing in the dark. "Whiskey?"

Jesse swirled the glass in his hand, tipped it back, and emptied it. "Was."

Now that his eyes had adjusted to the dark, he hunkered down to look beneath the swing. "Where's the bottle?"

Jesse snorted again. "I tossed it over in the bushes, so you and Tyler wouldn't know I'd been drinking."

Dylan clenched his hands into fists and then relaxed them. The need to pound something, or make that some-one, until he was senseless was so close to the surface it took all of his control to keep the lid on it. "Did you break it?"

Jesse looked over toward the barn and was quiet for so long, Dylan wasn't sure he was going to answer. "Only thing broke's in here." Jesse thumped a fist against his heart.

"Damn." Dylan's gut clenched. He knew exactly how his brother felt. "Been there, got over it," he said softly. "You will too. Give it time."

"The hell you say!" Jesse shot to his feet and shoved Dylan backward. "You never loved Sandy like I loved Lori."

Dylan's back smacked against the porch railing hard enough to feel the imprint of the wood grain. The lid shifted and some of his anger seeped out. He gave as good as he got and shoved his brother.

Jesse stumbled and landed on the swing. The impact forced it backwards against the opposite railing, the resounding crack echoed in the night a heartbeat before Jesse ended up on his backside with the swing splintered all around him.

"Shit for brains! Dad built that for mom right before he shipped out to Beirut."

Dylan's anger erupted. He dove for Jesse as his brother was gaining his feet. The two hit the railing like bulls at ramming speed. The rail broke, dumping the brothers over the side and into the flowerbed on the other side.

Jesse fought like a wild man, but Dylan was more than ready to meet his brother's fists with his own. The night echoed with the sound of fists meeting flesh and bone grinding against bone. Jesse got in a sucker punch that drove the air from Dylan's lungs. As he struggled to draw in a breath, the back porch light flicked on and bathed the scene in a soft golden glow.

"What the hell is wrong with you two?" Tyler was loaded and ready for bear. The sharply indrawn breath coming from behind him had Dylan shaking his head to clear it.

Damn, they'd woken Tyler and Emily up. Struggling to his feet, he reached out a hand to help Jesse up out of the trampled garden. He looked at Jesse, then Tyler, and answered, "Nothing."

Jesse nodded at him and turned to Tyler. "Now."

The oldest Garahan was visibly vibrating. Dylan and Jesse looked at one another and grinned. Dylan said, "Bring it on, Bro!"

The touch of a hand to Tyler's back stopped what would have been one hellacious brawl. They hadn't gotten into one in a couple of years. Dylan was sorry his brother stopped. "Could've gone another round," he grumbled.

"What's gotten into you two?" Tyler demanded.

He and Jesse looked at each other again and shrugged simultaneously.

Emily was standing next to Tyler with her arms crossed beneath her seriously stellar breasts. "Well, are you going to answer your brother?"

Dylan closed his eyes and cleared his throat. When he had his horns hidden again, he answered as politely as possible. "We did."

Tyler eyed him like he was something scraped off the bottom of his brother's boot. Dylan looked over at Jesse and noticed the youngest was having trouble keeping his horns from showing.

Needing to diffuse the situation before it ended in an all out brawl that would have Tyler's girlfriend reading them all the riot act, he grinned. "A shrug's the Garahan way of communicating."

Her hands were now on her hips. Lord, she was pretty when she was riled. No wonder Tyler agreed to let her hog-tie him. "A shrug could mean yes, no, or I don't know."

"See?" he said nodding at Jesse and then Tyler. "She's figured us out already."

Instead of the tongue-lashing he expected her to follow

up with, she started to laugh—a rich, throaty sound. Add that to the fact that she'd stood by Tyler when the odds and his ex-girlfriend were against him, and Dylan knew why the oldest brother would leg-shackle himself to the woman. She was definitely a keeper.

"Are you two 'bout done?"

Jesse shoved him. Dylan shoved back. They nodded to one another and turned to face Tyler and shrugged again.

Emily laughed harder. Dylan enjoyed the view. When she laughed, the strap holding up that excuse for a nightgown slid off her shoulder and threatened to expose what he knew would be perfection.

His brother's eyes narrowed. He said a silent thank you to God and braced himself, knowing they were a second away from a good old-fashioned family donnybrook. "Bring it on, Bro."

Tyler leaned forward about to leap off the porch, but Emily held him back with the strength of her words. "If you want to sleep downstairs on the sofa tonight, *darlin'*, you go right ahead and beat your brothers' brains out."

She turned on her heel, giving the brothers a view of her first-class legs.

The urge to fight left with Emily. Dylan cuffed Jesse on the back of the head. "Tomorrow I'll fix mom's swing."

Jesse looked at the pile of wood and nodded. "I'd apologize, but I'm not sorry for pounding on you."

Dylan grinned and swore; his fat lip split and started to bleed. He touched it with the tips of his fingers. "Lucky punch."

"Accurate punch."

Tyler smacked them both in the back of the head simultaneously. "We'll all help put mom's swing back together tomorrow."

They agreed and he added, "Next time, wake me up so I can get in on the fight."

The brothers were laughing as they walked inside and turned out the lights. "I've got to fix a few slats in Wildfire's stall tomorrow and patch where that shingle broke off before I head in to work at Ronnie's shop."

Jesse was halfway up the stairs. He called out over his shoulder, "I'll check your stash of wood and see if I can come up with a couple that are the right length or close to it for mom's swing."

Tyler put out his hand to stop Dylan from following too close behind. When their brother was far enough away not to hear, Tyler rasped, "Thanks."

Dylan nodded. He knew Tyler wasn't thanking him for repairing the gift their dad had given their mother all those years ago; he was thanking him for helping Jesse release some of the emotions bottled up inside of him before he self-destructed.

"Next time, we'll wake you."

His brother's quiet chuckle eased the rest of the tension still swirling around inside of Dylan. He might need a woman now and again, but his brothers shared a much closer tie; they were blood kin. You could get mad as hell at them, but when the chips were down and the bank was breathing down the back of your neck, just waiting to snatch one hundred fifty years' worth of Garahan sweat, blood, and tears out from under you, you could count on your brothers to help you through and guard your back. Well... once they pounded on each other, they'd be ready to take on the world.

Tyler took the stairs two at a time to catch up with Emily, who waited at the top. Dylan watched as Tyler scooped the laughing woman into his arms and carried his prize into his room, closing the door with his foot. Their muffled laughter eased the ache in his heart. Tyler deserved happiness as much as the rest of them, and had fought just as hard to hang on to Emily as she had to him.

It was hard not to be jealous of his older brother. A feminine squeal of surprised pleasure was punctuated by the slamming of his younger brother's bedroom door. Dylan shook his head. He knew it would take time for Jesse to get over Lori's leaving, but tomorrow, after they'd all done their part to repair the swing, he'd be more than ready to meet Jesse head-on again.

Still tangled up inside from wanting a woman who wasn't quite ready to trust him, Dylan knew he'd relish the idea of beating on his little brother until Ronnie was ready to let him ease his frustration inside of her amazingly responsive body.

And he just knew she would be. Hell, if her lips, mouth, and hands responded to his stealing a few explosive kisses, just imagine what the rest of her would do when he licked his way toward her sweetest spot.

"Man, I don't know how much longer I can wait to sample more of my East Coast woman." His heart echoed that he wanted way more than a taste of the woman. He wanted her heart, body, and soul... and not necessarily in that order.

Closing his door, he sat down on the edge of the bed

and pulled off his boots and socks. It was tricky unzipping his jeans with his johnson locked and loaded—from just thinking about Ronnie.

His sigh was long and low. "It's gonna be a long night."

Shucking his jeans, he stripped off his shirt and hit the sheets, amazed that he could close his eyes and drift off to sleep with a raging hard-on.

His last coherent thought was about her and whether or not she'd taste like wild honey or caramel cream.

Ronnie woke to brilliant sunshine streaming in through her bedroom window. She tried to close her eyes and ignore the fact that it was morning. She'd spent more time tossing and turning than sleeping after the pep talk Nonni had given her. But the sunlight on her eyelids was warm and welcoming. Giving in, she sighed, opened her eyes, and sat up.

"I feel like something the cat dragged in." She stumbled out of bed, dragging her sorry behind down the hall to the bathroom. "Well, crap." The image looking back at her *looked* like something the cat had mauled.

With an empty bladder, she headed toward the kitchen. "Coffee." That would fix everything; after two or three cups, she'd be awake and able to do something about her lack of sleep.

"That man's got me tied up in knots." And if that image didn't just add to the tension screaming through her body this morning, her neck had a crick in it from trying to get comfortable enough to sleep last night.

"Coffee first, yoga second." With her morning planned, she rinsed out the coffeepot and filled it with cold water. Finding the innards to the percolator proved to be difficult. The basket for the grinds wasn't in the dish drainer. After putting everything in the drainer away, she realized that the stand for the basket wasn't either. They weren't buried beneath the pots, pans, and bowls she'd used last night.

Scouting for parts to her percolator first thing in the morning without caffeine surging through her system was not how she envisioned starting her day. "Crap, crap... crap!" She opened and closed cabinets, but didn't find the essential parts to her glass percolator—the only shower gift she'd kept after severing her ties with her ex, the one from her grandmother who believed there was only one way to make coffee. Irascible as only an old lady could be, she'd been emphatic when she'd told Ronnie that drip didn't count as real coffee.

Ronnie's head started to ache from lack of caffeine, but she ignored it and yanked the refrigerator door open. "May as well have orange juice if I can't have coffee."

The basket for the coffee grinds was sitting on the shelf next to the orange juice. She pulled both out, poured a glass, and set the basket on the counter next to the stove. Shaking her head, trying to wrack her brains to see if she could remember what she'd been thinking last night, the image of a tall, dark, and handsome cowboy with callused hands filled her. "Dylan."

A full body shiver accompanied the butterflies in her belly, a reaction she was becoming used to where he was concerned. She opened the fridge to put the orange juice back and found the rest of the coffeepot's innards. The stand for the basket was nestled in with the eggs, and the basket lid was on the shelf by the bread.

"Lord, I really need this coffee," she mumbled aloud. "Where did I put the top to the pot?" She put the stand in the pot, added the basket, and counted out rounded spoonfuls of coffee. The scent permeated her bad mood and started to smooth out the rough edges waking up cranky had given her.

"Can't brew coffee without the damned top to the pot." Resigned, she reached for her purse to dig out her keys and money to buy a cup of coffee and found the missing top.

She pulled it out of her purse and stared at it. "I've got to do something about that man before he drives me crazy." *Short trip.*

Once the thought took hold, she started to laugh, a quiet chuckle that gave way to an all out belly laugh. She was wiping her eyes and putting the top on the pot before she stopped. It took the edge off the tension and had almost the same effect as a good cry. Who knew?

Now that coffee was at the end of her morning rainbow, she could cope. She made breakfast—no point in enjoying her morning cup without something to line her empty belly. Her grandmother always insisted that the morning meal was the most important and set the tone for the way a person's day would unfold. She wondered when it would be her turn to be right about something. Nonni couldn't always be right, could she? Thinking of a certain dark-eyed Irishman with a smoldering look that turned her insides to jelly, she knew she'd have to give the man a chance and stop thinking about the curse so damned much.

Maybe she was making it come true by trying so hard to avoid it, in some perverse inversion of the law of attraction or something. Maybe she should try to make the curse come true and then it wouldn't. The circular thinking was making her head spin.

The scent of frying bacon and percolating coffee filled her tiny kitchen, lightening her heart and soothing her frayed nerves. Scrambling eggs in the pan, she asked herself, "What am I going to do about that man?"

Without warning, the image of his broad and beautiful chest, sculpted pectoral muscles, sprinkling of dark hair between those amazing muscles, and emerald green shamrock tattoo filled her mind. She stopped and knew what she wanted to do with and to the man... it was how to get her brain to shut off long enough to follow where her heart wanted to lead her that she didn't know.

"I've followed my heart before and look where it got me."

She'd told her grandmother that same thing last night and Nonni had reminded her that she'd followed her head. Ronnie sighed and admitted that Nonni had been right once again: she had married Anthony Faustino because he'd convinced her he would always be able to provide for her. At the time, being able to have things and beating the DelVecchio Curse had been more important than finding what she suspected she'd discovered with Dylan—the promise of a love that grabbed you by the heart and made you dizzy with it while you waited to see if the lust that tied you up in knots would fulfill that promise or simply burn itself out.

As she sat down to eat, her brain kicked into high gear. There were times in life when you realized you'd been telling yourself something for so long that you'd come to accept and believe it to be the way things really happened. In that moment, Ronnie realized that she'd worked so hard to convince herself that she'd followed her heart where her first husband was concerned that she believed it. But the truth was that she let him convince her that she should marry him; his promise that he'd be faithful to her had been what she wanted him to say. In her heart, she hadn't really worried about it because she didn't really love him—but she had wanted to. It had become habit to think of him as the man she would marry and spend the rest of her life with. Her heart had willingly followed her head and disaster had followed in its wake.

Carrying her plate to the sink, she washed it and set it in the drainer. With Dylan, she'd had no control over her instant attraction to him. She'd felt the rope slip around her shoulders as the blindfold had been ripped from her eyes. His dark and dangerous eyes had beckoned to her as he reeled her in. One kiss and her world tilted on its axis. She had been functioning on a different plane of existence since he'd laid his lips on hers, coaxing a response from her.

Tingles sparked beneath her skin and shot warmth from her heart straight to her core. He set off a conflagration that had yet to be quenched. Was she just being pigheaded, fighting against what in her heart she knew was meant to be? Should she ignore the warning light flashing in the back of her mind, cautioning her to keep her heart safe from the man who was the DelVecchio Curse walking? Or should she trust in her grandmother and Mavis's advice and turn off her mind and trust Dylan?

"I need to clear my mind... yoga and then the hot

shower." Putting her immediate plan into action, she went to her bedroom and changed into the new workout clothes she'd bought before she left New Jersey. She slipped them on and immediately felt her mood lift. The pants were pale grey with *Bootylicious* emblazoned across the backside in lipstick pink with a sports bra in the same bright shade.

Stopping in the bathroom, she grabbed a hair clip and swept her hair up and out of the way. Ready to take on the world, or at least loosen up the kinks in her neck and shoulder, she walked into the living room and bent over to pull the yoga mat out from under the sofa.

The sunshine beckoned, so she laid out her mat in her favorite spot, right beneath the window. Inhaling a deep, cleansing breath, she was ready to begin with Mountain Pose. Moving fluidly through her routine, she was limber and ready for the Downward Dog pose. Ronnie felt the beauty of her mind and body perfectly in tune as she repeated the movements.

Reaching for the long-sleeved shirt on the arm of the sofa, she pulled it on and sat on her mat in the Lotus position. Extending her arms palms up, she closed her eyes and began to meditate.

Renewed in body and spirit, she put away her mat, ready for that hot shower.

―∾∿∾―

Standing beneath the hot spray after meditating always opened her mind. Usually, she could sort through whatever problems she had, but this morning, her thoughts kept coming back to Dylan Garahan.

His dark eyes held secrets and promises that beckoned

to her whenever their gazes met. She knew what he wanted; what she didn't know was whether or not she was ready to take that dive over the edge into madness. Oh, she knew she'd enjoy the ride and probably let him share her bed for the next little while. What worried her was that he'd be satisfied with one night, and she wouldn't, leaving her in the same position she'd been in before, wanting a man who was no longer interested.

Why was she thinking about that now? Dylan wasn't her ex. He couldn't be more different. Anthony dressed in Armani suits and handmade Italian loafers, while Dylan preferred well-worn denims, boots, and black Stetson. Her mind wandered as she dipped her fingertips into her favorite body scrub. She let the almond scent wrap around her as she smoothed it on and rinsed it off, mentally shedding her insecurities. Ronnie felt revved as she turned off the shower and reached for a fluffy yellow towel.

"Female rituals are so good for the soul," she told her reflection. "I wonder what Shannon and Lenore are up to today?"

A few minutes later, she was on the phone. "How are things over at the Mysts of Time?"

Listening to her friend, she smiled. She knew exactly what Shannon was going through, having to rebuild what she'd lost. "Did Emily recommend the same carpenter to you?" She hoped Emily hadn't; she didn't like the idea of her pretty blonde friend distracting the man who was about to become her lover. Which was the main reason she wasn't as close to Shannon as she was to Mavis—her past had taught her not to trust women friends her own age.

"Pam Dawson sent over this really great handyman," Shannon said. "He's got the job nearly finished."

Ronnie would have loved to have her shop back in one piece as quickly, but knew that Dylan was nearly working twenty-four/seven. She hoped he had it in him to finish the job; she'd be done if she had to put in that many hours of hard labor.

"How's it going over at your place?"

Ronnie hesitated. Should she tell Shannon everything that was going on? It had been so easy to talk to Mavis. The woman was old enough to be her mother and had been the first friend she'd made here in Pleasure. Would Shannon try to steal her man, as her ex–best friend had stolen her husband? Dylan was definitely worth stealing!

"Hey, is everything all right?"

The concern in her friend's voice helped her decide to reach out to her and share a little bit more. "Yeah. Sorry, I've been busy and what with Dylan messing with my mind—"

"Honey, I'd let that man mess with more than just my mind if I was you."

Ronnie's heart fluttered in her breast. "That's what has my mind in a twist."

Shannon's throaty laughter sparked her own. "I wouldn't mind getting twisted or tied up by that man."

She couldn't agree more. "That's the rest of what has me feeling upside down and backwards. I've never met anyone like him before. He's the complete and total opposite of my ex-husband."

"You've got an ex?"

"Yeah," she said. "Long story, ends badly."

Shannon was silent for a couple of minutes, then said, "Why don't I come on over and we can talk about it?"

"I don't want to talk about my ex," Ronnie insisted.

Her friend laughed again. "Hell, I don't blame you. I want to talk about Dylan."

This time, Ronnie's laughter bubbled up from deep inside as she made the decision to trust a woman her own age. "I'll put the coffee on. I'm waiting to hear from my insurance agent. They owe me a check."

"Tell me something about that Texas man that'll tide me over 'til I get there."

Smiling, she knew just the thing. "He's got this way that he looks at me, and I just know what it'll be like when he's tasting me one kiss, one lick, at a time."

Shannon cleared her throat and Ronnie swallowed, her mind working over time. The image of Dylan's biceps bulging, as he kept his deliciously naked body from crushing hers a heartbeat before he put his one hundred and eighty pounds of torque to work satisfying the gut-burning need she had to make love with the man, set her ablaze.

Fanning herself, she wondered if she'd ever be able to quench the need she had for this man. Would one night be enough? Would one hundred?

Time would tell.

"I'll be over in a few," Shannon said. "Oh, and I'm bringing chocolate."

"You're my hero."

Shannon laughed. "I bet you say that to anyone who promises you chocolate."

Ronnie felt better already. "Busted!"

Chapter 10

THE SOOTHING MOTIONS OF SAWING THROUGH A PLANK of wood eased some of the tension that spent the night between Dylan's shoulder blades. The rap of his nine-pound hammer driving nails into the wood beat the rest of it into submission.

Fitting the pieces back together and filling in where the slats had been totaled when he and Jesse had fallen into their mother's bench almost made up for the fact that they had blindly destroyed the precious gift.

"Grandpa would have had our hides."

"Only if he caught us," Tyler drawled. His brother opened the screen door and handed Dylan a steaming mug.

Dylan eyed it warily before accepting it. "Who made the coffee?"

"Jesse."

Dylan looked over his shoulder and watched as their younger brother made his way over from the barn.

"Horses and stock've been fed," Jesse rumbled. "You 'bout done?"

Dylan ignored his brother and blew across the surface of the coffee. "Not as good as Ronnie's." He grinned. "And not as bad as Tyler's."

He sidestepped Tyler's halfhearted punch, which missed him by an inch. "Your aim's off this morning." Dylan drained his mug and set it on the porch.

Tyler grunted in response and Jesse snickered. "That's 'cause a certain redhead kept him up half the night."

Dylan watched the grin on their older brother's face smooth into a smile. "Your turn will come, Jess."

Instead of the argument he expected, Jesse shrugged and joined them on the porch. With his brothers flanking him, Dylan nodded. "On three, you two lift your ends of the bench, and I'll reattach it to the chain."

When the bench was rehung, he stepped back and sighed. "I'll paint it later."

"No," Tyler said. "Leave it as a reminder as to why we need to pay attention to what really matters in life."

Jesse nodded and Dylan rasped, "Family and the Circle G."

⁓

"But there must be some mistake." Ronnie couldn't believe it. "I've always paid my bills on time—"

"I'm sorry, Ms. DelVecchio, but it's totally out of my control. You should be receiving our decision in the next week or so."

"But I need the money now… the damage to my shop and stock was devastating. I'm losing money every day my shop isn't open."

"I would call family members and see if they can possibly help you out in the interim."

"But—"

"Good-bye, Ms. DelVecchio."

She stared down at her cell phone, unable to believe that her insurance company wasn't going to be sending the check as promised. How would she be able to buy more stock? How would she pay Dylan for the supplies he said he needed to put her shop's walls and shelves back together?

"Bastards!" It wasn't much, but yelling helped get it out of her system and made her feel marginally better.

"And my day started off so well with a visit from Shannon and chocolate."

She didn't know what she was going to do. Dylan would be arriving in a little while and she needed to be able to focus and talk to him about the hold up in her funds. While she wasn't paying him for the labor, she was paying for any materials he couldn't salvage.

"And just how does that help the Garahans pay their feed bill if I can't?"

With a sigh, she resolved to take charge of what she could. Right now the only thing she had control over was herself. "I need another round of yoga if I'm going to be sane by the time he gets here."

A few minutes later, she'd changed into her exercise gear and was reaching under the sofa for her mat. Breathing in deeply, she centered herself and spread her feet hip distance apart, consciously adjusting her body into the Mountain Pose. The familiar movements demanded her full attention, not allowing her mind to worry over the possibility of her insurance company denying her claim.

Muscles warming with the routine, she bent in half, touching the mat with the tips of her fingers.

"Your body is so beautiful."

The deep timbre of Dylan's voice rolled over her like molasses on a warm day. The delicious image of his muscled perfection lying in her bed while she drizzled said molasses in a thin line from his neck to his knees filled her. She straightened and frowned at him. Damn him for ruining her concentration.

"The way you move, so smooth and fluid—it's like watching a ballet."

"You've seen a ballet?"

"Yeah," he chuckled. "I was forced, but it wasn't as bad as I thought it'd be."

Yet one more thing that added to her interest in the man. She sighed and gave in to need and let her eyes take a long and lazy journey across his broad shoulders, she shivered.

"Miss me?"

She swallowed to clear the tightness in her throat. "I'm not sure I should answer that question."

He tipped his Stetson back and that's when the light hit his face and she noticed the bruise along his jawbone and his fat lip.

"Did you have an accident?"

He chuckled, but shook his head. "No, ma'am."

"Did you walk into something?"

"You could say that." He looked like he was about to say more, but instead, he stepped closer, reaching for her. Unsure of what he was thinking or feeling, she took a step back. "Are we back to pretending you don't want me to touch you?"

She tilted her chin up. Their gazes met and held. She knew what he wanted. The dark and desperate desire in his eyes spoke of long nights filled with loving, and she wondered if he'd be a missionary man, or one who liked to go around the world. It had been a long time since she'd spent the night making love… hell, it'd been a long time since she'd made love at all. He stopped and crossed his arms over his massive chest and waited, watching her with eyes the color of sinfully rich dark chocolate. Eyes that promised heaven... What was her problem? He was hot sex in battered jeans. An orgasm waiting to happen. Was she crazy?

Certifiable, she realized, when his impossibly dark eyes beckoned to her. The man wanted her, she wanted him... where was the problem? Oh, yeah... the lack of funds.

"I was balancing my checkbook when the insurance company called. After talking to them, I needed to clear my head, so I was doing a little yoga." She looked up at him and sighed. "It was working until you showed up and started messing with my mind."

His grin was lethal, but not unexpected given the opening she'd just give him. "So you can't resist me?"

"If I work hard at it, I can," she retorted.

He frowned down at her, but before he could say anything else, she knew she had to tell him. They'd agreed to barter—his labor for her cooking—but she was supposed to pay for the materials the same as he was supposed to pay for the food she cooked for them. How could she do that if she didn't have the money?

"My insurance company just called."

"You said that already."

"I know but it's what we talked about that I need to tell you."

The look in his eyes changed to one of understanding. "The check's gonna be late."

She hesitated, needing to confide the rest of what she feared, even if it changed the direction of the relationship they'd been moving toward. The lyrics and melody of an old Eagles' tune flitted through her brain:

"You can't hide your lyin' eyes." She'd been lied to and wouldn't do that to anyone—ever! "Dylan, look," she began, "I'm not sure I'll be getting that insurance check anytime soon—or maybe at all. But I don't know because they aren't telling me." She hesitated before adding, "I'll understand if you can't finish the job the way we agreed to until I figure out a way to come up with the money for the materials."

Needing to do something with her hands, she bent over to grab the edge of her mat.

"Do you have to bend over like that?"

She finished rolling the mat and bent lower to shove it under the sofa before she turned around to face him. "Why? Is it a problem?"

His eyes were dark and dangerous again and her body reacted to the emotions simmering there. "Not if you don't mind me tossing you over my shoulder and dragging you off to strip you bare."

Damned if that image didn't replace the yummy one of him drizzled with molasses. She drew in a breath and forgot to let it go until she heard Mavis's voice in her head reminding her to breathe out. Placing a hand to her chest to ease the ache there, Ronnie relished the fact that the devastatingly attractive man standing in front of her wanted her as badly as she wanted him... but was waiting for her to give him the green light.

What was she waiting for anyway? She'd already given herself the talk, already knew what was important about the man—except for his past relationships, but did she really need that information?

"What happened to thinking me doing yoga was like watching a ballet?"

He took off his hat and smacked it against his thigh. Watching as he raked a hand through his hair, she glanced up and held her breath. His frustration was there for her to see; watching him wrestling with it made it hard to remember to breathe.

"Can't think straight when you start twitching your pretty little backside in my face."

"Really?" She liked that he was having the same trouble she was. "Well, it's hard to concentrate when you start flexing your seriously stellar muscles in my direction."

He chuckled, setting his hat back on his head. "Seems we have a similar problem," he rumbled. "Maybe we could help one another fix it." Before she could respond, she was crushed against his chest and kissed senseless.

When he eased her back, but kept her in the protective circle of his arms, she licked her lips. She could still taste him. Delectable as dark chocolate, heady as a shot of her grandmother's sambuca.

"I could ease some of that tension coiling up inside of you, darlin'."

She laughed—she hadn't meant to but couldn't seem to help herself. The man pulled emotions out of her that she'd thought long dead. Touching her fingertips to his mouth, she whispered, "I know you could, and I really want to let you, but I need to figure out how I'll survive until I get that check."

"I could use a break," he said. "Why don't you come on over here and sit down." He guided her toward the sofa. "Trust me."

Her gut settled and her heart urged her to follow. "OK, but I need—"

"To relax." He sat down and pulled her onto his lap and held her to his heart. The rhythmic beat did what the extra half hour of working out hadn't: soothed the craziness tying her up in knots.

"Dylan, I want—"

"Me to kiss you." His lips were warm and soothing as he pressed them to her forehead, cheek, and chin.

She giggled. "That wasn't what I was going to say."

He cupped her face in his big hands and smoothed a wavy strand of hair behind her ear. "Ronnie, you worry me."

"I do?"

"Yeah," he said. "I'm finding I want more from you than I'd first thought. I still want to get you naked, and know that making love with you will be memorable, but I'm wanting to take my time to get to know what's going on inside that clever brain of yours too."

"Uh… I—wow, I'm so glad."

Laugh lines formed at the corners of his eyes when he smiled. "So long as I know I'll be getting you in bed soon, I can wait. But for the moment, I need you to let me hold you."

Had God been listening when she'd said that particular prayer? Going with her instincts, she laid her head against his chest and let go of her worries one by one. Her body relaxed fully against him as she closed her eyes.

Dylan's arms tightened around her as he settled her in the crook of his arm. The kiss to the top of her head eased the rest of her worries; his sigh of contentment touched her on a level no man had touched yet. The hell with the curse—if she didn't mess things up, this man was the one she wanted to grow old with.

She jerked awake and smacked her head on some-thing hard.

"Ow!"

"I'm so sorry," she soothed realizing that she'd man-aged to hit his bruised chin.

He was shaking his head at her. "Must have dozed off." Staring at her, he brushed his hand across her shoulder and settled it against the small of her back ad-mitting, "I didn't sleep much last night."

"I didn't either." How much had she missed by fol-lowing her head rather than her heart the first time? Hell, those days were over. She was grabbing life with both hands and living it fully from this moment on. "How much time do we have?"

He grinned. "Not as much as I'll need the first time I make love to you, if that's what you're asking."

Disappointment eased contentment aside. Resignation filled her. "I really do need to get back to the world of high finance."

He pulled her closer and shifted on the sofa, rasping, "Wrap your legs around me, darlin'."

Eager to comply, she did as he asked and was re-warded when he cupped his hands beneath her back-side and pulled her close. The heat of him seared right through his jeans and her yoga pants. She whimpered, but his mouth claimed hers and her thoughts splintered apart as his lips and hands worked their magic. As she reached for the buttons of his shirt, he was easing her off of his lap. She shivered at the loss of heat.

"Ronnie, I've got some more to finish up, and I don't

want you to get mad at me for distracting you when your checkbook's waiting for you. How about we agree to take a break in about an hour or so. We could accomplish a lot in an hour."

She agreed. "Thanks for understanding what I needed. Even I didn't."

His gaze locked with hers. "My pleasure." The roughness of his reply went right to her heart.

A few minutes later, she was back in front of her laptop, ready to pull her hair out as the reality of her situation hit her hard. "How am I going to pay my credit card bill if I have no stock to sell? How am I going to buy more stock to sell if I don't pay my credit card bill?"

Slumping into the chair, she wondered if she should call her family. Her cousin Vito had always said family took care of family. But didn't you have to pay them back sometime? She didn't envision heading back to New Jersey and had no desire to get tangled up with owing anyone at this point in her life. She'd made it this far on her own and intended to keep going forward. Was she just being stubborn?

Too bad she'd hit a snag when she'd moved to Pleasure, Texas, and foolishly thought it was an idyllic community without crime. Imagine that. Crime was everywhere—just like back home. "And if Jolene and Emily were to be believed, the kids who did this were just bored and having themselves a time."

Instead of doing what she'd told Dylan she needed to, her mind drifted, remembering the shock that rooted her feet to the sidewalk outside of her shop. Her beautiful shop smashed to pieces and everything inside destroyed. The sheriff hadn't arrested anyone in connection with the break-in yet, but he was of the opinion that the same person (or persons) who had shot out the sign hanging outside of the Lucky Star was responsible for vandalizing her store and then repeated the performance at the Mysts of Time, Shannon's store.

Ronnie leaned her elbows on the table on either side of her laptop and let her forehead drop into her hands. What was she going to do? "I've already cashed in my half of the divorce settlement." The trip out West seemed to be just what she needed. She hadn't stopped until she saw a sign on the highway for Pleasure, Texas, Population 439. She'd grown up in a town with 60,000 people and couldn't even conceive of so few people in one town. "All things considered, I still think I made the right decision settling here. I like the people I've met and the sights I've seen—especially one dark-eyed, handsome hunk of cowboy."

Shutting down her laptop, she knew she wouldn't be headed back to New Jersey unless it was to visit Nonni. Once she'd turned off the highway and drove into the town of Pleasure, she knew she was going to stay. The quaint storefronts looked like something out of one of her grandmother's favorite TV Westerns. Harrison's Feed Store and Dawson's General Store were across the street from one another and housed in two of what she'd learned were a handful of historic buildings in town. Enjoying the idea of living out West, just far enough from where she'd left her past, she drove farther and saw a building with a signpost out front advertising it was for sale.

On autopilot, she had parked her car in front of the building and got out, walking toward it as if in a trance. It was perfect: two stories with a space for her shop on the first floor and living quarters upstairs. It needed work, but Ronnie knew in that moment that she was destined to end her journey in Pleasure, which sparked the name of the lingerie and perfume shop she intended to open: Guilty Pleasures. Maybe it would be harder to make her business work out here in the middle of a ranching community, but she would add an online store and she was willing to work hard to make her dream a reality.

The sound of hammering broke through her thoughts. Since she wasn't getting any paperwork done, it was time to start cooking, even if she wasn't certain she'd be able to continue with their bartering agreement. She needed to come up with a way to earn money fast, or her dream of owning her own business and flourishing out West was going to evaporate under the brutally hot Texas sun.

Cooking helped her mind sort through her troubles. She grabbed her frying pan and set it on the stovetop. Opening the cabinet, she found the Italian flavored bread crumbs, canola oil, and cooking sherry. Setting everything out on the counter, she opened the fridge and pulled out two eggs and the chicken breasts she'd bought earlier in the day.

Knife in hand, she started to debone the chicken.

Dylan's gut clenched with need, but he strove to ignore it as the vision that greeted him just a short while ago replayed in his aching head. He hadn't slept much, troubled with dreams that didn't make sense. Well, part of his dreams made sense—the ones where he'd emptied

himself into the brunette currently driving him crazy—
but the other part was actually what had given him the
ache at the back of his skull and between his eyes.

He'd dreamt of a man, a tall man with a build a lot
like his own, but the face wasn't Dylan's face. It was
similar, but more like their grandfather's. The man had
lifted a young boy up off the ground and tossed him
in the air, catching him at the last moment, thrilling
the boy. In that moment, Dylan had felt that thrill right
down to his toes and knew he was that boy.

Then the man turned to the other little boy and did the
same with him. Dylan's heart nearly broke all over again
as the man turned and set the boy on his feet and turned
toward a woman holding the youngest of the three boys.
She was his mother, and the man in the khaki-colored
uniform was his father. He'd left that day to go on a
peacekeeping mission in Beirut.

He didn't really remember, but he did remember his
mother telling Dylan and his brothers that they should
be proud of their daddy. He was a Marine. Three weeks
later, their lives shattered when his mother's worst fear
became reality and a dark sedan pulled up to the ranch
house and two Marines came to their door with a letter.

His mother held the letter to her breast but didn't
open it. The two officers saluted her as tears pooled in
her eyes and slipped down her cheeks. His father was
one of the 220 Marines killed when their barracks ex-
ploded, the act of a suicide bomber that, to date, was
the largest single-day loss in the Marine Corps since the
Battle of Iwo Jima during WWII.

Their lives had irrevocably changed with that single
act of terrorism. Their mother had gone on with their

lives because she had three reasons to—five-year-old Tyler, four-year-old Dylan, and her youngest, Jesse, just two years old—but she'd never really recovered from the loss of the man she'd loved her entire life.

Dylan blinked and reality painfully intruded as he hit his knuckles with the hammer instead of the nail. "Sonofabitch!" He set his hammer down and shook his hand; it never helped with the pain, but was something he'd been doing for as long as he could remember. His grandfather had taught them to walk it off if they'd fallen and to shake it out if they'd smashed their hands.

"That'll teach me to keep my mind on what I'm doing." Ignoring the throbbing in his hand, he went back out to his truck and hauled the first drywall panel over to the sawhorse he'd set up on the sidewalk. He measured twice and cut once, just as his grandpa had taught him. Armed with his reconditioned drywall screw gun, he was ready to rebuild the first of four walls.

The sound of footsteps overhead soothed the rough edges that remembering his dream had left behind. It must have been working with his brothers rebuilding their father's final gift to their mother that sparked the long ago memory. He didn't like to think about what might have been if his dad hadn't been in the Corps. Everything happened for a reason, his mom used to say. Although why God in His infinite wisdom decided he and his brothers would lose both parents before they'd learned to drive was beyond him. "Probably better that way," he mumbled as he screwed the drywall into place.

Easing back to eye up the drywall, he took a moment to check the fit before pulling the tape measure off his tool belt to check the measurement for the next sheet of drywall. Keeping his hands busy usually let his mind wander, but not when he was using power tools; the slip up with the hammer earlier was just that—a momentary slip up. He normally paid close attention to what he was doing when he was working. If he didn't, he'd have ended up like Tyler, head-butted into a barbed-wire fence, or worse, trampled by their steer. When doing carpentry work, he had to keep focused, or else he'd end up measuring wrong. As a rule, his side jobs didn't pay much, but would end up costing him to do business if he wasted time and materials.

"Frigging perfect!"

His mouth twitched as he fought to contain his smile, knowing it would only open up the split in his lip. "Wonder what's got Ronnie riled."

The overwhelming need to see her again, after holding her in his arms as they drifted off to sleep, had him heading for the stairs.

He walked into the kitchen in time to see her stick her bloody hand underneath the faucet. His gut clenched as he reached for the roll of paper towels. His hands weren't clean, but as long as they stopped the bleeding first, they could clean it out later.

"Easy, now," he soothed, putting pressure against the folded wad of paper towels.

Her eyes met his and he felt his gut clenching with need. They'd taken a big step forward in their relationship earlier. She'd fallen asleep in his arms, and from the look in her eyes was willing to trust him when she was injured. Surely she'd trust him with her heart soon. He struggled but managed to get his thoughts back to where they needed to be. Carefully blotting the wound on the back of her hand, he noticed the bleeding had slowed down. "I don't think you'll need stitches."

Her sigh of relief had him looking down to meet her gaze.

"How do you know?"

"I've had a lot of hands-on experience recently. I'm sure you heard about my brother Tyler's run-in with Widowmaker."

Ronnie nodded and leaned her head against his shoulder. "I hadn't met your brother then but I heard about what happened from Mavis."

He still had ahold of her hand and was reluctant to let go until he was certain he was right about the wound. "I need to take a look at the cut to see how deep it is." She agreed and buried her face against his side. His heart stumbled in his chest, and before he could step back, he was sliding headfirst down the slippery slope into uncharted territory.

Getting a grip, he uncovered her hand. Relief speared through him. It was an impressive slice across her knuckles, but when he gently manipulated the skin around the edges, he could see that he was right; it wasn't too deep. "A couple of butterfly bandages will hold the wound closed. We just need to clean it out with soap and water first, peroxide second."

"I don't even know what a butterfly bandage is." Ronnie sounded lost.

He brushed the hair out of her eyes and swept the tips of his fingers across her cheekbone. "I've got some in the first-aid kit in my truck."

"Is there a story behind why you travel with one?"

He shook his head. "My grandfather taught us to keep

one on hand; you never know when you're on a job or out on the range and need one."

"But if you're on horseback—"

"Most times we are, but we transfer the first-aid kit from one of our trucks to our saddlebags before we head out."

"So you're kind of like a Boy Scout."

He tilted his head back and laughed. The woman was pure delight. He was the one who'd found her and was keeping her. "Not hardly, but I have been known to help damsels in distress."

She smiled until Dylan started massaging his soapy hands over hers and then some soap went in the cut. She sucked in a breath and held it. "It only hurts for a little bit." He blew across the cut hoping to ease the pain and distract her. When she looked up at him, he gave into need and pressed his lips to the tip of her nose.

"Thanks." She looked down at her hand and the blood beginning to ooze out from the wound. "Are you sure about not needing stitches?"

He nodded. "Where's the peroxide?"

"In the bathroom."

He ripped off another bunch of paper towels and folded them neatly, holding them against her knuckles. "Wait here. I'll go and grab the bandages from my car and the peroxide from your bathroom."

"OK."

He ran down the stairs and sprinted out to his truck. He wasn't worried that she'd lose too much blood, but he didn't like the thought of her being alone and injured. He took the steps up two at a time and found her standing at the sink pouring the peroxide over her hand.

"I thought I told you to wait here."

She looked over her shoulder. "I'm still here."

He narrowed his eyes and frowned down at her. "You went to the bathroom."

She grinned. "I had to pee."

He shook his head. "You were supposed to stay put."

She laughed at him. "DelVecchio women don't like to be told what to do. You'd best realize that now."

He nodded. "Got it." When she set the bottle on the counter, he blotted it dry so the bandage would hold. "This won't hurt." Dylan carefully squeezed a thin line of antibiotic ointment on the cut—too much and the bandage wouldn't hold. Careful not to hurt her, he fastened the butterfly on one side of the wound and pulled it closed, pressing the bandage to the other side of the cut.

"Don't get it wet."

"Yes, doctor."

Their eyes met, and he saw the moment her guard slipped and hunger filled her gaze. It was torture, but he tamped down on the overpowering need he had to sweep this woman into his arms and take... just take, until they were both limp and satisfied. He could make his move, and he could have her, but he knew now wasn't the time. They'd already talked about it earlier and had reached an agreement of sorts. He might have more instant gratification, but would lose in the long run. Right now, he needed focus so he could work toward a future with Veronica DelVecchio. Quirks and all, she was the woman he needed.

But if it wasn't soon, he'd didn't think he'd be able to control the greedy need he had for her. It would be raw and primitive, and he didn't want their first time together to be their only time. He knew one taste wouldn't be enough.

Closing the cage on the beast inside of him, he drew back and breathed deeply. The scent in the kitchen enveloped him. "Whatever you're cooking smells amazing."

She smiled up at him. "It's just breaded chicken, but I thought you might enjoy it."

He walked over to the pan and looked down at it. "Where's the bread?"

Ronnie rinsed out the sink while she answered, "In the bread crumbs."

"I'm hungry."

This time she walked over to stand beside him and placed her good hand on his back. Not a tentative touch but the touch of someone who was familiar... like a lover. It was a start—a damn good start.

"Are you always hungry?"

He shrugged. "Mostly." He eyed the crisply browned chicken pieces as Ronnie splashed white wine into the pan and covered it. "Is that dinner tomorrow?"

She smiled and handed him an empty plate and nodded toward the dish. "No. I made it just for you." She set the timer and turned the flame down under the pan. "It'll be ready in five minutes. Help yourself." Dylan watched; he hadn't really watched a woman bustling around a kitchen since he'd been a kid. "What were you doing when you tried to slice your knuckles off?"

Her back stiffened, the only indication that she'd been affected by his question, but he didn't know if it was in a good way or bad. He'd have to ask.

"Washing dishes and thinking."

"It must have been some serious thinking, or else you wouldn't have cut yourself."

She surprised him by agreeing. "Sometimes my mind wanders and it takes awhile to get it back focused on the job at hand."

"What were you thinking about?" He watched the way her eyes changed from a soft spring green to brilliant emerald. Her cheeks flushed and her breathing became shallow. Lord what a picture his woman made when she was aroused. Moving in, he took the spatula from her hand and set it on the edge of the dish and pulled her into his arms.

"Kiss me back, Ronnie." He dipped his head and immersed himself in her taste, her scent, her need.

She pressed her agile body against his until there wasn't a breath of air between them. He wished he wasn't so noble and hadn't already decided to go slowly because the need to rip the clothes from her body had him clenching his hands into tight fists.

Ronnie traced the tip of her tongue along his bottom lip and moaned softly into his mouth. When she nipped his lip, he slid his hands to her curvy backside and plundered.

He needed her... now. He slid his hands back up to the collar of her T-shirt and grabbed a fistful with each hand, ready to rip.

"Ronnie, are you upstairs?"

She jolted at the sound of her name being called and eased back from him, forcing him to either let go or rip her shirt in half. He sighed and let go.

Mavis Beeton walked into the kitchen and said, "I,

um, ran out of mas—oh, sorry," she said with a nod toward Dylan. "I didn't realize you weren't alone."

"My tools and my truck are right outside." He wondered why the older woman was blushing. Imagine Mrs. Beeton blushing. "Is everything all right?"

"Oh, just fine." She turned toward Ronnie. "May I have a word in private?"

"Sure, we'll be right back."

Dylan watched the two walk down the hallway toward Ronnie's bedroom and felt the knife of need slice deeply. He wanted to take that particular walk and be the one going with Ronnie to her room.

Emotions roiled in his gut. Lust tangled with need and got all mixed up with an intangible feeling that he'd never felt before—something that he'd never experienced with Sandy, but was a part of his parents' marriage and it scared the shit out of him. Needing to get a grip, he picked up the plate and the spatula, serving himself chicken instead of kissing Ronnie. He skewered a forkful, blew on it, and took a bite. Tenderly cooked meat, perfectly spiced and lightly browned, had his mouth watering for another taste. "God, the woman can cook."

He was on his second piece when he heard the women coming back.

"Thank you, my dear," Mrs. Beeton said, gripping the brown paper bag with both hands as she walked out the door. "Now don't forget to keep that cut dry for a couple of days."

"I will," Ronnie promised, watching Mavis leave.

Taste buds humming, Dylan yanked her close. Her honey-sweet flavor mingled with the Italian spices, half of which he couldn't name, but the combination went to

his head like three fingers of Irish whiskey. His tongue
tangled with hers and his brain shouted *More!*

Hands urgent, mouth latched onto the side of her
neck, he gave silent thanks as she went pliant in his
arms, giving herself to him on this most basic level.
Lust had him by the balls and tied up in knots. "Ronnie,
darlin', ask me to stay."

She pushed against his hold. He wanted her so badly,
the claws of need raked through his gut and left him raw
and bleeding, but he wouldn't force her. He eased his
grip and she slipped out of his arms.

"I can't think straight when you kiss me."

"And that's a problem because…"

"I'm not sure I'm ready for this."

He scrubbed his hands over his face. "Which part of
this? Me staying over, or me making love to you until
your eyes cross and your head spins?"

Impossibly, she laughed. He was as serious as a heart
attack and she was laughing. He frowned down at her,
needing to make her understand that this was no laughing matter. Before he could speak, she held up both
hands. He froze.

"I want you so bad I've been on the brink of an
orgasm since the other day at your ranch. If you think
that's easy, you'd be wrong."

The image of Ronnie walking around with the female
equivalent of a hard-on had him grinning. "That a fact?"

Her eyes flashed the split-second warning before she
had her hands on his chest, shoving him backward.

But he was ready for his filly's temper. He grabbed
ahold and pulled her with him. The table jumped and the
chairs rattled as they hit the floor. The air rushed out of

his lungs and his back ached like a sonofabitch, but he protected Ronnie within the shelter of his arms.

"How long are you gonna make me wait, darlin'?"

She laid her forehead against his and sighed. "How long have I got?"

He slid his hands down the length of her spine to his favorite handhold, her curvaceous backside. Torturing himself, he stroked her rounded cheeks before splaying the palms of his hands on the apex of her curves and pressing down.

Her breath caught and her eyes flashed with desire.

"Time's up."

She matched his grin and lowered her lips to his. The first kiss was a tentative foray, like a lover's first kiss… chaste but sweet.

He groaned and she deepened the kiss, adding the tip of her tongue, amping up the torture, stoking the fires of passion burning inside of him. "Darlin', you'd better be sure before you go any further. There won't be any stopping this time."

———

Ronnie's mouth opened before her brain fully kicked into gear. "Do I have to worry about you lassoing my best friend and branding her too?"

Hurt flashed in his eyes, but before she could take the words back, he shifted her weight and slid out from beneath her. He stood looking down at her and opened his mouth to speak, but then must have thought better of it. Raking a hand through his hair, he blew out a frustrated breath, spun on his boot heel, and stalked out of the kitchen.

The sound of his footsteps echoed on the staircase. She'd ended a good thing before they'd gotten started. Tears filled her eyes, but she couldn't bring herself to blink them back. She'd done the unforgiveable... judged, tried, and hanged a man before he had a chance to defend himself.

Shifting onto her side, she curled up into a ball, but the memory of the hurt in Dylan's eyes wouldn't leave her. Funny thing was, she felt worse than the night she'd discovered her ex–best friend was having an affair with her ex-husband. This time it felt as if her heart were being ripped out of her breast while someone scraped her insides raw before pouring acid on them.

"Drawn and quartered," she murmured. "Just the punishment I deserve."

Chapter 11

"YOU GONNA TELL ME WHAT'S EATIN' YOU?"

Dylan ignored Jesse, grabbed another bale of hay, and tossed it down off the truck. He hurt, inside and out, like he'd had the ever lovin' shit kicked out of him and then rolled over so the black-haired filly could stomp all over him.

"Never even got to the good part," he mumbled. He sunk the hayforks into another bale, yanked up the bale, and tossed it down at his brother. Jesse swore as the bale hit him in the chest, but his brother's anger didn't faze Dylan. Not much would until he could figure out just what he'd done wrong last night. He hadn't made any promises that he'd broken... hadn't cheated on anyone, yet she'd all but accused him of it.

Hell, he felt worse than the night he'd walked in from putting in a full day riding and mending fences and bumped into Sandy on her way out the back door, bags packed, one in each hand. Shock had held him immobile while the woman he'd been planning on marrying carefully placed her bags into her trunk and slammed the lid and turned back to him. She'd had tears in her eyes, but she blinked them away and reached for him, hugged him tight promising to write once she reached her destination in Egypt, and asked him to remember to listen to the next woman who was lucky enough to have him in her life.

That was nearly two years ago and counting. She'd written letters and sent a couple of postcards, but he'd never written back. He didn't know what to say.

"Never told her I loved her."

Jesse paused and looked up at his brother. "Did you?"

"I just told you I didn't."

Jesse snickered. "No, Romeo, did you love Sandy?"

Dylan kept working, the movement kept his brain from short-circuiting over the green-eyed siren who'd pulled the rug out from beneath him last night. "I thought I did. We grew up together, spent so much time together, and made plans—well, that is, I made plans. She had other ones that I guess I didn't believe. I never thought she'd actually want to leave Pleasure. Life's close to perfect out here. Why would she go?"

Jesse shrugged. "Texas isn't for everyone, Bro." Wiping his sleeve across his eyes, his brother asked, "So what's eating you?"

"Siren-green eyes."

"Ahh." Jesse took off his gloves and slapped them against his jean-clad leg. "That makes sense."

Dylan snorted. *Didn't to him.* Hell, he still couldn't believe he'd been accused and convicted without ever having the chance to prove himself. "Women."

"Can't live with 'em," Jesse said cheerfully, walking over to the jug of sweet tea he'd left by the corral. Taking a swig, he wiped his mouth on his sleeve and lifted the jug and shook it.

"Not yet," Dylan said, declining the offer of a cool drink. "Why do women do what they do?"

Jesse shrugged, pulling his gloves back on. "Why do men keep fallin' for 'em?"

They looked at one another and grinned. "'Cause they think with their johnsons," they said simultaneously.

"Was Grandpa ever wrong?"

"Not yet," Dylan answered, forking and tossing another hay bale down to his brother.

They finished off-loading the pickup before Dylan stopped for a drink. "You make this tea?"

Jesse shook his head. "Emily did."

Dylan tilted his head back and drowned the dust in his throat with a gulp of sweet tea. "She's getting better at it."

Jesse snorted. "Yeah, last time she used ten tea bags."

Dylan snickered. "Jesus, I thought she'd killed me."

"Big Bro would have if he caught you laughing at his woman."

"Love's got him by the throat."

Jesse agreed. "But it works for him."

"She works," Dylan added. And for the life of him, he couldn't understand why Ronnie had struck out at him last night. "You understand women?"

His brother tilted his head and thought about it. "Enough to know some shoot to peak faster than others and that some have this sweet little spot on the side of their neck—"

"Not what I meant... but good to know you're learning." Dylan tilted his Stetson to the back of his forehead and rubbed at the line of sweat, adding a swipe of dirt. "I mean about the way they think, why their minds work ass-backwards."

"Nope." Jesse put his gloves back on and headed toward the barn, calling out over his shoulder. "Emily's in the kitchen. Ask her."

"Hell." He couldn't ask what he wanted to. How

could he phrase it so she wouldn't take a swing at him with the frying pan or other implement of destruction found in their kitchen?

"She should know," Jesse said, turning around, walking backwards toward the barn. "Let me know what she says."

He brushed at the bits of hay clinging to his shirt and legs and stomped onto the back porch.

"Wipe the pasture off your boots!"

"It's not Tyler," he answered, pulling the door open.

Emily put her hands on her hips and frowned at him. "Don't care. Wipe your feet before you track God knows what in. I just scrubbed the floor."

Embarrassed, Dylan backed up and did as he was told. *Women.* But maybe Emily would be able to help him understand how Ronnie's mind worked. "Emily?"

"Hmmm?" Her back was to him while she stirred a bowl filled with what smelled like chocolate cake or maybe brownies.

"What're you baking?"

"Brownies."

He'd heard from Tyler that she baked brownies when she was stressed. "Is everything all right?"

Emily looked over her shoulder at him. "Not sure how the new guy's working out."

Dylan's stomach clenched. "Doesn't he show up on time?"

"Most days."

Tyler's girlfriend had become a part of their family and didn't normally speak in one-word sentences. Something was on her mind. Wanting to help, he asked, "Is he giving you ladies a hard time?"

"Not exactly."

The need to pound on something started bubbling to the surface. His brothers weren't handy, so he suppressed the urge and tried to get to the bottom of the situation. "Then what's bothering you?"

"It's hard to put into words," she said, setting the spoon on the countertop. "I've got a bad feeling, but it isn't fair to fire him without giving him a solid reason, other than he makes me twitchy."

Dylan nodded. "Agreed." Watching her open the oven and slide the pan of brownie batter inside, he waited until she closed the door and turned back around.

Their eyes met and she asked. "Something bothering you too?"

His shoulders slumped. How did he ask a woman to help him figure out one of her kind?

"Is this about Ronnie?"

Her question had his gaze snapping up from his boots to meet hers. She tilted her head to one side waiting for him to answer. He shrugged and finally said, "She doesn't trust me."

"Why not?"

"I have no idea."

"Did you do anything that would give her a reason not to trust you?"

He shook his head.

"Then maybe it's not about you."

Irritation flared inside of him. "Then who?"

"Someone in her past taught her not to trust."

"Thanks."

Emily's words swirled in his head and he remembered Ronnie's question. Putting the pieces together as he walked through the kitchen, he suddenly changed direction and headed toward the second floor. He hadn't intended to go into town this early, but now that she'd put the thought in his head, it all started to make sense. What if he'd reacted differently to her question? What if he'd simply moved forward the way he wanted to, smoothly talking the woman into bed? He might not have spent the entire morning spoiling for a fight.

He grabbed a clean T-shirt and the deodorant stick he'd tossed on the bed just that morning. Ready to tackle the job he'd left unfinished last night and the woman he was ready to butt heads with so he could get tangled up with her later, Dylan bounded down the stairs. He waved at Emily on his way through the kitchen.

She had her hands in a sink full of suds. "Aren't you riding out to the western pasture with Tyler this afternoon?"

He shook his head, "Jesse'll do it for me. I've got things to take care of in town."

Emily smiled at him. "Good luck, Dylan."

He went with his gut and pulled her into his arms and hugged her. "I'm going to need it."

She smiled at him. "Give her a chance to confide in you." She patted his shoulder as he released her. "She needs a reason to trust you, Dylan. Whoever hurt her before did a number on her. It's not easy to lay your heart on the line after it's been stomped on."

"If Tyler ever changes his mind…"

Emily laughed and shook her head at him. "Not in this lifetime. Now get going!"

Dylan found Jesse out by the corral. "Hey, I've got to go to town early today."

His brother looked at him but didn't say anything.

"Tyler's headed out to ride fences later—"

"I've got your back."

Dylan opened the truck door and started to get inside, but Jesse's question stopped him. "You coming back tonight?"

He looked over his shoulder. His brother didn't look as bad as he had the day before. The desperate look in his eyes was gone. Good thing—his knuckles were still sore from punching Jesse in the face and he didn't think he was up to fighting with him tonight. "Not if things go as planned." He paused then said, "Thanks, Jess. I'll pay you back."

"Damn straight."

Putting the truck in drive he wondered if Ronnie would kick him out if he showed up at her door in the middle of the day. As he got out to open and then close the gate, he realized he couldn't blame her after the way he'd left last night. Hell, he was acting like a female. Emotions were not his department; their youngest brother had the lion's share in their family and had dealt with that sort of thing more often. He and Tyler didn't. Up until recently the oldest Garahan had pretty much kept to himself since his ex walked out, but then Emily burst into his life and everything changed.

Dylan acknowledged that he had a similar experience and hadn't been the same since he'd lassoed a green-eyed lady with long black hair.

What was it with Garahans and women walking out? Driving into town he mulled over that thought until he'd crossed into the town limits. He wasn't sure and would have to ask Tyler, but he wondered if their inability to voice their feelings had anything to do with the women leaving them. Then again, Jesse talked all the time and Lori still left him high and dry—twice, for the same loser!

Making a left onto North Main Street, he wondered if maybe it was the women they'd chosen the first time around and not so much something that was inherently wrong with the men of the Circle G. After all, if the women didn't fit, was it any wonder that he and his brother had trouble telling the women how they felt?

Pulling up outside of Guilty Pleasures, an ugly thought hit him. He might actually be headed down the rocky road to love alone. He parked, got out, and leaned against his truck. Up until they tussled on the floor, Ronnie seemed to feel the same way he did. They'd fallen asleep while she'd cuddled on his lap, like a couple that had been together for a while. She'd been right there with him, kiss for kiss, until he tugged her down onto the floor with him… maybe she really didn't like being manhandled.

The memory of the way her expressive green eyes went from pale, spring green to desire-filled emerald shot through him, having him shifting his stance to accommodate the tightness behind his zipper. She hadn't minded the manhandling that first night. What had changed?

"This isn't getting anything accomplished," he grumbled, pushing off the truck. "I've got work to do and then some." He looked both ways and strode across the street toward the shop. Odd, but it didn't look like anyone was there.

He knocked, but no one answered. Concern slithered through his gut. He knocked again. This time, he tried the door; it wasn't locked. Stepping inside, he shut the door behind him and called Ronnie's name.

Something was definitely wrong. Disturbing thoughts filled him, remembering what had happened over at the Lucky Star. His brother had been there to protect Emily during a break-in. Maybe someone had broken into Guilty Pleasures and Ronnie was upstairs... and in trouble.

His gaze swept the room. Nothing seemed out of place and everything looked exactly the way he'd left it last night. He headed for the stairs, focusing on one goal: protecting the woman he'd walked out on.

Ronnie breathed deeply and bent in half, letting mind and body work in tandem, allowing the deep stretch to work muscles that had spent the night knotted. She usually didn't take a break midday to exercise, but she needed it today. Following Shannon's suggestion, the soothing sound of harps filtered through the tiny ear buds attached to her MP3 player.

She stretched forward, walking her fingers out in front of her until she'd stretched out fully. Concentrating on the movement and the mystic music flowing through her head, she walked her fingers back until she was touching her palms to the floor.

Strong hands grabbed ahold of her waist, shredding the calm she'd worked so hard to achieve. Instinct had her drawing in a breath to scream, but the air burst from her lungs when she was tossed over a muscled shoulder. Panic morphed into fear as a large hand splayed across her backside.

It took every ounce of nerve she had not to give in to the fear. She pounded on the man's back with her fists and, just as she realized she recognized his scent, was tossed into the middle of her bed. Down but not defeated, she brushed the hair out of her eyes and pulled the headphones out of her ears.

"You scared the ever-loving crap out of me!"

Dylan's nostrils flared and his eyes darkened with need until she could see her reflection in their depths. He stood towering over her, vibrating with a potent combination of need laced with anger.

"A man can only stand so much torture, DelVecchio." He toed off his boots, pulled off his socks, and grabbed the hem of his T-shirt, yanking it over his head. The shirt landed on the floor behind him.

Ronnie's heart moved back down out of her throat. The man might have taken her by surprise, but he was a welcome intrusion and a magnificent sight. His pectorals glistened with a thin sheen of sweat, adding a magical dimension to the shamrock tattooed over his heart. With each breath he took, his broad chest expanded, emphasizing each and every sinew beneath the surface of his sun-bronzed skin. The need to touch tingled the tips of her fingers. She licked her lips and he narrowed his gaze.

"There's no turning back," he warned. "I've wanted you from the first night I saw you."

She wanted to tell him that it was up to her to choose her lover, but he'd unzipped his jeans and was in the process of shimmying out of them. Inch by delicious inch, his glorious body was revealed to her.

"You're not wearing any underwear."

His mouth lifted in what might have been a smile, but his raging erection distracted her.

The moisture left her mouth, as her body reacted, pooling the essential fluids where she would receive each and every tantalizing inch of him.

Her nipples tightened as his eyes focused on her breasts. Stepping out of his jeans, he slid onto the bed until he was leaning over her on all fours. Her body went haywire, sparks of lust shooting from her fingers down to her center. She wasn't sure he'd fit, but she sure as hell wanted him to do his damndest to stretch her to the limit, as he tested his one hundred and eighty pounds of thrust against her one-hundred-thirty-five-pound frame.

"I want you so bad, I ache," he admitted, pulling the sports bra up and over her head.

His eyes gleamed as he bent to take her breast in his mouth. He sucked her fully into his mouth and she shot straight to boil. She'd been primed and lubed, watching him strip; now she throbbed in time with his deep sucking motion.

The strangled sound had him releasing her breast and rearing back on to his heels. He yanked her pants and thong from her body in one swift movement that had her lifting her hips seeking more.

He shook his head and bent to take her other breast in his mouth. His lips and tongue tortured her, while his hands slid down her back to cup her backside, lifting her higher. She was powerless to move beneath the onslaught of his desire. She'd never been wanted like this.

He buried his face between her breasts for a second before his lips began a foray up the side of her neck.

She tilted her head to the side to give him better

access. He groaned as he licked and nibbled a path back down her neck, between her breasts. When he flicked her left nipple with the tip of his tongue, she went blind with need. Switching to the other breast, he played her body like an instrument of pleasure. When his fingers slid down over her abdomen, he lifted his head and waited a heartbeat.

She opened herself to him, offering everything she had.

His hands and mouth worked in tandem, building the tension within her to the bursting point. Just when she was about to cry out to him to take her, he pulled back, covered his erection from tip to base with latex, and thrust into her. The sensual shock to her system had her locking her legs around his waist, allowing him to go deeper. Harder. Faster.

She counted the first few thrusts, amazed at the power and pleasure she received with each one, until he drove so deeply inside her, he touched her womb. Rocked to the core, Ronnie felt the echo of that touch in her heart, cracking the walls she'd erected around it in order to survive her ex's betrayal.

Dylan's passion was raw, his lovemaking elemental, demanding she respond in kind. Her mouth latched on to his neck; he thrust and she sucked, until the need to move closer to the edge caught ahold of her. She nipped his neck then arched back, forcing him deeper.

They drove one another higher, closer to the edge with lips, tongues, teeth, and hands. Dylan was afraid he'd come before she did and started reciting the names of his high school football teammates in his head. Her body was agile, strong, and sexy as hell. How was he going to keep from losing it? Her hands slid down his back to cup his butt cheeks. When she squeezed him hard and lifted her hips up, his eyes crossed. He held on to his control with everything he had; she was so close. He slipped his hand between their bodies; one touch had her sucking in a breath before she shot up and over the peak, breaking apart in his arms. He drove deep and followed.

"Mmmm. You taste better than I imagined." Dylan dipped his head between her breasts and let his tongue ignite the embers of their passion still smoldering just beneath the surface.

"I can't possibly—"

Her protests were cut off by her strangled moan of pleasure. "Darlin', I'm counting on it."

He shifted and switched it to overdrive, and she was the recipient of his deliciously muscled frame molding her body to his, drawing every last drop of pleasure from her sweat-slickened limbs.

"Come with me, darlin'."

"Dylan, I just—" Her words slid back down her throat and a groan of pure pleasure slipped from between her lips.

Sated, satisfied, her muscles went lax. Her arms slid from around him; her legs quivered before releasing their ironclad grip around him. He rolled onto his side and she snuggled closer as the rhythmic beat of his heart and sound of his breathing lulled her to sleep, safe and warm in his arms.

"I was right."

Ronnie shook the cobwebs from her head and opened one eye. "About?"

"You pack a lethal punch."

She pushed against his shoulder until he rolled onto his back, taking her with him. Stacking her arms on his chest, she laid her chin on her hands and stared down at him. Lord, he was gorgeous. She hadn't wanted to take the chance, but now that she had, she may as well enjoy the benefits of her decision and enjoy what promised to be a wild ride.

"How'd you know?"

His crooked smile went right to the soft spot she'd developed where this one man was concerned. "Instinct."

"Oh really?" She didn't believe him but went along with the game. "From the first time you saw me?"

The rumbling chuckle wasn't quite the response she'd been hoping for.

"A blonde, a brunette, and a redhead walk into a bar…"

She knew where this was going. "Yeah, yeah," she chuckled. "Why do I feel like I've heard this one before?"

His chuckle deepened to a rolling laugh that soothed her irritation. "I could sell that blindfold and become a millionaire… I've never gotten so hard for a woman so fast."

"I just might have to look into marketing one."

"Come again?"

"It might take some time to convince my customers who normally purchase perfume and lingerie that they really need to add blindfolds for special occasions."

He shook his head but didn't say anything. Maybe he didn't believe her. But she was already thinking she'd contact her supplier and see if he'd want to add it to his catalog. His gaze narrowed and he waited for her to fill in the blanks. When she continued to watch him without breaking eye contact, he raised his eyes heavenward.

"Lord, save me from willful fillies." He rolled them over until he was on top again.

"Do you have to keep grouping me with animals?"

He rubbed his chin thoughtfully and tilted his head to one side. "A filly is a very special animal."

"It's just a female horse," she countered, irritation slowly beginning to build.

He shook his head and let his callused hand slide down to her backside, snuggling her female parts as close as they would go without being joined. "Not to a stallion," he said, lifting his hips, rubbing his semi-hard erection against her. "An exceptionally fine filly will twitch her tail in front of a stallion, tempting him to match his strength to her fire. Catching her scent, he'll strut his stuff in front of her, ignoring her until she starts raising a ruckus, and that's when the fun begins."

Ronnie could not believe that she was getting turned on listening to Dylan talk about the mating habits of horses. Was she insane? "Let me get this straight, we're talking about horses, right?"

His smile was seductively slow and full of promise, a definite turn on. Damn... she was going crazy.

"I pegged you for a smart city slicker from back East that night." His gaze met hers. "Seems I was right about that too."

When her mouth fell open but no words emerged, she knew she was in trouble... deep trouble.

He chuckled. "So tell me again, what else do you sell besides massage oil and perfume?"

"My online supplier has a catalog of specialty toys that some of my customers ask for, but I don't carry."

"And you sell a lot of online merchandise?"

She grinned up at him. "You have no idea."

"Women here in Pleasure buy your… uh… stock?"

She nodded, enjoying his discomfort, especially after likening her to a horse. "My online store does a brisk business and is actually the main source of income from the specialty side of Guilty Pleasures."

He stared at her for the longest time then nodded with a wicked gleam in his eyes before pulling her breast into his mouth.

Her body trembled with want. Trying to keep up, she couldn't imagine the stamina required to go another round. As if he could read her mind, he grinned down at her. "Have you got any protection in that stash of yours?"

"You'd be surprised," she rasped, as his delightfully taut butt muscles flexed and he brushed his erection against her heat.

His eyes turned that wonderful shade of molten chocolate a heartbeat before they glazed over. "Where?"

"Medicine cabinet in the bath—"

Dylan was out of bed and halfway down the hallway before she finished speaking, returning with a box of condoms clutched in his right hand. "Ribbed and lubricated—"

She got hot just listening to him reading the label on the box. "For her pleasure."

His gaze met hers, snagging her full attention when he ripped the foil packet open with his teeth, knelt on the bed, and blew into the condom. Distracted, she asked, "Why do you do that?"

He smoothed the protection into place. "Saves time," he said a heartbeat before he slid all the way home.

Buried to the hilt, he slowly drew back out. "More time in the saddle."

He thrust deep and slowly withdrew.

Words were beyond her as the tension began to build once more. Sparks ignited beneath her skin, igniting the conflagration she'd come to associate with the man in her arms, setting her free and letting her fly.

"Dylan!"

"Coming, darlin'."

Chapter 12

DYLAN WOKE TO THE SWEET SOUND OF THE WOMAN he'd branded snoring… he held his breath to better hear the snuffling coming from where she'd planted her face in the pillow. The urge to shout out with joy washed over him, but he didn't want to wake her just yet. He wanted to savor the moment and the woman.

She was always moving—at a trot, if he was to compare it to how quickly a horse would move. Must be an eastern thing; out West people used an economy of motion: fast when necessary, but most times slow and steady to work dawn until dusk in order to get the job done.

He let his gaze slide down the slender cream-colored curves highlighted by the late afternoon sun. Ronnie moaned in her sleep and shifted onto her side, snuggling her curvy backside in his lap. The breath he'd just inhaled rushed out as his body went on full alert and he drew in more air. Parts of him woke before others, and he went from semiawake to "I'm ready for more, darlin'."

Shock waves of pleasure washed over him as she shifted yet again, this time to her back, allowing him to look his fill. Her wavy black hair spread out over the white pillow only accentuated the beauty of her soft supple curves. The muscles of her upper body were toned and only added to the delightful sight of her creamy white breasts topped with rosy red nipples.

Like a kid in a candy store, he couldn't keep from reaching out to touch. Brushing the tips of his fingers across first one nipple and then the other, he was rewarded when they responded, tightening into firm buds, begging to be tasted.

Going with the flow, he shifted so he could lean down to sample the bounty before him. He blew across one rose-tinged peak then flicked out his tongue to dampen it. Marveling that the buds could become firmer, darker, he repeated the movement with her left breast. Giving in to desperate desire, he swirled his tongue over and around the areola, sucking her breast into his mouth.

She moaned, tossing her head from side to side on the pillow, but didn't waken. Her body warmed beneath his touch, flushing a delightful shade of pink on the parts he favored... the white parts. She'd obviously been in the sun and had worn a tiny excuse for a bathing suit, creating the intriguing triangles of creamy white outlining key points of interest to him. Not one to ignore a gift when it was being offered to him, Dylan straddled her and began to run his hands up and down her sides. The slender curves intrigued him, so he traced them again. Her satin smooth skin warmed to his touch. The swift rush of blood to his dick had him biting back against the need to simply take until he'd satisfied the lust burning a hole in his gut.

She had a mole beneath her right breast; he hadn't noticed it earlier. He took his time now, touching the dark brown spot with the tip of his finger; it wasn't as soft as the skin surrounding it. Indulging himself, he let his finger glide along the curve beneath her breast before switching to the other side.

Ronnie stirred beneath his touch and slowly opened her

eyes. Bright spring green darkened to emerald as desire flared to life. Rock hard, he shifted so he was nestled at the apex of her thighs, ready for her to give him the signal.

She licked her lips and lifted her hips.

Signal enough, he reached for the condom he'd left on the bedside table, opened it, and sheathed himself while she watched. Her eyes spoke more eloquently than words. Grandpa always told him that you could read a person's thoughts by looking into their eyes.

"Hot damn!" Dylan tilted his head back and howled.

Ronnie giggled and grabbed ahold of his hips. "I bet you do that for all the girls."

He shook his head and slipped inside of her, slow and smooth, watching her closely to gauge his movements to her responses. Hmmm... slow and smooth had her closing her eyes and lifting her hips languidly. He repeated the movement until she was putty in his hands.

The devil inside of him wanted to kick it up a notch; he pulled out slowly, then shifted and gripped her hips with both hands, lifting her up off the bed, burying himself to the hilt with one swift and determined thrust. Her eyes shot open and her nostrils flared a heartbeat before she lifted him up and off the bed with the power of her amazingly muscled glutes.

"Darlin' you're killing me."

She tilted her head back and let out a low guttural sound that had him answering in kind. He growled and her eyes glazed over. He dove deep and felt his eyes cross and his head spin. His brain shut down as his body flipped an internal switch to instinct. His muscles heated to the task as he thrust into her again and again, demanding she meet him and give him equal measure.

———⁓⁓⁓———

Ronnie had never been with such a demanding lover.
Her head tried to keep up, until the primal being inside of her took control and met him thrust for thrust,
the power of her muscles heating her blood as it sang
through her veins.

The beat of her heart urged the being she'd become
to sup, to take, to devour. Pushing against his shoulder,
she urged him onto his back and rode him as if he really
was a stallion. Thighs tightening around him when she
wanted him to thrust harder, loosening when she wanted
him to slow down. He responded to her every touch.

Tilting back, she angled her hips and opened more
fully to receive him, but it wasn't enough. She wanted
more... needed more. Leaning her forehead against his,
she rasped, "I need to feel you deeper."

Dylan's jaw clenched, but he eased her off of him and
spun her around, so she was on her hands and knees on
the bed. Pressing on her shoulders, he eased her down
until she was leaning on her forearms, until she felt exposed, vulnerable. "If deep is where you want me," he
drawled, "then trust me, darlin', you're gonna feel me
touch your heart."

When he thrust into her tight sheath, her inner muscles clenched and relaxed as her body wept with joy and
accommodated every single inch of him, deeper than she
had before. His grip on her hips tightened and her last
thought as he drove into her again and again was that
she'd never trusted anyone the way she trusted him with
her body. The reward was a blinding orgasm.

She had no bones; they'd disintegrated as she'd

shattered. She slumped forward. Dylan placed his callused palm against her heart, then shifted it to span the distance between her breasts, holding her up off the mattress. The angle rubbed her hidden nub of pleasure against the throbbing vein running along the length of him. She didn't think she had anything left to give him. She was wrong. Her passage wept again as he wrung out every last drop of moisture in her body as she rocketed to the stars.

Dylan held on to Ronnie as the feeling started sprinting through him. His brain shut off and his body took over as he drove into her again and again, mindless to everything except giving and taking pleasure from the woman in his arms. When she clenched tightly around him, he let go of his control and followed her into the madness.

She whimpered as he eased himself free.

"Oh God, darlin'." His hands were gentle as he laid her on the bed. "Did I hurt you?"

She licked her lips and tried to shake her head, but she didn't have anything left in her. Besides, she thought, she didn't have any bones to support her muscles.

"Damn it, woman, tell me where it hurts."

The concern in his eyes wrapped around her heart and added another dimension to their lovemaking. Added to the heat and lust that grabbed her by the throat, was the knowledge that she'd trusted him to take her around the world and make love to her from every position possible.

DelVecchio Curse be damned. Dylan was the kind of lover women dreamed about, wrote novels about, and used as a measure to uphold each and every other lover in their lives against. If she lived to be one hundred, she'd never meet anyone like him again. That he could be tender with her, concerned that he'd hurt her, after shattering her world with the longest orgasm of her life, was proof positive that he was a keeper. She'd worry about the possibility of twins later.

He grabbed her by the shoulders and pulled her into his arms. "I'm sorry, darlin', please," he begged. "Tell me so I can fix it."

Despite the seriousness of the situation, she laughed, a joyous, bubbly sound that came straight from her heart. He eased his hold on her so he could frown down at her. She laughed harder. His frown turned upside down and soon he was laughing with her, hugging her to his heart.

"Damn it, woman," he grumbled. "You scared the bejeezus out of me!"

Her bones magically knitted themselves back together, and she wrapped her arms around him, kissing him with all of the passion in her soul and love in her heart. "I couldn't move my arms or feel my legs."

He kissed her forehead and eased them down on the bed, wrapped in one another's arms. "I think I hit six with that last one."

"Six what?"

"Darlin'," he drawled, "if you have to ask, then I'm not doing it right." He brushed his lips across hers and chuckled. "You're supposed to say thank you."

"If you were trying to impress me, you more than met the mark."

He looked at her but didn't say anything.

Finally she couldn't take the silence anymore. "What's wrong?"

He shook his head. "I was just thinking."

"About…" She gave him the lead in, but he didn't take her up on it and tell her what was bothering him. She tried to hide her irritation. "Cat got your tongue?"

He laughed. "Did I mention how much I enjoy your fractiousness?"

"Yeah, now how about telling me what's on your mind?"

Dylan sighed, as if the weight of the world was sitting on his broad shoulders. "Must be because you're not from around here," he observed. "Otherwise, you'd know exactly what's on my mind. Are men that different back East?"

She bit her lip and thought it over. Her ex certainly was, but if she looked hard enough, she'd be willing to bet that there would be a man out West despicable enough to match her ex's betrayal. Just as she came to that conclusion, she realized he didn't really want to know the answer to his question—he was just being a wiseass!

She looked at her bare wrist. "Look at the time. Gotta go."

He reached out and placed his hand on her arm. She wanted to yank her arm from his grasp, but dug deep to control her rising temper and was rewarded when he rumbled, "Darlin', you blew me away."

Not exactly the poetry she'd hoped for. Good thing she didn't expect flowery phrases or words of undying devotion… at least, not yet. She smiled and snuggled back against him. "So, how about you tell me more?"

His smile was slow, sensual, and got her juices flowing again. Had one afternoon of amazing sex-capades turned her into a nymphomaniac?

"I'm a man of action," he said, lowering his mouth until it was but a breath from hers, "not words."

His lips tantalized, promised, then fulfilled as they took command and devoured her.

———

The sun was hanging lower in the sky when she forced herself to put a little distance between them. "I do have work to do, you know."

His eyes mesmerized her; their rich dark brown reminded her of her favorite flavor of chocolate: semi-sweet. The emotions flickering in their velvety depths amazed her. Although cool and aloof on the outside, the man was a boiling pot of emotions beneath the surface that she'd just barely scratched.

Would he want to let her in? Time would tell. Maybe she should say something that would urge him to tell her how he felt. Oh, Ronnie knew she'd satisfied his hunger for her. Heck, he'd done the same and they'd dozed off in one another's arms more than once since he'd flipped her over his shoulder and carried her up the stairs.

"Well, I'm a woman... we like to use words."

He snorted.

She scooted up against the headboard and crossed her arms beneath her breasts. "Being a man of action, I'm sure that snort has a translation."

His mouth quirked up on one side, still he said nothing.

She leaned over and poked him in the shoulder with her pointer finger.

The rusty, rumbling sound of his laughter was music to her ears. She'd loved that he'd laughed while they'd been making love. How they'd managed to cut through the first few layers of brand new relationship and settle themselves smack into what she'd say would be halfway through the first month, she had no idea. Maybe it was the way they'd met and the tension that spiked whenever the two of them were in the same room. He enjoyed what drove most men away after they got to know her: her temper and her quirky personality.

She glared at him and he laughed harder. Would this man always keep her slightly off-kilter? Finding out just might take the rest of her life and be worth every moment of the journey. Her heart jolted at the thought. She could just imagine the soft sound of her grandmother's laughter.

Finally, he spoke. "Women like to use twenty words when one will do."

"One?"

He nodded. "Words aren't often necessary."

"They are to a woman."

He reached for her hand and captured her attention as he slowly brought it to his lips without breaking eye contact. "Are they for you?"

She could feel the warmth of his lips where they hovered about her knuckles. The skin tingled, still he waited.

"Ronnie, darlin'."

She swallowed the pool of saliva in her mouth and asked, "What?"

He chuckled softly and pressed his mouth to the back of her hand, the rasp of his whiskers adding another dimension to the press of his lips and the warmth of his mouth. Her stomach clenched and an answering gathering of moisture in her center had her deciding he was the only man for her.

But his talent between the sheets wouldn't keep their relationship going for the long haul. They had to be compatible on other levels as well. She liked what she'd learned so far: he was considerate, had an affinity for one-word sentences, worked until he dropped, loved his brothers and their ranch.

"I know you like my cooking."

His gaze never left hers as he touched the tip of his tongue between the knuckle of her forefinger and middle finger. "Better 'n Tyler's."

"That's not a compliment." She tried to yank her hand back, but he held it firmly in his grip.

"If you'd ever had to eat my brother's cooking, you'd know it was. Just ask Jesse. Tyler can't scramble up eggs without burning them, or pan fry a steak without turning it to boot leather."

"I haven't made eggs for you yet and you haven't tasted my seared steak served on top of arugula and red peppers topped with fresh grated Asiago cheese."

His stomach rumbled and he grinned and scooted off the bed. "Got any handy?"

She shook her head. "Do men ever think of anything other than sex and food?"

He stretched his arms overhead and touched the ceiling. The man was tall and broad—a feast for the eyes with all those muscles playing just beneath the skin. Her head demanded that she stop drooling over the man and get her butt back to work; she had orders to process, books to balance, and mangled stock to finish sorting through… not to mention more meals to prepare for the hungry men of the Circle G.

"Sometimes we don't think about either."

Well, now that statement had her ears perking up. "Really?"

His smile was just this side of wicked. "Sometimes we sleep, darlin'."

She reached for his T-shirt and slipped it over her head. It would be work to get back into her exercise clothes and she wanted to wrap Dylan's scent around her for a little while longer.

"Help yourself." He was smiling as he pulled on his jeans and followed her to the kitchen. "So are you frying up a steak for me?"

Time to get down to business and keep one step ahead of the man, or they'd be right back where she needed to be: in his arms and in her bed. "Maybe," she called out over her shoulder.

Reaching for the dish detergent, she turned on the hot water and a hint of cold and began to wash her hands, careful not to get her cut wet. Drying them off, she opened the fridge and looked inside. "Hmmm, I'm not sure if I have any thawed."

She opened the freezer and found what she was looking for. "I've got two small steaks, all I have to do is thaw them." While he watched, she took them out of their package and placed them on a plate and defrosted them in the microwave.

Satisfied with the results, she took out her largest frying pan and coated the bottom with extra virgin olive oil and let it heat.

"What are you doing to the steaks?"

"Just adding crushed coarse black pepper and a spritz of salt for flavor."

"Before you fry them?"

She looked up and smiled at the concentration on his face. He looked like he was trying to memorize what she was doing to replicate it sometime in the future. She wouldn't mind having him in her kitchen while she cooked. The cracked wall around her heart shed a few more pieces.

She cleared her throat and said, "It enhances the flavor while the steak is searing."

"Cooking?"

"Yes." She smiled at her apt pupil. "At a very high heat, to brown the outside, but not overcook the inside which most people prefer rare to medium rare."

He grinned at her as she transferred the meat to the pan and added the pepper and bit of salt to the other side. "I prefer that mine doesn't moo," he drawled. "Just barely warmed would be good."

Her laughter got to him on a level he didn't know existed. Watching her prepare food in her tiny kitchen, the precise way she measured, stirred, chopped, and didn't waste any motion or time, had him realizing that she'd be a perfect permanent addition to the Garahan kitchen.

Whoa! Don't let's go crazy just because the woman is amazing in bed.

She looked up from where she'd been beating a half dozen eggs in a bowl and smiled. *Hell, Son, just admit it,* his grandfather's voice bit out in his head. *She's perfect for you too.*

His head felt light; he reached out to steady himself.

"Hey, are you OK?" Strong arms wrapped around

him and guided him to the closest chair, settling him on it. "The steak'll be ready first. Can you handle arugula and red peppers with it, or do you just want it as a side to your eggs?"

Did he dare tell her that he heard his grandfather's voice in his head at odd times and that it sounded so real it comforted him? "On the side."

Concern filled her gaze and his heart tumbled closer to the edge, perched to fall. In his mind's eye, it was a long way to the bottom, and not knowing what awaited him there, he dug deep for the fortitude to go forward knowing that he was on the verge of falling so far so fast, that he'd been dizzy with it.

Hell, she'd practically ripped his heart out of his chest and handed it back to him while they'd been making love. She gave one hundred percent, matched him stroke for stroke, thrust for thrust.

Ronnie set a plate brimming with food in front of him. "Dig in," she said with a hint of a smile.

He didn't need to be told twice. He scooped up a forkful of fluffy eggs, chewed, swallowed, and sighed. "I might just survive." His gaze met hers. "Thanks."

She turned around and flicked off the burner before the coffeepot boiled over. While it settled down, she served herself and placed the plate next to him, but she didn't sit down.

"Let me." He reached for her hand. "You made breakfast. I'm man enough to admit that I ran out of energy. If my grandfather were here, he would smack me on the back of the head if I didn't at least pour coffee for the woman who worked so hard to please me… in bed and in the kitchen."

"Does he still live out at the Circle G? I don't remember meeting him."

Dylan paused and his gaze met hers. "When he was alive, he used to—he's been gone for awhile."

Her eyes softened as she reached out to grab hold of his hand. Squeezing it, she pressed her lips to his knuckles. "My grandmother on my father's side is the only one still alive. I miss her. She's always reminding me to do the right thing and encouraging me to try things I'm afraid to."

He nodded. "If I tell you something, will you promise not to think I'm crazy?"

"Cross my heart!" She waited, breath held.

He'd come this far, he may as well tell her. "Sometimes I hear him talking in my head, things he used to say when he was alive."

Ronnie's eyes filled and she wiped at the tears. Undone, he thanked the Lord for a woman who understood the value of family. "I know my grandmother would love to meet you, but for now, you can talk to her. She loves to tell people what to do."

They were both smiling when he nodded. "I just might take you up on that, but my brothers might want to talk to her too."

Ronnie's laughter was light and lovely. "She will be in her glory."

Dylan got up and rooted through her cabinets until he found two mugs and poured their coffee. "Milk?"

"Please," she said, scooping up some eggs.

"Sugar?"

"Thanks."

He served her and gave in to temptation and rested his

cheek on the top of her head, inhaling her sweet scent
before he kissed the same spot. Ronnie was a woman
with a heart of gold. She understood that he'd told her
something private, and then offered to share what she
had with her grandmother. She was definitely a keeper.
He sat down and tucked into his meal.

*Take her out to the Circle G, let her loose in the
kitchen; you know she belongs there...*

Is that your answer for everything, Grandpa? Take the
women out to the ranch and see who's got the grit to stick
it out? Didn't work out the first time for Tyler and me.
Hell, for that matter, Jesse chose the wrong woman twice.

*That's because none of you were thinking with
your hearts.*

"Is he talking to you now?"

He chuckled. "Yeah."

"What's he saying?"

"That I should take you out to the Circle G and let
you loose in our kitchen."

She laughed as she started to clear the table.

He scooted her out of the way, so he could fill the
sink with hot water and soapy suds.

"This is my kitchen, damn it!"

He could tell she wasn't really angry. "And I'm doing
your dishes, darlin', so take a load off."

"You're in my way."

He grinned at the picture she made. Emerald eyes
flashing with pique, lips pouting, just begging to be
kissed. "Hell." He yanked her toward him and took as he
pleased, filling himself to bursting with the tart-tongued
taste of her. "Darlin', I'm wonderin' how long it'll take
until I get my fill of you."

She struggled out of his embrace and backed up. With a toss of her head, a strand of hair fell into her eyes. She batted it out of the way and grumbled, "Maybe I've had enough of you."

He laughed out loud; it felt so good to spar with his filly. "Liar." And to prove it, he picked her up, pulled her to his heart, and swung them around in a circle. Dizzy with the movement, dizzier from the woman in his arms, Dylan captured her lips in a kiss that promised everything.

She didn't respond until his tongue stroked hers and, like a match to tinder, she erupted into flames in his arms, threatening to burn the both of them alive. He let her slip out of his arms, pressing a possessive hand to her lower back, molding her to him. "Come home with me, Ronnie, darlin'."

"Now?"

He slid his hands lower, indulging himself by cupping her taut backside and hearing the catch in her breath right before he nipped her chin. "Right now."

She shook her head as if to clear it. "I need to get a few things together."

He brushed his lips to the spot he'd nipped and slid his hands up to her waist. "That'll give me time to get my lumber list together to finish the job downstairs. Right now, I've got this powerful need to see you at the Circle G… Besides, my brothers'll be finishing up the last of the before-supper chores and will be hungry as bears."

"Do you think they liked what I cooked the other night enough to want more?"

"Didn't you see the way they tucked into that pot of meatballs and sauce?"

She chewed on her bottom lip. "I… uh… was a little preoccupied and didn't notice."

He brushed his lips across hers one last time and then set her free. "If we're gonna get there before they get desperate enough to eat the varnish off the table, we'd best get a move on."

When she stared at him, he winked at her. "We're burnin' daylight."

She laughed a joyful sound that eased the worry hiding inside of him. "Give me fifteen minutes."

He headed toward the stairs. "Clock's tickin', darlin'."

Chapter 13

"ARE YOU CERTAIN YOUR BROTHERS WON'T MIND IF I stay the night?"

Dylan's smile was slow and sensual, igniting the embers of their earlier lovemaking. "Darlin', they'd walk on water if you'll cook more than dinner for them. Trust me."

Looking up at the man riding beside her, she acknowledged the gift for what it was: a sign that she hadn't made a mistake in trusting her body to the man, and now taking it one step further and trusting him with a bit more of herself. "I think I will."

He let his gaze slide to hers before focusing on the road before them. Rather than respond verbally, he grunted.

"What's that supposed to signify?"

He snickered. "Lord above, now you sound like Veronica instead of Ronnie, using fancy words when just plain English will do."

"But I got more than a grunt out of you," she said, crossing her arms beneath her breasts.

"Just adds icing to the cake, darlin'."

She wondered if he was referring to her or their budding relationship as the cake. In the past she would have let it slide and not asked, but that was the old Ronnie. The new Ronnie asked questions when they popped into her head... and damn the consequences.

"So, darlin'," she said, tossing his favorite expression back at her. "Am I the cake?"

He licked his lips and ground out. "Don't tease a man when he's driving."

Shifting on the seat next to him, she realized she'd been teasing herself as well. "You didn't answer me."

He signaled and pulled off to the shoulder and put it in park. His eyes were like molten chocolate, a sign he was either ready to turn up the tension and get down to getting busy or the other less favorable reaction—he might be getting angry.

"If you don't want me to toss you over my shoulder and into the truck bed to have my way with you while the entire population of Pleasure drives past, giving them a view of God's greatest creation—your amazing backside—then you'll let me concentrate on driving."

She licked her lips and he closed his eyes and groaned. "I'm not foolin', darlin'. Just sitting next to you knowing how quickly you shoot to peak has been messing with my mind."

Ronnie dared to touch the side of his face with the tips of her fingers and rasped, "I'm sorry."

He stiffened and moaned and reached for her. "Darlin', you are lethal."

She shifted and put up her hands, warding him off. "I've never had this affect on anyone before. It's kind of nice."

His nostrils flared and his brows lowered until he was glaring at her. "Nice ain't got nothing to do with what I'm feeling right now."

"Doesn't."

He shook his head. "Doesn't what?"

She laughed. "Ain't isn't a word."

"The hell it ain't," he said, sliding back over to his

side of the truck, irritation replacing the lust she'd just seen in his dark eyes.

At least they'd get farther out of town and closer to the ranch before she dared to tease the man beside her again. She planned to get a rise out of the man again soon… very soon. Ronnie needed to feed the fires of passion flaring back to life. Her fertile mind was trying to decide just how soon she could coax the man into bed with her.

The farther they drove, the more relaxed Dylan became. The scenery changed and the spaces opened up from the confines of town life to the acres of land owned by local ranchers. There was something about the land that called to her. Back home, she lived in suburban hell. She never really liked living on top of her neighbors, with so little space between the houses, but she hadn't had a choice until recently, when she'd packed her truck and pointed it toward the sunset.

"It's really beautiful out here."

He made a sound of agreement deep in his throat but didn't say anything, keeping his eyes on the road and his hands on the wheel.

Turning toward the window, she breathed deeply and was delighted with the sweet scent that filled her nostrils. "What smells so good?"

Dylan beamed. "Home." Putting the truck into park, he got out to open the gate and got back into drive through.

Before he could get out to repeat the process, Ronnie got out and closed the gate behind them. When she got back into the front seat, he thanked her. "Saved me a trip."

"My pleasure. Now tell me just what it is that smells so sweet out here."

"Hard to say," he answered. "My brothers and I narrowed it down to one or two possibilities over the years."

She watched his face, amazed at how different he looked when he was talking about the Circle G, how relaxed he appeared now that they were on Garahan land. "Are you going to make me drag it out of you?"

He tilted his head to one side and seemed to be thinking about it. "That could be interesting."

"Arrgghh… Dylan!"

At the fork in the road, he turned left. "In a few minutes, we'll be closer to one of the sources of the sweetest scents known to man."

They drove for about a half a mile before he pulled over next to a pond. This time he turned off the truck when he put it in park. He got out and opened her door for her. "Come on," he said reaching for her hand.

She swung her legs to get out and placed her hand in his. Skin to skin, palm to palm, felt good… felt right. Letting him lead, she willingly followed.

"Stand right here," he said, positioning her at the edge of the pond. "Now wait for it…"

"For what?"

"Patience," he said watching the tall grass on the other side of the water. "OK… now breathe deep."

She did and was rewarded with a lungful of the sweetest air on earth. "Is it the water or the grass?"

"Don't know. Tyler thinks it a combination of the grass, water, and good old Texas dirt."

She nodded. "I have noticed that different parts of the United States have different colored dirt. I suppose it makes sense that it would smell different too."

Dylan got down on one knee and dug into the dirt by

the edge of the pond. "Watch the grass and wait until it starts to sway toward us, then take another deep breath of the air, water, and dirt."

Ronnie did as she was told, watching Dylan's expression change from hesitant to expectant. She really was a goner if she was ready to sniff a handful of Texas dirt just because Dylan asked.

"Well?"

"I can't decide which of the three it is, but the air is definitely sweeter out here than in town."

Dylan tossed the dirt on the ground, brushed his hand on his thigh, and reached for her again. This time, he reeled her in and held her close. "What is it about you?"

She tilted her head back and looked up at him. "Maybe it's you."

He lowered his mouth; she licked her lips and stood on the tips of her toes, unable to wait for him to move closer. He shifted her closer until not a breath of air separated them and then simply devoured her. She melted against him, wanting him more than the next breath she took. Taking her cue from him, she let her tongue trace the shape of his mouth before delving deeply to tangle her tongue with his.

Dylan's moan of pleasure heightened her own. When he gently set her away from him, she wondered why, but didn't have a chance to ask.

"We really need to go now, or my brothers will be very hungry tonight, because I won't be going back inside until I've spent some time plumbing your depths."

She shivered at the thought of making love to her hot Texas hunk out by the pond. "Can we come back out here... later?"

245

Dylan grinned. "Darlin', you can count on it."

"OK, we'd better get going before I change my mind and jump you right here."

Dylan looked like he'd swallowed his tongue. He closed his eyes and drew in a deep breath before opening them again. "Ronnie darlin', you'd best get back in the truck. I'll follow along behind."

She reached for his hand, but he shook his head. "Not going to happen if we're going to make it back to the kitchen without tearing each other's clothes off before we go three feet."

Nodding, she dropped her hand and walked over to the truck and got inside. A few minutes later, he joined her.

The ride back the way they'd come seemed longer than the ride out to the pond, most definitely due to the fact that they were both trying to keep their hands to themselves and their lusty thoughts under control.

Finally, Dylan pulled up next to the house. Getting out, they walked side by side but didn't touch one another. Ronnie knew if she did, they'd have an audience if the loud voices coming from inside the house were real and not the TV or radio.

Dylan opened the door for her and she walked into pandemonium. She froze on the threshold and felt her jaw go slack. Tyler and Jesse stood in the center of the room arguing while a pan smoked on the stovetop, sludge bubbled in the bottom of the drip pot on the counter, and the sink was rapidly filling with water.

"What the hell is going on in here?" Dylan bellowed the question.

His brothers turned as one and started speaking at

the same time. Since it seemed that no one was going to take the pan off the burner, turn off the faucet or the coffeemaker, Ronnie did while the men argued.

Finally, she'd heard enough. "Will you three listen to one another?"

As one the men turned to face her. "Well, now, Dylan, why didn't you say that you had someone with you?" Tyler asked.

"Ronnie, how are you?" Jesse said, moving toward her with his hand outstretched.

Charmed, she grasped it and heard an odd sound coming from behind her. "Do you have a large cat?"

Tyler grinned. "No, what you're hearing is the sound of our brother outlining his territory."

Confused, she shook her head. "By growling?"

Jesse shot a look in his brother's direction and finally let go of her hand.

Dylan moved closer and wrapped his arm around Ronnie. He turned toward Jesse and ground out, "Stop horning in on my woman."

A thrill raced up Ronnie's spine. She looked up at him. "Yours?"

His nostrils flared and his gaze narrowed, connecting with hers. "Yeah. You got a problem with that?"

She felt the smile from the inside out. "Not on your life." Going with the flow, she slid her arms around Dylan's waist and hugged him tight. "Oh, by the way, guys, I turned off the stove, the coffeemaker, and the faucet. What were you two trying to do: burn the place down or flood it?"

Tyler shrugged, and Jesse put his hands in his back pockets and rocked back and forth but didn't say anything.

Dylan reached out and smacked Jesse on the back of the head.

"Hey, what did you do that for?"

"If you have to ask, then you're not as smart as you think you are," Tyler said with a grin.

"Are the three of you finished?" Ronnie asked, easing out of Dylan's embrace. "A fire in the kitchen is a serious matter. You should always pay attention and not leave the coffeemaker on so long that it turns the coffee into sludge."

Tyler nodded. "My fault, sorry."

"Who left the empty pan on a lighted burner? That's a bigger risk of fire than the coffeemaker."

"Sorry," Jesse said. "My fault."

"What about the sink?"

Tyler and Jesse looked at Dylan who raised his hands up in the air. "Can't pin that on me, guys. I was with Ronnie."

From the identical looks on the Garahan brothers' faces, she knew just what the men were thinking; she felt her cheeks flushing with heat. Oh yeah, they knew exactly what she and Dylan had been doing before they got here. To redirect their thoughts, she smiled and made shooing motions toward Tyler and Jesse. "Out of the kitchen."

Jesse stopped in his tracks. "But it's our kitchen."

She grinned up at him. "Ah, but you can't cook like I can."

He looked at Tyler for help. The oldest Garahan shook his head. "I'll start on the laundry if you'll start on the upstairs bathroom."

Jesse cringed. "Best two out of three falls, and I get to do the laundry."

Before he could carry through on his suggestion, Tyler grabbed the front of Jesse's T-shirt and pulled him toward the door. "Maybe next time. Come on, Bro."

"Alone at last," Dylan said wrapping his arms around Ronnie from behind and hugging her to him. "I could get used to seeing you in our kitchen." He kissed the side of her neck. "And out by the pond later."

Warmth radiated from the pit of her belly up to her heart; this time, she could swear she heard more cracks as bigger chunks of the wall around her heart broke apart. "Play your cards right, cupcake, and you could have both."

He spun her around until they were face to face. "I've warned you about teasing."

She slid her hands around his neck and met his hungry gaze and raised him one. "Who's teasing?"

Their lips met and her heart soared. When his hands swept down to grip her hips, she placed her hands on top of his as she firmly pushed him away from her. "I need some space if you expect me to cook dinner for your clan."

His eyes smoldered and he reached for her again.

Ronnie shook her head. "Think about where you'd like to start when we're out by the pond later beneath the soft light of the moon, while I rustle up something to make your taste buds stand up and sing."

Dylan's eyes spoke volumes. The want, the need, and the passion combined as one and called to her, tempting her to simply reach out and take his hand, but Ronnie was raised to do the right thing. She made a promise, and it was up to her to be strong enough to keep it.

"Later," she whispered. "Now skedaddle."

Dylan spun on his boot heel and stalked from the kitchen.

She knew he wasn't angry with her; more than likely he was trying to deal with the same sensory overload she'd been trying to cope with since they'd come apart in each other's arms earlier that afternoon.

Ronnie put her hands on her hips and surveyed her temporary domain. All was well. The frying pan had stopped smoking and the sludge in the coffeemaker was cool enough to pour down the drain. The only disaster looming was the water in the sink; it was a few drops short of overflowing.

She started rooting through cabinets and came up with a huge stockpot and a smaller saucepan. "Perfect." She carefully dipped the saucepan in the water and scooped some up, ladling it into the large pot. After the first few pans full, the sink was no longer in danger of spilling over onto the oak wide board floor, so she reached in to pull out the drain plug.

She poured the dregs of the coffee into the swirling water, diluting the sludge so that it wouldn't clog the drain or the pipes. Third disaster averted, she leaned back against the counter for a moment and took it all in: the height of the ceiling, the well-worn countertops, and the coveted farm-style sink, big enough to bathe twins in.

"Where the heck did that thought come from?" Shaken to the core, she brushed her hands on the seat of her denim skirt and opened the fridge. Dylan was right; it was well stocked. Deciding to go with something simple but filling, she pulled out two packages of beef cubes and rummaged in the cabinets until she had most of the ingredients she needed for beef stew. Reaching for her tote bag, she pulled out the spices she was never without: basil, oregano, and garlic powder.

"I wonder if they have any red wine." It was like playing a child's game, hunting up ingredients and the thrill of discovery when she found them. Finding a bottle among several others surprised her; she would have thought the Garahan brothers only drank beer.

"And that would be stereotyping," she chided herself. "And you know how much you hate when people do that to you just because you have an Italian last name, dark hair, and come from New Jersey."

Using the shortening she found among the cooking supplies, she added it to the Dutch oven and tossed the defrosted beef cubes in the bag of flour. The familiar motions of cooking soothed her frayed nerves and helped to center her focus on the job at hand, which was important because if she didn't she'd end up burning dinner.

A little while later, the stew was simmering on the back burner and she was studying the contents of the freezer once more, this time for dessert. "Jackpot!" Ronnie pulled a couple of packages of frozen mixed berries out to thaw.

"Lucky devils," she muttered to herself. "You're going to get my grandmother's triple berry pie."

Two hours later, the kitchen was cleaned and dinner was ready. "Now where did everybody go?" She wandered outside but didn't notice anyone right off. "Hmmpf."

She turned and started walking toward the barn. It was dark inside, and the soothing scents of hay and horse washed over her. It had been a long time since she'd done any riding, longer still since she'd competed in barrel riding. The soft whicker coming from the first stall had her stopping to greet the friendly animal.

"Hey," she crooned. "Nice to meet you." Ronnie stroked the star blazing between liquid brown eyes down to the soft muzzle. When the horse started lipping her palm, she giggled. "Sorry, I didn't bring anything with me." She looked over her shoulder and spotted a bag of grain. "I'll be right back."

Dipping her hand in the bag, she scooped up a handful of oats and a chorus of whinnies sounded. "Excellent sense of smell, guys. I'll get you some in a minute."

Going down the row of stalls, she greeted and pampered each and every horse. "Quarter Horses are so beautiful," she murmured, coming to the last stall. The horse raised his head and kicked at the sides of the stall.

"Easy, boy," she soothed all the while admiring him. "Aren't you pretty."

After he finished showing off for her, he tossed his head one last time, moved to the stall door, and nudged her shoulder. She laughed and offered the handful of oats.

Dylan couldn't believe his eyes. He'd come into the barn searching for Ronnie and found her petting Wildfire and offering him a treat. His horse wasn't known for taking to strangers—then again, neither was he—but he and his stallion seemed to agree on the woman from back East.

"I see you've met Wildfire."

She turned and smiled. "He's so beautiful... they all are."

Dylan's heart swelled with pride. They raised steer for beef at the Circle G, but they also raised Quarter

Horses to breed and to sell. The horses held a special place in his heart. "They're not just work horses—"

"Quarter Horses are bred to work the ranch, but are amazingly fast barrel racers," she interrupted.

He looked down at the woman and shook his head. "You always manage to surprise me, darlin'." Taking her hand, he lifted it to his lips and brushed a kiss across her knuckles. "How do you know about my horses?"

"I used to be a barrel racer... was pretty good at it too."

He grinned. "The more I find out about you, the harder it is to think about letting you go."

The solemn look on her face had his gut clenching. "Then don't let go of me."

He raised his eyebrows. "Ever?"

"Why don't we just take it a day at a time?"

"All right," he drawled. "I'll let you know if I'm keeping you after supper."

Her jaw dropped, and he touched the tip of his finger to her chin to gently close her mouth. "Careful, darlin'. Around here, you might catch some flies... really big ones."

She snapped her jaw shut and glared up at him. "If you're lucky, I just might let you eat the meal I cooked for your brothers."

"Just my brothers?"

"We'll see how I feel by the time I walk back to the kitchen." Spinning on her heel, she stalked back to the kitchen.

Dylan wasn't taking any chances. Dinner smelled so good, he nearly wept in gratitude. If it tasted as good as it smelled, he couldn't afford to let her get mad enough at him to deny him a sample.

He caught up to her and swept her up in his arms without breaking his stride. "Don't pout, darlin'. It gives you a wrinkle right here." He touched his fingertip to the frown line between her eyebrows. Unable to resist, he pressed his lips to the tiny line forming there.

The snarling sound coming from the woman in his arms had him chuckling. The elbow to his stomach had him stumbling and setting her down to draw in air. "You are the most contrary woman I know."

"Oh," she said sweetly. "Do you know that many?"

He started to answer, then thought better of it. "At the moment, you're ahead of the pack." Let her chew on that one and digest it.

"Hey, Dylan," Jesse hollered out the back door, "what's keeping you two?"

"Coming," he yelled, grabbing ahold of her hand and pulling her along behind him.

"I've heard that before," she sneered, slipping out of his grasp and running ahead of him. She paused at the back door, where Jesse stood grinning down at her. "You hungry?"

"Yes, ma'am," Jesse answered. "Smells good enough to eat."

She shook her head at him. "That's the plan." Before Dylan made it to the bottom step, she slipped her arm through Jesse's and pulled him into the kitchen.

Jesse kept looking over his shoulder, but she patted his arm. "Don't worry, he won't stay mad for long."

Jesse cleared his throat and mumbled, "Don't count on it."

"Did everybody wash up?" She was setting out a stack of plates when Dylan made his move.

He caged her against the counter and bent his head, whispering, "Jesse's right."

She got her gumption back and then some, pushing against him and spinning around in his arms. "Back off cowboy."

"Did you just call him cowboy?"

"Shut up, Jesse!" she and Dylan said at the same time.

Dylan fought against the urge to smile. Damn, but he really liked her moods... the meaner she got, the more attraction he felt. *Contrary*, his grandfather's voice echoed in his head. *Always were.*

"Not gonna happen in this lifetime," Tyler said walking into the room, with a disheveled Emily in tow.

Emily smoothed her hair out of her face but couldn't do anything about the telltale wrinkles in her once smooth T-shirt minidress.

"Are we keeping you two from anything more important?" Jesse teased.

Emily flushed a bright pink, but walked over to the youngest Garahan and hugged him. "Your brother is the best thing that ever happened to me."

Tyler's eyes darkened and Ronnie knew exactly what he was thinking; she'd seen the same look in Dylan's eyes. "I could save your dinner for you to nuke and eat later."

Tyler's eyes lightened and so did his mood. "It'd be mighty cold come morning." Turning to Emily he pulled her into his embrace and kissed her until she melted in his arms.

"Wow," Ronnie murmured to no one in particular. "I wonder if all of the Garahan men kiss like that."

Jesse stopped right beside her, plate in hand. "Want to find out?"

Dylan reached between the two and grabbed his brother by the front of his shirt. "Do it and die."

His brother flinched. "Uh… I'll take a rain check on that kiss, darlin'."

Dylan flung his brother against the cabinets. "Over my dead body."

"Jealous much?" Tyler interrupted, coming between the two.

Dylan flexed his muscles and gathered his control; it was the only thing that saved Jesse from being pounded into a puddle.

"Let's eat." Emily took Ronnie by the elbow and steered her toward a chair on the far side of the table. Inhaling, Emily said, "Smells wonderful. I can bake brownies, but I'm not a great cook."

Tyler chuckled. "Darlin', you do so many other things really well."

"Is this one of them?" Emily walked over and slipped her arms around Tyler's waist, pulling him close before pressing her lips to his.

When they finally came up for air, all Tyler could do was nod.

"Wasn't it against one of Grandpa's rules to be kissing in the kitchen?" Jesse asked.

Dylan locked gazes with Ronnie before answering. "Only if he caught us."

Chapter 14

DYLAN DISCONNECTED THE PHONE CALL AND SIGHED. He'd offered, and now he'd have to come through for Jolene… starting tomorrow night and for the next few days. "Why did I make that damned offer?" *Because you never thought she'd take you up on it, Son.* "Gee thanks, Grandpa."

But his grandfather was right. He never thought she'd take him up on it. "Damn, she'll probably start asking me about that damned all-male revue again."

Jesse walked up behind his brother. "What revue?"

"That crazy woman Jolene—" His gaze met Emily's. "No offense, ma'am."

She smiled warmly. "None taken."

"Jolene wants to have an all-male revue for Take Pride in Pleasure Day, featuring some 'real' cowboys with her dancers."

Jesse looked thoughtful. "Sign me up. It sounds like fun."

"We're holding some of the events in the town square," Emily said, "so all of our dancers will be wearing jeans, boots, and Stetsons—no shirts."

Dylan sighed and looked at his brothers. "We're going to have to do the damned revue, aren't we?"

"We owe Jolene," Tyler said quietly, locking gazes with Emily.

"Come on," Jesse said, punching Dylan in the shoulder.

Dylan punched him back as Ronnie walked back into the room.

"For heaven's sake!"

Ronnie looked at Emily, but Emily shook her head. "Don't ask me. I warned you the Garahans were mixers—they enjoy brawling."

Ronnie shook her head and sighed. "I guess I didn't realize they were so physical about it."

It was Emily's turn to laugh. "Honey, that's the best part of relationship with a Garahan man... the physical part."

Tyler pulled Emily into his arms and kissed her soundly. "Amen to that." Putting his arm around her, he swept her toward the door. "Come on, darlin'," he crooned. "Time to remind you just how good the best really is."

Jesse glowered at the empty doorway. "I'm going out to the barn."

"Didn't you already take care of the horses?" Ronnie asked.

Dylan knew what his brother planned to do. "Yeah, but there are a couple of feed bags that we toss around when we're angry." He watched the door bang twice against the frame and hoped Jesse would come around to their way of thinking and forget the woman who'd broken his heart... twice.

"Seriously?"

"As a heart attack, darlin'. Come on," he urged, after his brother made it over to the barn. "There's a spot I want to show you out by the pond."

"Oh," Ronnie said, her eyes bright with anticipation. "Where the air smells so heavenly?"

"You can touch heaven there, darlin'."

"Really?"

He pressed his lips to the side of her neck. "Oh yeah," he rasped. "And I'm just the man to show you the way. Wait here." He sprinted toward the front of the house.

"Where are you going?"

"I'll be right back," he called over shoulder, hoping she wouldn't follow him. That would just take more time, because he'd have to pull her into his arms and kiss her some more, and with the way need was burning a hole through his gut, he'd be taking her against the damned wall in the upstairs hallway.

"Well, I can—"

"Ronnie, darlin'," he interrupted. "Please don't move. I'm going to get a quilt and don't want to waste any more time than we have to before I make love with you."

Her mouth rounded in a kissable O. He winked and ran for the stairs. Two minutes later he was in the kitchen with his right arm wrapped around his woman and his left holding his grandmother's quilt.

"Time's a wastin', darlin'."

Ronnie's breathless laughter echoed deep inside of him. "We're taking the truck?"

"What part of 'darlin', I can't wait,' didn't you get?" His grin must have been contagious; she smiled back at him.

"Lead the way."

He opened the door for her, waited until she was inside, and closed the door. Placing a hand on the hood of the truck, he vaulted over to the driver's side. Inside, he slammed the door and revved the engine. When she grabbed ahold of him, he was concentrating on backing up. "If you touch me now, we won't get to make love out by the pond, and my little brother's still in the barn."

She let her hand drop to her side. "You're burning starlight."

He had to laugh. His woman was something. Man, when had he started thinking of her as his? Did he really want to keep her? *Last night* and *yes*, his lust-addled brain managed.

"The expression is daylight, tenderfoot."

"Tenderfoot?"

"That's right, you're not from around here, and it shows." His hands tightened on the wheel as he slowed down to turn at the fork in the road. "Almost there."

"Is it a problem for you that I'm not from Texas?"

Her brow was wrinkled and her eyes weren't as bright as they'd been a few moments earlier, by the light of truck's cab. She was worried. Did that mean she cared? Hell, she'd better care; he was halfway down the slippery slope to love.

"Not in this lifetime. It's what makes you special."

In the glow of the dashboard, he saw her expression soften. "You think I'm special?"

He slowed down to park alongside the pond and yanked her to his side of the truck and into his arms. It was a tight squeeze, but that just amped up the lust that was quickly burning out of control. Her lips softened beneath his, but he didn't have time for a gentle tasting with the choke hold his libido had on him.

He plundered and she moaned. "Damn," he said, pulling back from her. "I'm getting out of this truck and you'd better be right behind me, because if I touch you again, it'll be to bend you over the bumper."

She laughed and scooted over to her door. "You don't scare me, Dylan."

His nostrils flared as her laughter wrapped around his heart and squeezed. "Maybe you should be scared." He was scaring himself. Wanting her was driving him crazy. Needing her like his next breath he'd worry about later. Right now, he needed to bury himself to the hilt inside of her welcoming warmth.

She reached for the quilt and spread it out on the grass, smoothing her hand over the tiny stitches. "This is beautiful."

"It's prettier in daylight. My grandma liked to sew."

"Are you sure we should use it?"

He reached for her hand. "We can talk later." He yanked and she fell into his arms. Kisses mingled with their shared laughter. His boots went flying—one to the left, landing against the base of a tree, the other he didn't bother to track. He had a gorgeous woman in his arms with her lips latched onto his neck.

"Why can't I get enough of you?"

His heart lurched. "I've been suffering here too."

She started to push him away, but he let his weight settle him more firmly against her, pressing her against the soft cotton bed they'd made beneath the stars. "Talk later… kiss me now."

He stripped the clothes from her slender body. "I'll go slower next time." Her nipples pearled as a wisp of a breeze blew across the pond, and he bent and sucked first one breast and then the other deeply into his mouth.

Her groan was so close to agony, he almost stopped to ask if she was all right, but she lifted her hips and

he knew she wasn't in pain. She was right there with
him. Licking and kissing a path along her collarbone, he
stopped to tease first one rosy peak and then the other.

"Dylan!"

He didn't bother to answer. Pressing his lips over her
heart, he slid his fingers from beneath her rib cage to the
dip of her belly button and followed the path, first with
his tongue and then a gentle breath, blowing until he
could feel her shiver.

Plumbing her depths with his fingers, testing her
readiness, it was his turn to groan. "You're so wet...
so hot."

She wrapped her arms around his neck and pulled
his mouth back to hers, pouring everything she felt into
the kiss. Lifting her hips, she offered what he craved.
He paused to cover himself then sank into her depths.
I'm home.

———∿∿∿———

Ronnie's heart stuttered in her breast as Dylan thrust
again and again. She gave him all she had and then offered more. "I can't wait—"

Arching his back, he drove into her, lifting her up off
the quilt. Grabbing ahold of his amazing backside, she
hung on for dear life as he plunged into her over and
over until her body took over and she ceased to think
about holding back. Heart pounding, mind racing, she
soared over the edge into madness, trusting the man to
keep her safe as she shattered around him.

The moonlight illuminated the hard planes of his
cheek and jaw. The man was so beautiful it made her
heart hurt. "Wow."

He snickered. "Gee thanks, babe," he rumbled. "Glad you approve."

She smacked him on the back of his shoulder. "My brain's not catching up as quickly. Give me a few minutes."

He rolled over until their positions were reversed and she was on top. Leaning her elbows on his chest, she sighed. "Now that you've snapped off a piece, I don't suppose I could interest you in another?"

His eyes narrowed and he stirred and stretched inside of her, but he pulled out of her and reached for another condom.

"You are amazing."

He slid his hands to her backside, pinning her to him like a butterfly to a swatch of black velvet. The words evaporated as his hands massaged her butt cheeks; the rhythmic movements of his hips mesmerized her. "Dylan, I've never—" She wanted to tell him she'd never been this lust-crazed in her life. He wasn't her first, but he was by far the best.

"Darlin', you sure about that?" Shifting his grip and his hips, he urged her to keep up.

Following his lead, she rode him hard, until he flipped them over again and plunged deep, pumping into her until he was empty.

His let his forehead rest against hers. "Darlin', you're going to kill me."

"Oh, I don't know about that." Energized, she hugged him to her and pushed his shoulder until he rolled onto his side. Pressing her lips and then her cheek against his heart, she snuggled in and closed her eyes. Safe and secure. Happy and loved in his strong arms.

He tried to move his arm, but she protested. "This is my comfy place. Don't move."

He laughed and reached out to grab a corner of the quilt, wrapping them in a cocoon of soft cotton. Sliding his arm back around her, he asked, "Better?"

She sighed. "Amazing."

His breathing evened out and became deeper. Before he could fall asleep, though, she wanted to tell him what being with him meant to her. "Dylan?"

"Mmmpf."

"Are you asleep?"

"Almost."

"I meant what I said."

"Which part?"

"I've never been with anyone like you before."

"Damn straight, darlin'. Once you've had a taste of Texas you never go back."

She pinched his butt.

"Hey!"

"Just testing the Grade A perfection of your rump, darlin', to make sure I wasn't dreaming."

"Veronica?"

Lord, she loved when he drawled out her name. "Yeah?"

"Shut up."

"Jerk."

"Shrew." She struggled to move out of his embrace, but he wouldn't let her. "Lord, you're temperamental."

"Are we back to you comparing me to a horse again?"

"Darlin', I live and breathe horseflesh."

"But I'm not—"

"You're fiery, strong, passionate, and fierce in your

lovin'… just like the best filly… the one you want to breed to your strongest stallion."

"I still don't like it."

He pressed his lips to her forehead, cheek, and chin. "You surely do, darlin'. Better catch some z's. Morning comes early at the Circle G."

Wondering if her heart could take waking up next to him without the promise of a lifetime scared her right down to her toes. "Are you a morning person?"

"I wake up locked, loaded, and ready for bear."

"Well—"

"Better shut your eyes. You'll be needin' your rest come sun up."

"Promise?"

"Cross my heart."

With Dylan's arms wrapped around her, she closed her eyes and snuggled against him, falling asleep to the sound of the wind gusting across the pond and the steady beat of his heart.

She woke at sunrise with his lips on her heart, branding her. There was no going back, only forward. *God, please let this man feel half of what I feel for him.*

Her morning prayer said, Ronnie greeted him with a smile as she slid her hand between them, finding and testing the satin smooth length of him. Two strokes later, he jerked and swore.

"I'm sorry… did I grip you too hard?"

He closed his eyes. "Not nearly hard enough, darlin'. Don't let me keep you from your explorations."

Intrigued that he'd let her take the lead, she tested the length and strength of him again, pressing her lips to his as she flicked the tip of her finger across the soft, smooth, blunt tip of his erection. She was rewarded with a bead of moisture. Swirling it over him, she listened for the catch in his breath. Encouraged, she took him in hand and stroked him, coaxing more, listening to his ragged breaths and pounding heart.

He was on her in a heartbeat, buried to the hilt, pressing his lips to her heart. "Now!" he urged.

She gave herself over to the splendor of his lovemaking. Hard, fast, urgent, powerful. If she lived to be a hundred, she'd never have another lover like Dylan. He plunged in deep, touching her womb, his hot seed emptying into her.

"Oh crap!"

"Not exactly the words I long to hear after waking up my woman with lovin' at sun up."

She grabbed the sides of his face and tilted it up so their gazes met. "Tell me you used a condom."

His blank look was her answer.

She was on her feet before he could stop her. "What part of the curse didn't you understand?"

"I'm sorry, darlin'—"

"Don't darlin' me," she bit out.

He stood up, towering over her, and his confusion washed over her. "Look, all I know is that you have a family curse, you never explained what it involved. Besides I don't believe in that kind of stuff."

"But you're Irish!" Tears pooled and slid down her face. How could she have ignored the warning signs? "I'm not ready to grow as big as a house and carry your twins."

His eyes were dark and dangerous. "Are you telling me you wouldn't want the children I could give you?"

She'd been stupid to let her lust rob her of the ability to think, the ability to act and prevent a possible pregnancy. Rattled to the bone and embarrassed to the core, she grabbed her clothes, yanked them on, and started walking toward the ranch house.

"Ronnie, wait!"

She sniffed back the tears and shook her head.

He was angry and still naked when he caught up to her. "So am I a pity fuck?"

That got her full attention. "Excuse me?"

"I thought we had something good going here, but if I'm not good enough for you, just say so and I'll have somebody give you a ride into town."

How could last night's loving and this morning's early wake-up call end so badly? "We did... I mean we do—"

"Then what's your problem? Maybe I didn't make you pregnant. It was only one time... God, that sounds lame, but maybe luck will be on our side." When she didn't say anything, he grabbed her by the upper arms and shook her. "Damn it, you get to me. My brain shut off—O.F.F.—when you grabbed ahold of my dick."

He stood there vibrating with anger—with an emotion close to the fear slashing through her brimming in his dark and dangerous eyes—and she believed him. Dylan was an honorable man who'd been blinded by the lust that she'd stirred him to. How could she stay mad at him?

She stifled the snicker. "Nice mouth, Garahan."

He pressed it to hers. "Likewise, DelVecchio."

She melted against him and confessed, "I thought I'd have more time before the curse was fulfilled."

"You really believe in it?"

"Not until I met you."

He sounded like he was pleased. She looked up at him and frowned. He was smiling. "What's so funny?"

"You are, darlin'."

"I told you not to call me that. That sexy Texas drawl is how we got in this predicament."

"No use closing the barn door now that the stallion's been set free."

"I thought it was a cow," she grumbled.

"I prefer to think of myself as a stallion."

Her lips quirked as she fought the need to smile. "I just bet you do."

"Can we worry about what might be later?" His sincerity struck a chord.

"I guess we could."

"I've got to get going on my chores."

She didn't like the way he was frowning at her. "So do I, so I'll let you get to it."

"You won't shut me out?"

Ronnie thought about it, but it was wrong to place the blame squarely on his broad shoulders when she'd been the one to tempt and tease him into a frenzy that ended up with them making love without protection. "I'd be the jerk if I did."

"So don't be," he urged, running his hands up and down her arms.

"All right."

He took her hand and started walking. "Let's go get some breakfast."

Her laughter felt good and stopped him in his tracks. "What's so funny?"

"Aren't you going to put your pants on?"

"Damn," he said, looking down. "I'd be breaking one of Grandpa's rules if I showed up to breakfast naked with women in the kitchen."

She followed him back to where they'd spent the night. "Are you making that up?"

He shook his head and reached for his jeans. Pulling them up, he fastened them and sat down to pull on his socks. "Nope."

"But why would you show up to breakfast naked?"

"That's how I sleep."

"But aren't you embarrassed?"

He grinned at her over his shoulder as he hunted down first one boot and then the other. "Are you?"

"Well, not if it was just the two of us, but I'd never show up for a meal that way."

"Never?" he asked, walking toward where she stood bent over folding the quilt.

She straightened and handed it to him. "It's a little damp on the bottom from the dew."

"No problem. It's hardy, like my grandparents." He stuffed it under one arm and took her hand again.

She liked the way it felt: strong and sure. "Dylan, what if our luck doesn't hold out?"

He walked a little ways before answering. "Then we'll just have to keep trying until we get you pregnant."

Love for the man filled her to bursting. "You wouldn't have to be responsible—"

"Don't even go there. Garahan men don't walk away from trouble… they run toward it."

"But it was my fault—"

"Darlin'," he said, tossing the quilt in the truck bed. "We're in this together. Hell or high water." He kissed her briefly and patted her on the backside. "We've got to haul our asses or the day'll pass us by."

"I just want you to know…" She swallowed against the lump forming in her throat. She wasn't the same woman who'd left her past behind. She was stronger, she was resilient, and she was head over heels in love with a Texas cowboy. Going for broke, she spit it out, "I love you."

His eyes rounded in shock and his mouth opened but no words came out.

Perfect, she thought. They may have sealed the deal and activated the DelVecchio Curse for this generation, and he didn't feel the same way about her.

"No," she said holding up her hand. "Don't say what you don't feel."

Instead of apologizing and pouring out his heart, the way she'd hoped, Dylan rounded the truck and got into the driver's side.

Shock held her immobile.

"We're burning daylight."

No mention of her play on words last night, using starlight in place of daylight. No mention of the love they'd made or the possibility of pregnancy. Drawing in a deep breath, she got into the truck and slammed the door. Maybe it was lust and her feelings were all one-sided.

Dylan pulled a U-turn in the middle of the road, tires spitting out gravel as he floored it back to the ranch house. Her heart hurt watching the man who vowed Garahans ran toward trouble get out of his side of the truck and leave her there.

Maybe she'd hurt his feelings more than he let on.

Then again, maybe he really didn't care if she ended up pregnant.... maybe he was like her ex.

That thought stopped her cold. Dylan Garahan was the complete polar opposite of her ex. Time to give credit where credit was due.

He held open the back door. "You coming?"

He didn't sound mad; he sounded preoccupied. Maybe she was making a mountain out of a molehill, time enough to sort things out later that night when he came by to work on the shelves in her back room.

"Be right there," she answered. "I'm going to hang up the quilt."

He looked down at her and his eyes warmed by degrees. "Thanks. I'll start breakfast; my brothers probably ate everything that wasn't nailed down. Ronnie?"

She looked over her shoulder at him, surprised to see his look of frustration. "What?"

"I don't know much about love."

She swallowed the comeback and waited for him to say more. When he turned and walked inside, she knew she'd chosen a long row to hoe.

Don't give up so easily, bambina.

Removing a couple of clothespins from the line, she smoothed the quilt over it and refastened the clothespins. "It's so hard," she whispered, tears filling her eyes, tension clogging her throat.

That's because he's worth it.

Chapter 15

"Ronnie, dear," Mavis Beeton's voice mail begin, "I'm over at the Smith place and had a great idea. Call me."

"What in the world is she up to now?" Ronnie was used to Mavis's coming and goings and the unusual orders she placed with Guilty Pleasures from time to time.

They finished eating and Dylan wasted no time or sweet words on her—just a tip of his hat on his way out to saddle his horse. It wasn't until after she'd heard hoofbeats racing past the house that she realized she had no way to get to town... well, unless she hot-wired his truck.

She called Mavis back, but didn't have a chance to speak to her, just listen. "I'm in a hurry—can you meet me at my place?"

Ronnie agreed and ended the call.

The kitchen was clean, the dishwasher was running, and steaks marinating for dinner. After the way Dylan had hightailed it out to the barn, she didn't figure there was any reason to stay. "Was he thinking I'd just sit out here and watch the grass grow?"

Ronnie thought about leaving him a note, but what the heck—he hadn't kissed her good-bye, so she'd return the favor. One more glance around the room satisfied her that she'd left it cleaner than she'd found it. With dinner soaking up her favorite marinade in the fridge and the makings of her peaches and cream cobbler on her grocery list, she closed the back door and sprinted toward Dylan's pickup.

She just stood there for a moment admiring the stepside pickup, her favorite body style. "Well, a woman's got to do what a woman's got to do."

Opening the driver's side door, she got in, reached under the dashboard, pulled the wires that were already visible, and touched them together until the engine caught and started to idle. Sliding out from under the steering column, she sat on the front seat and looked down at her hands and smiled. She'd learned how to hot-wire anything with wheels, but hadn't been able to learn how to play piano.

"Weird," she mumbled. "Well, time to head on into town and see what Mavis is up to."

Thinking and driving usually got her into so much trouble that she'd end up on the wrong road going in the wrong direction, so she flicked on the radio and kept time with the music, tapping on the steering wheel.

"And for you oldies fans out there, here's one from Conway Twitty."

Ronnie kept time not really paying attention to the lyrics until she heard the refrain—"I don't know a thing about love"—and thought of Dylan and his heartfelt confession.

"When will you learn to keep your mouth shut?" she asked aloud, putting the truck in park and getting out to open the gate. Once she'd driven through, she remembered Dylan's shell-shocked expression and total lack of response to her declaration. "Stupid," she said, putting it in park again. For a heartbeat she thought of leaving the gate open, but wasn't sure why they kept it closed other than to keep people out.

Did their cattle wander this close to the property line, or did they graze elsewhere? She hadn't seen any, but that didn't mean there weren't any nearby. Her responsible side had her closing the gate, but then hesitating as she flipped on the turn signal.

You shouldn't steal.

She'd placed herself in the line of fire again, knowing the reason why cut her to the core. Her damned wounded pride. Stomping on the gas, fishtailing onto the main road, she headed into town. "I'm just borrowing his truck. I'll bring it back in time to cook dinner."

Just under an hour later, she was pulling up outside of Mavis's house. Her friend was waiting for her. She looked at the truck and asked, "Isn't this Dylan's truck?"

Ronnie grinned. "Yep."

Mavis shook her head. "Interesting." When Ronnie didn't say anything else, Mavis said, "You should host a lingerie party and let us come up with the guest list."

Ronnie laughed. "You're a constant source of inspiration."

"Good, because Jolene thinks it's a great idea and we've already invited people."

Ronnie turned onto North Main Street and pulled up outside of her shop. "In that case, give me a minute. I'll be right back."

"Aren't you going to turn the truck off? It's a waste of gasoline."

She shook her head. "I'd rather keep it running than have to hot-wire it again."

The sound of Mavis's laughter followed her into her

shop, lightening her heart. She ran upstairs and found the box she'd received the day before and headed back downstairs and outside.

"So, are the ladies meeting us at the Lucky Star?"

Mavis nodded. "Between my connections and your stock, I think we could keep you in business even if the whole block burned down."

When they arrived, Jolene was waiting for them. "Come on in. I've put coffee on." When they walked into the bar, Jolene grabbed a tray of mugs and the pot. "Caffeine anyone?"

Ronnie smiled. "Thanks. Well," she said, "what do you think?"

Jolene looked at Emily and nodded. "I think we should keep it small, by invitation only. The ladies will feel pampered. While you show them your lingerie, perfume, and massage oil, we offer them some of Lettie's special sandwiches."

Mavis agreed. "Lettie's chicken salad is always a hit."

"I've been experimenting with two new types of frosting for my signature brownies," Emily said. "I could donate dessert."

Ronnie's eyes filled. "You're all so generous… willing to help me when I haven't really done anything to earn your generosity."

Mavis patted her arm and handed her a tissue. "We women have to stick together, especially in times of trouble."

"If you give us the list, Mavis," Jolene said, pushing her chair back and standing up, "we'll start inviting people."

She really loved it here. "When I'm up and running, I am so paying you all back."

Jolene stared at her and narrowed her eyes. "Convincing Dylan that he and his brothers should be a part of our all male revue during Take Pride in Pleasure Day will be all the payment we need."

Ronnie winced. Dylan's truck! "Hey, I've got to go, um—"

"Return a truck?" Mavis asked sweetly.

Ronnie laughed. "Something like that."

"I can't believe Dylan let you drive it," Emily said. "Garahans don't give the keys to just anyone."

"He didn't actually give me the keys."

All eyes turned toward her. "I, uh…"

"Hot-wired it?" Jolene suggested.

Ronnie beamed. "My cousin Vito taught me years ago."

"Useful skill," Gwen said.

"It has come in handy over the years."

"Ever go to jail for it?" Emily asked.

"Not yet," Ronnie said with a grin.

Jolene looked at the clock on the wall. "Best be getting out to the Circle G."

Ronnie grabbed her box and thanked everyone. "I'm forever in your debt."

Mavis waved her away. "Friends lean on friends… friends lean back."

Ronnie looked at the group surrounding her, acknowledging, "It works."

Hot-wired and headed back to the ranch, Ronnie wondered how best to approach Dylan after leaving the ranch without a word… or note. She thought of then discarded so many ideas that by the time she got out to open the gate, there was a steady pounding at the base of her skull.

There were no other vehicles parked outside when she pulled up, leaving her to wonder if she'd taken their only means of transportation. Ignoring the ache in her head, she got out of the truck and walked up the steps to the back door. The swing caught her eye, and at any other time, she'd have sat down and enjoyed the simple pleasure, but this evening, she had steaks to broil and a man to grill.

No one was in the kitchen, but that was probably for the best. She could have dinner broiling and ready to serve by the time the men arrived.

By the time she was setting the cobbler on the stovetop to cool, Jesse and Tyler came in from outside. "Hey, Ronnie. We were wondering where the truck went. Everything all right?"

She nodded. "Perfect timing. How do you like your steak?" Looking behind them she watched the back door for Dylan to arrive. "Did you wash up?"

Tyler answered for the both of them. "Rare. Yes, ma'am. We'll finish setting the table." Turning toward his brother he said, "Grab the forks and knives."

Dylan still hadn't shown up by the time she'd put dinner on the table. She couldn't stand the suspense and finally asked, "Is Dylan feeding the stock?"

Tyler stared at her for a long moment before answering. "He… uh… had to go into town."

Jesse wouldn't meet her gaze, instead, he tucked into the meal before him, filling his mouth so he wouldn't have to speak.

The fact that they weren't going to tell her was

painfully obvious. Either Dylan asked them not to tell her where he was going and when he'd be back, or it was a brother thing... covering for one another.

She swallowed her feelings and started to straighten up.

"Aren't you going to eat with us?" Jesse asked.

"I've actually got things to... uh... do at home." Before the tears welling in her eyes fell, she turned around and finished washing the pots, pans, and dishes she'd used preparing their meal.

"We'll load the dishwasher," Jesse offered. "Dinner was great."

Tyler smiled down at her. "Dylan will be sorry to have missed you."

She couldn't meet his gaze for long. "See you tomorrow."

Before they could call her back, she was out the door and almost to the truck before Jesse caught up to her. "Hey can I give you a lift?"

She stopped with her hand on the driver's door. "I'm so sorry. I wasn't thinking."

He watched her as if waiting for her to say something else. When she didn't, he shrugged. "No problem. Dylan rode Wildfire into town. We're never really stuck unless we want to drive down to Brownsville."

She didn't know where it was or why it was significant, but she nodded, hoping he'd stop talking to her.

Jesse wasn't in on her plan; he'd talked her ear off by the time they'd made it to town. When he pulled up in front of her place, she grabbed her box of lingerie and bolted out of the truck, thanking him on the fly. She didn't turn around to see if he was planning on getting out of the truck, and was relieved when she heard the sound of him pulling away.

She opened her door and closed it quickly behind her, leaning her forehead against the back of it, finally giving in to the pain welling up inside of her. "I hate to cry," she ground out as the first tears fell. "Gives me a headache."

Pushing away from the door, she turned and walked upstairs. "Matches the one in my heart."

Listless, she shuffled down the hallway and fell face down on her bed. It wasn't comfortable, so she rolled onto her side. "Face it, girl, he's long gone. You pushed him away with your hissy fit and lack of enthusiasm when he asked you whether it was babies in general or just his babies that you didn't want to be pregnant with."

"*Stoonad*," she chastised herself. *Stupid*. She'd spent the most incredible night of her life making love with Dylan. He was passionate, his lovemaking raw and untamed, just like the man. But there's more to a relationship than just sex.

Watching the play of light on her ceiling as a car drove down the street, she wondered what he was doing in town. Was he with someone? And why would she even think along those lines after the way they'd burned each other up beneath the star-filled Texas sky?

"Certifiable," she mumbled. "Crazy. Dylan was a generous lover." And why the hell was she thinking of him in past terms? "Will he come back or will he hate me forever?"

"Arrgghh." Needing to move, to do something, anything except lie alone in her bed, Ronnie did what she always did to unwind: yoga. Changing into her favorite workout clothes, she stood barefoot on her mat in front of the picture window. The light was too bright, so she turned it off, relying on the glow from the incandescent bulb in the overhead kitchen light.

She went through the motions, relying on her inner copilot to remember the moves that would have been far too much for her brain to conjure up at that point. A half hour later, she was on the floor in the Lotus position, clearing her mind and finally finding inner peace.

Rolling up her mat, she stored it beneath the sofa and headed to the kitchen to fill the teapot. She always had the need for a hot cup of tea after she meditated. "Cinnamon Spice should do it." Once the burner was heating up, she reached into the cabinet and found the tea.

The pot whistled before she realized enough time had passed for the water to heat. She wandered around her apartment, wondering why she'd given her ex even a portion of the house they'd purchased. He didn't deserve it and her lawyer was certain he could get her more, but something had held Ronnie back—probably the fact that she didn't really want any reminders of their brief time together.

"Water under the bridge," she murmured into her mug. Too bad she'd finally found her comfy place… and it was in Dylan's arms. All of the earlier emotions she'd been battling came back in a resounding wave of despair. Digging deep, she wiped away her tears and wandered back into the living room by the window. Leaning against the window frame, she watched the way the moonlight illuminated the street below and thought of the song she'd heard earlier.

Her heart twisted a little remembering the way his lips had pressed to her heart as he pulled her closer and loved her while the sweet breeze blew across the pond, rustling the grass until it sang a soft and gentle melody.

A dozen fractured thoughts filled her mind, but she pushed them away, concentrating on sipping her tea and keeping a lid on the tumultuous feelings inside of her that were struggling to break free. It was hard to be wanted the way Dylan seemed to want her last night, but it was harder still to be tossed aside, forgotten amidst the ashes of their shared passion, wondering if he'd be coming back or moving on to another conquest.

"One look at the man and you can imagine women lining up around the block just to have the opportunity to look at him." She sighed. "He's gorgeous... all those beautifully sculpted muscles... and those powerful thighs. And I know for a fact he can grip more than the sides of his horse with them."

A shiver wracked her tired body. "Damn... I'm sleeping alone tonight." She sighed and drained the rest of her tea. "One night... well, actually, one amazing afternoon, and one stellar night with the man, and I'm looking for forever."

Carrying her empty mug into the kitchen she looked at her reflection in the dark window. "What is wrong with you?"

Standing up straighter, she tilted her chin up. "Nothing that time and a little distance won't cure." Ronnie flicked on the overhead light and reached for the book on the top of the stack. "Nora," she said holding the book in both hands. "I really need you to take me as far away from Texas as I can get tonight."

With help from one of her favorite authors, Ronnie let herself be swept away to Connecticut. An hour later, she was embroiled in someone else's romantic problems—a wedding planner and a mechanic.

—✺—

"She show up yet?" Dylan demanded. He couldn't believe that the woman had managed to tie him up in knots for most of the day and had hot-wired his damn truck. He knew she had because the only set of keys had been hanging on the cup hook in the kitchen when he'd left earlier.

"Yeah, everything all right?"

Jesse's question was a loaded one. Dylan snickered. "Just fuckin' dandy."

His brother sighed. "She kept looking for you."

"That a fact?" He wouldn't admit that he'd hoped to see her before he had to go into town and save the butts of two pretty little redheads by doing something he'd sworn never to do again in this lifetime: strip. He hadn't even had the chance to talk to her after their argument that morning. Hell, if that wasn't something… Dylan Garahan wanting to *talk* to a woman.

"Did you even tell her where you were going tonight?"

"Nope."

"Look, Dylan, I'm no expert in matters of the heart—"

"Will you just bring the damn truck and leave it at the Lucky Star?"

Jesse's grumbled response had Dylan's mouth quirking up on one side. "Yeah, women are all of that and more. Ms. Harrison said I could stable Wildfire over at the feed store, but I'd rather not have to. The women here are acting like they'd never seen a man ride a horse before. It's downright creepy."

His brother's laughter eased one of the knots in his gut. "See you later."

"So, cowboy," Jolene called out, "you find a safer place to leave your mount tonight?"

"Damn, quit callin' me that."

"I call 'em, like I see 'em... cowboy."

He shook his head and stroked Wildfire's neck. "Come on, boy, we're going over to Harrison's. They've got oats."

Wildfire's ears twitched. "Might be an apple in it for you if you go quietly." He swung up into the saddle and half a dozen women groaned out loud.

He glared at Jolene, who gave him that annoying fingertip wave and warned, "Hurry on back, cowboy. You don't want to miss your number."

He used his thighs to urge his horse in the direction of the feed store. "Jesse's coming to take you back to the ranch and bed you down for the night."

The horse's answering whinny eased another knot. Too bad for him the rest could only be undone by a woman with raven hair and ruby lips.

"Does everything I'm thinking have to remind me of lyrics to a damned song?" Too late, the rhythmic cadence of his horse's hooves hitting the pavement was in perfect time to the Eagles' tune running through his mind—"Witchy Woman." At Harrison's he took the saddle off and used his hands to rub Wildfire down. "Jesse'll rub you down right with your favorite curry comb when you get back to the Circle G," he promised.

The horse nodded then nudged Dylan in the shoulder.

"I didn't forget." Laughing, he fed the stallion a handful of oats, loving the feeling of the animal's lips seeking out more of the grain long after it was gone.

"Give me a minute, boy." Dylan dug his pocketknife out of his pocket and quartered the apple he'd snagged out of their kitchen before leaving home. "Be good while I'm gone," he warned, closing the door to the stall.

The horse watched him leave but didn't make a sound.

"You know I always keep my word."

Wildfire finally snorted his agreement.

Dylan felt a little bit lighter walking back to the Lucky Star—not because he had to survive another night up on stage with all those women hootin' and hollerin' at him, but because he was fortunate to still be able to keep Wildfire and the rest of their Quarter Horses. They hadn't had to sell them in order to pay for the feed bill and mortgage. If he had to work at the Lucky Star to keep from selling Wildfire and the other horses, he'd do it.

He loved working with wood, and would welcome any other jobs Emily would send his way, but he'd long ago decided it would always be a hobby; the ranch had to come first. Rounding the corner, he shook his head. Damned if every one of those females wasn't waiting for him to return. Standing dead center was the redheaded troublemaker who'd hired Tyler a while back, tricked him into thinking he'd be hauling kegs and stocking shelves when all the while she'd been hiring him to be her new headliner after the last one got caught with his pants down.

"Seems to be a pattern here," he grumbled low enough so no one would hear.

"We decided to wait for you." Jolene was grinning ear to ear and damned if every one of the women there started clapping. "You see, cowboy," she said, nodding to the ladies, "they've missed you."

"Damn."

"Come on, ladies," Jolene urged. "Dylan'll be on stage shortly. You won't want to miss what the man can do with a coil of rope."

He tipped his head back and sighed, but the night sky didn't hold any answers for him. The small hand cupping his ass had him spinning around and grinding his teeth. One look from Jolene, who'd been watching everything and had seen it too, had him clamping his jaw tight. He could abide her rules for another night or two, but beyond that...

When he drew closer, she whispered, "Thank you, Dylan. You really are a lifesaver."

All of his mad melted away because the softer side of Jolene reminded him of Emily, and for his brother's girlfriend, he'd walk through fire. It was the least he could do since Emily'd done that and more for Tyler.

"Have you seen Ronnie this evening?"

Now why would Jolene want to know that? Before he could ask, she patted his arm. "It's going to be a boon to her business."

He was about to ask what the hell she was talking about, but Natalie called out to Jolene and the two disappeared inside.

He had no choice but to follow. Inhaling the familiar scent of warm rain had him grumbling again. "Just how the hell do they do that? Pipe the scent in?" Ignoring the mirrored walls, he shook his head. "Forget how, why?"

His questions went unanswered as he tried to slip through the crowd to the stage door.

"Oh, Dylan," a little blonde sighed, "we're so glad you're back."

He tipped his hat.

A redhead had her hand to her heart and a brunette was fanning herself. What the hell was wrong with these women? They'd all grown up in the area. Pleasure and the neighboring towns were filled with men who worked the land, raised cattle, and rode horses.

"You're one fine-looking cowboy," a voice crooned.

He spun on his boot heel and his stomach iced over before he realized it wasn't Sandy.

He tipped his hat to the brown-eyed blonde and moved to walk past, but she grabbed ahold of his elbow. "You sure are a looker, handsome."

He stopped and stared at her. What the hell did she want from him? The woman didn't even know him... not like Ronnie did. Hell, he should have talked to Ronnie before she left. Talking wasn't his strong suit, but he owed it to her because he wanted to spend the rest of his life with her. His silence must have become uncomfortable, for the blonde let go of his arm. Opening the stage door, he wondered what the hell made people tick. The brunette he craved and thought would be sharing his bed for the next little while didn't want to have his children—not that he was so all-fired ready to have any, but that wasn't the point. Now here he was back at the Lucky Star, and women he didn't even know were convinced they would be just the one for him.

"Women are trouble."

One of the other dancers walked toward him. "Hey, glad you could fill in for us tonight. Jolene was worried."

Dylan shook his head. "But she's already got two dancers. Why does she need three?"

Joe shrugged. "Seems to work for her and the crowd that keeps getting bigger by the night."

"So she really caught the new guy in the act?"

Joe grinned. "Yep. In the pantry sampling the local honey."

Dylan couldn't help but smile. "That a fact?"

Joe started to laugh. "Jolene tried to break it up by hitting him with a broom."

"I'd have paid good money to see that."

Joe nodded to Dave, who'd finished his act and was walking back stage. "Dylan was asking what happened to the new guy."

Dave shook his head. "Jolene's got good aim."

"What else did she do?" Dylan had the perverse need to know.

"When the broom didn't work, she grabbed a bottle of seltzer from the bar," Joe said.

"And hit him in the ass with it," Dave finished.

"She's quite a woman," Dylan had to admit.

"Chet looked over his shoulder at her and she shot him right between the eyes."

The three men shared a laugh. Dylan wondered why anyone would want to strip for a living, but these two hadn't given him any concrete answers when he'd asked before, he doubted they would now. *Best to let it go. Just do the job, Son, and hightail it back to the Circle G.*

Yes, sir.

"Hey," Dave said. "Did you get a load of the boda-cious blonde with the big brown eyes?"

Dylan shrugged.

Joe nodded. "I think she's looking for some action." He turned toward Dylan and asked, "You interested?"

"I'm taken."

Dave nudged Joe and said, "Good to know."

Dave rubbed his hands together and grinned at Joe. "You want first crack at her?"

"Go for it. You saw her first," Joe said laughing. "I'll catch her on the next go-round."

"Your rope's over there," Joe called out as Dylan walked over to where three pair of chaps hung and one coiled lasso hung on the wall.

"I hope everyone's decent," Jolene called out before poking her head around the edge of the door. "Damn, my luck's just not holding out, all y'all are still dressed."

Dylan shook his head. "Trouble really is your middle name."

She laughed and held out her hand. "I thought you might want to have a brand new pair of briefs to wear."

He stared down at the offering and wondered how the hell he'd sunk so low as to be wearing black spandex again. "I prefer boxers." Her hoot of laugh-ter took the edge off his frustration. "I like a woman with a sense of humor." Thoughts of Ronnie's throaty laughter plagued him. Damn why couldn't he just forget her?

"It looks like you have a lot on your mind. I'm a re-ally good listener," she offered, laying a hand on his forearm. "You can call anytime."

Dylan couldn't resist the urge to tease. "You sure

Jake won't mind me callin' an hour or so after we close down tonight?"

Her lips twitched as she fought against the urge to smile. "Don't you worry none; I can handle him."

The chuckle came from deep inside of him, loosening up a couple more knots of tension. "I do believe you've met your match, Ms. Langley."

Jolene's eyes softened and he knew he'd been right about the couple. "I'm right partial to Pleasure's fire marshal."

"So tell me, Jolene," Dylan began, "did you really shoot my replacement between the eyes with seltzer?"

She frowned. "After I gave him a couple of solid whacks with my best cornhusk broom. Couldn't get him to stop, though," she said. "Since I didn't have a garden hose handy, I grabbed the next best thing."

Dylan's snort of laughter caught him by surprise. "Maybe I could ask Tyler to rig something up for you in the bar's kitchen… he installed a Y hose splitter at the back of the house that'd do the trick."

Her green eyes lit with mischief. "I may need him to install one… depending on who I get to replace you."

"Didn't you go over the rules with the guy?" Dylan couldn't believe she hadn't.

She frowned and shook her head. "I did, but I didn't catch him in the ladies' room or the men's room."

Dylan patted her shoulder needing to reassure his boss that she hadn't been wrong. "He had no call sullying your club's reputation by getting busy in the pantry."

Her head shot up. "Oh Lord, I never thought of that. What will my customers think?"

Dave and Joe walked over to join in the conversation.

"You might need to make some sort of announcement before Dylan takes the stage."

She looked at Dylan. "I run a decent place. Women are safe here, but they have to know that there's a line no one can cross here. There's not going to be a need for Sheriff McClure to come back because of an FIP."

Dylan grinned. "Fornicating in public—Sheriff Wallace lectured us all about it in sixth grade... was it an ARI?"

Jolene tilted her head to one side. "That's a new one. What does it mean?"

"I think Tyler was the first one of us brought home in the back of the sheriff's cruiser because of an ARI—alcohol related incident."

"How old was he?"

"Thirteen."

"So young?"

"Sometimes you have to grow up fast," Dylan said, not going into detail. Hell, it wasn't his story to tell. Jolene's gaze was still locked on his when he shook his head. "You'll have to ask Tyler if you want to know why."

"You want Joe and me to go outside and start the ladies line dancing?"

Jolene smiled. "I think that'll really help keep the ladies involved and coming back. Watching all y'all dancing and stripping is fun, but women really like to dance."

The two left, discussing which dance to begin with. A few moments later the music stopped and they heard Dave asking everyone to line up for some good old-fashioned fun.

"You remember the routine Natalie and Jennifer

taught you?" Jolene asked. When he nodded, she continued, "I'll go out a few minutes before you do. When the lights dim, you stride forward in that loose-limbed walk of yours."

"What are you going to say?"

"I'll recite the rules I have for my dancers. I'll let everyone know why I have those rules and why no customer is allowed to cross that line either."

"That'll work. Short but sweet, and to the point."

Dylan watched her leave and knew he had a little time before he had to get undressed for his act. He pulled his cell out of his pocket and swore. "Hell, I don't have her phone number."

Resolving to get it from Jolene after his act, he got ready for his routine. Fingering the rope, he was reminded of a woman with green eyes and kissable lips. He'd be better off not getting involved, but that wouldn't get rid of the ache in the vicinity of his heart.

He'd been there before, but this time things were different. His working the ranch had never been affected like it had today. And he sure as hell had never wanted to track a woman down before to sort things out; he'd let the others walk away... but Veronica DelVecchio wasn't walking out of his life now that she'd stormed into it.

"Women!" he grumbled, reaching for the rope. The heft of it felt right in his hands; he could pretend he was out working the ranch with his brothers... well, up until he had to toss his rope around the designated birthday girl.

"I'd rather get thrown off Wildfire into a stand of cacti than be here tonight."

That thought led to another. "Maybe my back East lady would volunteer to pull the cactus spines from my wounded hide."

You'd better find that woman and make up with her.

"Maybe I will."

Chapter 16

RONNIE CLOSED THE BOOK WITH A SIGH. "I REALLY love a great romance." Setting the book on her shelf, she looked at the clock by her bed. "Not the first time I've read past midnight... won't be the last."

Needing a breath of air, she headed downstairs and outside to sit on her front steps—not quite like back home, but close enough. Breathing deeply, she started to feel a little better. The air was warm and the stars were bright.

The sound of someone calling her name had her looking up and recognizing Dylan's truck driving toward her. Her heart lurched in her breast, beating double time, until she realized it wasn't him when the driver turned and grinned. It was Jesse who waved and whistled at her.

"Nice outfit, slim," he called out as he drove by.

Looking down, she saw what he must have: bare feet and a baggy shirt slipping off her shoulder—that was it.

Her phone vibrated and she answered it.

"Ronnie?"

Dylan's voice wrapped around her like a hug, but having spent the night reading a romance novel instead of wrapped in his arms, she held back the reaction screaming inside of her. "How'd you get my number?"

The sharp intake of breath told her she'd hit her intended mark—payback was a bitch, but his reaction wasn't quite what she expected. "Darlin', I've surely missed your sassy mouth."

"Damn it, what do you want?" The man got to her on all levels, and she was afraid that if she didn't disconnect the call soon, she'd start crying like a baby. A girl had her pride.

The heartbeat of silence had her biting her tongue. When would she learn to control her temper?

"Darlin', you can kick and bite all you want, but you're going to be in my bed tonight."

Her heart began to pound. "Maybe I'm not interested."

"Liar," he rasped. "You know you want me as bad as I want you... I'm planning to make you crazy later. You'll be screaming my name, wrapping your legs around my waist, and begging me to fill you."

The picture he painted was so real, so vivid, she had to swallow the saliva pooling in her mouth. "Not gonna happen," she rasped.

"Wanna bet?" he asked. "Pack a bag, darlin', 'cause when my shift's over, I'm coming to pick you up."

"What shift?" The voices cheering in the background all sounded female. The light went on... someone was finally home. "Are you at the Lucky Star?"

"Yep."

"I thought your last night was a couple of days ago." What was he doing back working for Jolene? Why didn't he tell her? And why the hell should she care?

"I'll be there in an hour."

The devil in her bit out, "I'm busy."

But he didn't answer her; he'd already disconnected.

"Damn man," she swore. "I'm not interested in him anymore."

Now what was she going to do? Walking back inside, she slammed her front door and mumbled, "Maybe I don't want to see him again."

Looking down at her hands, she noticed they were trembling. "He's right… I am a liar."

Heading upstairs, she went over her choices aloud. "I can stay here and be mad at the man who bruised my heart." By the time she reached the top step, she added, "Or I could pack an overnight bag and be ready when he picks me up and waylay him with teeth and tongue." She knew just where to touch to drive him up and over the peak into madness. "I could hold him hostage here until he admits he should have said good-bye earlier today."

Lighter in heart, she was already formulating her attack. "I think I'll start with that sweet spot he has at the base of his neck and work my way along his collarbone until I can trace a path from the base of his throat to his navel."

Grinning, now that the plan was hers and not his, she sprinted down the hallway to her bedroom and threw a tote bag on her bed and tossed in jeans, underwear—super skimpy—and a skinny T-shirt.

Then she headed to the shower and turned it to scald. She was going to be loose, limber, and ready when her man came to call.

He looked across the room and met Jolene's direct gaze. Damn. He'd given his word; he didn't have a choice. With a slight nod toward the brown-haired woman standing stage front, Jolene confirmed what he'd feared. *Damn.* His back was tired and she was a big old girl.

Suck it up, he told himself as he raised the rope over his head and began the smooth, circular motions necessary to work the rope. Satisfied with the motion, he let the rope fly. It landed around his target's middle; he flicked his wrist and it tightened around her.

Her surprised expression changed to one of pleasure. At least Jolene'd be happy that he'd made the birthday girl smile.

Dylan finished his act and made a beeline for back-stage. Dressed, he set his Stetson on his head and headed for the other side door. Looking to the left and then the right, he slipped out the door, grateful the crowd hadn't made it around back yet. His world shifted toward nor-mal as he spotted his truck, right where his brother prom-ised he'd park it. "You can always count on a Garahan."

Driving over to Ronnie's, he wondered if his little filly would be giving him a hard time or trying to get him hard. A shiver wracked his frame as anticipation lit a fire in his gut. He'd been afraid she wouldn't speak to him after the way he'd let her leave the Circle G without saying good-bye. He knew she'd still be there and was sorry he'd acted like an ass. But he was ready to make it up to her, as soon as he kidnapped her and drove her back to the ranch. Then he'd have his way with her and convince her he was worth the effort to keep up with his temper and his moods.

Mostly difficult moods, if his ex was to be believed. He thought he was a peach, but then again, he didn't see anything wrong with waking up and punching one of his brothers before coffee. They were Garahans, they had tempers, they defused each other's tempers. End of story.

He pulled up in front of Ronnie's shop and wondered

what kind of reception he'd receive. He hadn't given her a chance to say much on the phone. Walking to the door, he decided he would roll with whatever kind of mood she was in. He knocked twice and then let himself in. She knew he was coming, so he didn't see any need to stand outside waiting.

With his back to the room, he closed the door and heard someone on the stairs. He looked over his shoulder and just about swallowed his tongue. Ronnie stood on the stairs wearing next to nothing and his brain simply short-circuited.

He didn't remember moving, but then she was in his arms, nibbling his chin, sliding her tongue along the rim of his mouth before she tangled her tongue with his.

"Ronnie, darlin'," he whispered against her lips before sliding his hand down the length of her spine and molding her to him. "I'm sorry I didn't wait for you," he murmured against her lips. He was a fool to let his temper dictate his actions. She was his woman, his match in bed and out. Her temper more than matched his. How could he let anything get in the way?

"I'm sorry I let you leave without saying good-bye." He crushed her to him and lost himself in the honeyed sweetness of her lips. Anger forgotten, he gave in to the need that had been clawing at his gut all day. Blood racing, heart pounding, he deepened the kiss, tongues tangling, hands seeking her secret places, pushing her as close to the edge as he was.

When she wrapped her legs around him, he gripped her thighs and sampled the side of her neck, inhaling the delicate scent that was uniquely hers. "I have a fierce temper."

Ronnie sighed and tilted her head farther to the side, allowing him to nibble on the tendon, eliciting tiny moans from her luscious lips. "Forgive me?"

~~~

Ronnie couldn't think, could barely breathe. Her plan was going awry. She wanted to be in charge, she wanted to call the shots, but his wicked lips were wrecking havoc with her heart and messing with her mind.

"Just tell me what you want, darlin'." His lips blazed a trail over her heart and between her breasts. "And I'll make it happen."

His vow released the words she'd hidden in her heart after he'd left her hanging at the ranch. "Love me, Dylan," she cried out as his lips toyed with her breast before pulling it into his mouth. "I need you to love me."

He released her breast and reared back, nostrils flaring, eyes dark and compelling. "Don't let go."

Her head felt light, her voice nonexistent, but she managed to nod. He brushed a hand across her thong-clad backside, making her squirm in anticipation. She wanted him deep inside of her.

Dylan bent his head and traced the outside edge of her ear with the tip of his tongue. The rasp of his zipper had her shivering again, but she needed her brain to work, she needed to be sure he protected her.

"Help me," he whispered, tracing his tongue along the line of her cheek, while walking toward the wall and leaning her against it.

"How?"

"Lock your legs and lift your sweet backside, so I can cover myself and protect you."

Heart in her throat, she tensed her thighs and lifted, and Dylan groaned.

"Darlin', you're killing me."

"But—"

She felt his hands moving, brushing against her sensitized backside as he opened the foil packet and covered himself.

"Ease up, darlin'."

Legs shaking, she did as he bid, loosening her hold on him but not letting go, even when a cramp settled itself in her left butt cheek. She sucked in a breath but rode through the pain.

His lips found hers as his hands instinctively found the knotted muscled and massaged it loose. With a deft touch, he lowered her and slid all the way home.

She arched back to take more of him. He held on to her hips with a grip of iron as he pulled back and then plunged again. He picked up speed as his lips traced a path along the line of her jaw. She gave herself over to the magic of his mouth and hands, reveling in the strength of him, the rigid length of him, and was rewarded with a mind-melting orgasm that stole her breath.

But Dylan didn't stop; he slid in and out of her, increasing his pace, adding to the tension building inside of her. A low, throaty moan of ecstasy fueled her passion, pushing her closer to the edge.

She clamped her legs around him with all of her strength and grabbed ahold of his muscled backside, urging him to take all, to give all. His hoarse shout of triumph sent her spiraling into oblivion with him.

"Darlin', you've got to let me go."

"Mmmm…" Deliciously languid warmth filled her. "No."

"My legs have about three seconds before they give out," he warned as he eased out of her and swayed, and nearly lost his grip.

Reality intruded… the bitch. "Sorry," she murmured. Placing her lips to his pounding heart, she uncrossed her ankles and let her legs glide down the long length of him, brushing against denim as she did, reminding her that he couldn't even wait to take his pants all the way off before he made love to her. "You are lethal." She locked her arms around him when he teetered toward her. "Lean on me."

His weight shifted and she braced herself, laughing. God, it felt good to laugh. "I didn't think you'd lean all of your weight on me."

He moaned. "You drain me dry, tell me I can lean on you, and then change your mind?"

"No, I didn't."

"Drain me dry?" He chuckled. "Darlin', it's gonna take some time to refuel and reload."

"I mean I didn't change my mind." Her gaze met his and she welcomed the passion, encouraged the desire, and hoped he felt a fraction of what she felt for him.

"I'm only giving you half my weight." The devil gave her his full weight and toppled them toward the floor.

"Dylan!"

At the last moment, he turned them and took the brunt of the fall on his back. The whoosh of air told her it wasn't a pain-free landing.

"Are you all right?" Worry had her tracing her hands along his shoulders and down his arms, trying to reach his back.

"If you move 'em just a little bit lower, I'd be much obliged, ma'am."

The girlish giggle sounded foreign to her ears. "You, sir, are making fun of me."

"Not on your life, darlin'. I've got this cramp—"

"Oh, I'm so sorry." She sat up and his low moan told her more than words. "Just where is this, uh, cramp?"

His gaze locked with hers and his slid his hands down to cup her cheeks. "You're sitting on it."

She bent down and nipped him the chin. "I thought you needed to refuel before reloading."

"Kiss me, darlin', so I can refuel."

Ronnie wasn't sure she believed him. "You can't possibly have anything left inside."

"My heart's so full right now, darlin', it'll last a lifetime."

Tears filled her eyes and spilled down over her cheeks onto his forehead.

"Ronnie, darlin'," he whispered, "don't do that." He shifted her to his lap, sat up, and cradled her to his chest.

Words caught in her throat, but they weren't necessary. She wrapped her arms around him and let his gift of love pour through her. Oh, he hadn't said the words yet, but he came close... so awfully close.

For now, it was enough.

Chapter 17

"ARE WE GOING TO SLEEP ON THE FLOOR ALL NIGHT?"

The comforting sound of Dylan's voice rumbling beneath her left ear woke her. "Depends on whether or not you're going to be rolling over any time soon."

His chuckle was music to her ears and should have been her warning. "I'm thinking about it—right now."

She squealed with laughter as he yanked her closer and rolled until she was beneath him.

"Interesting position," he murmured kissing her forehead, nose, and chin. "But I was serious about you in my bed. I want to wake up with you at the Circle G."

"I already slept with you at the ranch."

He brushed his lips across her cheekbone. "Ah, but that was to satisfy my need to make love with you beneath the stars on Garahan land."

She watched him closely, waiting for him to laugh. When he didn't, she frowned up at him. "You aren't kidding?"

"About which part? You in my bed or you beneath the stars?"

"The part where we're on your land."

"Goes without saying, darlin'. We Garahans are proud of what we've made. My brothers and I have been struggling lately, but we're hanging on to what our great-great-grandparents built with everything we've got. We'll do anything to save the Circle G."

"I know how you feel," she whispered, stroking the strong line of his jaw with the tips of her fingers. "I've put everything I had into this business, and I don't intend to run scared because some teenager trashed my store. Pleasure's where I live now... I'm staying... and I'm fighting back."

Her gaze met his and she saw that he understood. "What do you have in mind?"

"Mavis asked me to compete in the rodeo to help raise money for the town. I hadn't planned on competing again, it's been awhile, but for Mavis and to earn my place in this town, I'm riding."

"How long has it been since you've been on a horse?"

"Too long." Running her hands along the breadth of his shoulders, she sighed. "Your strength is one of the first things that hooked me."

He pressed his hands flat on either side of her head and rose up on his toes. In pushup position, he lifted himself up and then lowered himself until his lips were a breath away from hers. "Is that a fact?"

Her breath snagged in her lungs; it was work, because the man drove her to distraction, but she focused so that she could exhale and then draw in a much needed lungful of air.

Turning her head to the side, she stared at his hand. "You have the most intriguing scars. Is there a story behind all of them?"

"Funny thing about a bow saw," he began only to be interrupted by her.

"Are you making that up? I've never heard of a bow saw."

"No," he grumbled, "I'm not. Now where was I?"

She clamped her lips together and waited for him to continue.

"When you're holding the wood still, make sure to move your hand out of the way of the blade, or you'll run the teeth of the saw right over it."

She shuddered. "That had to hurt."

He leaned all of his weight on one arm and lifted his hand to examine it. "Yeah," he rasped. "Thought I'd cut it clear down to the bone, but the good news was that the blade wasn't all that sharp."

She knew she should say something, but the man was deliberately teasing her, testing her, by doing one-arm pushups. When she was able to make her mouth work concurrently with her brain, she asked, "So it didn't cut too deep?"

"No," he answered. "But it was a ragged mess. Tore the skin up real bad."

An echo of his pain lanced through her and had her reaching for his hand. The crosshatch of lines confirmed his story. "How old were you?"

He lowered himself to within an inch and lined up their lips. "Does it matter?"

The desire churning in his eyes warmed her from the inside out. "Yeah," she whispered, tracing his lips with the tip of her finger. "It's a part of what made you the man you are today."

He opened his mouth and sucked her finger into the velvety warmth. The movement of his lips and tongue mesmerized her and had an answering pull tugging at her core. Her body knew what it wanted: Dylan. But could she keep him? She closed her eyes. He wasn't a lost puppy; he was a man.

He brushed against her as he shifted, redistributing his weight. Opening her eyes slowly, she watched him rein himself in, banking the fires of passion burning brightly inside of him.

She could tempt him and rekindle those flames, but she wanted to know more about him. Spending time with him at the ranch might give her the answers she needed—to the questions she had yet to ask.

"We're wasting time, darlin'." Before she could refuse, he had her hand in his and was tugging her to her feet. "You planning on wearing that bit of nothing again soon?"

She looked down at the sheer black miniscule chemise and then up at his face. From the way he frowned, she couldn't quite tell if he wanted her to. She toyed with the skinny shoulder strap and slid her fingers down along the ribbon running between her breasts. His eyes followed and his nostrils flared. Gotcha!

"I could throw on my nightshirt over top of it."

He closed his eyes and groaned. "You will pay for teasing me, darlin'."

She smiled and hugged him close. "I plan to, darlin'."

His rumbled laughter was the sweetest sound. "Grandpa was right."

When he didn't say anymore, she prompted him. "About…"

"Women."

"And?"

He shook his head. "If we don't get going, we're going to end up staying here, and you'll miss out on a chance to ride some prime horseflesh."

She couldn't resist. "Will I get to ride your prime flesh too?"

He swallowed and ground out, "Get your bag, woman, and save that thought 'til we get to the Circle G."

It felt so wonderful, teasing Dylan and being wanted to the point of desperation. Taking pity on him, she sprinted for the stairs and called out over her shoulder, "Yes, sir."

On the ride over, she scooted over next to him on the bench seat and reveled in the fact that they could be comfortable enough with one another to ride in relative silence and know that words weren't necessary—being together was.

A light was burning in the kitchen, but the rest of the house was dark. "Will anyone be up?"

"No." Dylan parked the truck and got out and walked around to her side of the truck, holding the door she'd just opened. "I want to kiss you so badly my gut is churning."

His confession tugged at her heart and had her leaning close. "What's stopping you?"

"My brother's window is right up there." He pointed to the middle window on the second floor. "And you're loud."

"Kissing you?"

His eyes swirled with a heady mix of passion and lust. "We wouldn't be kissing for long."

"Oh." Her fingertips tingled as her blood began to race. "We could sit on the swing."

He shook his head. "We just put it back together."

"It looks solid," she said, walking toward it.

He seemed to gather himself in as he spoke. "It was the last gift my dad gave my mom."

As if she understood, she said, "She'd think of him every time she sat on it."

His serious expression lightened. "Yeah. We all did."

Knowing his parents weren't around and not wanting to bring up what could be a painful subject, she hooked her arm with his. "We can have coffee out here in the morning."

"Darlin', it's already morning."

She looked up at the sky. "It's still dark."

"The steer don't tell time by the darkness of the sky."

"How do they tell time?"

He opened the back door. "Do you really want to know?"

Oddly enough, she did. "Yes." She let herself be led through the kitchen.

"By their inner clock... probably their hunger." He pulled her toward the stairs and she willingly followed. "We have one too." Putting his finger to his lips, he whispered, "Right now mine says it's time to hit the hay, but I may have some energy left for a little early morning lovin'."

She felt the smile blossoming from the inside out. "Promises, promises."

He yanked her against him and swept her into his arms. "Get ready to ride, darlin'."

Dylan put his shoulder to his bedroom door and gave it a nudge with the heel of his boot to close it. The soft snick of the latch closing seemed to satisfy him. He knelt on the bed and placed Ronnie in the middle. His movements were slow and deliberate.

Where was the flash, the frenzied movements she'd grown accustomed to? "Dylan are you—"

He leaned over her and brushed his lips across hers lightly, gently. "Let's try something different."

Her heart began to pound. "Different how?" She remembered the night he lassoed her and hoped he wasn't into really tying her up; she wasn't sure she'd be into bondage.

He must have seen the worry in her eyes because he cupped her face with his hands and kissed her with a reverence she'd never experienced. "I want to take my time. I want to savor your sweetness."

Her mouth opened, but no words came out, only a strangled moan of pleasure as his lips brushed feather-light kisses on her cheek and chin before beginning a journey that led him to the base of her throat.

He was destroying her, fueling the fires of passion by taking his time. "Dylan, I—"

His lips silenced her again. "Let me love you, darlin'."

How could she refuse?

He lifted her up and pulled the T-shirt over her head, revealing the sheer chemise. Instead of taking that off too, he pressed his lips to her heart and kissed her. The warmth of his mouth created a moist pocket of air beneath the fabric.

She shivered.

He groaned.

He moved to her breast and suckled her through the fabric. The rasp of sheer, damp voile had her belly fluttering. When he switched to the other breast, her inner muscles started twitching.

"Dylan—"

Again, he answered her with his mouth. His supremely talented mouth set off a trail of sparks leading from her breastbone to her belly. She sucked in a breath when he swept aside the fabric and nipped her hipbone.

Grabbing ahold of him, she tried to bring him back up to her breasts.

Reading her body and the tension in her limbs, he lifted his head and rasped, "We can save what I had in mind for another time. There's plenty of territory to conquer without getting to your honey-sweet center."

"It's just that I—"

He shifted so he could press his lips to hers. "Do you trust me?"

She felt the tension leaving her by degrees. She nodded.

———~~~———

"Excellent." He took the same path as before, sampling and savoring her along the way. He didn't want to force her too fast too soon. He needed to build her trust in him so that she'd offer him everything he wanted: all of her.

He'd worry about the whys and wherefores later. Right now, he had uncharted territory to cover. He could get really close to her honey without actually sipping from her sweetness.

And he intended to get as close as she'd let him.

"Easy," he soothed as he traced the rim around the dip of her belly button, eliciting another shiver of pleasure from the woman he worshiped with his mouth and tongue.

Need filled him, the need to show her tenderness and passion instead of the raw, unbridled lust he'd shown her up until now. He slid his hands slowly up her sides, testing the fullness of her breasts, cupping them, before bending to swirl his tongue around their rose-tinted peaks, amazed at how quickly they pearled beneath his attention.

Her lips lifted upward and her head tilted back as she arched toward his touch, seeking more. Dylan dug deep to control the urge to devour and found he had the capacity to give more.

He shifted his hands so they lifted her up until she was dependent upon him to hold her right where she wanted to be: on the receiving end of his full undivided attention. The color of her eyes deepened to emerald. He didn't have the words to tell her all that he was feeling, all that he wanted her to feel, but he could show her.

He brought her closer and suckled her left breast, then slid his tongue across the valley between her breasts before suckling the other, lavishing it with equal attention. Her short, sharp panting breaths told him more than words. His woman wanted him, needed him as much as he needed her. He *loved* her.

Dylan released her breast as his mouth opened in shock. His head spun as his breath clogged in his lungs, and his heart beat double time. He couldn't possibly love her. The word love wasn't in his vocabulary, hadn't been since the day he and his brothers laid their mother to rest beside their father.

But Ronnie didn't notice his turmoil; she was still clinging to him like a burr on a horse's hide. When she called out his name, he knew he couldn't just stop. He'd shown her he could be gentle with her, that he cherished her. *Damn*. It wasn't too soon. A man didn't want to cherish a woman he planned to mattress dance with; he cherished the woman he wanted to spend the rest of his life with.

She's the one.

'Bout time you woke up and smelled the coffee, Son.

His rumble of laughter had her easing back from him,

but before she could ask him what was wrong, he bent his head and fitted his mouth to hers, molding her lips with his. His traced the lush shape of her lips with his tongue, encouraged when her soft moan allowed him to stroke the velvet softness of her mouth and tangle his tongue with hers.

When she pressed her hands against his chest and tried to push back, he eased his hold, wondering what was wrong.

"You're killing me," she rasped before pulling his head back down so she could reach his lips. When her teeth nipped his bottom lip, it was his turn to groan.

He eased her down on the bed and got up, grumbling, "I should have done this part first, damn it."

She was smiling up at him as he toed off first one boot and then the other.

"But then I'd have missed watching you undress."

He bent over to remove his socks and she sighed. "You have the best ass."

His snort of disbelief escaped before he could work to hold it in. "Now there's where you're wrong," he said climbing onto the foot of the bed. "You, on the other hand," he murmured, flipping her over onto her stomach, "have a magnificent ass."

"What are you going to do now?"

His laughter was just this side of wicked. "Why, darlin', I thought you trusted me."

She mumbled something into the pillow.

"I didn't hear you. What was that?" he asked, pressing his lips to the curve of her ankle before sliding his tongue along the line of her calf muscle.

"Oh, God."

Encouraged, he tested the uncharted territory, the virgin skin on the back of her knee, with his lips and tongue.

She was squirming in earnest now. "Dylan, please don't make me beg."

"Hold on, darlin'," he urged. "I'm not finished yet."

She bucked beneath him when his tongue touched the dip at the back of her right knee. Lord, his filly was sensitive there. "Tell me you hate it and I'll stop." He pressed a kiss in the dip and heard her moan, but she didn't ask him to stop.

Good thing, because he was so tense, he'd have imploded if she asked him to stop before he had a chance to test the firm white skin on her amazing backside. He set his teeth on her and she growled at him. "You do not fight fair."

"Ronnie, darlin', if you think this is fighting, I must not be doing it right."

He couldn't decide if her snort was one of derision or temper. Fillies have been known to snort when the temper was on them.

"If you don't turn me over right now, there is definitely going to be a fight."

His good mood was slipping away from him. He flipped her over and ground out, "I'm trying to show you my tender side, damn it."

She wrapped her arms around his neck and brought his lips down to meet hers. "I appreciate the sentiment, darlin', but you left something turned on at home."

He didn't register what she was talking about until she brushed her heated core against his erection. It didn't take a rocket scientist to figure out that the woman was burning with need.

"Again?" he teased, before kissing her with everything he felt, showing her with lips, tongue, and a nip of his teeth for good measure.

"I need you now," she demanded, sliding her hands down to grip his muscled backside.

"Let me protect you." He eased back, found the condom he'd left in his bedside drawer, smoothed it on, and covered her from head to toe with his body.

"Now, darlin'," he drawled. "Where was I?"

She lifted her hips and he slipped into her with a swiftness that stole her breath. "Here?"

She tried to answer him, but he didn't give her the chance. He wanted her to remember that he could be gentle; he could cherish her, damn it. Then her hips rocked up against his and every last thought was sucked out of his head, in a vortex of desire so strong it took them both under and whipped them up over the peak into madness.

Her finger poking him in the shoulder had him reluctantly moving, but he braced himself on his arms and looked down into her siren-green eyes.

"Tender nearly killed me."

He crushed her to him and rolled onto his back chuckling. "God, I love you, Ronnie."

She tried to smack him, but he rolled back until she was beneath him again. "I thought that's what you wanted to hear."

Her green eyes flashed with temper. "So you just said it because you thought—"

He shut her up by kissing her. "I've never said I love you to another female—except my mom—and that was a long, long time ago."

Her eyes filled with tears, but she was smiling… and he knew that was a good thing.

"I love you back," she rasped.

"Let me hold you, darlin'."

She sighed, snuggled close, and drifted off to sleep.

Chapter 18

"I'VE GOT TO GO, DARLIN'."

Ronnie opened one eye and groaned. "What time is it?"

"Four thirty. I'm working a second job, so my brothers let me sleep in."

She brushed a lock of hair off her face and opened the other eye. It was work; even her eyelids were tired. Looking up at him, she realized there was just something about a man with rough edges and a little wear on him that appealed to her—on all levels.

"Morning," Dylan rumbled, pressing his lips to her forehead.

The sweetness of his kiss seeped into her bones and wrapped itself around her heart, smashing what was left of the wall she'd built to protect it. "Good morning," she whispered.

"I brought you a cup of coffee."

She smiled and reached for the cup. Blowing across the surface she took a sip and started choking.

He was grinning when he said, "Jesse got up first and made the coffee."

"Is that what this is?" She'd never tasted anything quite like it. "Did he add a strip of leather from the bottom of his boot to the grinder this morning?"

"Beggars can't be choosers." He nodded toward the cup. "If you want better coffee, you can wait for Emily to get up or make it yourself."

"If you get a coffeemaker with a timer, Emily could set the pot up at night to go off at whatever unearthly time you guys start your day."

"It was a revelation to us when Tyler came home with that drip coffeemaker. We'd always made coffee like you do... Grandpa wouldn't drink it otherwise."

"I couldn't picture Emily out here until I saw the way she fits in."

Dylan grinned as she dared another sip. She grimaced and he chuckled. "Emily's as close to sainthood as a woman can get... she's Tyler's saving grace."

She almost blurted out that Dylan's was hers, but she caught herself in time. He hadn't repeated the words she still held close to her heart, but she wouldn't forget that he had said them. Knowing he was not long on words, the importance of the fact that he told her loved her was not lost on her.

"Tell you what," she said slipping out of his bed. "I'll make you coffee and breakfast."

He shook his head. "I'll take you up on the coffee, but I already ate. The stock doesn't sleep in."

"OK," she said. "Will you wait for the coffee?"

He let his finger slide along her collarbone, stopping in the hollow at the base of her throat. She shivered and he pressed his lips where his finger had been. "I'll put the horses in the front pasture and feed and water them, and come back for coffee."

She imagined she could brew a pot of excellent coffee and whip up a batch of corn bread while he worked. "You bet." She walked into his arms and hugged him tight. When he loosened his hold, she stood on her toes and kissed his cheek. She knew when to tempt and when to hold back.

He laid his cheek on her head and inhaled; he let the breath out slowly as if savoring it. "Why do you always smell good enough to eat?"

She laughed. "I have no idea, but if you really want a great cup of coffee, you won't give me any ideas about distracting you from taking care of Wildfire and the gang."

He pushed her gently back and laid his hands on her shoulders. "There's a lot about me that you don't know."

She nodded. "You could say the same about me, but we have time... don't we?"

Dylan bent his head and gave her a swift but devastating kiss. "As long as it takes."

Before she could ask him to explain, he spun on his boot heel and was gone.

"Time's a wastin'," she mimicked his Texas drawl and opened up her tote bag, pulling out jeans and a T-shirt. No point in spending the extra time to put on underwear; she was going to hit the shower right after she was finished in the kitchen.

Amazed at just how dark it was at this hour, she was careful not to make too much noise as she walked by the only closed door in the hallway. Making her way downstairs, she noticed that it might still be dark, but it wasn't quiet. The cheerful sound of birds chirping floated in on the early morning breeze.

Washing her hands in the sink, she noticed a feeder hanging from a hook just outside the window. She'd have to make a point to look later when the sun came up.

The coffee was dripping into the pot by the time she was scooping corn bread into a glass baking dish. Sliding it into the oven, she gauged her time and hoped

it would be ready before Dylan headed out to do whatever chore he had to tackle next.

The room was noticeably lighter by the time he
walked in the back door. "Hello, darlin'."

She handed him a mug and nodded to the stovetop.
"There's hot corn bread if you want a slice."

His gaze locked with hers. "I love corn bread."

She grinned up at him. "Mmmm… I know."

He set his mug on the countertop and wrapped her in
his arms. "Have I told you how much it means to me to
see you here at the Circle G?"

He had, but she hadn't a clue why. "Yeah, but why—"

He tilted her head back and pressed his lips to the
tip of her nose. "Garahans have owned the Circle G for
over one hundred and fifty years. We've fought Indians,
drought, and survived more than one range war. We're
a part of this land: worked it, lived on it, and are buried
in it."

"I thought that was just a figure of speech."

"No, ma'am. I can show you the graves later." He
kissed her forehead and hugged her tight. "It's sharing
what's part of me with you, and seeing the way you just
fit in here, that warms my heart and feeds my soul."

Tears welled in her eyes, but she didn't bother to
blink them away. She needed Dylan to know how much
his words meant to her. "There's this feeling I get being
here, even when you're not in the room, it's like I'm
where I belong… I'm home."

He captured her lips in a soul-searing kiss. When he
drew back from her and leaned her against the counter,
he was grinning. "No, don't distract me, woman. I need
a hunk of that corn bread and have to get on to the next

chore on my list or I'll never have the chance to drive
out to your place later today and finish up priming the
drywall or putting up the shelves."

She placed a hand to her lips and sighed. "I guess I'll
hang around, unless I can borrow your truck."

He bit off a piece of corn bread and groaned. "Almost
as good as my grandma's."

She paused with her cup partway to her mouth.
"Excuse me?"

He chewed and swallowed. "Darlin', ain't nobody
who can top my grandma's corn bread, but this is so
close it's almost heaven."

"Hmmpf." Mollified, she waved at him to get him to
move away from the counter. "I need to put plastic wrap
on it, or it'll be hard by the time you come in for lunch."

"Hang on a sec." Dylan cut out a huge chunk, pulled
off two sheets of paper towel, wrapped it up and kissed
her on the cheek. "Thanks. This'll hold me until lunch."

He stopped in the doorway and looked over his shoulder. "You plannin' on takin' my truck again?"

She smiled. "Well, that all depends."

Dylan waited. Finally, she shook her head. "I'll be
here for a while. We're having lasagna, roasted garlic
with Italian bread, and a nice salad."

His eyes glittered. "With the same sauce you made
the other day?"

"Maybe, but not if you don't give me some space so I
can start cooking. That sauce has to simmer for a couple
of hours."

"Can you make a double batch?"

"For you, darlin'," she drawled, "anything."

His eyes darkened as he drew in a ragged breath.

"Don't be temptin' me when I've got to concentrate on my chores."

Her lips twitched, but she fought the urge to smile. "See you later."

He nodded. "If you want to practice barrel riding later, we've got a couple of real good cutting horses."

He was on the back porch when she called out, "Can I ride Wildfire?"

"He doesn't take to other riders."

"But what if he does?"

"I'll be riding him out by the North pasture after lunch, but you can pick any one of the other horses."

"Thanks. Maybe I'll wander on over to the corral after I'm finished in here and see who wants to let me ride them."

"Now you're talking like a woman who's been living on a ranch all her life."

She was still smiling when she heard the sound of hoofbeats as he and Wildfire rode off. Looking around the kitchen she sighed. "This is about as far as I could get from suburban living in Jersey."

Wiping down the countertops, she started gathering what she'd need to create Nonni's red sauce. The familiar scent of garlic and onions sautéing in olive oil soothed her. By the time she had the sauce simmering on the back burner, she checked the clock. "Just enough time to grab a quick shower before those wild-eyed Texas boys invade my kitchen—"

She had to hang on to the back of a chair to steady herself. "It's not my kitchen."

The thought that it could be had a feeling of déjà vu washing over her.

"OK, let's not go crazy here. I'm in a relationship with a volatile, scrumptious cowboy, who busted down the walls I built around my heart after my ex stomped all over it. That doesn't mean it's time to break out the orange blossoms, white lace, and rice."

Unless you love him. Her brain was working over-time as her head listened to what her heart had been trying to tell her. "I really do love him." Drawing in one deep cleansing breath and then another centered her. She let go of the chair and walked upstairs to take a hot shower.

Her cell phone was ringing when she walked into the bedroom. Keeping her towel from slipping with one hand, she answered it.

"I was just about to leave you a message."

"Sorry, I just got out of the shower."

"Really?" Mavis asked. "Do tell."

Ronnie laughed. "What's up?"

"Are you free this afternoon?"

Ronnie smiled. "I could be. What do you need?"

"I've called a few friends and they can't wait for the lingerie party. Can you meet me at the Lucky Star?"

"I was going to spend part of this afternoon practicing my barrel riding. It's been a while."

"Maybe you could squeeze in two hours in town," Mavis suggested. "Say from two o'clock until four?"

Ronnie thought about it. The potential for more sales and new customers outweighed the need to prac-tice what she knew would come back in a heartbeat. Barrel riding was a lot like riding a bike—you never forgot how, and if the horse was as good as Dylan said he was, it would be a lot easier. Barrel riding was a combined effort: your talent and skill added to your horse's.

"I'll let Dylan know I'll be at the Lucky Star for a while this afternoon. See you later."

As she hung up, she realized that her box of lace-covered confections and perfumes was at her shop in town. "Damn. I've got to go through it and see what I have and what I can download from my website to use as flyers in case anyone wants to place an order."

After she got dressed, she went to check on her red sauce. The spicy aroma wafted toward her as she walked into the kitchen, welcoming her. "Let's see if it tastes as good as it smells."

Dipping the spoon in the sauce, she touched the tip of her tongue to it—perfect temperature—and tasted it. "Hmmm... needs a dash more salt." After sprinkling some in the pot, she stirred and then tested the sauce again. "Mmmm... perfect."

Ronnie was adding the top layer to the lasagna when Tyler walked into the kitchen.

"Smells amazing in here."

She ladled sauce on the noodles then added a few handfuls of shredded mozzarella. "Tastes better."

He nodded. "Any chance of getting that for lunch?"

Jesse walked in with Dylan, distracting Ronnie from answering. Her gaze sought Dylan's. When he looked over at her, her insides got all gooey. The man definitely had a hold on her.

"Is that lunch?" he asked, pointing to the baking dish she lifted from the countertop.

"Dinner," she said covering it with foil and placing it in the fridge. "I wanted to make sub sandwiches, but you don't have the right kind of rolls, so I made Dagwood sandwiches instead to go with the potato salad... I made both kinds."

"What's a sub sandwich?" Tyler asked.

She closed the fridge and looked over her shoulder at him. "You're kidding, right?" He shook his head and started to reach for a sandwich. "Did you wash up?"

They all nodded. "At the pump outside," Dylan answered for his brothers. "So what's a sub aside from what the Navy uses underwater?"

She laughed. "Who would have thought the food would be so different out here? It's a specialty back home in Jersey. You take a nice Italian roll, half the size of a regular loaf of bread, and layer it with salami, ham, cappicola, provolone, tomato, lettuce, onion, spices, and vinegar and oil."

"Sounds good," Tyler admitted.

"It goes great with a frosty glass of cola—"

"Or a longneck?" Jesse asked.

She nodded. "That too."

"So why are we getting cartoon sandwiches?" Dylan asked.

She grinned up at him. "So you know what a Dagwood is?"

"Our grandfather was a *Blondie* fan." He added, "He used to have one of us read from the funnies while he made us all Dagwood sandwiches. We still get a kick out of reading it in Sunday's funnies."

"My Nonni loves that comic strip." She smiled and said, "When I get back from town, I'll hopefully have the makings for subs for you guys."

"You're going to town?"

She nodded. "Mavis called. The ladies have arranged a get together with some of their friends over at the Lucky Star around two."

"Girl stuff?" Dylan asked.

She tilted her head to one side and said, "I'm going to bring my lingerie and scented oils to show a few invited guests. Hopefully people will want to buy something silky or sweet-smelling. It'd help me keep my business afloat while you're rebuilding my shop for me."

The brothers looked at one another and Jesse shook his head. "I guess we're not invited."

Tyler scooped up some potato salad on his plate and pointed the serving spoon at the second bowl. "Women need to spend time together. Hey Ronnie, I recognize potatoes in there, but why doesn't it have mayonnaise on it?"

"It's German potato salad, made with vinegar, oil, onions, and parsley… no mayo or celery."

Dylan picked up a fork and dove in. His surprise showed on his face. "It's good… different," he told his brothers, "but good."

"Gee, thanks, Dylan."

He smiled at her and nodded. "We're pretty adaptable around here. Hey," he said slowly, "any corn bread left?"

She laughed. "You took most of it with you this morning."

Jesse pushed his way past his brother. "You made corn bread? How come I didn't get any?"

Dylan reached out and hauled her into his arms. "'Cause she likes me better than you."

Love for the man simply swamped her. From the way

he was gazing down at her, she had a feeling he felt the same way too. His lips captured hers in a fiery kiss that liquefied her bones, reassuring her.

"If you're not gonna share," Jesse growled, "then cut it out."

Dylan eased his hold on her, shifting her to fit against his side. "Sorry."

"No," the youngest Garahan grumbled, "you aren't."

Dylan's sigh was long and just a bit patronizing. "Hell, when you're right, you're right."

Jesse looked like he was ready to start swinging, and might have if Tyler hadn't stepped in front of him. "Let's eat. We've got more range to cover this afternoon before we can come back and have some of that lasagna."

Having three men with healthy appetites to cook for was satisfying. She loved to cook and wondered if Emily didn't.

"Does Emily ever cook for you?"

Tyler grinned. "She bakes the best brownies."

She waited for him to continue. When he let it go at that, she finally asked, "So she doesn't like to cook for you?"

Jesse snorted in response and Dylan chuckled. "She might if Tyler would let her out of the bedroom for more than just to go to work at the Lucky Star."

Tyler grinned. "Woman's smart," he said looking over at Ronnie. "She knows her place is in my bed."

"Well, really," she grumbled. "That's just simply medieval."

Tyler was still smiling when he added, "Works for us."

Her lips twitched as she fought the urge to smile. "Good to know."

When the men had decimated the plate of sandwiches and three quarters of the salads, Tyler and Jesse thanked her and left. Dylan waited for them to leave before drawing her into his embrace. "I thought they'd never leave."

She giggled. "They were hungry."

He tipped her chin up, lined up their mouths, and swept her mind clean with a soul-searing kiss. Coming up for air, he rasped, "Me too."

He kissed her again and asked, "Why can't I get enough of you?"

Ronnie leaned against him. "I have no idea, but I'm not complaining, because I feel the same way."

"Good to know," he said, nipping at her lips. "I've got work."

"OK," she sighed, squeezing him in a bear hug. "I'll see you at dinner time… Oh! Can I borrow your truck?"

His grin went straight to her heart. "You're asking me this time?"

"Yep."

He brushed the tips of his fingers along the line of her jaw. "You want to borrow the keys?"

She placed her hand on top of his where it rested on her face and sighed deeply. "I don't need no stinkin' keys."

His laughter reassured her that he understood her reference to an old Humphrey Bogart film and she didn't have to explain. "I'll be back in time to warm up supper."

"If you aren't," he warned, "I'll come looking for you."

She stepped back into the circle of his arms. "Promise?"

He dipped his head and captured her lips one last time, drawing everything she felt from the depths of her soul and filling it back up with his.

"Promise."

Chapter 19

MAVIS WAS WAITING FOR HER OUTSIDE THE LUCKY Star. "Word's spread about our little get-together this afternoon."

Ronnie's face lit up. "That's really great news."

The older woman shook her head. "Not if it involves the Rotary Club or the Women's Club."

Clutching her box tighter, Ronnie forged ahead; she'd hit roadblocks before and detoured around them successfully. This was just a minor bump in the road, not a full-fledged roadblock. "Instead of worrying about it, why don't you tell me what happened while I set up inside."

Mavis shook her head. "Later," she said, opening the door to the club. Ronnie inhaled and was instantly at ease as the scent of fresh rain washed over her. Turning to Mavis she smiled. "I usually have incense burning in the back of my shop. Maybe I'll have to rethink that and have the scent infused into my air conditioning and heating system like it is here."

"It always smells wonderful in here," her friend agreed, "and sets the tone for the evening ahead."

"There's a grocery store back home that uses cinnamon from about Halloween on through the holidays," Ronnie said. "But on really warm fall days, it's a bit much."

"You've got some time to decide what scent you'd

like to use," Mavis assured her. "Will Dylan be finished with the repairs anytime soon?"

Ronnie paused on the threshold of the barroom and shook her head. "He's got a full plate with the repairs at my place and the possibility of one or two other side jobs that he was telling me about the other day. Then there's the never-ending list of chores to keep the Circle G running smoothly."

Mavis hooked Ronnie's arm with hers and gently tugged. "That man works hard, but so do you. Let's see if we can keep your business afloat with a few more sales."

"Hey y'all," Jolene greeted the women. "Are you two ready to party?"

Emily walked out of the downstairs kitchen with two trays laden with food, one with tiny delectable-looking sandwiches arranged like a tower, and the other filled with yummy-looking brownies. "Gwen's bringing the pitchers of cold tea—one sweet and one with lemon."

Ronnie grinned and set her box down. "You ladies are the best." Her eyes teared up, but she blinked them away. "I can't thank you enough."

Jolene reached for the box and grinned. "Maybe you can give us a major discount on your collection of lacy teddies."

"Done," Ronnie agreed.

Gwen grinned and asked Jolene, "Is the big bad fire marshal partial to lace?"

Jolene's grin said it all. "I thought it would be right neighborly," she said, "if we all chipped in and bought something for Anne Marie and Janet."

Gwen snickered. "Ronnie doesn't carry what those women need in her store."

Jolene tapped her chin and asked, "What about your online store? Do you have any toys?"

Ronnie laughed, imagining the looks on the two ladies' faces when they opened their gifts. "My distributor would love if I'd add vibrators to my online store."

Emily nudged her cousin. "Maybe we should go with something small; we wouldn't want them to feel awkward that they don't have something to give us in return."

Moving over to stand beside Ronnie, Emily reached toward the rainbow-colored satin and lace spilling from the box. "May I?"

"Please," Ronnie said. "In my store, I encourage my customers to touch. I have some fabulous satins and silk, but then, for those who prefer natural materials, I've got this cotton batiste that is to die for."

Emily held up a swathe of black lace so tiny, she giggled. "What is the point?"

Ronnie held up another lacy thong in red. "If you have to ask—" Voices interrupted what Ronnie was going to say as a group of women walked into the barroom.

"Welcome ladies," Jolene said motioning toward Ronnie. "Your hostess this afternoon is the owner of Guilty Pleasures. You all heard what happened to her shop. While Dylan's rebuilding her shop, Ronnie's going to be holding parties here at the Lucky Star."

"Why don't all y'all help yourselves to something to eat and drink, and then browse her collection?"

"Thanks, Jolene," Ronnie said, truly grateful. "I've seen some of you in town, and maybe one or two of you in my shop before. Unfortunately, none of the lingerie was salvageable, except for some bits of lace and satin that I'm planning on piecing together into a wall hanging to hang in my store to show whoever did this that I'm not easily intimidated and I'm not leaving."

The round of applause was totally unexpected. She felt her face grow warm. "I'll get down off my soapbox for now." She scanned the group gathered around her. "I just received an order in the mail, so I've got some lovely lingerie to show you. I have a handful of reproduction antique perfume bottles and a small sampling of fragrances that can be added to massage oil. Ask me anything you like."

While women chatted amongst themselves and helped themselves to the food and drink, Ronnie watched as Jolene lifted one see-through chemise after another for inspection. A little old woman with snow-white hair and piercing blue eyes approached. She smiled down at her. "Yes, Mrs. Peterson?"

"Do you have anything that would tempt my Jonas?"

Ronnie looked at Emily and Jolene, but they looked at their feet. No help from that quadrant. She noticed that the room had gone quiet, and she realized that if she was going to build a business and name recognition in this town, she'd best keep on going the way she'd begun when she opened the doors of Guilty Pleasures: by being honest and forthright whenever possible.

"Actually I do... what's his favorite color?"

One by one the women gathered around the lovely bits of lace and satin draped on the ebony bar. The black was a perfect backdrop for displaying most of her collection.

"He's right partial to red."

Ronnie nodded and lifted up a knee-length chemise

with a peekaboo lace panel from the V-neck to the hem. "What about this?"

Mavis nodded. "That'll get his attention, Mille."

Mrs. Peterson frowned. "I just can't imagine how it would look on." Shaking her head, she sighed. "You know how a dress that looks great on the hanger, looks awful on you—you're not built like a hanger."

Inspiration hit Ronnie. "We should have a fashion show! I've got a mix of sizes here. Why doesn't everyone pick something and go change in the dressing room at the back of the stage? Is that OK with you, Jolene?"

Jolene grinned and said, "Absolutely. Who's first?"

The women divided into groups, half of them sorting through the chemises and teddies to select one in their favorite color and the other half waiting for the makeshift dressing rooms to free up.

Mavis wrapped her arms around Ronnie and hugged her tight. "Our town's founding mothers would have taken to you right off, Ronnie."

Mrs. Peterson nodded and said, "Like most everyone gathered here, I've lived in Pleasure all my life, and I agree. The Donovan sisters would have welcomed you with open arms." She nodded to the group at large, and said, "How can we do any less? Welcome to Pleasure, Ronnie dear."

The women took turns hugging Ronnie or shaking her hand. A feeling of contentment flowed over her, relaxing her. Their acceptance meant the world to her. "You have no idea how grateful I am—"

"They do," Mavis interrupted. "We have a solid core of independent women here in town, but there is a small group determined to take over and change the way things have always run here." Nodding to Jolene and Emily, she continued, "But we aren't about to let that happen, are we, ladies?"

Everyone started talking at once, and Jolene spoke up, "Thanks, Mavis. We love living here and providing a service to this community."

Ronnie agreed and decided it was time to bring the conversation back to safer ground. "Amen to that. Did you know that aside from some regular customers, I have had a few adventurous men wander into my shop buying gifts for their wives or girlfriends, but they've detoured past my personalized massage oils? Anyone want to create their own free sample?"

While the women gathered around her, she passed around small vials of essential oil. "These two are my favorites: vanilla and almond. I add them to my home-made sugar scrub. It's a fabulous exfoliator, but leaves a hint of scent that your man will appreciate. So think about his favorite scents and I'll add a couple of drops to the massage oil I've brought with me."

"Can't you just create one because you like the way it smells?" one of the women asked.

"Absolutely," Ronnie said with a smile. "Not every woman has a man in her life or wants to complicate her life with a man, no matter how good looking or sexy he is."

"Well now, darlin'," a familiar voice drawled, "I'm here to change your mind."

Ronnie whirled around and watched as Dylan's eyes bugged out, but he wasn't staring at her; he was looking at the stage. "What the hell is going on here?"

She looked over her shoulder at the group of ladies

who'd decided to take her suggestion to heart and were
twirling up on the stage in various stages of undress—
mostly scandalously skimpy. Clearing her throat, she
answered, "What do you think?"

He tore his gaze from the stage and the women
modeling Ronnie's lingerie and frowned down at her.
"I thought you were just showing your underwear to
the ladies."

His Adam's apple bobbed up and down and his eyes
widened as the elderly Mrs. Peterson walked stage front
in her peekaboo lace-paneled chemise and called out,
"What do you think, Ronnie dear?"

Before Ronnie could answer, three more ladies—all
of them Rubenesque in build—walked out modeling her
signature line of teddies, garter belts, and stockings.

Dylan opened his mouth to speak when he was interrupted by one of the ladies holding out a brightly colored
catalog that Ronnie hadn't realized had been in the bottom of her box. "Can I order this Venus Butterfly from
your online store?"

Dylan's jaw dropped, his eyes glazed over, and he
slowly shut his mouth.

"Veronica DelVecchio," a deep voice ground out,
"you're under arrest."

Ronnie whirled around and stared at Sheriff McClure.
"Surely there's some mistake," she said.

"Now hold on, Sheriff," Dylan began, but McClure
ignored him.

"For encouraging pillars of our community to be in-
decently exposed and for selling pornographic material
without a license," the sheriff said, slipping handcuffs
around her wrists.

The irony of being in handcuffs while holding her supplier's catalog of pleasure toys wasn't lost on her. Since she was going down, she'd go down in flames. "Why Sheriff McClure," she purred, "what a great idea. I'm going to have to start selling handcuffs along with my create-your-own fragrance massage oil."

The man's face shot straight to purple. "Let's go." He yanked and pulled her along behind him. "You ladies get dressed," he ordered.

Ronnie noticed that he had a tic beneath his right eye.

"Somebody box up that evidence," the sheriff bit out, "or you're all going downtown."

Not one woman moved. "Are you crazy?" Jolene said, stepping in front of the sheriff. "Last time I checked, it's not against the law to have a party in this town."

He glared at her, but she didn't budge. Emily got in his way, standing next to her cousin. "You cannot tell us how to celebrate or have fun."

He stared at Emily but didn't speak; he stepped around the women, dragging Ronnie and the catalog she still held. Incensed that he wasn't listening to anyone, Ronnie whacked him on the back of the head with it.

He stopped and looked over his shoulder at her. "Assaulting an officer of the law while trying to perform his duties is going to add to your jail time."

Dylan got between them and the door. "Now hold on there, Sheriff—"

Instead of the reaction either of them expected, the sheriff put his free hand to the holster at his hip. "Step back, Garahan," he warned. "I don't want any trouble from you and don't need your interference upholding the law in this town."

When Dylan opened his mouth to speak, Ronnie expected him to stick up for her and give the sheriff a piece of his mind while rescuing her from spending time behind bars. When he closed it just as quickly and stepped aside, her heart plummeted to her feet and her euphoric feeling of not only being accepted in town, but also being rescued by the man she loved, evaporated.

Dylan stared at her, but his expression was closed, unreadable. What was he thinking? *Would he just let the sheriff haul her off to jail? Weren't they a couple? Shouldn't he be sticking up for her?* The sheriff hauled her away before she could ask.

Dylan pulled his phone from his hip pocket and hit the speed dial. "Come on, Bro," he grumbled, "pick up the phone."

"Hey," Jesse answered. "What's keeping you and where's our cook?"

"I need you and Tyler to back me up."

His brother didn't hesitate or disappoint him. "When and where?"

"I'm at the Lucky Star. Ronnie's just been arrested."

"Yeah right," Jesse drawled. "Are you two staying at her place? You'll miss her awesome lasagna... it even tastes great uncooked."

He couldn't believe his brother was jawing about food when Dylan's woman had been dragged off to jail! He balled his free hand into a tight fist, clamping down on the urge to put it through the wall. He looked up, relieved to see Emily and Jolene standing close. "Put Ty on the phone. Emily'll explain everything."

Handing his phone to her, he planted his boot heel and spun around, sprinting down the hall after the woman he'd move heaven and earth to see safely back at the Circle G. Damn, why hadn't he just said something? Why did he just stand there?

Must have been the vision of Mrs. Peterson in the peekaboo lace. Now go and get that woman!

His grandfather was on his side and pulling for him, and his brothers were on their way. It was time to go after Ronnie.

When he opened the door, the sheriff was pulling away from the curb with the red light flashing and the siren wailing. "There're not enough people breaking the law around here," he grumbled opening the driver's side door to his truck and sliding on the seat. "Sheriff should be out trying to catch the sonsofbitches who destroyed Guilty Pleasures… not arresting the store's owner."

Before he could put his truck in reverse, the passenger door opened and Mavis Beeton got inside. "Well don't just sit there," she said. "Follow that car!"

He grinned at her, absurdly grateful that she was with him. "What are we going to do?" he asked, putting the pedal to the metal. His truck lurched away from the curb and ground through the gears as it gained speed.

When he would have turned left, Mavis grabbed his arm. "Turn right; you need to drive to my house."

"Not now! I've got to get to Ronnie."

She smiled at him. "Not without the ammunition you need," she told him.

"I can't think straight right now, Mrs. Beeton, not until I can see her and explain…"

"Explain?" Mavis prompted.

"Why I didn't do anything back there," Dylan ground out.

"Why didn't you?"

He shook his head. "I don't know; must have been the fashion show."

Mavis chuckled but quickly covered the sound by clearing her throat. "Well then, are you ready to act now?"

He didn't hesitate. "Yes, ma'am."

"Willing to set her free at any cost?"

"Yes," he rasped. "Just tell me what to do."

"I've been studying our town's history—"

He cut her off. "No offense, Mrs. Beeton—"

"None taken, Dylan," she reassured him. "Now do me a favor and shut up."

Shock had him closing his mouth. She continued, "We have a few laws that have been on the books for over one hundred years."

He clenched his jaw tighter but continued to drive to her house instead of where he wanted to be—needed to be—the jail.

"One, in fact, that set your great-great-grandfather free."

Dylan shifted his gaze from the road ahead to her face. "I'm listening."

"Finally," she said. "Mine is the third house on the left."

He pulled up and put it park but didn't kill the engine. "Time's a wasting. Keep talking."

"The Donovan Marriage Ordinance clearly states that as long as the crime isn't cold-blooded murder, a woman—or man—could have the prisoner released into their custody."

"Just like that?"

"Not quite," Mavis said, opening her front door.

Dylan wanted to yell in frustration but kept a lid on his temper and followed along behind her.

She didn't waste any time or steps; she walked into her kitchen, grabbed a ragged ledger book, and grinned. "Let's go get your bride."

That stopped him in his tracks. "My what?"

Mavis didn't laugh at him, but he wondered if she was thinking about it, noticing the way her lips were twitching.

"We have a few more minutes. Sheriff McClure might be angry right now, after the way your bride whacked him in the back of the head with that sex-toy catalog."

"Why do you keep calling Ronnie my bride?"

"Sit down, Dylan."

"I've got to get to the jail before she closes herself off from me completely. You saw the look on her face; she thinks I'm not coming after her."

Mavis patted his arm and urged him to sit. "If you go there now, what are you going to do? Browbeat the sheriff into letting her go?"

Dylan stopped and thought about it. "Maybe."

"Think, Dylan," she urged. "You need a bona fide reason for the sheriff to release Ronnie."

"My fists might be enough—"

She shook her head at him. "Then you'd be right there in the hoosegow with your bride."

"Why do you keep calling her that?"

She opened the ledger and tapped the first page. "Here is the list of Pleasure's early laws."

He ground his teeth in frustration but didn't say anything; he was afraid of what he might say, and Mrs. Beeton was only trying to help.

She flipped through to another section. "And here's where they record the list of prisoners and their crimes."

When he didn't speak, she added, "And the dates they were released."

He pushed to his feet; Mavis grabbed his arm. "August 4, 1912, was the first time the Donovan Marriage Ordinance was invoked."

Dylan turned slowly and stared down at the older woman. "The fourth of August?"

She nodded and grinned. "1912." She waited and patted him on the arm. "Does the date ring a bell?"

"Yeah, but I'm not sure why."

Mavis pointed at the ledger, halfway down the page. "It says right here that one of the prisoners, Judson Garahan, was released into the custody of a Miss Deidre Flaherty on August 4, 1912."

Dylan sat down hard. "That's my—"

"Great-great-grandfather's name," she said. "I know. Judson was released as soon as he said 'I do.'"

"I do?"

Mavis frowned up at him. "What part of 'Marriage Ordinance' didn't you hear?"

The light went on inside Dylan's head. "He married her to get out of jail?"

Mavis nodded. "Are you willing to marry Ronnie in order to set her free?"

He set his jaw and slowly rose from his seat. "I meant what I said. I'd do anything to get her out of there."

The older woman was smiling as she pulled Dylan toward the front door. "Let's see if we can get the sheriff to listen to reason, now that you have some leverage."

On their way outside, a car pulled up behind his truck. Emily got out of the passenger's side saying, "Tyler said they'll meet you outside the jail... and to wait for them!"

"It's a forty-five minute drive from the Circle G to town."

Emily shook her head at him. "They're already on their way and will be here in ten minutes."

"How—" he said before it hit him. "Jesse's driving."

She nodded. "Come on. Jolene's driving and the ladies are all meeting us at the jail."

He didn't even pause to wonder why; he opened the door for Mrs. Beeton and felt an immense sense of relief filling him seeing the ledger on her lap. "Will he let her go?"

Mrs. Beeton answered his question with a question, "Will you marry her?"

His heart leaped in his chest. "Yes."

She patted his hand. "Then, yes. He'll have no choice but to release her."

"May I borrow your phone, Dylan?"

He handed her his cell and focused all of his attention on getting to the jail in record time. A few minutes later, she handed him back his phone. He pulled up outside the jail and was surprised to see the number of cars parked and women waiting.

"'Bout time you got here," Gwen grumbled.

Dylan didn't even acknowledge her comment; he beat Mrs. Beeton to the door and held it open for her. "Mrs. Beeton—"

"You can thank me later. Wait for your brothers. That'll give me time to soothe the sheriff's ruffled feathers."

"I don't give a damn about McClure."

"Which is exactly why you'll give me a few minutes while you wait for your brothers." Her tone didn't brook any arguments.

When he tried to follow her, she reminded him, "They'll be here in a minute or two. A united front will impress the local law. Please wait for them."

He stepped back and turned around, surprised by the group of women that nodded as they filed into the building behind Mrs. Beeton.

The screeching of tires and spitting of gravel had him turning toward the street. His brothers were calm, cool, and just this side of arrogant as they strode toward him. Familial pride filled him. "I didn't know what else to do—" he began.

"I hear Mrs. Beeton's got a surefire way to get the sheriff to release her," Jesse said.

"Is it true?" Tyler asked, his eyes brimming with laughter. "Was she having a lingerie party and did she really whack the sheriff?"

Dylan shook his head. "Look, we'll talk later," he said. "There's a woman inside who thinks I've abandoned her and lied when I told her I loved her."

Jesse stopped in his tracks. "You actually said the words?"

Dylan grabbed Jesse's left arm while Tyler grabbed Jesse's right, pulling the youngest Garahan toward the door. "Yeah," Dylan ground out. "Let's finish what we've started. It's time for the Garahans to save the day." He looked at Tyler and grinned. "Again."

Tyler nodded. "One of us falls," he rasped, "and the other two will be right there to pull him back up."

Faith renewed, determination filling him, Dylan stormed into the jail, ready to tear ass and take names.

Chapter 20

RONNIE DUG DEEP FOR STRENGTH AS THE SHERIFF instructed his deputy to fingerprint the criminal—her!

She'd never have believed this could ever happen to her. She never broke the law, always drove within the speed limit, never double-parked or jaywalked.

"Ms. DelVecchio, I need your right hand first."

She tried to pay attention, but her mind kept returning to that awful moment when Dylan stepped aside and let the sheriff haul her off to jail. *How could he?* She'd never let Dylan get hauled off to jail without a fight.

"Damn his eyes."

"Can't you keep the prisoner in line, Deputy?"

"Yes, sir," he answered before looking down at Ronnie. "I'm going to have to ask you to refrain from using foul language."

Ronnie's simmering temper reached the boiling point. "Bite me."

The deputy's eyes widened and his face turned beet red.

Satisfaction took an edge off her anger, but it was short-lived. She heard the scrape of a chair and saw the sheriff rise and walk toward her, but then he stopped in his tracks, stood straighter, and slid his hand to the gun at his hip.

Turning to look in the direction the sheriff had, Ronnie's hand flew to her breast to keep her heart from pounding out of it. Walking toward her was the man she'd thought had abandoned her to her plight.

As he stepped in from the narrow hallway, his brothers stepped alongside, flanking him. Dark-haired, dark-eyed, and glowering, the middle Garahan brother was enough to set her heart aflutter and bring tears of relief to her eyes—that his brothers were there too just added to the feeling.

"I'm here to demand you release Veronica DelVecchio."

The sheriff didn't miss a beat. "That a fact, Garahan?" Looking from one brother to the next, he asked, "You three planning on starting a brawl in my jail?"

Dylan and his brothers looked at one another and then at Mavis, who still held that battered book she'd brought with her. "That won't be necessary, Sheriff McClure," she said cheerfully with a nod in Ronnie's direction. "I'd like to bring your attention to the Town of Pleasure's Ordinance Number Five."

Clearing her throat she looked over her shoulder and called out, "If there are any other people who'd like to act as witnesses, now would be the time to come forward and be counted."

Ronnie couldn't believe her eyes. Jolene, Emily, Gwen, Natalie, and Jennifer led the way as Lettie and Pam Dawson, and Minnie Harrison walked into the room, followed by every single woman who'd been at the Lucky Star just a short while ago.

"Wait for us!" Shannon and Lenore McKenna bustled into the room. "Sorry we're late; we came as soon as Jolene called."

The women of the town were there for her, to support her. Surrounded by her contemporaries, she straightened her shoulders and faced the woman who she knew made it all happen. "Mavis—"

Her friend shook her head at her and Ronnie fell silent.

"Now, Sheriff," Mavis said, "if you'll let me continue."

The lawman vibrated with anger but managed to nod instead of pulling his gun on the Garahan brothers, which was what Ronnie thought he'd been about to do.

"Any resident of Pleasure, man or woman, has the right to invoke this Ordinance and the law has to release the prisoner into their custody."

"Let me see that," McClure ground out, reaching for the ledger.

Mavis handed him the book and moved to stand beside Ronnie. She leaned close and whispered, "Don't say anything until Dylan's had his say."

"What?"

Mavis patted her on the arm, put a finger to her lips, and moved away.

Dylan nodded to his brothers and stepped forward. "I hereby invoke the Donovan Marriage Ordinance and ask you to release Veronica DelVecchio into my custody."

He turned toward Ronnie and rasped, "I promise to love her, cleave to her, and keep her out of jail for the rest of our married lives."

"Marriage Ordinance?" Her head felt light, her thoughts fuzzy, and her body detached. When all eyes turned toward her, she moistened her parched lips with the tip of her tongue and looked at the man who standing in front of her. "You're asking me to marry you?"

Dylan nodded.

"And I'll be free to leave this jail?"

Again, he nodded.

She looked over at the sheriff and asked, "Otherwise I'll have to stay locked up?"

McClure nodded. "You do the crime... you do the time."

She swallowed against the lump in her throat and faced Dylan. "I thought you were leaving me to twist in the wind."

He stood straighter and glared down at her. "Not in this lifetime."

"Well, you didn't say anything in my defense and you let the sheriff cuff me and drag me out of the Lucky Star."

"Mrs. Peterson's... uh... outfit distracted me. I'm sorry, Ronnie, but there's just some things a man's not ready to see."

Her lips twitched, but she dug deep fighting the urge to smile. "What about the DelVecchio Curse?"

"I've already told you it would be pure pleasure if you carried my children. I'm partial to twins."

"A curse? Hey, Bro," Jesse said, "are any body parts going to fall off?"

"What curse?" Tyler asked.

"Later," Dylan ground out. "Can't you see I'm busy here?" He pulled Ronnie into his arms. "Well?" he asked. "Will you marry me and start on the next generation of Garahans?"

She looked over at Mavis, who had tears in her eyes, and then back at Dylan. "What if the curse is a dud and I can't have children?"

He lifted her chin with the deft touch of his knuckle. "I need you to marry me, Ronnie," he rasped. "I love you for your fractiousness and the fact that you would take on the law with the power of your convictions and your stock of lingerie and scented massage oil."

Ronnie grinned and asked, "Can I ride Wildfire?"

His eyes widened, but instead of answering he covered her mouth with his, lips teasing, tongue tangling. When he ended the kiss, she hugged him tight. "How could an East Coast girl like me resist the awesome power of pure, unadulterated, Texas testosterone?"

"Marry me and come live with me out at the Circle G."

"Are you sure about this, Ronnie?" Shannon asked.

"Hey," Jolene called out, "now would be the perfect time to ask him."

Ronnie shook her head to clear it. "What are you talking about?"

Jolene crossed her arms beneath her breasts and then threw them up in the air and grumbled. "Take Pride in Pleasure Day—the all-male revue…"

Ronnie grinned. Not that she didn't think Dylan meant what he said, but just to prove a point and test Dylan's conviction to marry her, she said, "Since you've agreed to let me ride Wildfire, I have one more request."

Dylan's eyes swirled with a combination of desire and love. Her heart melted, and for a moment she forgot what she wanted to ask him.

"Ask me anything, darlin'," he rumbled, pressing his lips to her forehead.

"Will you and your brothers be a part of the Lucky Star's all-male revue in the Take Pride in Pleasure Celebration and Rodeo?"

He eased back and glared down at her. For a heartbeat she'd thought she'd gone too far, overestimating how much he loved her or how far he'd go to keep her out of jail.

He let go of her, drew in a deep breath, and crossed his arms over his broad chest. If possible, his glare was more intense and just this side of disconcerting.

Hell, she should never have asked. Wasn't it enough that the man asked her to marry him to keep her out of jail? But no, she had to go one step too far and ask him to parade around on stage with his brothers, shirtless, while women hooted and hollered—

His sigh was loud and long, and for a second, she thought he'd capitulate. Instead, he turned his back on her.

Tears filled her eyes, but she'd be damned if she'd let Dylan Garahan know how badly he'd hurt her. DelVecchios went down fighting!

"Ty, would you and Jesse be willing to help out Jolene and Emily and be a part of their damned all-male revue?"

Tyler started laughing while Jesse started cheering. "Hoowee! I'm gonna call our New York City cousins back and tell them we're in and they should book their tickets now!"

Before Ronnie's mind could process the fact that he was asking his brothers to be a part of something she knew he dreaded doing, Tyler spoke up. "Hell, if you and Jesse are willing to strip down in public—"

"There will be no stripping in public, damn it," Sheriff McClure roared.

Jolene started laughing. "Don't you worry none, Sheriff," Jolene drawled. "There will be no stripping— just a lineup of dark-haired, dark-eyed, handsome cowboys dancing on stage in their jeans, chaps, boots, and Stetsons."

The sheriff glared at her but finally agreed. "SIPs usually lead to FIPs."

Ronnie tilted her head to one side. "What does SIP and FIP mean?"

Dylan yanked her close and chuckled. "'Stripping In Public' and 'Fornicating In Public.'"

She pushed against his shoulders and he eased up his hold on her. "You've got to be kidding."

He shook his head and drew her back to within kissing range. His lips descended toward hers, but before he could kiss her, Ronnie decided to tempt the man who would be driving her crazy for the rest of their lives. "I know how much you love pecans," she rasped. "I've got this killer praline recipe." She leaned closer, blew in his ear and then whispered, "I can warm it up on the stovetop and then drizzle it all over you... then I'll just have to lick it off."

Dylan's eyes darkened as he cleared his throat and grabbed her hand. "If you'll excuse us—"

"Not so fast, Garahan," the sheriff rumbled, handing the ledger back to Mavis. "You're not leaving this office until you're married to the prisoner."

Mavis turned and smiled as a man in long black robes hurried toward them. "I got here as soon as I could, Mrs. Beeton."

"Thank you, Judge Gambling."

Standing in front of the couple, the judge nodded. "Now then, if there's no one here who'll object to the marriage of these two fine upstanding citizens—"

"The prisoner was arrested for selling pornographic materials!" a shrill voice called out from behind them.

As one, she and Dylan turned. The president of the Rotary Club stood shoulder to shoulder with president of the Woman's Club. Before Ronnie could tell the women where to get off, Mavis beat her to it.

"Well now, ladies, since you weren't invited to our little gathering earlier, I'll just have to assume, you're feeling a mite left out." Mavis turned to Ronnie. "Do you have any more flyers left?"

When Ronnie nodded, the blonde opened her mouth to speak, but Mavis kept talking, "After all, Jolene and Emily know how much Janet and Anne Marie look forward to spending time at the Lucky Star—maybe a couple of your toys will keep them off the streets at night."

"Well," Anne Marie shrieked. "I never—"

"That's not what I heard," Pam Dawson said.

The noise level of the room soared as the two women tried to argue with Pleasure's one-woman wrecking crew—Mavis Beeton.

Ignoring the ruckus, the judge continued, "Do you promise to love and honor Veronica from this day forward?"

Dylan pressed his lips to her forehead. "I promise to love, honor, and keep my little filly out of jail for the rest of our married lives."

Ronnie sputtered, "Filly?"

Dylan cupped her face in his callused hands and rasped. "Fractious, hardheaded, and just plain perfect, you're my little filly, darlin'." He dipped his head to press his lips to hers. A soft, sweet kiss filled with promise. He slid his hands along the slope of her shoulders, down to the curve of her waist. The heat of his hands, combined with the strength she knew he held in check convinced her she wouldn't regret marrying him.

She felt as light as a cloud. Free and unencumbered by the past, she looped her hands around his neck and felt her heart soaring free. She couldn't wait to call Nonni and share the news.

The judge's next question brought her back to the present. "And do you promise to love and honor Dylan in return?"

Ronnie smiled up at the man holding her close. She touched her fingertips to his cheek, leaving a streak of black ink. She held her laughter inside of her; she'd tell him about the streak later. "I promise to love, honor, and keep all pornographic materials behind closed doors—ours."

"I now pronounce you man and wife."

Dylan slid his hands to her back and splayed them at the base of her spine, holding her against him, as he bent his head and sealed their vows with a gentle kiss, a promise from his heart.

Ronnie laid her head on Dylan's chest and sighed. "You're sure you won't too get tired of being tied down to a rabble-rouser from back East?"

Dylan gathered her close and kissed the breath out of her. When he came up for air, he asked, "What part of 'I love you' didn't you understand, darlin'?"

"Now who's being fractious?"

He laughed and crushed her to him. "Kiss me back, darlin'."

She tilted her head back and smiled up at him. "With pleasure, darlin', I surely will." And she did.

Acknowledgments

To my family… thank you for your continued support and willingness to be used as *visual* stand-ins for my characters, and to act as a buffer to the real world while I finished this book. I'd be lost without you guys; you ground me and keep me sane. I love you.

Thank you to my wonderful editor, Deb Werksman, for her vision, attention to detail, and amazing ability to push me to dig even deeper, helping me to become a better writer. If my characters don't always listen to me, at least they listen to you. I'm so grateful to be working with someone who really understands the way my mind and my characters work. Thanks, Deb.

To the whole Sourcebooks team… thank you! You ladies totally rock!

About the Author

C.H. Admirand is an award-winning, multi-published author with novels in mass-market paperback, hard-cover, trade paperback, magazine, e-book, and audio book format.

Fate, destiny, and love at first sight will always play a large part in C.H.'s stories because they played a major role in her life. When she saw her husband for the first time, she knew he was the man she was going to spend the rest of her life with. Each and every hero C.H. writes about has a few of Dave's best qualities: his honesty, his integrity, his compassion for those in need, and his killer broad shoulders. She lives with her husband and their three grown children in the wilds of northern New Jersey.

She loves to hear from readers! Stop by her website at www.chadmirand.com to catch up on the latest news, excerpts, reviews, blog posts, and links to Facebook and Twitter.

Read on for an excerpt from

Jesse

Coming July 2012
from C.H. Admirand
and Sourcebooks Casablanca

Chapter 1

JESSE GARAHAN HIT THE GAS AND BREATHED IN THE hot Texas air. He loved the feel of the wind in his face and engine rumbling beneath him as the hot sun smiled down on him, trying to parboil him to the driver's seat.

He'd left the ranch in two pairs of very capable hands—his brothers. Tapping his fingers on the steering wheel, he wondered if he could find a wild woman like the one Garth Brooks was singing about on the radio. Hell—he didn't have time for romance right now, too much to do and not enough time to get it done in. Setting that thought aside, he concentrated on the road ahead of him and coaxing as much speed as possible out of his truck.

Flooring it, tearing ass along the road to town, he grinned. He loved driving and figured he missed his calling having to work at the ranch with his brothers—but Garahans stuck together no matter what, and as long as the ranch still had life left in it, a Garahan would be running it. With enough work for ten men, most days he and his brothers were worn to the bone, but not ready to roll over and give up.

A speck of color off in the distance at the side of the road, had him cutting back on the accelerator. Could be one of the Dawson sisters, Miss Pam had told him she'd been having a bit of trouble with her old pickup. Slowing it down, ready to lend a hand, he sucked in a breath and held it. Steam poured out from under the hood of a car that a very curvy, compact, jean-clad blonde was opening the hood to. When he noticed the rag in her hand, he knew what she was going to do.

"Damn fool woman!" He feathered the gas for more speed, cranked the wheel hard to the left, whipping the car in a perfect 180. Gravel spit out from beneath his tires as he skidded to a halt behind her vehicle.

When she jumped back with a hand to her heart, he threw the truck in park and swung his door open with enough force to move the dead summer air like the early morning breeze coming across the pond at the Circle G. Stomping over to her, he grabbed her by the elbow and pulled her off to the side, out of harm's way.

When she yanked free of his hold, he was more than ready to read her the Riot Act. Drawing in a deep breath, he was about to let loose, when he heard a little voice calling.

"Mommy?"

"Lacy, honey, I told you to stay in the back seat until I fixed the car."

Looking down, he noticed a pint-sized cowgirl staring up at him, her big blue eyes wide with wonder. Not much surprised Jesse Garahan, but the little bit of a thing, no bigger than a fairy, was wearing pink—from the top of her head to the soles of her feet—and stood out like a swirl of cotton candy at the county fair.

"Go on back now; I have to thank the man for trying to help us." The woman's voice was firm, but the little girl wasn't listening. Before he could process that fact, the vision in pink was tugging on his jeans and asking, "Are you a good guy or a bad guy?"

He shook his head at the incongruity of the situation. He'd intended to put the fear of God into the woman foolish enough to open the cap of her over-heated radiator while she stood in front of it, and instead here he was staring down at the tiniest, pinkest, cowgirl he'd ever seen.

"I uh—" he didn't know how to answer. If he'd done what he'd intended to do—yell at her mother—the little girl would probably be crying now, and positive he was a bad guy. "I stopped to help."

When the little one nodded, but refused to let go of his jeans, the woman came closer and soothed, "He's a good guy, honey."

The little girl tilted her head to one side and frowned up at him. "But he gots a black hat—Gramma says good guys wear white hats."

Jesse chuckled. "Is your grandmother a fan of Gene Autry or Roy Rogers?"

Her little head bobbed up and down, and her cowgirl hat slipped off her head and would have hit the ground, if not for the bright white cord attached to it. She was still looking up at him when she said, "Uh huh."

"That was a long time ago, and only on TV," the cowgirl's mother told her. "The good guys wear white or black hats now."

The little one bobbled and grabbed ahold of his leg with both little hands and whispered, "Daddy wears a black hat."

He didn't need to know that. Concentrating, he couldn't figure out a way to delicately loosen the little one's grip without scaring her. Her mother surprised him, by kneeling next to him. Looking down at them, he remembered the times his mother had gotten down to eye level with him when he'd been scared as a kid. It always helped ease most of his worries—except for the biggest one—why wasn't his father coming home?

To keep from letting his mind go down that rocky path, he focused on the still-steaming engine and grumbled, "Don't you realize how dangerous it is to open the cap on an over-heated radiator?" He'd learned that particular lesson from his grandfather years ago, his pride had taken a direct hit, but he hadn't ended up disfigured from steam burns.

The blonde's head snapped up and their eyes met. He couldn't help but notice the frosty blue daggers pointed directly at him.

"I was going to be careful to keep the cap facing away from me." She cupped her hands around her daughter's, where she still held tight to his leg and urged, "Come on Lacy, you can let go now."

To his relief, the little one finally did as she was told. When her mother lifted the itty-bitty cowgirl up in her arms, he relaxed. The only kids he came into contact with were the handful of teenagers who came out to the ranch, working off a debt they owed to his older brother Tyler and his fiancée Emily.

"But, mommy," she whispered, "I gots to ask him."

He was standing close enough to hear. "Ask me what?"

"Are you a real cowboy?"

Before he could answer the little girl added, "I never seen one in my whole life!"

"Your daddy's a cowboy."

"Nu uh." Lacy shook her head. "He rides bulls, not horsies, 'member, mommy?"

Jesse couldn't keep the chuckle inside; the rumbling sound seemed to capture little Lacy's interest because she poked her tiny pointer finger in the middle of his chest.

"Lacy, what did I tell you?" Looking up at him, the blonde's eyes were troubled, "I'm sorry, she's curious about everything. We're working on keeping our fingers to ourselves." She smoothed a hand over the fly-away hair on the top of Lacy's head and said, "Aren't we, sweetie?"

"I was trying to find the sound, mommy," the little girl admitted. "His lips din't move."

Not much touched his heart since the woman he'd been planning on marrying changed her mind, but this pint-sized, cotton-candy cowgirl had the walls surrounding it cracking. He smiled down at them and it felt good inside. "Name's Garahan, ma'am," he said, tipping his hat to the little lady. "Jesse," he said, staring into the mother's cool blue eyes.

Her cheeks flushed a tender pink, reminding him of the sweet peas climbing on the fence by the back door that his new sister-in-law, Ronnie, had planted. "Pleased to meet you, Mr. Garahan."

Lacy bounced in her mother's arms, "Me too, me too!"

Her mother hugged her daughter and looked up at him; her slow smile stole the breath from his lungs. He'd seen a lot of pretty women in his time, and loved his fair share, but something about the pair in front of him just got to him on a level he didn't quite understand. It was new to him, and he wasn't quite sure how to react or what to say. Lucky for him the little one kept babbling about cowboys, black hats, and funny rumbling sounds until his brain kicked in and he realized he'd been staring at the little one's mother.

She kissed the top of her daughter's head, and he'd swear he heard another crack echoing deep inside of him.

"Does your mommy have a name, Miss Lacy?"

The girl beamed up at him and nodded.

Satisfied that he'd find out the woman's name, since she hadn't offered it yet, he grinned and Lacy answered, "Mommy."

He pushed his Stetson to the back of his head and let out a breath, "Hel—er heck, Miss Lacy, I already knew that."

She tilted her head to one side and studied him for a moment. "I like him," she said in a stage whisper. "Even if he wears a black hat like daddy."

The look of sadness in her mother's eyes was swift and filled with pain. "We'll talk about that later, sweet pea." She looked at him and said, "My name's Danielle Brockway, and you already know this pint-sized cowgirl is Lacy."

"Pleasure to meet you both." And it was, when the two were laughing, it was contagious and for the first time in weeks, he felt lighter, happier. Wanting to keep the feeling going just a bit longer, he nodded toward her still-steaming car. "Can I give you and Miss Lacy a lift into town?"

"Shouldn't we crank open that cap first?"

He shook his head. "It'll cool off better if you let it sit. I'll stop by on my way back to the Circle G and check the radiator and coolant level for you. Where can I drop you ladies off?"

When she looked at him and then over her shoulder, he knew she was going to refuse. She shifted Lacy in her arms and reached into her back pocket and pulled out her cell phone. After pressing a couple of buttons, her troubled gaze met his. "The battery's dead."

"S'OK, mommy," Lacy patted her on the cheek. "You can plug it in the car, 'member?"

She hugged her daughter with just a hint of desperation. "I don't have a charger, Lacy, honey, this is our new phone. We had to give the other one back."

Her gaze shot to his, and he knew she hadn't meant to mention that last little bit of information. No surprise, women liked to talk, except when a man was trying to find out what he wanted to know. Then all of the sudden a woman had nothing to say. Her eyes filled with sadness and for reasons he couldn't understand or explain, he wanted to do something to help.

Why did they have to give their damned phone back?
Where the hell was Lacy's daddy?
And why was Danielle sad?

Before he could ask, she was thanking him for his time and trouble. "We'll be fine. My uncle will be worried if we don't show up soon; he'll come looking for us."

"And he'll know just where to look because?"

The light of irritation in her pretty blue eyes made him feel a whole lot better. He liked a woman with a little temper but as of late preferred redheads to blondes. Blondes only led to trouble. He'd better be wary around this one.

The longer he stared at her, he noticed there was something familiar about her. "I'm trying to help you," he ground out. "Not hurt you."

Had they met before? Had he broken a promise or worse, her heart? A feeling of dread swamped him.

"Who's your uncle?"

She shrugged and Jesse was starting to get a clearer picture about these two damsels in distress: Lacy's daddy wasn't in the picture, they'd traveled far enough driving a car that either had little or no maintenance done on it—or one with a crack in the radiator—either option would cause the car to overheat, and the chances were pretty good that her uncle had no idea she and Lacy were headed into Pleasure to visit with him.

He asked again, and this time she answered. "James Sullivan, he owns—"

"Sullivan's Diner," he interrupted. *Crap*.

"Thank Mr. Garahan for stopping to help us, Lacy."

"But I—" his words died in his throat as the little girl practically leaped out of her mother's arms reaching for him. "Whoa there little filly," he warned, taking a step closer.

Breathless belly laughs had the little girl tumbling farther out of her mother's arms. He reached for Lacy as her mother changed her grip to keep her daughter from falling on her head. Jesse was faster. And before his head could warn his heart to be careful, the ladies were cradled in the protective circle of his arms, warming him from the inside out.

"You saved me!" The little girl's squeal of excitement was a totally foreign sound to him. Uneasy and unsure of the feelings he wasn't used to experiencing, he settled her safely in her mother's arms and stepped back.

But the pint-sized cowgirl wasn't through. "Leggo, mommy. I gotta thank my hero."

Jesse rolled his eyes, another phenomenon, men didn't roll their eyes. Hell, he'd only been in the company of these two females for fifteen minutes and already he was acting like someone else. Shaking his head, he held up his hands and said, "My pleasure, ma'am."

Lacy seemed disappointed, but he had other worries on his mind. "You can use my phone." He reached into the breast pocket of his shirt, then offered it to her. "Call your uncle."

He thought she'd refuse, and wondered what it was about him that worried her. Most of the women in town were happy to have his help—some more than others. After a few moments, she finally reached for the phone and dialed.

He was surprised when she handed the phone back to him. "Uncle Jimmy wants to talk to you."

He took the phone, met her gaze and smiled. A deep, gravelly voice on the other end demanded to know what the hell happened and who the hell was he talking to. Putting himself in the other man's shoes, he calmly answered, "This is Jesse Garahan, Mr. Sullivan." He waited for the owner of the diner to say something about the time he and his brothers got caught stealing a pie from the windowsill of the damned diner.

It wasn't long in coming. "What the hell did you do to my niece's car? Don't think I don't remember you and your brothers, Garahan." He felt like he was a kid again, caught with the pie in his hands. Tyler had passed it off to Dylan, and Dylan to him, as Sullivan was hollering at them from inside his diner. They'd nearly gotten away, but Jesse had tripped and fallen on top of the pie. They'd had to make it up to Sullivan, their grandfather had insisted.

To this day, he always steered clear of the diner.

Too bad, Jimmy Sullivan made the best damned pie in Pleasure.

"Did you hear me?" The man's question brought him back to the present. "Yes, sir. I'm sorry, sir. I was driving by on my way to town and noticed them stranded by the side of the road. Their car overheated. I'll check things out later. Yes," he answered, wishing he could ease the frown lines between her eyebrows. "Not a problem, I'll make the time."

After reassuring her uncle that he wasn't going to go back and steal her car, or let her stand by the side of the road baking her brain in the hot Texas sun, he handed the phone back to her. "Your uncle wants to talk to you."

She narrowed her eyes and frowned up at him. He shrugged and walked back over to her car. It should be cool enough to add more fluid to the radiator by the time he was on his way back to the Circle G. Damn but her uncle had a way of making him feel like an irresponsible kid again. Lost in thought, he didn't hear her approach.

"Mr. Garahan?"

He looked over his shoulder. "I guess you don't remember me... I'm only a couple of years older than you. Call me Jesse."

She squinted at him. "Vaguely."

Once he'd made the connection, he remembered meeting her at Dawson's, she'd been pestering her uncle for a chance to ride a real horse and not a stupid old pony. The memory made him smile.

"Jesse, then," she grumbled. "If you're sure it's no trouble, would you please drop us off at my uncle's diner?"

"None at all, ma'am." Placing his hand beneath

Danielle's elbow, he led her toward his truck. "Can you slide into the middle, Miss Lacy?"

"Uh huh!"

He waited until they were settled on the front seat before he closed the door and rounded the cab to get in the driver's side. The odd thought that he'd like to keep them and bring them back home to the Circle G had him shaking his head as he slid onto the seat. Closing the door, he waited while Danielle buckled the seat belt around her daughter, and then herself, before he put the truck in drive.

Cruising along the road at a more sedate pace, Jesse had the feeling that these two ladies had just changed his life. While they chattered back and forth about the hole in the knee of his jeans and the smear of dirt on his shirt sleeve, he wondered if it was too late to head for the hills and regroup. Women were trouble, and in pairs—dangerous.

He shook that thought from his head. Garahans don't back down and they sure as hell don't retreat. He gripped the steering wheel tighter and concentrated on getting them into town so he could drop them off at Sullivan's Diner. Distance was required in order to clear his mind and deal with his reaction to the ladies.

Tyler

by C.H. Admirand

———w———

Desperate times call for desperate measures…

When Tyler Garahan said he'd do anything to save his family's ranch, he never thought that would include taking a job as a stripper at a local ladies' club. But the club's fiery redheaded bookkeeper captures Tyler's attention, and for her, he'll swallow his pride…

And one good turn deserves another…

Emily Langley feels for the gorgeous cowboy. It's obvious that he's the real deal and wouldn't be caught dead in a ladies' revue if he wasn't in big trouble. And when he looks at her like that, she'll do anything to help…

Working days on the ranch and nights at the ladies' club, Tyler is plumb exhausted. But could it be that his beautiful boss needs him just as much as he needs her…

———w———

Praise for C.H. Admirand:

"Admirand's second frontier romance features clever and well-crafted plot lines." —*Publishers Weekly*

For more C.H. Admirand, visit:

www.sourcebooks.com

Red's Hot Cowboy

by Carolyn Brown

He wasn't looking for trouble…

But when the cops are knocking on your door, trouble's definitely found you. And this is where Wil Marshall finds himself after checking in to the Longhorn Inn. It could all be a big mistake, but Wil's not getting much sleep. Then the motel owner—who is drop dead gorgeous and feisty to boot—saves him from an even worse night behind bars. Now he owes her one, big time…

But Trouble comes in all shapes and sizes…

Pearl never wanted that run-down motel, but her aunt didn't leave her much choice. And then this steaming hot cowboy shows up looking for a place to rest. Next thing she knows, she wants to offer him more than just room service. But if he calls her Red one more time, he won't be the only one accused of murder…

Sparks are definitely flying and before long, the Do Not Disturb sign might be swinging from the door…

Praise for Love Drunk Cowboy*:*

"Brown revitalizes the Western romance."—*Booklist*

www.sourcebooks.com

Tall, Dark and Cowboy

by Joanne Kennedy

She's looking for an old friend...

In the wake of a nasty divorce, Lacey Bradford heads for
Wyoming where she's sure her old friend will take her in.
But her high school pal Chase Caldwell is no longer the
gangly boy who would follow her anywhere. For one thing,
he's now incredibly buff and handsome, but that's not all
that's changed...

What she finds is one hot cowboy...

Chase has been through tough times and is less than thrilled
to see the girl who once broke his heart. But try as he might
to resist her, while Lacey's putting her life back together,
he's finding new ways to be part of it.

Praise for Cowboy Fever*:*

"HOT, HOT, HOT...with more twists and turns than
a buckin' bull at a world class rodeo, lots of sizzlin'
sex, and characters so real you'll swear they live down
the road!" —Carolyn Brown, *New York Times* and
USA Today bestselling author of *Red's Hot Cowboy*

Cowboy Fever

by Joanne Kennedy

—⁓—

She thought she had it all...

A modeling contract with Wrangler got this Miss Rodeo Wyoming a first-class ticket out of town, but somewhere along the way Jodi Brand lost her soul. When she gets back to her hometown, her childhood friend Teague Treadwell's rugged cowboy charm hits her like a ton of bricks...

He believed he wasn't good enough...

Teague is convinced Jodi's success lifted her out of his reach. Now he's got to shed his bad boy image to be worthy of the girl next door...

But whoever heard of a beauty queen settling for a down and dirty cowboy...

—⁓—

Praise for Joanne Kennedy:

"Bring on the hunky cowboys."—Linda Lael Miller, *New York Times* bestselling author of *McKettrick's Choice*

"A delightful read full of heart and passion."—Jodi Thomas, *New York Times* and *USA Today* bestselling author of *Somewhere Along the Way*

www.sourcebooks.com

One Fine Cowboy

by Joanne Kennedy

―〜〜―

The last thing she expects is a lesson in romance…

Graduate student Charlie Banks came to a Wyoming ranch
for a seminar on horse communication, but when she meets
ruggedly handsome "Horse Whisperer" Nate Shawcross, she
starts to fantasize about another connection entirely…

Nate needs to stay focused if he's going to save his ranch from
foreclosure, but he can't help being distracted by sexy and
brainy Charlie. Could it be that after all this time Nate has
finally found the one woman who can tame his wild heart?

―〜〜―

Cowboy Trouble

by Joanne Kennedy

All she wanted was a simple country life, and then he walked in…

Fleeing her latest love life disaster, big city journalist Libby Brown's transition to rural living isn't going exactly as planned. Her childhood dream has always been to own a farm—but without the constant help of her charming, sexy neighbor, she'd never make it through her first Wyoming season. But handsome rancher Luke Rawlins yearns to do more than help Libby around her ranch. He's ready for love, and he wants to go the distance…

Then the two get embroiled in their tiny town's one and only crime story, and Libby discovers that their sizzling hot attraction is going to complicate her life in every way possible…

Praise for Joanne Kennedy:

"Everything about Kennedy's charming debut novel hits the right marks… you'll be hooked."—*BookLoons*

For more Joanne Kennedy, visit:

www.sourcebooks.com

My Give a Damn's Busted

by Carolyn Brown

———〰〰———

He's just doing his job…

If Hank Wells thinks he can dig up dirt on the new owner of the Honky Tonk beer joint for his employer, he's got no idea what kind of trouble he's courting…

She's not going down without a fight…

If any dime store cowboy thinks he's going to get the best of Larissa Morley—or her Honky Tonk—then he's got another think coming…

As secrets emerge, and passion vies with ulterior motives, it's winner takes all at the Honky Tonk…

———〰〰———

Praise for Lucky in Love:

"A spit-and-vinegar heroine… and a hero who dances faster than she can shoot make a funny, fiery pair in this appealing novel."—*Booklist*

For more Carolyn Brown, visit:

www.sourcebooks.com

Hell, Yeah

by Carolyn Brown

———

She's finally found a place that feels like home...

When Cathy O'Dell buys the Honky Tonk, the nights of cowboys and country tunes come together to create the home she's always wanted. Then in walks a ruggedly handsome oil man who tempts her to trade in the happiness she's found at the Honky Tonk for a life on the road with him....

Gorgeous and rich, Travis Henry travels the country unearthing oil wells and then moving on. Then the beautiful blue-eyed new owner of the Honky Tonk beer joint becomes his best friend and so much more. When his job is done in Texas, how is he ever going to hit the road without her?

———

Praise for Carolyn Brown:

"Carolyn Brown takes her audience by storm... I was mesmerized." — *The Romance Studio*

"Carolyn Brown creates a bevy of delightful and believable characters." — *Long and Short Reviews*

For more Carolyn Brown, visit:

www.sourcebooks.com

I Love this Bar

by Carolyn Brown

—◦◦◦—

She doesn't need anything but her bar...

Daisy O'Dell has her hands full with hotheads and thirsty ranchers until the day one damn fine cowboy walks in and throws her whole life into turmoil. Jarod McElroy is looking for a cold drink and a moment's peace, but instead he finds one red hot woman. She's just what he needs, if only he can convince her to come out from behind that bar, and come home with him...

—◦◦◦—

Praise for One Lucky Cowboy*:*

"Jam-packed with cat fights, reluctant heroes, spirited old ladies and, of course, a chilling villain, Brown's plot-driven cowboy romance... will earn a spot on your keeper shelf." —*RT Book Reviews*, 4 stars

"Sheer fun... filled with down-home humor, realistic characters, and pure romance." —*Romance Reader at Heart*

For more Carolyn Brown, visit:

www.sourcebooks.com

Getting Lucky

by Carolyn Brown

—✎—

Griffin Luckadeau is one stubborn cowboy...

And Julie Donovan is one hotheaded schoolteacher who doesn't let anybody push her around. When Griffin thinks his new neighbor is scheming to steal his ranch out from under him, he's more than willing to cross horns. Their look-alike daughters may be best friends, but until these two Texas hotheads admit it's fate that brought them together, running from the inevitable is only going to bring them a double dose of miserable...

—✎—

One Lucky Cowboy

by Carolyn Brown

—⁓—

No big blond cowboy is going to intimidate this spitfire!

If Slade Luckadeau thinks he can run Jane Day off his ranch, he's got cow chips for brains. She's winning every argument, and he's running out of fights to pick. But when trouble with a capital "T" threatens Jane and the Double L Ranch, suddenly it's Slade's heart that's in the most danger of all.

—⁓—

For more Carolyn Brown, visit:

www.sourcebooks.com

Lucky in Love

by Carolyn Brown

—⁓—

Beau hasn't got a lick of sense when it comes to women

Everything hunky rancher "Lucky" Beau Luckadeau touches turns to gold—except relationships. Spitfire Milli Torres can mend a fence, pull a calf, or shoot a rattlesnake between the eyes. When Milli shows up to help out at the Lazy Z ranch, she's horrified to find that Beau's her nearest neighbor—the very man she'd hoped never to lay eyes on again. If Beau ever figures out what really happened on that steamy Louisiana night when they first met, there'll be the devil to pay...

—⁓—

For more Carolyn Brown, visit:

www.sourcebooks.com